SHAKESPEARE'S WITCH

Pages of Darkness Book One

SAMANTHA GROSSER

SAM GROSSER
BOOKS

Shakespeare's Witch

ISBN: 978-0-6483052-5-5

Cover design by Elena Karoumpali at L1graphics

https://www.samgrosserbooks.com

London

1606

Chapter One

IMPERFECT SPEAKERS

Despite the dark it was still early, the long nights of winter stretching far into the day. New-lit torches throbbed in a chill breeze that swept off the river as the shops and stalls began to close their shutters for the night and housewives hurried to make last-minute purchases. A pieman passed them, the last two pastries in his basket sweetly scenting the air. Briefly, Sarah remembered it was suppertime, but she forgot it just as quickly as they followed Master Shakespeare and their mother through the busy Bankside streets. Once or twice she threw a glance behind as though a force in the dark were stalking her.

'No one is following us,' her brother murmured, pressing his hand closer on hers. 'But I feel it too.'

Past St Saviour's Church, the lanes narrowed and pockets of liveliness arose from the taverns and alehouses. Men's voices raised by drink skirled in concert with the high-pitched laughter of whores. But the way was well known to them all and they walked easily through the dark behind the single torch that Will carried: by the time the high white walls of the Globe loomed up in the darkness, she was breathless and warm.

Inside the theatre, Will touched his torch to the others in their sconces, and the shadows bobbed and danced as the small party made their way across the broad yard and up onto the stage.

'Here?' Will asked Sarah's mother.

Elizabeth nodded. It was a good place to scry – quiet and dark and open to the sky.

Sarah stepped away from the others to the edge of the stage and looked out into the empty darkness, allowing the activity behind her to ebb into the background of her thoughts. Above her the painted heavens marked the positions of the stars in hues of gold and blue, and beyond the roof that covered the stage, the night sky hovered velvet black, pinpricked with the first real stars of silver. Even in the shadows she knew every detail of the playhouse – the wide yard before the apron and the three tiers of wooden galleries that circled it, the sweep of the stage to the tiring house behind with its three floors of dressing rooms and storerooms, and at the top, the wardrobe where she worked with her brother to sew the actors' costumes.

She was aware of it all, a place of magic even in the silent evening dark, and she allowed her breathing to soften, opening herself up to the promise of the night. Then, when she sensed that the others were ready behind her, she turned around to face them. A single candle flickered lightly on the small table they had placed centre stage, and the shewstone lay on a linen cloth before it, its surface smooth and dark and inviting. Her brother gestured to the stool he had set before it, and though she was aware of the eyes of the others watching her as she took her seat, she took time to make herself comfortable, straightening her skirts, tucking back stray hair from her face. Her own gaze never left the surface of the stone. When, finally, she was settled, her mother and brother took their places just behind her and placed a hand on her shoulders: she could feel the strength of their connection as the shewstone beckoned, insistent, demanding her attention. The candle flitted and danced at the edges of her vision, and the blackness of the stone seemed to deepen. Behind it, across the table, she saw Will take his seat, nervous hands smoothing back the thinning hair and a sheen of sweat across the unnatural pallor of his forehead. She had never known him so unnerved.

His gaze travelled to her mother. 'Sarah will scry?' he asked.

'She has a greater gift than I,' Elizabeth answered.

He gave a quick nod and Sarah lifted a small smile of reassurance towards him. But as the shewstone began to shimmer its offer of foreknowledge, the weight of the hands on her shoulders began to seem a heavier burden. With a sudden rush of apprehension, she wished he hadn't asked for this; she sensed already she would see only pain, and sometimes it was better not to know.

'What would you like to ask of the spirits?' she said. Her voice sounded strong and even, no trace of the tremor of her fear.

'I want to know,' he replied, and his voice was equally calm, 'if the play I am writing now will have good fortune.'

'The name of the play?'

'*Macbeth.*'

She nodded once to show she had understood, then closed her eyes, aware of her breath permeating all the angles of her body, connecting. A warm light passed through the hands of the others, suffusing her with its energy: she was conscious of the solid earth beneath her, the freedom of the air above. The stars pulsed in their places in the heavens and she surrendered herself to their call, imbuing her spirit with their mystery and power. For a moment she remained in this heightened state of being, open to the universe, before she let the shewstone draw her gently back and opened her eyes to focus in the blackness of its depths, secrets ready to be yielded in the world it would reveal.

The once-black surface began to shift with colours that swept across it left to right – red turning crimson and darkening to purple before clearing into bright sky blue, like clouds blown away before the wind. She gazed into the clarity, patient and waiting, as images began to form and slowly coalesced into focus deep within the stone. At times she felt as though she could step right into it, and she was glad of the anchor of the hands on her shoulders that kept her moored and safe.

'What do you see?' Will asked.

'Hush,' her mother's voice sounded softly beside her. 'Hush now, and let the spirits show us what they will.'

He fell silent again but she could sense his impatience across the table and the effort it took for him not to speak. Sarah followed the visions as they turned and slid and changed, mutable and ineffable as air, scenes falling away before her as her mind reached out to grasp them, a myriad of possible futures shifting with the fates. But she knew now to be patient and to let the visions rise and fall as they would: in time they would settle and reveal their truth. Waiting, her body seemed to grow light, without substance, as the scene in the stone hardened at last into a future she could see and hold on to. Then she watched in silent horror, unable to speak what she saw, fate playing out before her. Unconsciously, she lifted her hand to reach out to the images as though she might be able to change the future with a touch, and she stopped only when she felt Tom's fingers tighten on the muscle of her shoulder, drawing her back, keeping her safe. The vision lingered, hovering in all its awful warning, and she closed her eyes for a breath in vain hope of unseeing what she'd seen. When she looked again, the stone was blank – a cold black piece of obsidian that told of nothing.

'What did you see?' Will asked again.

She swallowed, her mouth dry, pulses hammering. She was acutely aware of the weight of Tom's hand on her shoulder, and she lifted her own hand to grasp his fingers. Reluctantly, she raised her head to meet Will's question. His eyes were dark and restless and deep with his fear as he fixed his gaze on her, desperate. What had he suspected she'd see? she wondered. How much was already known to him? She took a deep breath. 'This play,' she began, and her voice left her lips as a whisper, 'deals with sorcery?'

He nodded. Tom's fingers tightened around hers and she was grateful for his touch.

'And what else?'

'There are … witches,' he offered.

'The play has conjured evil spirits,' she said. 'These are what haunt your dreams. Your words have opened doors to them.'

'What must I do?'

'Close them.'

'And the play? Can I still use the play?'

She shook her head. 'You cannot,' she whispered.

'What will happen?' he demanded. 'What did you see?'

She could not tell him, images too dark to speak of, her innards hollowed out.

'What if I rewrite it?'

'I cannot give you the answer you seek,' she said.

4

He leaned across the table and placed an ink-stained hand on her wrist. His fingers felt like ice and she had to fight the instinct to drag her arm away from his touch. 'It's good, Sarah,' he breathed. 'The play is good, as good as anything I've written.'

'It will bring only evil,' she told him. 'Nothing good will come of it.'

He snatched his hand away from her and stood abruptly, then paced the stage, once more every inch the dramatist. 'It is only dreams, after all,' he muttered. 'Only dreams.' He moved downstage and stood looking out as though playing to an imaginary audience, before he turned back towards her and Sarah lifted her eyes to look at him once again. He looked beaten, weary. 'But they are dreams unlike any others I've ever known,' he said. 'Some nights I dare not even sleep.'

'You must close the doors,' she repeated.

He gave her a small smile. 'It is my work. It's what I am. I cannot let it go.'

She swallowed and dropped her eyes to the table. The shewstone had never revealed such images before, and for the first time in her life her gift seemed more of a curse.

She did not return his smile. 'Then I can help you no more,' she said.

He took a deep breath and nodded. 'I thank you. All of you,' he said. Then with a bow he turned and was gone, swallowed into the darkness of the playhouse, the candle flame lifting and falling with the sudden draft from the opening door.

'What did you see?' Tom demanded, turning her by her shoulder to face him and squatting down before her, grasping her hands, peering up into her face. 'What did you see?'

She shook her head, still full of the images.

'Tell me.' He squeezed her hands harder, as though he could force the words out of her.

'I cannot,' she whispered. 'I dare not.'

'You must tell us.' He lifted a hand to brush her cheek, and reluctantly she raised her eyes to meet his. They were dark and ardent and she hadn't the will to refuse him. But the words were hard to utter: once spoken they gained new power – a life and force of their own.

'I saw death,' she breathed, 'and madness and pain and imprisonment ...'

'Whose death?' Tom asked. But his question was more gentle this time and she heard the doubt in his voice.

'Ours,' she replied, holding his gaze with hers. 'Your death and mine.'

He let go of her hands as though they had burned him and stood up, taking two steps away, turning his back towards her and breathing hard.

'We must go,' their mother said in the silence. 'Before your father misses us.'

Sarah rose without another word and went to her brother, sliding her arm around his waist, drawing him close. 'It is only one future,' she murmured, but the words were empty and she believed them not. 'There are many that are possible.'

'When has the stone ever lied?' he returned with a wry smile. 'Can you tell me?'

'We should go,' she said. There was no answer to his question, no salve for the blow, and their father's wrath was something to avoid.

He nodded and put his arm about her shoulders and placed a kiss against her head. Then they turned once more to their mother, carried the table and stools back to their place, and together left the stage.

Chapter Two

ALL HAIL MACBETH

The first day of rehearsal and she walked to the playhouse reluctantly, with none of the excitement that she usually felt, just this heavy weight of foreboding and a chill inside she couldn't shake despite the spells of protection they had woven. On her way through Borough Market she dawdled, hoping to distract herself with the earthy pungency of fish and livestock, and the shouts of the traders who called out as she passed, but it did nothing to help. Now she waited, unnoticed at the side of the stage, observing the ragged circle of players as they prepared to begin the first read-through of the play. Will Shakespeare had not yet arrived and the atmosphere was excited and charged. There was much laughter and pulling of legs. Only Richard Burbage seemed indifferent, but she suspected the nonchalance was merely an act – he felt himself too venerable to indulge in such frivolity, above such things, though she knew once rehearsals began he would forget the posture and give his all to the play. He was the leader amongst them, the actor each one of them aspired to be. There was not one man in the Company who was not in awe of his talent.

Except perhaps for Nick Tooley, she mused, who fancied himself as Burbage's successor, leading-man-to-be. Certainly he was talented: hungry and intense, he brought a charge to the stage Sarah found hard to look away from. Apprentice, boy actor, hired man and recently made a sharer in the Company, he was not without ambition and he had come a long way from low beginnings. She watched him laughing with his apprentice, the boy actor John Upton, who hung upon his master's every word. Then, dragging her gaze away from Nick, she passed it over the other men in the circle: John Heminges, Henry Condell, William Sly, Robert Armin. Along with Burbage they were the stalwarts of the Company, and the major roles would go to them. Fine actors all. The smaller parts would be given out amongst the hired men and apprentices, and the women's roles to the boy actors. Her brother, Tom, as Company wardrobe-keeper, might also act a line or two. She caught his eye and he smiled, and in the excitement of it all she forgot to be afraid, smiling at him in return.

Then Will arrived and the work began.

'So tell us, Will. What is the play?' Burbage asked.

Surprisingly, Will hesitated, casting a glance towards Sarah before he answered. He was still pale, she thought, and the dark circles beneath his eyes spoke of nights disturbed. He was still dreaming then, the spirits still haunting his sleep.

'It's a Scottish play, based on Holinshed. The murder of a king, ambition's undoing of a man ...'

'Yet it opens with ... witches?' Burbage was skimming through his pages. He seemed unimpressed.

Again Will flicked a look towards Sarah, who tilted her head in a half-shrug. Tom registered the exchange from his place in the circle and shot her a questioning look. She met the question blankly – she knew no more than he.

'The witches set events in motion,' Will answered in a louder voice this time, a deliberate attempt at confidence. 'They predict Macbeth's rise to kingship. All that follows rests on his belief it's his fate to be king.'

There was silence in the circle but she could not have said what prompted the unease: there had been witches on the London stage before without this same tense disquiet. She lifted her gaze briefly to her brother, who met the look with clear, grave eyes. He felt it too, then – the stirring of a darkness, malign forces at work beyond their ability to see.

'What?' Will demanded. 'No one turned a hair at Marlowe's *Faustus* …' Which wasn't true, Sarah knew: she'd heard tales that many believed real daemons had been summoned, the actors spending nights in prayer and fasting. 'And yet,' Will continued, 'you are afraid of playing *witches*? This is the theatre, and we are *actors*. Are you men?'

There was a general shaking of heads and murmuring of dissent. He had appealed to their pride – no man likes to be accused of being afraid.

'We're not afraid, Will.' Nick spoke for all of them. 'Just wary. The King may object to witches on his stage. Especially Scottish ones.'

'The King will not object. The Master of the Revels has already approved it.' Will was no longer nervous, buoyed up by his pride in his art and the need to persuade the others. Or perhaps it was himself he needed to convince. 'The witches are as evil as the King could wish,' he said. 'They wreak only havoc and harm. Those who practise witchcraft will gain no supporters from this play.'

'Then tell us our parts,' Burbage said. 'And let us read.'

And so the first rehearsal began.

By the second scene, Tom had forgotten his fears, the words weaving their magic and binding him into the fate of the characters. And though he knew this first depiction of the witches to be false, the malevolent hags of popular superstition, their words were real enough to compel belief in their power. Then the boy John Upton spoke as Macbeth's Lady, and Tom was spellbound.

He had seen him act before – a few nights since, he had played Goneril in *King Lear* – but this time the transformation was astonishing. The gawky boy was now a woman: the ungainly limbs were elegant and lithe, and the callow green eyes were knowing, cat-like. Even seated on the low stool beside his master as they read through the lines, his posture had changed. He sat up straight-backed, making quick, graceful movements with his hands or a tilt of his head, and the wide lips were sensuous beneath the sculpted cheekbones. He was beautiful, Tom realised, this boy-woman on the cusp of his manhood, and he couldn't tear his eyes away. His cock began to stir in response, warmth rising in his groin, and he shifted the pages of the play to cover his lap. Self-consciously, he flicked a glance to his sister, still watching from the side of the stage, but she too was transfixed by John's performance. The speeches were long but he barely faltered – beside such skill, even Burbage's great light seemed dimmed.

The messenger missed his cue and the illusion shattered as Will abused him with uncharacteristic temper. John dropped the mask and watched as the players shifted in their seats, waiting until they could resume the reading, but something of the beauty remained. Tom could hardly bear to shift his gaze away, lust billowing through him, his breathing ragged.

In the pause he cast his mind back over recent months, trying to recall if he'd ever seen John with a woman. Nights at the bawdy house with the other actors flickered through his memory, but he could find no remembrance of it. Still, the boy was sixteen; surely he must have known a woman by now. By that age, Tom had been a veteran already. And if he had tasted the pleasures of a woman, Tom thought, mayhap he would be easier to persuade. Most men, he had learned, preferred to try a woman's touch first, although for himself he had not been so picky: he had always taken his pleasure wherever he could find it.

The messenger read his line and John became the Lady once more.

'... Come, you spirits
    That tend on mortal thoughts, unsex me here,
    And fill me from the crown to the toe top-full
    Of direst cruelty ...'

Once more, Tom glanced towards his sister. She caught the movement and met the look with eyes that were full of misgiving. He gave her a smile that he hoped was reassuring, then slid his attention once more to the play.

~

At dusk Tom walked with Sarah through the darkening streets. A bitter wind had risen during the day, blowing off the river with a promise of rain, so they cut quickly inland, following Deadman's Place south towards the High Street. Despite the cold and growing dark, the day was still lively: the change of shift between the workers of the day and those who haunted the pleasures of the oncoming night. Torches flared beside the doorways, billowing and restless. Sarah huddled inside her cloak and picked her way carefully across the rutted mud, shoulders hunched, and the cold air hurt her lungs to breathe.

'What are your thoughts?' she asked.

Tom tilted his head, considering. 'It's a good play, no doubt. One of his best.'

She nodded. She too had been drawn in, spellbound by the magic of the words despite their call to dark forces, the awakening of evil. For it was not only the witches who appealed to the night; the Lady had summoned the spirits too. Was it her words of conjuration, she wondered, that would bring about the ill-fortune she foresaw in the shewstone? Her death, her brother's death?

'And it is only a play ...' he offered.

She nodded, wanting to believe it, desperate to forget the dreadful certainty of the shewstone. 'If I had not seen ...' she began. 'If he hadn't asked me to foretell ...'

'We cannot unsee the things we have seen. But the play is out of our hands now. Will is set on it and it will go its own way. We can only watch and hope and try to keep ourselves safe.'

They reached the High Street, the main thoroughfare that led to London Bridge, and it was packed with the rush of the last people who had crossed from the city, heading out of town. Carts and horses vied for space with travellers on foot, and tavern workers stood in the doorways, shouting out to entice them in from the cold for ale and meat and a bed for the night. They walked among them in silence and it seemed to take a long time to get home.

~

Later, at the Castle on the Hoop, Tom drank steadily, waiting for the others to arrive. A young girl with her breasts pushed up and a painted face came and sat close to him, a hand on the inside of his thigh.

'Good even, Tom.' She smiled, inviting. She was still young and still pretty; the rough life of her trade had not yet taken its toll. He lifted a hand and tucked a stray strand of hair back behind her ear.

'Jane.' Gently, he nudged her hand away from his leg. Tonight he was in no mood for women, despite the looseness of the ale in his limbs.

She tilted her head and pouted. 'You don't want to play tonight?'

'I'm waiting for friends.'

'Girlfriends?'

He shook his head.

'Then perhaps I can play with you all?'

'Later perhaps,' he offered. 'Or perhaps not.' He shrugged. He had given her good business in the past and though he liked her, he felt no obligation.

She considered him for a moment, then let her fingers caress his thigh once more. 'You know you're my favourite customer …?' She arched an eyebrow. A new mannerism, he thought. She was getting harder. Soon all the softness would go out of her and she would be just one more painted harlot, riddled with disease and the disappointment of a life of hard use. For a moment he pitied her – in a different life he might have thought her sweet enough to court.

'And you, Jane, are my favourite whore.' He pushed her hand away, less gently this time. 'Next time I want one, I'll come find you.'

Rejected, she swung away from him and left without another word. He watched her go and move on to the next man with a slight shadow of regret. The man was fat and ageing, with a mop of greasy hair across a scabby pate, and he grabbed at Jane's arse with a hand that expected obedience. He watched her squeal in mock offence and play the game she hoped the man would pay for. No wonder the girl had hoped to entice him, Tom, to her bed: young and attractive, he had never deliberately hurt a woman in his life. He took another mouthful of ale and turned his eyes away from her, his mind still turning on the play, the witches' words running through his mind.

His thoughts were broken when the others arrived, their cloaks damp with the first fall of drizzle and eager for the fire. He picked up his ale as they moved to a table closer to the hearth, and he took his seat close to John with their backs to the fireplace. He could feel the skin across his back reddening in the heat. Nick sat across from him, and Tom took a moment to examine him: the regular features, a square jaw and strong shoulders, the stubble of his beard, good teeth. But it was his eyes that made the whole attractive – intense and searching, and something sad behind them. He understood what Sarah saw in him, though he was unsure if she realised it herself as yet. He had seen her watching him today and recognised the hunger in her look, but she was still an innocent with men, still just a girl. Well, she could do worse than Nick, he thought. He would be a passionate and tender lover.

William Sly brought a jug and mugs from the bar and sat his bulk down next to Nick. Ale slopped from the jug across the table and Sly cursed as it dripped off onto his leg. John Heminges laughed and said something that Tom couldn't hear, raising a retaliatory obscenity from Sly. Burbage and Will took their places and continued a private conversation until Nick raised his mug and called a toast.

'To *Macbeth*,' he said.

'*Macbeth*,' the others echoed, and drank.

Tom turned to John, the desire he had not felt for Jane finding its mark at last. He could feel it in the quickened heartbeat, the heightened sense of touch. He placed a hand on John's shoulder and it was narrow and bony under his palm. Heat shifted inside him. 'You read well today. You are a most convincing lady.'

John smiled with pleasure and lowered his face away, made shy by the praise.

'Truly, you have quite a gift.'

Nick leaned in to join the conversation. 'He speaks for all of us. When you become a man, Master Burbage had better watch out.'

Burbage turned at the mention of his name. 'Eh? What was that?'

'We were just saying, Master Burbage,' Tom explained, 'that John's skill as an actor may one day rival yours.' He winked at John, who was looking uncomfortable.

Nick smiled and took another drink. It was good sport baiting Burbage, who, to his credit, always took it well.

'I think I'm safe for the moment,' Burbage answered. 'It'll be a while before he's old enough to play a hero. But yes, I'll grant you, he has great talent.' He lifted his mug towards John. 'I salute you, my Lady,' he said. Then he took a swig of his ale and turned back to talk once more to Will.

'Whereas you, Nick,' Tom murmured, 'are a more immediate threat.'

'Hush, Tom,' Nick replied. 'I am young yet. My time will come.'

Tom nodded and returned the smile, but he guessed Nick's easy acceptance was a mask for his true ambitions. It had to be. For what actor did not desire to play the lead? He was not so young after all, middle-twenties, mature enough for a prince or king. And Nick had a true skill – a quieter, tenser passion than Burbage, something always in reserve, a quality that was hard to look away from.

'Have another drink, John,' Tom said, filling the boy's mug from the jug. John smiled his acceptance awkwardly. Even after two years in the Company as Nick's apprentice, he was still ill at ease in the midst of his fellows. Despite his talent and his growing repertoire of leading female roles, he seemed to be unwilling to accept the easy camaraderie of the others. Tom could not recall that a single conversation had ever passed between the two of them.

'So, John,' Tom began, turning to face the boy, giving him the privilege of his full attention. 'Like you the life of an actor?'

'I like acting,' John answered.

'Ah, but that is not an answer to the question I asked.'

John looked down into his ale and licked his bottom lip and said nothing.

'You can tell me,' Tom coaxed, laying a reassuring hand on John's arm. The warmth of the touch travelled through him and he swallowed, forcing his breathing to evenness. 'Are you unhappy?'

John's glance snapped briefly towards Nick, now in conversation with Sly, the older man's laugh ebullient and hearty. He let his gaze drift back to Tom and their eyes met briefly. 'No,' he said. 'I'm not unhappy.'

'For such a fine actor,' Tom said, 'you're a terrible liar.' For himself, he found an inability to lie bewildering – his own facility with deception had always been endless. Perhaps it came from the instinct for self-preservation that was natural to a wayward child: his skill had saved him from more than a few boyhood beatings. What was John's background, he wondered, that he'd had no need of such a skill? He tried to remember how John came to them – an orphaned nephew of someone, perhaps? He couldn't recall.

'It's easy to be someone else,' John said. 'Harder to be myself.'

'Then be someone different,' Tom replied with a shrug. 'You can change. You of all people should know that. You don't have to remain the same person all your life. You can be whoever you want. Become someone else.'

'Who? Who should I become?'

'Who would you like to be?'

John's gaze wandered instinctively towards Nick. Tom smiled and squeezed John's arm again. 'You cannot become Nick Tooley. You can only become a different version of John Upton. But you can become more like Nick if that is what you wish. You can learn from him …'

John nodded, clearly uncomfortable with the conversation. But when he looked up, his gaze held Tom's with a steady, cool insistence that was surprising. 'And have you always been as you are now?' he asked.

Tom tilted his head, considering. It was a good question. 'I change my face to suit my company,' he replied, after a moment. 'I've always done so.'

'And when you are alone?' John said. 'Who are you then?'

He shifted back a little, breaking the web of tension between them. He could not answer.

'Tom?' John prompted.

'That I cannot answer,' he murmured, with a small shake of his head. 'I don't rightly know.'

John regarded him for a moment, thoughtful, and in the pause, Tom recovered himself and laughed. 'What serious things we speak of,' he said, taking up his mug once more. The others were getting to their feet, readying themselves to leave. The table juddered as they bumped against it. 'But I am glad to talk with you so. We will talk again.'

'I'd like that,' John said.

Then they stood up themselves, and made their way to the door.

Chapter Three

THE INNOCENT FLOWER

Sarah was in her chamber when Tom came home, preparing to scry her own future in the shewstone. Beyond the window the first squalls of rain whipped at the glass, and she was glad to be indoors. She had lit a fire in the hearth and sat now before its warmth in the flickering half-light. Her father disapproved of fires in the bedchamber, regarding such luxury as sinful, but its liveliness was welcome against the darkness in her mind and she hoped he would not know. On the table the shewstone sat ready as she closed her eyes and breathed slowly, trying to find the peace within she needed to continue, but her thoughts tumbled one over the other in vivid jumbled words and images: she was too weary to tease them into order.

The door swung open and a drift of cold air from the passage outside fanned the flames in the hearth. Tom stood in the doorway, his head tilted in question. She nodded – there was no point in consulting the stone tonight. She had not the clarity of mind, the concentration, it required. He closed the door and settled himself on the rug before the fire next to her, peering into her face.

'Sarah?'

She got up in one movement. 'I'm tired merely.' She did not feel like explaining herself, even to Tom: she wasn't sure if she could describe the turmoil of emotions within her.

'No.' He shook his head, looking up at her from his place on the floor. 'It's more than that.'

She shrugged. 'I don't know what it is ... I'm out of sorts, is all.'

He observed her for a moment and she wondered what was in his mind – she had never been able to read him as he could her. It had been a game they played as children that often ended in tears of frustration, but she was more accepting of it now. Besides, she had come to understand that there was much in Tom's life she was sure she would prefer not to know.

'What were you going to ask?' he said. 'Of the spirits.'

'Nothing. It's not important.'

'Tell me. If it was important enough to scry for ...'

She sighed. It was pointless to argue with him; he would persist all night if need be. But still she was reluctant. The play had unsettled her, the message in the stone still resonating. Will's witches should have no power to frighten her – they were stage hags from a fireside tale to scare puritans and children, a mishmash of traditions that bore scant relation to any witchcraft she had ever learned. But they had yet possessed a power she didn't understand, something evil, something secret. And Tom had been one of them, words of dark sorcery on his lips. She no longer felt so safe in his presence. And in the midst of her fears there was Nick. The familiar sense of hopeless desire hardened in her belly: if he noticed her at all, he thought of her as nothing more than a child.

Tom was still watching her and she turned away, irritated by his scrutiny and the knowledge that she would end up telling him all.

'Sarah, sit with me,' he said. 'Come.' He reached up his hand to coax her, lips lifted in a smile, eyes warm and friendly. There was no sign of the witch in him now, and in spite of it all she returned the smile. Did he do this with all the women in his life, she wondered, win them over with a charm that was impossible to resist? She suspected he might – a light touch of his hand, a well-timed smile, the deceptive innocence in his eyes. She shook her head, exasperated, and lowered herself once more to the rug beside him. They sat a moment in silence and gazed into the flames in the hearth, the fire burning low, beginning to die. The embers gleamed and glittered and she watched the images shift and change. There were some who read signs in the embers but she had never been gifted to do so. It was a pity, she thought. The fire was hypnotic in its beauty.

Tom touched her arm and she turned towards him. 'So?' he said. 'What were you going to ask?'

She took a deep breath. It seemed trivial beside the dangers of the play, the foolish desires of a lovesick girl. But the pain of it was real and she had fought to suppress it long enough.

'About Nick,' she whispered, sliding her eyes once more towards the hearth. 'I wanted to know if he would ever see me as a woman that he might ...' She trailed off with a shrug. Such things were hard for her to speak of: it was a world she had only recently entered.

'That he might love?' Tom finished the sentence for her.

She nodded, pulling a face of embarrassment. 'It's foolish, I know.'

'Not foolish at all.' Tom was quick to reply. 'How is it foolish to want such a man? He would be a good match for you.'

'A match?' Anger lit inside her and she shifted away from him, sliding back across the rug. 'You sound like Father.'

For once Tom was speechless. 'Then ...?' he managed to say, one hand turning in the air to complete the question.

'I want him to desire me.' She breathed out the words through lips taut with fury. 'To touch me, to kiss me, to know what his body feels like ...' She stopped. She had no need to supply him with the rest of her imaginings. She was sure he could understand it well enough.

Tom lifted his eyebrows and tilted his head in acknowledgement. Then he smiled. 'In that case,' he said, 'I doubt you need to ask the spirits.'

'How so?' She looked up at him quickly, suspecting a joke.

He reached out a hand to smooth back a hair from her temple. 'You're a woman, Sarah. A young woman with a clever mind and a pretty smile. You can win him easily.'

She stared.

'I will teach you.'

'Teach me?' She was bewildered. 'Teach me what? Teach me how?'

'What – to weave a spell without magic, to be cunning. How – by showing you how to be with him, how to hold your head and smile, how to move your body when he's near, how to flatter and charm and be aloof all at once, how to stir his jealousy. I promise you, he will come.'

Sarah ran her tongue across her lips. 'Is this how you win a woman?' she asked. She knew he never lacked for lovers, but she had always assumed his youth and good looks and natural wit had simply brought him good fortune. She had never considered he might consciously use cunning.

'The same principles apply,' he replied.

'Then let us start,' she said with a smile. 'I am eager to learn.'

'Tomorrow, sweet sister,' he said, getting up, then taking her hand in his to help her to her feet. 'It's late and I'm tired.'

She nodded.

'Think on it,' he said, 'and ask for dreams to help you. Tomorrow we'll begin.'

He bent to kiss her cheek and squeezed her fingers. Then he was gone and the door swung to gently behind him.

In the morning the whole household was at breakfast: mother, father, brother, sister, servants, and Simon the apprentice, taken on when Tom had refused the position, preferring instead to use his knowledge of tailoring as the Company's wardrobe-keeper. The bitterness of his refusal still hung in the air even four years on: Tom had never once accepted his stepfather's authority, and he had laughed in the older man's face when he tried to force him to accept the apprenticeship. Sarah still admired her brother for his courage but there were times when she wished for a more peaceful house – the constant hostility wore at her nerves.

There was silence at the table, no one daring to speak unbidden by their master, and Sarah picked at her bread and butter. She had no appetite after the night of dreams, her mind still chasing the images. Absently she watched the apprentice as he helped himself to more herring. He caught her eye and smiled, thin lips creasing, and she looked away, embarrassed he had caught her. She hoped he would read nothing into it; she had noticed recently he was smiling at her more. Perhaps he was thinking of another way to ensure his place in the family inheritance. God, she hoped not. She flicked a glance towards Tom, who returned the look with an almost imperceptible tilt of his chin. He had noticed it too, then, and her hopes were in vain.

Her mother's voice interrupted her thoughts. 'Stop picking at your food, Sarah. Either eat it or leave it.'

'I'm not hungry.'

'Then leave it.'

She pushed the trencher away, sullen, resentful of her mother's scolding. 'I'm not a child,' she said.

'Then don't eat like one.'

'Excuse me,' Sarah said, standing up. Her father lifted his eyes from his food and looked her over as though she were a piece of cloth he was thinking to buy. But he said nothing and after a moment lowered his gaze once more to the bread in his hand, continuing to chew his herring with a regular and persistent slopping that revolted her. 'I have things to do.' Clamping her jaw against her resentment, she left the chamber and fled up the stairs to her room. There she stood at the window, looking down into the street. A cart had got a wheel stuck in the mud a few doors down and the carter was trying to enlist help from passers-by to shift it. Two gentlemen in fine velvets stood to watch with encouraging jeers until a couple of passing journeymen pitched their strong shoulders against it and the spectacle ended.

Turning from the window, she saw her brother leaning his narrow frame in the doorway. She hadn't heard him come in. Light from the window brushed his face, highlighting the sharp high cheekbones, the straight and narrow nose, the angular jaw. His eyes were clear and blue grey today – the same eyes as hers, people said. But he was so familiar to her that she seldom actually saw him, and in the glow of the morning sun she remembered he was handsome.

'She treats me like a child,' she said.

'But you're not a child' – he shrugged – 'so why let it bother you?'

She smiled at his logic. 'Old habits, I suppose.'

'Then it's time to learn some new ones.'

'Don't you have to be at the playhouse?' She had not expected him to teach her this morning; she had thought she would have to wait until evening.

'A few minutes,' he replied. 'That's all we need.'

She took a deep breath and remembered the lust of her dreams. With the memory she felt a flush cover her neck and cheeks, and she touched her fingers to her face to feel the warmth.

'You need to make him notice you first,' Tom said. 'When he isn't onstage, what does he do?'

'He watches. Sometimes he reads pages of the play. Often he is with John.'

'Then you need to be close to where he is. Find some excuse to be near him. Here, pretend I'm Nick.' He leaned against the door, half examining his nails, half giving his attention to something in the distance. For all the world he could have been Nick at the theatre.

She laughed and swung away, self-conscious.

'Do you want him or not?' Tom demanded.

'I want him,' she said, swallowing down her embarrassment.

'Then …?'

She took a deep breath. 'Good morning to you, Nick,' she offered, taking a step closer. Then she looked towards the imaginary stage, feeling foolish. 'It's good, isn't it?'

'Come nearer,' Tom said.

She took another step. Impatiently, he reached out a hand to grab her arm and pulled her closer until she was standing right by him, her skirts brushing his legs, her face at his shoulder.

'So near?' Tom becoming Nick confused her: it felt dangerous, this closeness, and inwardly she shrank away.

'Stand up straight,' Tom told her. 'You have a pretty figure, use it.'

'I'm flat as a board,' she answered, looking down, running her hand over the bodice of her dress. It was a great source of disappointment. 'There's nothing to use.'

'It isn't important. But if you think it would help then do something about it. You're a seamstress, aren't you? Alter the dress. Give yourself something to use.'

She laughed with embarrassment. She had thought of it before but it seemed like a falsehood, a trick a lady at Court or a harlot might use, and beyond her own means.

'You have your whole body,' Tom was saying. 'The touch of a hand, the sway of a hip. Let your dress brush against him. Touch your hair, run a hand across your belly. Make him aware of your body as a woman. Now let's try again.'

She stepped back away from him and he pretended once more to be absorbed in the play. Attempting to clear her mind as though she were preparing to scry, she took a deep breath and moved forward again, coming in close beside him this time. It felt strange to be so near him with such unsisterly thoughts in her head, and with a jolt she realised she'd never been conscious of Tom as a man before: he had just always been her brother, and the new heightened sense of him threatened her understanding of the world – everything she had thought till that moment seemed abruptly changed. Was this what it meant to become a woman and leave childhood behind? Heat flickered over her skin as a blush, and she swallowed, struggling with unfamiliar emotions, forcing herself to be calm, to remember what Tom had just taught her. She waited a moment, trying to imagine again that she was at the theatre and that the man beside her was not her brother at all but Nick, the man she desired. By force of will, she mastered her nerves and heard herself say, 'It's good, isn't it?'

Tom turned his head towards her as though surprised by her sudden appearance. His face was very close to hers. 'Yes, it's very good,' he said.

There was a moment of silence, and she could feel the sudden tension between them, a heat passing one to the other, a quickness in her blood. She was aware of the rise and fall of his chest, the warmth of his breath, the weight of his gaze on her face. Overwhelmed by confusion, she backed away, turning her attention towards the window, away from her brother. When she looked towards him again, he was still watching her, a slight smile in his eyes.

'Do you think he will notice you now?' he asked her, his voice soft.

She nodded, her senses still prickling and her pulse running quickly. She was uncertain what had passed between them; she only knew it had excited her.

'Then let's go.'

He turned abruptly and snatched open the door, and she followed him down the wooden stairs and into the drizzle of the morning.

At the playhouse, rehearsal was just beginning and the various members of the Company were spread around the theatre to watch. Sarah sat herself on a bench with her sewing in the downstairs gallery to watch too. Nick was nowhere to be seen. He was probably in the tiring house behind the stage, or upstairs, she thought, perhaps rehearsing lines with some of the others. She would wait until he came to the yard. She felt a surprising calm beneath the nerves, the excitement of a coming adventure rather than the fear she had expected. The strange moment with Tom she had pushed out of her mind: she did not want to think of it. But whatever had taken place between them had imbued her with a new sense of courage.

They were blocking the first scene, the witches on the heath. Tom, Robert Armin, and Will Sly. It was clever casting, she thought, one young, one old, one fat. They came and went through the trap-door, appearing as if out of nowhere. With smoke in performance to hide them they would indeed seem as spirits. Will stood to one side of the stage, directing. There was no sign now of sleeplessness or fear in his face. He seemed his usual self, absorbed only in his work, passionate and certain. His self-possession was comforting: perhaps whatever he had conjured had gone on its way and let him be. Perhaps his dreams were no longer haunted. She touched the small charm she kept closely hidden in her skirts, one of the poppets that she and Tom had made for protection, and closed her eyes in a brief prayer to Hecate that it was so.

Onstage the witches were circling.

'Hail.'
'Hail.'
'Hail.'

Burbage and Nick – Macbeth and Banquo – wheeled slowly after them, following their movements.

> *'Lesser than Macbeth, and greater.'*
>> *'Not so happy, yet much happier.'*
>> *'Thou shalt get kings, though thou be none ...'*
>> *'Stay, you imperfect speakers, tell me more ...'*

Macbeth's eyes lighted on Tom, the nearest of the witches, who shook his head with a sly smile of denial as he backed away. Thwarted, and his gaze still following Tom's movements, Burbage took a step back, forgetting that the trap was still open. He fell hard into the space below with a cry.

For a moment no one moved, frozen by surprise, but as Burbage began to wail and moan, the whole Company ran forward to peer through the opening. Sarah was the last to get there to see Richard lying crumpled at the foot of the little wooden ladder with Nick crouching next to him, a gentle hand on the other man's shoulder.

'Let me through,' Sarah said.

They moved apart for her and she let herself down through the opening and knelt beside the injured man in the semi-darkness. 'Where are you hurt?' she asked him.

'My arm,' he said. 'And my back.'

She lifted her head for a moment, searching for Tom among the faces that were looking down. He caught her meaning at once and set off at a run to bring their mother, who was skilled in healing, her years as a midwife teaching her all manner of cures. Sarah was only beginning to learn but she was not without some skill.

'Let me see your arm,' she said, and gently folded back the sleeve from his wrist, running her fingers across the skin and finding the fracture beneath.

'Is it broken?' Richard asked, grimacing.

She nodded, the break unmistakable beneath her fingertips. He winced with her touch. 'My mother will know best what to do. We must get you upstairs.'

Richard moaned.

Sarah turned to Nick. 'Can we lift him up?'

He nodded. John Heminges dropped down through the opening and together they managed to manhandle Richard back onto the stage. Then between them they half carried, half dragged him through to the tiring room and laid him on the couch that lay against one wall.

Everyone looked to Sarah. She swallowed and forced herself to speak with confidence. 'He needs a pillow for his arm and a cold compress across the break,' she said. 'Then we must wait for my mother.'

They helped him to settle on the couch and Sarah stayed with him, attending to his arm with the compress someone brought, making sure he was comfortable before she sat on a low stool by his head to keep him company while the others withdrew, their voices hushed with concern and dwindling to murmurs. Only Will remained.

'What of Lear tomorrow?' Richard asked. 'I cannot play.'

'I know,' Will answered with a sigh. 'We will play something else.'

'But the bills have been printed.'

The playwright shrugged.

'You could do it,' Richard said. 'You know the lines …'

'Aye,' Will replied, turning away. 'I do know the lines.'

Then neither spoke for what seemed to Sarah to be an age. She was aware of Will pacing at her back and concerned, she guessed, for the days to come. Performances were scheduled and their leading man was down. But the Company was versatile, their repertoire extensive, and she had no doubt the plays would still go on. Richard struggled to sit up straighter, following Will's movements, and Sarah reached to shift the pillow that supported his arm. A grimace of pain passed across his face as he moved.

When her mother finally hurried in, out of habit Richard tried to rise to greet her, only to fall back with a groan. Mistress Stone came to the playhouse rarely these days but she was well known to the older members of the Company: her first husband, Tom's father, had been wardrobe-keeper in the early days, and Will had remained a constant friend. It was a source of great discord in their family: her second husband hated the playhouse and its players with all the passion of his Puritan faith, and Elizabeth had kept her distance from it to keep the peace.

'Mistress Stone,' Richard said. 'Forgive me.'

'Hush,' Elizabeth replied. 'And let me take a look at you.'

She bustled her daughter out of the way and took her place at the stool, running expert fingers over Richard's arm, examining his back. Sarah shared a glance with Tom, standing close to her, but she couldn't read his expression. His fingers brushed the back of her hand and she squeezed them. The accident and her mother's presence had unsettled her earlier confidence. Tom leaned in close and breathed in her ear. 'You did well. And you look beautiful.'

She took in a sharp breath of shock, but his words had their effect and she straightened herself up again, remembering she was a woman, not a child. She flashed him a glance and smiled.

'Good girl,' he murmured.

'We must get Master Burbage to his home,' Elizabeth pronounced at last, turning to look up at the waiting players who loitered near the door to the stage. They moved forward, anxious for news, and she got up to address them.

'His wrist is broken but it will mend,' she said. 'And his back is strained. But he must have rest. I'll prepare compresses of herbs to apply every day.' Then she directed her gaze towards Will, and Sarah saw the sympathy between them, an understanding she had seen many times before. It was a look she had never once seen pass between her parents. 'You must needs find a cart to take him,' her mother was saying. 'He can neither ride nor walk for many days yet.'

Will bowed slightly in answer and left. The others followed at a distance, and Sarah and Tom trailed out behind them, leaving Richard with their mother. The rest of the Company sat in small groups around the theatre, waiting, lounging on the benches or on the floor of the yard. Nick stood alone at the edge of the yard, leaning against one of the pillars with his arms crossed, apparently deep in thought.

'Go,' Tom said.

She nodded and let go of her brother's hand. Then, with one slow breath for courage and a movement of her fingers against the small charm in her pocket, she crossed the yard and went to stand beside him.

Chapter Four

BIRTH-STRANGLED BABE

In the evening after the tavern, Tom came to find her in her chamber once again. She was sewing by candlelight, the fabric close to the flame as she worked on the bodice of her dress to round out her figure. She had made pads to insert to push up her breasts, but it was less easy than she'd thought and she was beginning to wonder if she'd ruined a perfectly good bodice.

Tom stood at her shoulder for a moment, watching. Then he said, 'Do you still think you need them?'

'They can only help.'

He nodded, turning to lean his hips against the table, close beside her. She finished the stitch and tied off the thread. Then she sat back and looked up at him. He was pale, she thought, and his cheeks seemed gaunter than before. 'Are you all right?' she asked.

'Of course I'm all right.' The question seemed to irritate him. 'I'm always all right. And I came to talk about you, not me. So tell me. What happened with Nick?'

She smiled, revisiting the moments. The memory flickered bright and delicious in her thoughts as she framed the words in her mind to recount it all to Tom. Finding the phrases she needed, she laid down her sewing and took her brother's hand in hers, giving him all the light of her attention and her gratitude.

She had done just as they practised it, she told him, and he smiled and squeezed her fingers.

She had stood close beside him, looking out across the theatre for a moment before she spoke. Then she had asked, 'What will happen now? With the play?'

Nick turned his head toward her. She had never been so near to him, never so conscious of the smell of him, his warmth. It was hard to resist the desire to reach out and touch him. He tilted his head in a half-shrug. 'Someone else will play the part.'

'Who, do you think?' she said, meeting his eyes for a moment and registering the change she saw in his look as he reappraised her. She shifted her position slightly, touching fingers to her hair, and the consciousness of his full attention brushed her cheeks with pink. She wondered if he would notice.

'Perhaps it will be me,' he said, and smiled.

'I hope so,' she answered.

'D'you think I can? It is a weighty role.'

'Oh yes,' she breathed. 'You would be a fine Macbeth.'

He waited so she filled the pause, hoping she would not spoil things by saying too much. 'But I think you will play him very differently from Master Burbage. Quieter, more intense, less regal perhaps and more of the soldier?'

He nodded, sliding his eyes away to consider her words and then back again to regard her once more. 'I have thought so,' he agreed, 'that I would play it as you say.'

'Then let us pray you get the part.' She smiled again.

The slam of the outside door and Will's reappearance as he strode across the yard brought the moment to a close, acknowledged between them with a nod. The players stirred from their apathy and made their way towards the foot of the stage, forming a loose circle round Will. Sarah kept her place at Nick's right hand, assuming a new position for herself in the Company. Before today she would have hung back, afraid to overstep in this world of men. But no one paid her any mind, too intent on Will's decisions to be concerned about her.

'How is he?' Nick asked.

'In pain,' Will answered. 'But he'll recover. He just needs to rest.' He took a deep breath and looked around at them all as she waited, breathless to know who would take the part, her hopes bound up with Nick's. Then he said, 'Rehearsals will commence again tomorrow morning. Nick will take the part of Macbeth. Henry, you must be Banquo. I'll rearrange the other roles tonight and tell you your parts in the morning.'

'And Lear tomorrow?' Nick asked.

'I will play it,' Will said.

The players drifted out of the circle and Sarah risked a glance at Nick, who raised his eyebrows with a quick smile of complicity. She returned the smile, and on an impulse, touched her fingers briefly to his arm. To her surprise, he placed his own hand over hers and squeezed. 'Thank you,' he murmured, so that only she would hear him. 'Your prayers seem to have worked.' Then he let go her hand. 'Till tomorrow.'

'Tomorrow.' She backed away a couple of steps and dipped into the briefest of curtseys, which was met with an answering bow. Then she turned on her heel and paced across the yard toward the door before anyone could speak to her and notice the redness of her cheeks or her breathlessness.

Now, in her chamber with Tom, the recollection brought the flush to her cheeks once again and quickened her heartbeat. She looked up at her brother in the light of the candle and smiled, waiting for his praise.

'Good girl.' He gave her shoulder an affectionate squeeze. 'He's as good as won. I'm proud of you.'

'And tomorrow?' she asked. 'How should I be with him tomorrow?'

'Let him come to you tomorrow,' he said. 'Be friendly but not too much so, and a wee bit coy. Now he needs to work a little to win you.'

She nodded, fixing his advice in her mind, already thinking how she might behave.

'Now get some sleep,' Tom said.

'I need to finish the dress first,' she replied. 'Or I shall have nothing to wear.'

'And that would never do.' Pushing himself off the table, he stood up. 'Don't stay up too late – you need your beauty sleep. Good night, gentle sister,' he said, and bent to kiss her cheek. She held her face up for his kiss and the light stubble was rough against her skin.

'Good night, Tom.'

She watched him leave and, aware of her attention, he turned back at the door and blew her a theatrical kiss before he bowed and made his exit. She laughed and turned back to her sewing and worked for another hour until the dress was done.

~

She was woken in the night by the light of a candle in her face and her mother's hand shaking one shoulder.

'Wake up, Sarah,' her mother's voice was urging.

She struggled to rouse herself from deepest sleep, her mind groggy and confused. In her dreams she had been elsewhere, and the abrupt drag back to reality was a disappointment. Reluctantly she let the images trail into the darkness.

'What is it?' she mumbled.

'A birth. We must go. Now.'

She nodded and swung herself out of bed. The cold air stung against her skin and she regretted the warm blankets she had left. Dressing hurriedly as her mother helped to tie her skirts, she was ready within a few minutes and following her mother silently down the wooden stairs in the shifting light and shadow from her mother's candle.

At the front door Elizabeth took up a torch and lit it with the flame of the candle. Then, stepping outside, Sarah turned to lock the door behind her as her mother hurried away along the street, a dark shape against the torchlight. With a sigh, Sarah took off after her, holding her cloak close against the night air. The street was deserted – the small quiet hours between the late-night revellers and the labour of the early morning. The peace was disturbing, and instinctively she raised her eyes to see the sky. The moon peeped through the shifting clouds, waning just past the full and gibbous, and one or two stars tried bravely to shine their light on the mortals below, but the gathering clouds muffled their glow, threatening more rain. She lowered her gaze to her feet and ran a few steps to catch up with her mother.

They left the High Street and cut through the silent market toward the poorer, rougher streets of Bankside, where the theatre and the bear-baiting ring rubbed shoulders with the taverns and the bawdy houses that faced upon the river. They passed the Globe and the still-empty land that held the ghost of the Rose, closed now these last two years or more, the Admiral's Men settled in their new home north of the city. Around them nestled a host of tenement buildings – rooms to rent to suit all purses. A rat scurried out of her way down an alleyway and she thought she saw a glimpse of a figure in the dark. The streets at this hour were unsafe for women out alone, though she had never known her mother to be afraid. She wished she had the same confidence.

'We should have brought Tom,' she said, drawing level. 'It would have been safer.'

Her mother turned her head briefly towards her daughter. 'He was not in his bed when I looked,' she replied. 'So we are alone.'

'And Father?'

'I've never asked for your father's help in this and I never shall.'

'Why doesn't he approve?' She had asked this many times: his disapproval of her mother's midwifery was hard to understand – it was a respected profession after all, and a godly calling. But her mother always refused to answer, thin lips sealing closed in a line, jaw hardening in response. Still Sarah kept asking, hoping in the end she would know.

'Now, we are almost there,' her mother said, by way of answer.

It was a poor room in a tenement block set hard by the river beyond the strip of brothels. The wooden beams were dank and rotting and a smell of mould hung in the air. The child who had sent for them waited in the doorway as they went through to find a pale young girl sweating on a threadbare pallet. A solitary tallow candle threw an uneven light across the chamber, and though an attempt at a fire had been made in what passed for a fireplace, the wood was damp and the room had filled with smoke. Sarah's eyes began to water. The girl was about the same age as herself, she judged, perhaps fifteen or sixteen, and she felt a sudden rush of gratitude for the life she had been given – a good family and a full belly. Squatting down, she set about fixing the fire to give some warmth to the room, and placed some water to heat in the battered kettle that had been left on the hearth.

Elizabeth sat on the edge of the bed and took the girl's hand in hers, observing, assessing. 'What's your name?' she asked.

'Joan,' the girl said.

'And you are alone?'

Joan nodded. Elizabeth slid a glance to her daughter. 'This is your first?'

'Third. But none still alive,' the girl answered.

'How long have you had the pains?'

'Since not long after dark … Can you help me? I've nothing to give you.'

'I'll help you. Someone must.'

Joan gave them a grateful and unbelieving smile and they settled down to business.

The baby was born with the dawn, light creeping over the city behind the hanging clouds, barely noticed. Sarah held Joan's hand and stroked her brow as the girl screamed and wailed and pushed her new child into the world, Elizabeth helping to ease its way.

Sarah knew something was wrong as soon as the baby was out. Her mother's face remained closed, no instinctive smile of the joy of new life, no shared excitement. She gave her mother a questioning glance as Joan slid back into the pillows, too exhausted and sad to even ask for her baby. Wordlessly, Elizabeth cut the cord and wrapped the child, who took her first reluctant breaths with a muted cry, as if unsure whether or not she should make an effort at this life. Then, handing the baby to Sarah, Elizabeth bent once more to take care of the afterbirth.

Sarah held the child and examined her, lifting the corners of the swaddling cloth to see better the little body that she held. The child blinked silently once or twice, then gave up the effort and lay still, eyes closed. Sarah touched her fingers to the little hands, and saw what her mother had seen: six full fingers on the baby's left hand. She took a deep breath and swallowed, then wrapped the cloth tightly once more and handed the child to her mother.

Joan took the bundle without a word or apparent interest as Sarah tried to show her how to feed, but the baby seemed indifferent to her efforts and lay against her mother's breast without stirring. They remained so for what seemed like a long time as Elizabeth finished her work and Sarah was silent, wondering what she should say to the new mother, if she should simply let the girl find it out on her own. It was tempting, but it seemed cruel when she so obviously had no one to turn to, and she wondered what had happened in Joan's short life to render her so completely alone.

'What do you think of her?' she began.

Joan shrugged. 'She's a baby. Same as any other.'

'Not quite,' Sarah said. 'Have a look at her.'

Elizabeth, standing up to stretch out her back after so long bent over, gave a subtle shake of her head. Sarah ignored it.

Reluctantly, Joan struggled to push herself up in the bed a little, Sarah helping to move the pillow. Then the girl looked down at her child for the first time. The daylight had crept in, the morning fully born, and though it would never be bright in such a room, there was light enough to see by. The candle had guttered to a finish long ago. Joan observed the baby she held, this mouth she would now need the means to feed, and touched her gently, acquainting herself with the little puckered mouth, the wisp of hair, the hands waving lightly in the air. Then the girl saw the extra finger and recoiled with a gasp, shoving the child away from her, turning her face to the side.

''Tis only a finger,' Sarah said, lifting the baby, attempting to return her to her mother.

'I don't want her. She's cursed,' Joan hissed. 'All my babies are cursed. It's better that she dies.'

Sarah looked to her mother, who lifted an eyebrow as if to say *I told you so*. But how could she have left them? This child-mother and child. And if the mother's life was already beyond redemption, perhaps they could at least save the baby. But who would take in a six-fingered orphan?

Her mother stood before the fire, which had all but died, damp ashes and a trail of smoke all that remained. Then she turned once more towards Joan, holding the baby in her own arms now. 'Why do you say your children are cursed?'

The girl shook her head. 'It makes no difference why,' she said. 'Take her away. Do what you want with her. Her father was a devil and the Devil takes his own.'

'Where is the father?'

Joan gave a sharp bark of laughter and derision. 'Long gone on a ship. To a heathen land far away for all I know. And good riddance.'

Sarah nodded. They had no choice but to take the baby – if they left her with her mother she would die.

Elizabeth swung from the fire with a sudden movement and stood over them both. 'We will take the child to the orphanage and I will give you herbs to help you repair. But you'd do well to keep your legs together next time you're with a sailor, because, God help me, I will not help you if you breed again.'

Sarah dropped her gaze. Her mother's anger was harsh and complete and stubborn. She was glad it was not directed at her, but the girl was not cowed.

'I open my legs to eat, Goodwife Stone. So judge me if you will.'

Girl and woman locked eyes for a moment, one insolent, one judging, but it was the girl who looked away first. Sarah stood up with the baby and made towards the door. She was glad to be leaving such a dismal place, and in the street she breathed deeply, though the air was still dank and foetid even outside. She glanced along the lane. In the daylight she saw the meanness of the houses, rotting tenements and shacks set in filth, and children in rags running wild. A woman in a tattered shawl stood in a doorway, a thin and whining toddler at her feet, watching them go with despair in her eyes. Sarah dropped her own gaze to the ground at her feet and they hurried away, picking their footsteps carefully through the rutted earth. She was glad she hadn't fully realised the poorness of the place in the darkness.

They made their way along the river toward St Saviour's, which towered over the surrounding low buildings, an ancient godly bulwark against the sprawl of decadent humanity that lay all around it. The churchyard was overgrown but the solid stone of the walls and the dark wood door gave a sense of permanence. Inside, the air was sweet, and the floor had been scrupulously swept and mopped, the walls fresh white and clean. The curate came out at the scraping of the door on the stones and greeted them.

'Mistress Stone.' He bowed. He was a young man with a doughy complexion and earnest eyes still clouded with sleep. His faith must be strong to minister here, she thought.

'Curate.'

'Another for the orphanage?' He held out his arms to take the baby from Sarah, pity and resignation in his eyes as he smiled his thanks.

'Just born this night,' her mother said. 'A girl with no name yet. She has six fingers and her mother thought her cursed.'

'Poor little mite. We shall call her …' He looked to Sarah for inspiration.

'Elizabeth,' Sarah said. 'After the woman who delivered her.'

Her mother rolled her eyes. 'Don't be so sentimental.'

'Mary then,' Sarah offered. It was her own middle name. She turned to the curate. 'Call her Mary.'

Elizabeth nodded her satisfaction with the choice, and the curate flicked a glance to Sarah that was somewhere between humour and embarrassment. 'We shall call her Mary,' he said. Then he looked again to Elizabeth. 'God thanks you for the work you do here. He has surely sent you to us on His behalf.'

'He's very welcome,' Elizabeth answered. Then she dropped her head in a nod of farewell, turned and walked away.

In the churchyard she stopped and looked to her daughter. 'Perhaps now you understand why your father wants no part of it. But I …' She stopped and corrected herself. 'But *we* have been gifted with skills and it goes against nature to use them only for those who can pay us.'

Sarah nodded. She had attended births before, learning her mother's way with herbs and healing, but only at the confinement chambers of more well-to-do women – merchants' wives, shopkeepers, women with husbands and able to pay. She understood her mother had been protecting her, waiting until she was old enough and skilled enough to understand the responsibility the part of a midwife involved.

'Ours is not a path to tread lightly,' her mother warned. 'But the cycle of life needs attendance, and those poor children born to drabs and whores, unsought and unwanted, deserve the same chance at life as any other.' She turned and began to walk briskly away. Sarah followed, jogging the first couple of paces to catch up. Walking with her mother had always been so, mother striding on ahead and daughter struggling to keep up. She could remember getting lost at markets when she was little, letting go of her mother's hand when she was tired or distracted and her mother's form disappearing into the crowd in moments. She recalled the excitement of those moments of freedom, and the fear until her mother came striding back to find her. Only once did she get properly lost, hours of lonely separation that had lasted long after the first flush of excitement, and it had been Tom that found her and took her home. She could still remember the joy at seeing him, the hug he gave her, the sense of safety when she was wrapped up in his arms. He had said to her then that he would always find her: no matter where she went, whatever she did, he would always be there to keep her safe, and he had never yet given her cause to doubt him.

Now she bustled along towards home a pace behind her mother, the weariness of the night catching up with her at last, as well as sorrow for the little girl, Mary, whose life, if she survived, had begun so inauspiciously. Perhaps it would have been better if she had gone the same way as her older siblings, she thought. Perhaps a child with six fingers is truly cursed.

At home she drank a little ale as breakfast, ignoring her mother's order to take some bread, then hauled herself up the stairs to her bed. Tom was nowhere to be found and she guessed he had left already for the playhouse. She would have liked to be there at the first rehearsal with Nick as Macbeth and she considered it for a moment, gazing out of the window of her room, tracing the journey to the Globe in her mind, but the call of the weariness was stronger, so she dragged off her boots, slid under the covers and within moments she was asleep.

Chapter Five

CAN THE DEVIL SPEAK TRUE?

In the morning Tom bought a piece of apple pie for a penny from a street seller he passed on his way to the playhouse. He had not slept and he could taste the weariness and the headache that was starting to build behind his temples. But the food helped, the pastry still flaky and warm from the oven, and it shifted the bad taste from his mouth and gave him some energy for the day's rehearsal and performance ahead. He wanted to be home in his bed but he refused to allow the desire any space in his thoughts.

He had left the house late, creeping out through the door from the kitchen at the back of the house. There were no bolts on the inside, just a heavy key that worked from both sides, and he had long since had a key of his own to open it. Leaving the house unnoticed was a skill he had learned as a very young boy; he was at home in the Bankside streets, becoming known in the taverns and alehouses, attaching himself to those men who interested him – men who had something to give or to teach. Quickly bored with the education at school, he had sought out other learning, filling himself with an understanding that no schoolmaster could have ever given him.

Spending his nights in the inns and bawdy houses, he met men of all sorts with knowledge he could take and enticing tales of distant places: dark handsome women whose breasts were bare, and women with veils and skin that was sweet with scented oils. He heard of fabulous spices and jewels, and of palm-fringed islands with pellucid waters full of bright and vari-coloured fish. He learned too of different gods, and of rituals to commune with daemons and the dead. He absorbed it all, unafraid to ask for their knowledge and willing to do whatever they asked of him in return. For a time he toyed with the notion of taking to a ship to experience it all first-hand, but the life of a sailor held no appeal – he knew himself too well to think he would enjoy the deprivations of shipboard life, so he chose to let the learning come to him and keep the comforts of a dry bed, with good food and wine and women.

But he kept on searching, spending his nights quizzing strangers who passed through the Bankside taverns, probing for some truth that might one day satisfy his yearning. Sometimes he wondered where it came from, this insatiable desire that burned in him at times to the point of physical pain. He had met other men who sought truth and knowledge also, but he knew of no one else who suffered for it as he did. His sister's faith in the ancient magic of the earth and the symbols of the heavens was not enough for him: he had always craved something more, a desperation in his need to know all of life in its entirety.

Now he wandered on through the early morning, finishing the pie. With the coming of the dawn the bridge gates opened to admit the travellers who had stayed in Southwark overnight, and the streets were coming alive in the growing light. A trail of carts trundled from the farms of Kent, the air rowdy with their calls for buyers as their voices vied with the shouts and clatter of stall holders opening up, shutters flinging to. Apprentices and housewives swept their doorsteps clean, and two prostitutes, weaving their way home arm in arm, staggered into his path. They looked him up and down, and one of them reached out and trailed her hand across his face and over his chest with a gap-toothed smile of encouragement. He preferred the hidden darkness of the night-time: in the daylight hours too much of life was out on show.

'Two for the price of one?' she offered, stepping closer, her hand shifting down, fingers pulling at the waistband of his breeches. 'For a fine gallant like yourself?'

'Another time perhaps,' he answered, taking her hand and removing it.

'All right, my sweet wag.' She grinned and stepped back. 'We'll be waiting.'

He dipped his head with a smile of acknowledgement. A small band of horsemen clattered through on their way to the bridge and into the city, retainers for some nobleman in a livery he did not recognise riding fine horses in rich apparel, and he stood back to let them pass. Finishing his pie, he watched their backs grow smaller until they were swallowed up by the crowd. Then he turned off the High Street and skirted the market as it stuttered into life, heading towards the river. Though the morning was cold and damp with drizzle, he was early yet for rehearsal and he took his time. Only when the unseen church bells tolled the hour of eight did he finally bend his steps with purpose to the playhouse.

The players slipped into their new roles with ease. Nick's Macbeth was chilling, a dangerous intensity in the soft-spoken words, and it was easy to believe the dark forces at work within him, the conflict of his flesh and spirit. Even now, in these early rehearsals with the lines as yet unlearned and constant interruptions, there was a latent power in his delivery. It was a world away from the kingly projection of Burbage's portrayal, and Tom found himself rapt, his own duties as wardrobe-keeper forgotten and neglected as he spent every spare moment enthralled by each unfolding scene. He understood his sister's desire – Nick would be a passionate lover, he thought again, ardent and intense. His own passion began to stir at the idea of it, heartbeat quickening, and his gaze wandered across the yard toward John, who was sitting alone close to the stage, observing his master at work, head tilted in concentration.

Tom wanted to go to him, to sit beside him and savour his close-ness, but he guessed John would not welcome him now and he knew that timing was everything. So he watched from afar, studying each slight movement John made, each small change in expression, committing them to memory. Knowledge is power, someone once told him, and he had never forgotten it.

The scene ended and the players left the stage for a break. His own scenes over for a while, Tom was considering going up to the wardrobe to begin work on the costumes when Nick came and sat beside him and the half-formed thought was forgotten.

'How goes it, Tom?' Nick asked, settling himself on the bench, lifting one foot to rest it on the seat in front. 'You look tired.'

'A little,' Tom replied. 'But not so much I don't want to watch.'

'Too much ale and company of women?' They had parted at the bawdy house the night before as Jane had settled herself between them.

He shrugged. 'Perhaps. You should have stayed.' Then, 'Why didn't you?'

Nick gave a small wry smile. 'I've no more stomach for whores – they leave me cold.'

'There's someone else?' Tom was quick to ask.

'Aye. In my dreams. But she's long been out of my reach and I am nothing to her.'

'And still you want her?'

'I will always want her.' He looked at Tom with an expression that was hard to read. Regret, perhaps? Resignation?

'She is at Court?'

'She was.'

'Have I seen her?'

Nick shrugged. 'Perhaps. Her name was Catherine Shawe. Now she is *Lady* Catherine Thomas.' He sneered her title with all the derision he could summon. 'And her new master has taken her away from Court to breed for him.'

'You'll find another,' Tom said, gently. 'Time will mend thee.'

'Ah, but you didn't know her. She was a woman like no other.'

'They are all women like no other,' Tom laughed. 'Trust me. You will find some other woman that will move you the same, and she may be closer than you think.'

Nick nodded, and turned away with a deep breath, silent with his thoughts.

They sat quietly then until the rehearsal began again.

Sarah came to the playhouse late in the morning and brought bread and sweet omelette from home for her brother. Tom was still watching the rehearsal: he loved these early days of production as the players discovered the characters they inhabited and made their first steps to bring the world of the play alive. Each day brought surprises – a new meaning, a new connection.

'What, can the devil speak true?' Banquo's words sounded across the theatre as Sarah sat down beside her brother. She was wearing the altered dress, new curves shaping her breasts. But she was pale, he thought, and her eyes spoke of sleeplessness and bad dreams.

'Are you well?' he asked, taking the hunk of bread she gave him, picking at it with his fingers.

'We attended a birth last night, a drab in a low place by the river. She was barely more than a child herself.' She shook her head as though to dismiss the memory. 'The child had a six-fingered hand and the mother disowned it as cursed. We took it to the orphanage.'

'I'm sorry,' Tom said. He could think of nothing else to say. She rarely spoke of the births she witnessed, the mysteries of the confinement chamber a secret shared only by women. It was a world of magic denied to men, a ritual of creation he would never know, and a part of him envied such knowledge.

She gave him a half-shrug of resignation. Then, nodding towards the stage, she said, 'How goes the play?'

'It goes.' He smiled. 'Slowly, as always at this stage.'

She nodded and took out the omelette in its wrapping from the basket, holding it between her hands. He waited patiently for her to give it him but her mind seemed to be elsewhere, her gaze roaming the playhouse without apparent purpose.

'The dress becomes you,' he said, to break the silence.

His voice snapped her thoughts back to the present. Looking down she saw the omelette in her hands and laughed as she passed it to him. Then she ran her hands across the bodice. 'Do you like it?'

she asked. 'I look down and they look like someone else's breasts. I hardly know myself.'

'It suits you,' he said.

She smiled, still regarding her own body with doubt, fingers tracing the lines of the bodice. He watched her for a moment as she learned to appreciate this new facet of herself. But the dress was merely a prop, a tool that gave her faith in her womanhood. She was starting to bloom and ripen, he thought, her sweetness almost ready to be tasted.

He said, 'Have you spoken to Nick today?' He made a gesture towards the stage, where the players were in heated discussion with Will about the scene.

'Not yet.' Her eyes followed his to rest on Nick. Her lips quivered almost imperceptibly at the corners as she watched him, and Tom wondered what dreams she had of him, the reach of her imagination. She was still just a girl after all, still an innocent, dependent on a man to lead her into knowledge. He was glad it would be Nick, for he guessed that he would lead her there with tenderness. Then he hesitated, uncertain whether to tell her or not, afraid of denting her new confidence. But he decided she had the right to know.

'I found out something this morning,' he began.

She turned to him, eyes awakening with interest. A pang of misgiving for his next words pulsed through him. He hoped it was the right decision.

'Nick has feelings for another woman,' he said.

She took in a sharp gasp of shock and the smile she had been wearing gave way to lips drawn tight in pain.

'In love?' she breathed. 'And she with him?'

'I don't know. But either way, it's over. She is married now and gone from Court.'

Sarah turned her face away from him, gazing out across the playhouse towards the stage, eyes unfocused, unseeing. He observed her face in profile, the jaw set taut against emotion, her mouth clamped and hard, the full lips pulled to a narrow line.

'I'm sorry,' he said. 'But I thought you should know.'

She swung toward him, her disappointment finding its mark. 'You said I could win him. You said he was as good as won. And now you tell me this?' The actors on the stage flicked glances towards them – her voice, in its anger, had carried.

'Hush,' Tom said. He went on in a whisper. 'I didn't know. But it isn't hopeless, Sarah. It's over with this woman – you can help him to heal. And I can still help you win him, I promise. We will just have to try a little harder.'

Her eyes half-closed in disbelief, she shook her head. But the first spark of temper had passed and lasting anger was not in her nature. 'Do you know her?' she asked.

'I've seen her. At Court.' He remembered the last time they played there a few weeks before, and the gaggle of ladies who came to see the players afterwards, giggling and flirtatious, looking for danger. Except for one who had stood apart and not said a word, her attention fixed on Nick. Tom had thought little of it at the time but he was sure now that she was the one, a small drama enacted between the two of them, unspoken and invisible to all but themselves.

The rehearsal ended with the morning, the church bells striking noon. *Macbeth* was forgotten and all minds turned to the business of *King Lear*. The flag was raised above the theatre to summon the crowds – black for tragedy – and the players began their preparations, practising new lines as the roles were rearranged.

Sarah attended to Will in the tiring house, making last-minute alterations to the robes of the king – a stitch here and there to adjust them to fit their new bearer – and helping with the chalk and soot to age him. Will was distracted; his talent was for writing, and the role of Lear was no easy task. He snapped at his seamstress, uncharacteristically tetchy, and she let him be, though the work was only half-done. But all of them were on edge – Burbage's fall had unsettled them and upset the balance. He was their leader on the stage, and without him their confidence was dented. Then Will took the stage and there were ripples of disappointment around the galleries, and in the yard there were jeers.

'Where's Burbage?!' someone shouted. 'We want Burbage!'

Another man threw a half-eaten apple which failed to connect, splattering instead across the wooden boards. The actors paused for just a moment and Sarah saw the collective deep breath they drew before Will spoke his first line.

'Attend the lords of France and Burgundy, Gloucester.'

The hubbub dropped a notch.

'I shall, my liege.'
    'Meantime we shall express our darker purpose ...'

Will's voice carried over the grumbling, which began to dwindle slowly as their interest was lured once again by the words of the play, and their desire to see Burbage was forgotten.

He would pass, Sarah thought from her place behind the curtain, and though he lacked the gravitas of Burbage, she could believe him as the king. Slowly the audience came to think so too, drawn in at last and caught up in the illusion. And when Will left the stage at the end of the scene, the relief was clear in his face. She smiled, and he raised his eyebrows in answer. It was going to be all right.

Nick had known that it could not last forever, and that one day Catherine Shawe would be sold off in marriage to someone else, a man with money, power, status. But he had lived for a year in hope that somehow the Fates would save them, each moment precious, each memory hoarded against the pain he knew must eventually come. The conversation with Tom had stirred up the feelings again, the images of another man's hands touching Catherine's pale body, kissing her, entering her, another man with mastery over her happiness. He wondered if her husband would realise she was not a maid, and he closed his eyes against the thoughts, but the images remained.

'Are you all right, Master Tooley?' John's voice nudged at his thoughts, disturbing the recollections.

They were seated before the hearth at home in the small house Nick had bought with the money his father had left him, an inheritance he never expected to get. Whatever he had thought of his father he would always be grateful for the legacy – it had bought him a home and a share in the King's Men, and with them a more certain future.

'Master Tooley?' John repeated.

Nick opened his eyes and looked across to his young apprentice, seated now on the rug before the fire, the pages of the play open in front of him. He wondered how much the boy knew, how much he had observed. Only a little, he guessed. For all his talent and the time he had spent in the Company, John was still an innocent, eyes wide at the world as though it shocked him.

'Is something amiss?'

Nick shook his head in answer and drained off the last mouthful of wine in his cup. 'I'm just tired,' he said. 'It was a long day.'

'But it is going well, I think?' John ventured, hesitant, as if afraid to irritate his master. Nick wondered what he had ever done to deserve such fear – he had never so much as raised his voice to the boy, had only ever been kind. He couldn't imagine how hard it must be for a man to be so afraid of the world, but he had no idea how he might instil more courage. As John's master he felt responsible – the boy had no father to teach him. Then he remembered John's transformation on the stage and it bewildered him. How could such uncertainty transfigure itself so utterly? It was impressive to be sure, an act of magic for which he had no explanation.

'It is a good play,' Nick replied, sitting up straighter, blinking himself more awake. 'Very powerful.'

'Would you like to go over the lines?' John asked, indicating the pages he had been studying.

Nick smiled and shook his head. 'No. I'm too tired and I shall only stumble over them. We should probably take ourselves to bed.' He took a deep breath and unfurled himself from the chair, standing before the fire and stretching. John nodded, unable to hide his disappointment, and levered himself to his feet, the script held tightly in one hand.

'Don't fall asleep reading,' Nick warned.

'I won't.'

They each took a candle and Nick snuffed the others. The fire was almost out, embers pulsing with a final glow, and they left it for the servant to clear out in the morning when she came. At the top of the stairs they bid each other good night and took to their separate rooms, but despite his claims to tiredness Nick had no desire to sleep, and he sat at the window for a long time into the night, thinking of Catherine.

Chapter Six

HOW WILT THOU DO FOR A FATHER?

The tailor's shop was shut when Sarah arrived home, the workers gone for the day, and the torch was lit at the threshold, flickering bravely in the dark. Candlelight glimmered bright through a chink in the curtains in the window up above. She hammered on the door with her fist – the rain had made her cold and she was eager for the fire.

One of the maids let her in on her way upstairs with a tray of spiced wine. Sarah followed, the scent of warm cinnamon and nutmeg warm and inviting. In the main chamber above the shop a bright fire crackled and roared in the great stone hearth, spitting now and then with drops of rain through the chimney. It was a cheerful room with a generous window that looked out over the street, and the oak wood panelling that lined the walls lent the chamber a welcome warmth. Rush mats covered the wooden floor, and candles flickered brightly from the sideboard and the table. Sarah paused at the door to greet her parents with a small curtsey, then went to stand before the fire, stretching out her hands as her skirts steamed slightly with the heat. Her mother brought her wine and she took it gratefully, cradling the cup between her palms.

'How was the rehearsal for the new play?' her mother asked softly.

'It's coming along fine,' she replied. She was reluctant to say more, wary of lighting her father's disapproval. It was only with great reluctance he let her go there at all, trusting to her brother to keep her out of trouble. Better there, in one place and under Tom's protection, he reasoned, than collecting piecework from all and sundry. But she was aware it was a precarious privilege.

'What is the subject this time?' Her father looked up from the ledger he was studying at the table.

She took a deep breath to steady herself, cautious of his interest. 'Ambition,' she replied, carefully. 'A lord who wants to become a king.'

'And does he become a king?'

'Yes,' she replied. 'For a while. But it doesn't last – the crown was not rightfully his to take and he is corrupted by its power.'

Her father nodded, apparently satisfied, his attention wandering once more towards the ledger. Sarah took another sip of the wine and felt its heat thread through her body and touch her thoughts. She waited. He did this sometimes, allowing her to think his questions were finished, then springing more at the last moment.

'It will play at the Globe?' he asked.

'Yes,' she said with a smile. Then, after taking a last mouthful of wine, she said, 'I must go and change these wet clothes.'

No one answered but she was aware of Simon's gaze, so she kept her eyes averted as she stepped across the rugs, placed the empty cup on the tray on the sideboard and left the room.

In her chamber Sarah peeled off the damp outer layers of her clothing and shivered as the cold air brushed her skin. The hearth was grey and cold and she rubbed at herself with a towel, pale skin reddening. Then she dressed herself again, in plain dark wool that felt good and warm, hanging up the damp clothes and hoping the bodice would be dry by the morning; she wanted to wear it again. She had liked the new shape of her body and had seen Nick pass his eyes across her with pleasure more than once. For a moment she sat on the edge of her bed, reluctant to go back downstairs and face her parents, in spite of the cold. She wanted to think about Nick and recall the look in his eyes when he saw her. The thought of it kindled a heat inside her, a new and unfamiliar warmth – she wondered what he was doing now, if he was still drinking with her brother or if some whore had taken his fancy and was giving him pleasure. She sighed, envious; she had only the vaguest notion of the ways a woman might pleasure a man. It was not something she could ever ask her mother: her mother's sternness discouraged such intimate questions. Perhaps she should ask Tom, she thought. She knew without a doubt that he was skilled in such things.

Standing up, bracing herself to go downstairs for supper, Sarah ran her hands once more across her bodice and down the lines of her hips and her thighs, attempting to feel her body as a man might do and understand. Heat prickled again through her limbs and she swallowed, aware of her breathing, a new light-headedness. An image of Nick played across her thoughts, his fingers caressing the ample bosom of a whore, his other hand lifting her skirts. She hesitated, the feelings new and disturbing: she was uncertain how to respond to them, and their intensity left her breathless. She stood for a moment in the cold room, struggling to calm her breathing and quiet the restlessness in her body. Finally, when she thought she was once more in command of herself, she took a single deep breath, squared her shoulders and headed downstairs for supper.

Downstairs, the table had been cleared of books. Her father and Simon had repaired to the fireside, legs stretched out towards it. Master and apprentice spoke intermittently and they shared an easy rapport, a relationship built through long days in the shop and a mutual interest in the world of its business. Like a father and son, she thought, and tried to recall a single time she had seen her father be so at ease with her brother. There was no memory to call on and all she could bring to mind were the fights between them. Tom had never learned to accept his new father, and Master Stone had responded by trying to force his respect. Perhaps if he had tried to love Tom more, she thought, or even tried to win him by some small kindness, he would have succeeded better. But Tom, both as boy and man, would never bow to coercion, and beating after beating had only ever hardened his hatred and resolve. Now he rarely showed his face at home and their father did not seem to miss him.

Her mother was setting the table. The two servants lived out and went home with the end of the day, but supper was prepared, set out in dishes already on the sideboard. She watched her mother working for a moment. She had inherited the same body shape, she realised, slight and boyish: her mother had no bosom to speak of either. But there the similarities ended. Her mother's face was thin and pinched. Narrow lips pursed under a beakish nose, and the lines were not of laughter but were formed of furrows across her forehead and puckers around her mouth. Thick grey streaks coursed through her hair, and for the first time Sarah understood that her mother was ageing and that her life had not been happy. A rare wave of affection filled her and when her mother lifted her eyes from the dish of boiled chicken she was holding, Sarah smiled.

'Let me help you,' she said, taking the dish and carrying it to the table. 'It's heavy.'

Her mother said nothing but simply turned away to fetch the bread.

Over supper the talk was of the shop – two gentlemen customers asking for what the tailor considered outlandish garb, the kind of thing that Frenchmen wore. Slashed sleeves with red silk inserts. But they were prepared to pay handsomely and so the work had been accepted. The two men talked of it for most of the meal, occasionally addressing remarks to her mother, until finally the subject was exhausted.

A long silence followed, growing awkward after the conversation of before. Sarah kept her eyes on her food and ate without pleasure. The meal was plain, boiled meat and bread, pickles and cheese, some raisins – the simple fare befitting a Puritan household. Then Simon, sitting across from her, looked up from his food.

'So, Sarah, tell us more of this play,' he said.

She was so surprised she almost choked, a piece of bread going down the wrong way, making her cough. She wondered if he understood how much her father disliked the theatre, how hard he had tried to stop his children being part of it. Apparently not. It was hard to believe he would ask such a question otherwise. How could he be such a fool? She took a swig of ale to soothe her throat and paused to recover her breath. Simon was watching her, waiting patiently.

'It's called *Macbeth*,' she said, when at last she could speak. 'By William Shakespeare.'

'Scottish?' Simon ventured.

'Yes. 'Tis is a tragedy.'

The apprentice nodded. There was another silence. Then her father said, 'And does your brother play in it?'

Sarah hesitated, sliding a brief glance to her mother, who sat impassive. She had never been able to read her mother, never had the slightest idea of the thoughts that passed behind that face. Her father was watching her, waiting for an answer.

'Just a bit part, Father,' she evaded. 'His main role is wardrobe-keeper, as you know.'

'A lord, perhaps?' Master Stone persisted. 'A soldier?'

For another heartbeat she paused, but there was no point in lying – Tom would tell the truth of it without a second thought. 'He plays a witch, and a gentlewoman,' she murmured.

'A witch?' Her mother's shock sounded low and breathy in the silence. Behind her the fire popped and spat as a squall of rain found its way down the chimney.

Sarah nodded. 'It is but a small part,' she said.

'Dear God!' her father exclaimed, standing up, throwing down his knife so that it clattered and skidded across the table, coming to rest just in front of her. 'A son of mine on the stage as a woman, as a witch! It is more than I can bear.'

Her mother cast a glance up towards him and there was fear in her eyes.

'It is just a small part, Sarah said, Husband,' she soothed. 'A minor role.' She slid a questioning look to her daughter, an invitation to contribute.

'A few lines only. Right at the beginning,' Sarah lied. 'To set the scene merely.'

Master Stone shook his head. 'If even half of what I hear about your brother is true then I am glad he is no true son of mine. I would be ashamed to call him so. Since the very first he has tried me almost beyond my patience to endure. And now this ... Is it not bad enough he earns his bread in such a low and sinful place?' He rounded on

Sarah, pointing a stubby finger towards her. She shrank away instinctively. 'Did he take the part to mock me?'

Elizabeth stood and touched a hand to her husband's arm. 'My dear ...'

He swung towards her, sweeping her hand away. 'I've put up with enough from him. Years of insolence, years of debauchery. I have brought him up as my own in good faith and he has thrown every kindness back in my face. He has never tried, never once shown me respect!'

'It is just a few lines,' Sarah protested.

'It matters not how many lines,' he spat. 'I should have stopped it years ago. The shame of it.' He shook his head, jaw working with tension, and for a moment it seemed that the outburst was over. Then he lifted his head to look at his daughter again.

'Does your brother think I know not how he carries on? How he brings shame on us with his lechery and his low desires? That such a boy should belong to me ...' He drew in a deep breath, tapping blunt fingers on the table top in front of him. 'And it started with the play-house, that hall of the Devil.'

Sarah held her breath, dreading what might be about to come. A glance towards her mother gave her no clue; the older woman's eyes were turned away and lowered.

When Master Stone spoke again the words were directed at no one, seeming as if he were merely thinking aloud, turning over a decision to be made. 'And yet he is a man now – godless, shiftless, steeped in vice.' He lifted his shoulders in a shrug of resignation. 'I can do nothing more for him but pray for God's mercy on his corrupted soul.'

There was another silence that was filled with the tapping of his fingertips against the table and the hollow roar of the fire in the hearth. All of them waited for him to speak again. He sighed and sat down. Then, with another shake of his head he said, 'I can bear it no more. No more.'

Sarah's mother lifted her head and her gaze grazed Sarah's as it slid toward her husband. 'What mean you by that, Husband?'

'I mean that I have done all I can for him and I will do no more. He is no longer welcome under my roof and I will no longer call him my son. He can make his own way now – I'll see him no more.' He gave his wife a small, thin smile. 'But I will pray for him as I have always done.'

The silence tightened. Sarah swallowed and sought her mother's eyes, but she had turned her head away with a sniff. Sarah rose from the table and went to her, placing an arm around her shoulders. Her father looked stonily ahead, and Simon stared morosely into his supper. For long moments the silence remained until finally her father got up from his stool without a word and walked away. They heard his footsteps tapping down the stairs, and the front door open and shut. Sarah stared at her mother, amazed.

'Did you know?' she asked. Her voice sounded loud in the hush. 'Did you know this was coming?'

Her mother swallowed and shook her head slowly. 'Your father tells me nothing, Sarah. We live together, we share a bed. But we talk of nothing save the household business and God. I barely know him. I married him when Tom's father died to keep the roof above our heads. That is all.'

Sarah said nothing, no words to offer against her mother's confession: though she'd long suspected it was so, it still hurt to hear it spoken.

'I should go,' Simon said, leaving the table. 'You have matters to talk of.'

The women gave him no answer. Simon disappeared to his room downstairs behind the shop and they heard the muffled sound of his door latching to.

'Did you love Tom's father?' Sarah said then.

'We were happy.' Her mother nodded, and a wistful smile touched her lips. 'He was a good man and, yes, we married for love.'

'I'm sorry he died.'

Elizabeth's lips compressed into a line that masked the emotion behind it. She said, 'Your father has fulfilled his side of the bargain. That's all I ever asked. He gave us a home and a hearth, a measure of comfort. And he is not an evil man; he is just devoted in his faith and afraid for all our souls, especially your brother's. You should not judge him too harshly. Tom is grown now and he's chosen his own way. I can do nothing more to protect him.'

'But surely …' It seemed impossible that her father could cut him away so abruptly, so finally, and nothing to be done, no argument made in his defence.

'We can do nothing more,' her mother said, in a tone that closed the discussion.

Sarah was silent, but she would not let her brother go so easily. She nodded in feigned acceptance, then rushed to help as her mother began clearing away the remnants of supper.

Later, slipping out through the back door as she knew Tom had done a thousand times, she heard a voice say her name. She froze, hoping she had imagined it, the product of her fears.

'Sarah?' She heard it again. A male voice, spoken low. She turned toward it and saw Simon in the passage. His face loomed in the flickering light of the torch. 'What are you doing?' he asked.

She hesitated but no plausible excuse came to mind. She had not thought to be stopped by him.

'Where are you going?' he said in the pause. 'The streets aren't safe for a woman after dark.'

'I'm going to find Tom,' she replied. 'To warn him what is coming.'

'To Bankside?' His horror at the thought of it was clear in the tone of his voice – his own Puritan tendencies rising to the surface. 'How do you hope to find him? Surely you can't think of going into those places by yourself?'

She shrugged. What else could she do?

'I'll come with you,' he said.

'No,' she answered quickly, backing away. 'No. I don't need your protection.' She could move quicker and more discreetly by herself and she knew the streets around the playhouse well.

'If I let you go and anything happens to you, your father will kill me. If it makes you feel any better I'm doing it for me, not for you.'

She said nothing, unconvinced by his argument. She had seen the way he looked at her over breakfast, over supper, and she did not want his company.

'I'm not letting you go alone. We can stand here all night and argue if you wish.'

She sighed. He would follow her regardless; she had no choice. 'Very well,' she said. 'Let's go.' She set off quickly, bending her head against the rain, across the garden and over the wall, refusing the help he offered her, irritated by his presence. He was soon breathing hard; in his life as a tailor's apprentice he barely ever went outside, and Sarah was well used to walking.

'Keep up,' she said, when finally he stopped to catch his breath, his hand at his chest, breath coming laboured and rasping.

Nodding, he pushed himself on, plodding valiantly beside her as she wondered where Tom might be in the myriad of taverns, dice dens and bawdy houses that were the lifeblood of Bankside. She guessed she should begin at the Green Dragon, where she knew he had begun the night. After that, she had no clue. Perhaps someone there would know his whereabouts. Perhaps someone would help her.

Leaving the High Street at the market, they turned into Foul Lane. The maze of empty stalls and lanes was different in the late-night darkness, more threatening, and though she doubted he would be much help if they met trouble, she found she was glad of Simon's presence – it was reassuring not to be alone. He trotted along behind her, his breath still coming hard, but she did not slow her pace.

At the door to the Green Dragon she stopped and swallowed hard. It was a place she knew the players haunted often, and she cast her eye across the narrow front of it, observing the archway to one side that led to the stables and the yard with rooms where you could sleep for a fee. It was one of the larger taverns, she knew, and attracted a better class of customer than some of the others, mostly travellers caught on the wrong side of the bridge and waiting for the gates to open with the dawn. But she had never been inside such a place before. Her heart was hammering and her mouth was dry. Simon stood at her shoulder, no more experienced than she was, but his presence reassured her: a woman on her own must surely be in danger. Then she cast a quick glance at him and saw he shared her fear.

'Shall we?' she asked him, and he nodded and pushed open the door.

The door opened onto a low-ceilinged room with a wide hearth, tables and chairs strewn randomly at odd angles. There was dirty straw on the floor, and small groups of men of all sorts sat drinking. A couple of low-looking women in gaudy clothes were looking bored by the fire, and a great dog of some unknown breed padded across to sniff them, before turning away, uninterested. No one else paid them any attention. There was no sign of Tom or any of the others of the Company. Sarah took a deep breath and wove her way between the tables and chairs towards the women. They looked up at her approach with curiosity.

'Good evening to you,' she greeted them, dropping her head politely.

'Good day to you, mistress,' one of them answered. 'What can we do for you and your friend?'

Ignoring the suggestion and the sly smile that went with it, she hurried on. 'I'm looking for someone – a man named Tom Wynter. He was in here earlier with a company of players from the playhouse just across the way.'

The younger woman's expression changed from bored curiosity to concern. 'You want Tom?'

'You know him?' Sarah asked.

'I might do,' the girl said carefully. She was very young, Sarah realised, perhaps fifteen or so, and she had pretty eyes. Then she thought of the girl Joan with her dead, cursed babies, and wondered if this girl would end up the same. 'What do you want with him?'

'He's my brother and I have grave news for him.'

The girl flicked a glance to the older woman, who shrugged and turned away. 'I might know where he is,' she said.

'Thank you,' Sarah breathed.

'Come with me.' She led them back across the room and into the street, where the drizzle had hardened into a steady downpour. The girl had no cloak to cover her but she bowed her head into it and kept walking towards the river, her footsteps sure in the stickiness of the mud. Sarah pulled her own hood further forward and the water dripped off its edge before her face. After a few minutes, the girl turned in at another door and down a flight of stairs to a cellar that rang with voices, the hubbub echoing off the low ceiling. Halfway down the steps, she stopped, casting her eye across the drinkers. One of them recognised her and yelled out, but she merely cocked her head at him and turned on her heel.

'Not here,' she said.

They followed her into three more places that seemed the same, all the time moving closer to the water, skirting the church and Winchester Palace along tortuous lanes that Sarah had never ventured into before. They found him finally in the Castle on the Hoop by the river, still drinking with Nick and John and a couple of the others. 'He's over there,' the girl said, pointing. 'Tell him Jane helped you. I've got to get back.'

'Thank you,' Sarah said, but by the time she had reached into her purse for a coin to give her, the girl had gone.

Sarah moved through the crowd towards her brother, Simon at her heel. It was the most crowded place they had been to, and the jostling as she made her way across the room was disconcerting. She was aware too of the looks she was drawing, so she kept her head down and pushed on. This was no inn for travellers. Finally she reached Tom's table, but it was Nick who saw her first. He stood up and guided her to a stool beside him, his arm protectively around her. For a moment her errand was forgotten, all her senses alive to his closeness and relief at knowing she was safe.

'Sarah!' he exclaimed. 'What on earth brings you here?'

'I was looking for Tom,' she replied.

Her brother leaned across the narrow table and took her hand in his. 'What's happened? Why are you here?'

'Father has disowned you …'

Confusion crossed her brother's face, and disbelief. 'But why?' he managed to say. 'What have I done?'

She shook her head, overwhelmed by all of it now that her brother was found and her message delivered. Tears prickled in her eyes and she blinked hard and set her jaw.

'Sarah?' Nick's face was close to hers. 'Are you all right?'

'If I talk I'll cry,' she told him and he smiled, drawing her closer in towards him.

Someone gave her a cup of ale and she drank it. Then Tom changed places with another man and sat on the other side of her. She shifted a little away from Nick and turned to her brother, who refilled her cup. She drank more. It was watery and bitter but she felt the beginnings of a pleasant wooziness in her thoughts and a warmth inside.

'What happened?' Tom asked again.

'He asked about the play,' she began, 'so I told him and he said he could bear no more from you and that you are no longer his son.'

Tom drew back from her a little and slid a glance across the table towards John, who was watching it all, leaning in close to hear better. 'I have never been his son,' he said.

'You can't come home.'

'He can stay with me,' Nick said, touching a reassuring hand to her arm. 'There is room enough.'

She smiled, grateful, and then she remembered about Simon and lifted her head to look for him, but he was nowhere to be seen. He must have gone home, she guessed, once he had seen her to safety. She hoped he would find his way back without mishap.

'How did you find me?' Tom asked.

'Jane,' she said, and told him what had happened.

Someone refilled her cup again. She was feeling light-headed now, unfamiliar sensations pulsing through her. She smiled up at Nick, content to be near him, their shoulders touching as one or other of them shifted in their seats.

Nick spoke to Tom above her head. 'This is no place for your sister to be.'

'I can't take her home,' Tom answered.

'My house, then.'

Tom took her hand and led her through the crowd to the door.

Nick's house was small – on the end of a row of houses just south of Paris Garden, timber framed, wattle and daub, red tiles on the roof. Lead-lighted windows gave myriad reflections of the torch that Nick carried to light their way in the dark. But it was well kept and pretty, with trees beside it that bordered the lane. From the hallway a door opened into a wide, low-ceilinged room, and inside John set to making a fire. The room warmed quickly, the chimney drawing well. Sarah looked around her, content, still fuzzy from the ale. The room was simply furnished – a dark wooden table and chairs, a sideboard with a few pewter plates, a hardbacked chair either side of the hearth. Fresh rushes were strewn across the floorboards, and a single Turkey rug lay before the fire. She took her place on it, curling her legs beneath her.

'It's a fine house,' Sarah said, when Nick took his seat by the fire.

He smiled. 'Thank you.' Then, holding out the jug, 'Wine?'

She hesitated, her head still light, but the others were drinking and she wanted to be part of it all, so she accepted the cup and sipped at it cautiously. It was a world she had never thought to join, this male club of players, and to be so near to Nick was intoxicating. There was a pause, a moment of awkwardness, and she realised that she was the cause, their easy familiarity thrown by the presence of a woman.

'Please,' she said. 'Don't mind me. Pretend I'm not here.'

Nick laughed. 'Why would we want to do that?' he asked. 'It isn't often we have a pretty girl in our company.'

She felt the flush brush her cheeks and looked away. The wine was very strong and her thoughts were beginning to blur. To cover her embarrassment she took another a mouthful.

'Will you be in trouble with your father tomorrow?' Nick asked.

'I'm hoping he won't ever know that I was gone. My mother would never tell him.' She looked across to Tom, who shrugged. 'She tried to change his mind,' she told him. 'She tried to make it better.'

'She never stood up for me before,' he said. 'Not once.'

She was silent for a moment. His bitterness against their mother was unexpected – she had always thought them united as a band against her father, the magic of the ways they shared together binding them against his Christian zeal.

She said, 'She married him so you would have a father. She has no more love for him than you do.'

'I know.' He nodded. 'But still …'

She knew that there was more he would have said to her alone, but Nick and John were listening and so she changed the subject. 'What was your father like?' she asked. 'Can you remember much?'

Tom gave a half-smile, half-shrug. 'Only a little. I was very young when he died. But I remember that he sang all day, and if we ever heard music in the street we would have to stop and listen till it was done.'

'That's a lovely memory,' she said. 'I'll have no recollections like that about *my* father.'

'Nor I about mine,' Nick said. 'I can only recall the hard work and the beatings.' He paused, recollecting. Then he said, 'My father kept a roadside inn and the work was endless. Which is why I ran away when I was fourteen years old and the players came. I'd never seen anything so magical, nor even imagined such a world could exist. I was hooked from the very first moment.'

'What did they play?' She was enthralled, well understanding the spell of the theatre's world of shadows and dreams.

'*A Midsummer Night's Dream*,' he said. 'I wanted to be Puck.'

'Me too,' Tom laughed. 'I still do.'

'And me,' John said.

They sat in comfortable silence then for a time, watching the fire. She drank more of the wine and her eyes began to feel heavy. It would be nice, she thought, to lie down before the fire and sleep for a while. It was warm and comfortable and she felt safe with her brother and Nick. She was glad she had come.

Finally, Nick got up and stretched, yawning. From her place on the rug she could see the pink flesh of his cheek inside his mouth and she turned her face away. When she lifted her face again he was looking at her. 'You can have my bed,' he said. 'I'll sleep by the fire.'

'No,' she said, shaking her head. 'I can't turn you out of your bed.'

'It's not fitting for you to sleep here. You have my chamber. Come, I'll show you.' He reached down a hand and she took it, her small hand encased in the long strong fingers as he helped her to stand. She stood for a moment, slightly off balance, and he kept hold of her hand to steady her.

'Good night, Tom,' she said, turning. 'John.'

They nodded their good nights, and she followed Nick up the stairs to a tiny landing with a door on either side of it and another staircase that led up to an attic. He gave her the candle and opened one of the doors.

'Sleep well, Sarah,' he said. 'Sweet dreams.'

'You too,' she replied. There was a brief moment of hesitation, standing close to him in the darkness, aware of his breath, his warmth, the memory of his hand against hers. For a heartbeat she thought he would kiss her. Then the moment passed and she stepped through the door and closed it behind her.

Tom followed John to the other chamber, the single candle flickering against the darkness inside, the one large bed dominating the room. Tom walked to the window and leaned against it, looking out, but he could see nothing but the shifting reflection of the room. He turned and rested his hips on the ledge and watched as John stripped off his outer clothes in readiness for bed, narrow limbs shivering in the cold. Then he stood by the bed in his shirt, pale skin wan in the sickly light from the candle.

'Are you coming to bed?' John asked. 'It's cold.'

'I'm coming to bed,' Tom replied. John was still just a boy, he thought. Still so innocent. He turned his eyes away and shook his head, trying to shift the images that persisted, the urges that incited him on. It would be so easy to take him tonight, he thought, and to corrupt him against his will, but it was not the path he wanted to follow. He wanted John to turn willingly, to have him surrender through his own desire. It was a longer game and more of a challenge, and he was uncertain how to begin. He started to undress, aware of John watching him from the bed, the covers pulled up now around him against the night air. He felt his cock stir and turned away. It was too soon for that, he knew. He had to be careful.

Forcing his mind to an image of his father, a memory of harsh and brutal beatings, the desire slid away for long enough that he could undress and hide himself beneath the covers. When he was settled, John blew out the candle and they lay there side by side in the darkness. The knowledge of the young body next to his so close in the bed stirred the lust again, making him hard.

'Are you sleepy?' John whispered.

'Not really.'

'Me neither. Can we talk for a while?'

'If you like.'

'What will you do now your father's disowned you?'

'I suppose I will work to keep myself until I can work no more and then I will die poor, same as most others.'

'Can you not talk to him? Ask him to change his mind?'

In the dark, Tom smiled. 'You've not met my father.'

There was a silence. Then John said, 'I wish I could help.'

'Thank you,' Tom replied, and reached across the space of cold sheet that lay between them and squeezed John's hand in gratitude. John returned the pressure of his fingers and Tom allowed his hand to remain so that they lay there for a while hand in hand, until finally he heard the change in John's breathing, slow and quiet and regular. Then slowly, careful not to startle him, he withdrew his hand and silently, quickly, gave himself up to the lust.

Downstairs, Nick lay sleepless too before the dying fire, wrapped in a quilt and blankets that did little to soften the floor under his shoulders. Shifting in his makeshift bed, he tried vainly to get more comfortable. Then he thought of his own soft bed upstairs and Sarah, sleeping in its comfort. He let his mind linger on the thought, taking time to create an image of her in his mind, lying in the bed in her shift, no longer a child. He had noticed her as a woman the last few days, aware of her body and her eyes, the fullness of her lips. She was pretty, he thought, and young and unspoiled, and after tonight he suspected she might harbour feelings for him. He wondered if she was sleeping now or lying awake, restless as he was. A memory of Catherine Shawe in the same bed trailed across the corner of his thoughts and he brushed it away. She was as good as dead to him now and he had been a fool to think it could end any other way. She had loved him solely for the adventure of it, the danger of courting a Bankside player – he was sure of it; anything more had been an illusion. But the knowledge did not assuage the hurt. That, he guessed, would only come with time.

Still restless, he sat up again and hugged his knees, watching the ashes that glowed, pulsating in the dying throes of their heat, and struggling with the thought of the girl in his bed upstairs. It was tempting; she had been giddy with wine and ale and he was certain she would give herself willingly, but she was not some drab to use and cast aside, and he was unsure yet if he wanted anything more. In spite of all he knew of Catherine, his heart still ached with want for her, and he was unsure if Sarah could fill the void, if he should even try to yet. He sighed and pulled the covers closer round his shoulders.

His mind turned, searching for something else to occupy his thoughts, but they caught again and again on the image of Sarah, half-naked in his bed. Eventually, he simply let the image stay, travelling his imagination across her body, remembering the moment at her door when he might have kissed her. He should have, he reflected now. Just a kiss and nothing more. He smiled to himself at the thought of it, then lay himself back down on the rug and in minutes he was asleep.

Chapter Seven

THE CRY OF WOMEN

I n the morning they rose early and Sarah's head ached from the wine. She walked with the others as far as the playhouse, then bid them farewell and headed on towards home. The rain had stopped overnight, but the clouds were still heavy and the ground underfoot was soft and slippery. She tried to avoid the worst of it, picking her way carefully, but by the time she reached Narrow Lane, her boots were coated and the hem of her skirt was heavy with wet. Near the house she slowed, nerves weighting down her steps with the fear of discovery, and she sent a silent prayer to the spirits for aid.

Outside the house she paused a moment, looking up to cast her eyes across the three storeys of the narrow building, one in a long terraced row at the southern end of Southwark, nestled amongst a myriad of artisans' shops and merchant houses. The tailor's sign hung silently in the still of the morning – on a windy day it squeaked and rattled as it swung. The shop window was already propped open and she could see the bolts of cloth and a half-made jerkin on the dummy. With luck her father was already at work, safe out of the way in the back of the shop, though she could not see him. Perhaps he was further inside, out of sight. She hoped so. Then, taking a deep breath, she shoved open the heavy front door and trotted up the stairs to find her mother.

In the first-floor chamber the family was still at breakfast. She halted in the doorway, taking in the scene as dread swept up from her gut. Her father saw her first and fixed her with a glare.

'Close the door,' he commanded.

She did as she was told and took a couple of steps closer. Her father rose from his place at the table and came towards her. She swallowed and cast a nervous glance towards her mother, who looked away. She had rarely raised her father's anger, though she'd seen it often against her brother, and she braced herself for what was coming. Breathe, she told herself. Just breathe. But her pulse still hammered and the ache in her head shifted forward. He stood a foot away, and she could smell the ale he had drunk with breakfast on his breath.

'Where have you been?' her father said. His lips barely moved, the grey-whiskered jaw tight with fury.

She swallowed. Lies clustered behind her teeth on the tip of her tongue, but there were none she thought he might believe.

'I went to find Tom,' she said. 'To pass on what you said.'

Her father raised his hand and brought it hard across her face. Shock mingled with sudden pain and she dipped away, her own hand lifting to cover the smarting cheek, tears rising that she could not check.

'How dare you take such a thing upon yourself? How dare you sneak out of my house at night like a common slut? Did you visit the alehouse too? Did you mix with drunkards and whores?' His eyes slid towards Simon. Had he betrayed her after all? Was it his word that had brought her to this? Panic welled, limbs trembling, heartbeat racing. It was all she could do to stand straight and breathe. She lowered her head and said nothing, afraid to inflame him further.

'That a daughter of mine should go to such a low place and do such a thing!' He swung toward his wife, as if Sarah's behaviour could only be the fault of her mother. Then he turned once more to his daughter, stepping closer so that his face was only inches away. The sallow cheeks were trembling and there was spittle on his lips. She could not remember ever seeing him so close before. Swallowing, she had to use all her willpower not to step back and away from him. He grabbed her arm and held it, fingers digging into the muscle.

'Tom is no longer your brother, do you understand?'

'He will always be my brother,' she heard herself saying, though she felt her fear flicker through her limbs. 'Not even God can change that.'

Her father's face flushed and the anger seemed to travel through him in a tremor. She watched him, surprised she could be so detached as to notice such details. 'I have let you run in your ungodly ways for too long,' he went on. 'I should have stopped it years ago. I should have stopped you both. Your brother has damned his own soul and I can do nothing now to save it. But *you*? You are still my daughter and you will never go to the playhouse again. I have spared you the rod for too long and God has punished me with your wickedness. There is too much of your brother in you, and I mean to drive it out.'

She raised her eyes then, incredulous.

'Get you to your chamber while I decide what to do with you.'

She needed no second telling. She turned and fled upstairs to her room, slamming the door behind her in her haste. Then she leaned her back against it, breath coming in silent sobs, hard inside her chest. She stood there for what seemed a long time until she could bring herself to push away from the door and cross the room to the window, where she stood with dry, sore eyes while her breathing quieted to small and intermittent sobs that forced their way out of her, unbidden. Down below in the street outside the shop, a baker's boy was selling pies from a basket and flirting quietly with a maid, who held a held a load of laundry on one hip. They were laughing and she wondered how such a normal day could be passing outside her window when her own world had just come to an end.

After a while, when the baker's boy and the laundry maid had parted company and gone their separate ways, she heard her father's steps on the stairs, slow, measured and heavy. It was a sound that had quickened her heartbeat with dread for as long as she could remember. Most times it was Tom's door he was heading for and she would listen at her own door to the low rumble of the lecture and the repeated thwack of the strap against Tom's legs, though never once did she hear her brother cry out: he would have bitten off his own tongue before he gave the old man the satisfaction. But this time she knew he was coming for her, and her breath grew short with fear.

She moved to the window and stood with her back against it, as far from the door as she could go, the bed as a shield. The door handle lowered and she stared at it, waiting, pulse hammering. Just breathe, she told herself again. Just breathe.

Then the door swung inward and her father was there in the doorway, closing the door behind him with slow deliberation. When he turned to face her she saw the strap in his hand. Tears rose and she swallowed, forcing them down. Be like Tom, she scolded herself. Don't let him see you're scared. Don't give him the pleasure. Drawing herself up, squaring her shoulders, she faced him and waited. He stood silently for a moment, allowing his presence to have its effect on her. She observed him: thick and stocky, turning to fat, shoulders hunched from too many hours at his trade. His hair was growing thin, she noticed, with flecks of grey at the temples.

'Your days of wickedness are over, Sarah Stone,' he said. 'Get on your knees.'

She hesitated, caught between her desire to thwart him and her fear of the strap, and in the pause he launched himself towards her and grabbed a handful of hair in his fist, forcing her to her knees at his feet. Instinctively she cried out, trying to twist away, but he was stronger and yanked harder, pulling her down before he shoved her towards the bed, one hand still twisted in her hair. With the other he lifted her skirts, slowly and deliberately, placing them carefully across her back so they would not be in the way. Then he lifted the strap and brought it down across the backs of her thighs. The pain was blinding and she clawed at the bedclothes with her hands, shoving the quilt into her mouth to stifle her cries, thinking of Tom. How many times had he suffered this? Her father tightened his grasp on her hair, pulling her head round at an angle so she could not move. Then he struck her again, across the buttocks this time. Tears began to stream across her face and she could do nothing to stop them as the strap fell again and again. She lost count in the end, all thought vibrating in the pain, and when it was finally over and her father had carefully replaced her skirts to cover her modesty, she was almost insensible with humiliation and rage and hurt.

He released her hair from his fist and, taking her arm instead, dragged her roughly to her feet. She stood swaying and trembling, her face wet with tears, salt on her lips, and her father bent his face close to hers.

'Now I will leave you to think on your sins and to pray for forgiveness,' he breathed. 'I expect you to be on your knees for the rest of the day. Do you understand? And when you are chastened, when your suffering has brought you closer to God, we will talk again – it is time to think on your future.'

She nodded, still struggling to remain upright.

Then he turned on his heel, opened the door and was gone.

Chapter Eight

NIGHT'S BLACK AGENTS

At the Castle on the Hoop, the players discussed the day over bowls of leathery mutton stewed with figs, and Jane made herself at home on Tom's knee. He let her stay for a while, grateful for the help she had given his sister, and she ran her fingers up and down his neck, encouraged. But his attention was on John and gradually she grew frustrated by his indifference. She leaned in to whisper in his ear. 'What do I have to do to entice you? I'll do anything you ask for. Anything at all …' She bit his lobe gently before she sat back to look at his face.

He tore his eyes from John and met her gaze, but not before she had seen more than he hoped. She smiled and stroked his cheek. 'I'll turn over for you,' she purred. 'You can pretend I'm him.'

'Not now, Jane,' he murmured back. He was aware of John watching him, and an unexpected flare of shame lit across his chest, flushing his neck.

She was undeterred. 'Or would you like me to break him in for you and you can watch? I'd wager he's green – he'd go with a woman first, most like.'

He swallowed. It was a tempting offer – he had thought the same himself. His gaze wandered back to the boy, listening now to some story Nick was telling, his young face rapt with attention. Where did he find the knowledge to play the Lady when he was so innocent?

Tom wondered. Where did such an understanding of the power of sex come from?

'It won't cost you any extra to watch …' She tucked her finger under his chin and turned his face to her. He looked up and smiled.

'Do you think you can tempt him?' he asked her. 'He is very green.'

'Are you doubting me?'

He grinned, and ran his hand across her breast, and down between her legs. 'Not for a moment.'

'Are you sure you want to do this?' she asked him.

'Oh, I'm sure,' he replied. 'I'm very sure.'

They gave John more ale. Nick and the others left with knowing smiles. John half rose to leave with them but Tom placed a hand on his arm. 'Stay awhile, John,' he coaxed. 'It is early yet and there is much to talk of.'

John cast a wistful glance towards Nick, almost at the door, and settled back onto the stool. Jane filled his cup again.

'You should have seen him today,' Tom said to Jane. 'Our John has fulfilled his promise as an actor.'

She took the cue and turned to the boy. 'What is your part?'

'I play the Lady,' he replied, flicking a look towards Tom. 'The wife of the main character – that's Nick.' The words came out too fast in his nervousness, and his breathing was shallow.

'What's the story?' Jane laid an encouraging hand on John's arm and he jumped as though she had burned him. Hiding her surprise beneath a smile, she slid her hand away.

John turned to Tom. 'You tell it, Tom. You can tell it better.'

Jane moved closer to him. 'You tell me,' she insisted. 'Tom talks too much. I'd like to hear it from you.'

John swallowed and drank off some of his ale. Tom refilled the cup and put it back in his hand.

'There is a Scottish lord, Macbeth, and after a battle he meets three evil witches who make him promises – he will become a greater lord, and then be king. He tells his wife of the prophecy and then they plot to make it true.'

'They kill the king?' Jane's interest was genuine, and Tom smiled.

'They do,' John answered, beginning to forget his nervousness, engaged in the conversation. 'But it doesn't end well. Macbeth is racked with guilt because he has to kill again and again to hold his throne – his friend, women, children – and his Lady loses her mind.'

'When can we see it? When will it be ready?'

John looked to Tom for the answer.

'Before Easter at the playhouse.' Tom said, reaching across in front of John to touch her hand. 'I'll let you know when.'

She lifted her eyes and held his look for a heartbeat with an expression it took him a moment to read, before Tom understood with surprise that she loved him. He breathed in sharply and dropped his gaze, uncertain what to do with the knowledge. Then he said, 'Would you like us to show you backstage? We could take you there now.'

'In the dark?' John's voice quavered.

'We can take torches, light candles. Come, it will be an adventure.'

'Can we?' She was like a small girl, promised an unexpected treat. 'Please, John? Please can we go?'

'I suppose it would be all right,' John said. 'But I don't have a key.'

'I have one,' Tom said. 'To the wardrobe door upstairs. We can take the outside steps.'

They drank down the last of the ale and stepped outside into the evening. The clouds had cleared and the air was damp and cool and the sky was soft above them. Jane linked arms with Tom, and John followed behind as they turned away from the river and walked the short distance to the Globe, heading around the high wall to take the wooden steps that led up to the wardrobe, where Tom spent most of his hours. Inside, gowns and cloaks hung on racks around the edges of the room, and between them and under them stood large oak chests which held the bulk of the costumes, folded away and lovingly retrieved and repaired for each performance. In the centre of the wooden floor was a large high workbench with two stools drawn up either side. Sarah's sewing basket sat atop it along with the tools of

Tom's trade, which were laid out neatly at one end: scissors and measures and spools of thread, pins and needles, chalk.

The wardrobe smelled of old fabric and sweat and timber. Tom inhaled. He loved this place – he had slept here often, unbeknownst to the Company, and it was more of a home than ever his stepfather's house had been. He lit candles and gestured the others towards a low couch against one wall where he had slept many times. Jane took the boy's hand and led him towards it. He followed her with reluctance and sat at one end, as far away from her as he could. His shoulders were hunched as though he had turned in on himself. Jane slid an uncertain look towards Tom, who shrugged. It seemed this would be harder than they'd thought. Undiscouraged, she shifted closer until her skirts were touching his thigh, and Tom sat on the floor before them, John's uneasiness unsettling them all. Then Jane turned her body to face him and rested her hand on his arm. 'How old are you, John?' she asked.

'I'm almost a man,' he answered quickly, his face averted, staring down at his hands.

'Fifteen? Sixteen?'

'Sixteen.'

'And have you ever kissed a girl?'

He swallowed and shook his head.

'Would you like to?'

He shook his head again.

'Go on,' she urged. 'You might like it.' She shifted one hand to rest on his thigh and the other reached to curl his hair. He jerked his head away and she laughed. 'Well, you are a shy one. But no matter. We'll get there ...' She ran her fingers up his thigh and brought them to rest at his groin, gently feeling through the fabric for his cock. For a few moments he made no resistance, allowing the caress, but when he raised his head to look at her his face was etched with pain. 'Please stop,' he said.

Ceasing the movement of her hand but letting it still rest in place, she straightened to look at him. 'Don't you like me?' she asked.

'Ye-e-es,' he breathed. 'I like you fine, but ...'

'But ...?'

'I don't want this.' He turned to Tom. 'Please, Tom, make her stop. Please?' His voice trembled with desperation.

Tom sighed, suspecting they would have no joy with him tonight. 'Leave him,' he said to Jane. 'Just leave him. Just go.' He tossed her a shilling. 'Take the torch from the sconce on the wall outside and go.' She pocketed the coin and he looked away from the hurt in her eyes.

'Tomorrow?' she asked.

He shrugged. 'Perhaps. Now go.'

Her footsteps were quick and loud across the boards and the door slammed behind her as she left. He could hear the steady tap tap tap as she made her way down the steep wooden stairs to the street below. He had paid her well – he had no cause to feel guilty. But still, a sense of regret shimmied through him, a recollection of the look she had given him earlier. Perhaps he would see her tomorrow after all and make it up to her.

Shifting across the floor, he sat at John's feet. The boy was hunched forward, head bowed over his knees, arms wrapped around himself as though he were in pain. Tom touched his arm gently.

'John? It's all right. She's gone.'

John lifted his head a little and cast a glance around the room as though to check if it were true. Satisfied, he straightened up a little and uncurled his arms.

'What happened?' Tom asked softly. He was wary of feeding the boy's fear. 'Did she not please you?'

John shook his head a little, his eyes still lowered, still trembling.

'You don't think she is pretty?'

The boy lifted his gaze then and Tom had never seen such despair. 'Yes,' he whispered. 'She's pretty. And I wanted to like her. I still want to like her. But I don't. And I can't. I just can't.'

Tom shifted closer, beginning to understand, his heart quickening with hope. 'Tell me,' he whispered.

'I cannot.' John shook his head, lips tight and quivering with the effort not to cry. 'I am a wicked person, Tom. The Bible tells us so, and I will burn in Hell for my wickedness …'

'Then I will see you there,' Tom said. 'I'll be burning just the same as you.'

John raised his head and stared in bewilderment. 'But you … you

and Jane ...' He shook his head in confusion. 'And others ... I have
seen you go with other women too ...'

'I go with both, John. Women and men. I take love where I find it.'

'Can it be love between two men?'

'Truly.' Tom slid forward to kneel between John's legs, reaching to
touch his face with one hand and stroke the still-smooth cheek. He
heard the sharp gasp of surprise and lifted himself upward so that
their faces were level. He could feel the boy's warm, sweet breath and
he had to force himself to be slow, to be gentle, when his whole body
was screaming for release. 'Let me show you,' he murmured. He
leaned in to kiss John's cheek, then ran his lips downwards across the
jawline to the delicate warmth of his neck.

John rolled his head back with pleasure at the touch, his breath
deepening, quickening. Undoing the tie at the neck of his shirt, Tom
exposed the boy's shoulders to the air and ran his tongue and teeth
across the cold skin, brushing his lips around the salt of his armpit,
sliding across to find the nipple, biting gently. John lay back to accept
the caresses with his eyes closed, and Tom quickly fumbled with the
fastening of his breeches, forcing them down until he could wrap his
fingers around John's hard cock and take it in his mouth. John
moaned, giving himself to the unfamiliar pleasure as Tom struggled
to undo his own breeches with his other hand, freeing his own cock,
hand and head starting to move in rhythm. For several long breaths
they moved together in pleasure, John hard and smooth and sweet in
his mouth.

Then out of nowhere, John lashed out wildly in a sudden parox-
ysm, lurching forward, catching Tom hard in a blow to the side of his
head, knocking him to the ground.

'No!' John was screaming. 'I cannot ... I must not ... You are
wicked to do such things to me. I am lost ... I am lost ...' He fell to his
knees and clasped his hands before him in agonised, murmured
prayer as Tom sat up slowly, watching him, rubbing at his temple
where the blow had landed, still in shock and waiting for John to
grow tired of prayer. But the boy showed no signs of stopping, the
murmured litany of sins still tumbling from his lips, eyes closed,
hands clasped in frantic supplication.

Tom rose to his feet and moved away, disturbed by the boy's

devotions and hating the God who had just spoiled his pleasure. He thought of his stepfather and the dismal Sundays of his childhood, spent on his knees in prayer and repentance for as yet unknown sins. Even then he had hated the Church, chafing against the rules and restrictions. There had been no joy in the house after his own father died, no laughter, no games, only harsh words and discipline, punishment for his failure to feel the fear of God his stepfather urged. No wonder he had turned his back on it.

Standing at the bench, he turned his gaze once more to watch John as he prayed. He felt no guilt. The boy had told him he lusted for men – what else should he have done? He sighed, losing patience with John's piety. If he couldn't have him, he wanted to be alone, not listening to a hum of mumbled prayer that returned him to his own miserable childhood. 'Go home, John,' he said.

The prayers continued. He seemed not to have heard. Tom approached him and squatted down in front of him until their faces were almost level. 'Go home.'

John's eyes slid reluctantly towards him. They were wide with fear and surprise and he sidled backwards, away.

'Go home,' Tom repeated.

'You are evil to tempt me so,' John whispered, 'to lure me into sin. Surely the Devil himself has sent you to snare my soul …'

'No.' Tom shook his head. 'No, I was just mistaken. I thought you wanted me …'

John stared.

'Didn't you?' Tom persisted. Surely he couldn't deny it: his desire had been plain to see. Tom sat back on his heels to put some distance between them. He was beginning to regret he had started any of this, but it was too late to retreat altogether. Besides, he knew now for sure that John desired him; it could only be a matter of time until he fell. He would just have to be patient. 'Go home, John,' he said again. 'Go home.'

'What about you?' John was already scrambling to his feet and moving away like a frightened animal before a hunter. It was almost comical.

'I'll sleep here,' he said.

John said nothing more but turned and fled, pausing at the door only a moment to allow his eyes to adjust to the darkness outside. Tom heard the rhythmic patter of his feet as he hastened down the stairs. Then he sighed, vacillating, wondering if he should seek out Jane again and slake his lust with her, but he was weary with all the emotion, and the new knowledge that she loved him weighed him against it. He would sleep on the couch and see to his own pleasure.

Sometimes, he thought with a wry smile, it was just the easiest thing to do.

Chapter Nine

THIS SLUMBERY AGITATION

Just before supper, Sarah heard her mother's light footsteps on the stairs. A small flare of hope lit inside her that she might be reprieved from the fireless, candleless dark of her confinement. Remaining huddled in the bed, the only way to keep warm, she waited and watched the light of her mother's candle wax and wane through the narrow space above the door. Then the door opened and the straight, narrow figure of her mother entered, closing the door quickly behind her, before she crossed to the bed.

'I brought you some bread and butter, and some salve for the welts,' she whispered. 'Your father is still in the shop.'

'Thank you.'

She put the hunk of bread and a jug of ale on the small table beside the window. Then she turned back to her daughter. 'You found your brother last night?'

'He's staying at Master Tooley's house. He'll be all right.'

'You stayed there also?'

She pretended not to hear the subtle question underneath, averting her eyes from her mother's scrutiny. 'Yes,' she replied. Her mother sat on the edge of the bed and took her hand, holding the fingers tightly, warm and strong and reassuring. For a moment they remained so in silent, affectionate connection. Then Sarah said, 'Is there nothing we can do?'

'For you or for Tom?'

Sarah gave a wry smile. 'For either of us.' Then, 'What does he plan to do with me?'

'He will marry you to Simon,' her mother answered. 'Even so young as you are.'

She said nothing and her heart seemed to drop inside her breast. She had known, of course, that her father had wanted the marriage, but she was still so young – she had thought she had years left of freedom, years in which the world might change its course. Regret heaved in her innards, a physical ache. It was hard to imagine she could be a wife so soon and that Simon would be the man to break her into womanhood when Nick had been so nearly in her reach. They had been so close; the almost-kiss at his door, the softness of his bed, all snatched away in a moment. Her future stretched bleak before her, and the darkness of the fate she foresaw in the shewstone overshadowed it all.

'You could do worse than Simon.' Her mother smiled.

'I could also do better.'

'Perhaps. But it's not your decision to make.' She paused. 'Nor mine.'

'He is set on it, then?'

Her mother nodded. 'I'm sorry – I know it isn't what you hoped for. But Simon will be a kind husband and there's much to be said for that.' She gave her daughter a rueful smile and slid her eyes away.

'You've known both kind and unkind, I think.'

Elizabeth nodded and patted her daughter's hand.

Then Sarah said, 'And Tom? Surely we can do something for Tom?'

Her mother shook her head gently. 'Your father has only ever tolerated your brother, and Tom has surely not helped himself. He set his heart against him from the first. He was willful, always inso-lent. Even at a tender age he would goad him into fury, both of them too proud to bend. And now ... this ... when he knows what his father thinks of such things.' She gave a small shrug of hopelessness.

'He did not choose the part.' It was instinct to defend him.

'He chose the playhouse,' her mother said. 'Your father wanted him as his apprentice – he would have forgiven him much if Tom had agreed to it, for what father does not want a son to follow him?

But Tom wouldn't have it. And the playhouse is everything your father despises: ungodly, sinful, a mire of wickedness, full of whores and rogues.'

'You know that it isn't so, don't you? There are good and bad, same as anywhere.' She couldn't bear to hear the people she loved and the world she adored so reviled.

'Of course I do. I loved the playhouse. Will was Tom's father's dearest friend.'

Sarah hesitated a moment. 'And he is still yours?' she ventured.

Elizabeth gave her daughter a reluctant smile. 'Yes, he has remained a good friend through all these years. Quietly, secretly, loyally, his friendship has been constant.'

Sarah returned the smile. It was good to know her mother was not alone.

'Now I must go,' Elizabeth said, 'before your father discovers me here. I'll leave you the candle.' She bent forward and kissed her daughter's cheek. 'Blessed be,' she murmured.

'Blessed be,' Sarah returned. Then she watched her mother slip silently away and back to her life beyond the door before she turned to the tray of food her mother had brought and began to eat.

She dreams she is in a forest of pine at night, walking barefoot on the cold, soft earth. A full moon glimmers through the branches of the oaks overhead, brushing silver hues across everything it touches, and a stream trickles lazily beside her – she seems to be following its path upstream, searching for the source, and despite the darkness, she finds her way easily, unafraid.

In time she comes to a clearing where the stream begins, emerging from an outcrop of rocks to spill into a pool that fills before it overflows and runs off along its way. Stepping out of her shift, she slides into the water and lowers herself down until the surface laps around her shoulders. It is cool and clear and sweet, and she is tempted to submerge herself, to give herself to the sacred water and stay in this place always.

Then, one by one, four men approach to stand at the edge of the pool, one at each point of the compass. She feels no shame at her nakedness before them, no fear, content and at ease in the pure crystal water. She has no doubt this is where she is meant to be. Wheeling slowly, the rock hard and smooth beneath her legs, she regards each of them in turn. As she turns, each man holds out a hand to beckon her to them, and she sees then that they too are naked.

She goes first to stand before her father, out of habit of respect and obedience, and he speaks to her, though with no voice she can hear with her ears.

Bride thou shalt be, obedient daughter of Christ.

Placing one hand on her shoulder, and the other on her breast, he rests them there until she steps away and drops back into the water to wash herself free of the taint of his touch.

Then she turns to Simon.

Wife thou shalt be, loving mother of children, though none of mine.

He too places one hand on her shoulder and one on her breast, until she slips away from his touch also to rinse herself clean in the pool.

Then she goes to Tom, whose skin is taut and pale in the moonlight: his nakedness before her quickens her breath. He steps closer.

Lover thou shalt be, spirit of the earth.

For a long moment she waits before him, and when finally he lifts his hand to her breast, she gasps as a charge fires between them. She steps closer, her breasts pressing against his ribs and his member hard against her belly. Desire flares through her before he takes her hand in his and leads her to stand before Nick. She waits, drinking in the beauty of the man who stands before her, his muscles strong and vivid in the silver light.

Mistress thou shalt be, if thou so wills it.

He reaches for her hands and lifts them to his lips, drawing her closer in towards him. Then she stands against him, and with his touch to her breast, she feels herself begin to fall, floating and free.

When she woke, it was morning and the window was bright with the early sun. The dream was still clear in her mind, and the sense of its freedom suffused her, desire and confidence mingled and intoxicating.

In the dream she had chosen her path.

She could not obey her father and she could not marry Simon. Her fate lay with her brother and with Nick, a freer world, in spite of the difficulties. The only way out was to flee, but beyond that knowledge she hardly dared to think. She would be a woman alone with no father or husband to protect her, and no place under the law. An image of the girl with the six-fingered baby bore into her thoughts. Would she end up the same, she wondered, forced to sell her body to survive, to men far more repulsive than Simon, men who would beat her and force her to do unspeakable things? The prospect of such a fate filled her with terror but she closed her mind to it: she had Tom to help her and her skill with a needle, a small income from the playhouse.

But was it possible?

And always, behind all the doubt, lay the shadow of the death she had foreseen in the shewstone.

At the playhouse Nick went to find Tom upstairs in the wardrobe. The younger man was working at his bench, bent over some breeches he was stitching for one of the lords, and he turned at Nick's approach and laid down the sewing. He looked tired, Nick thought, too many late nights and too much ale had leached the colour from his cheeks and darkened the skin around his eyes. Soon he would lose the beauty of his youth.

Nick pulled up the other stool and sat at the bench so that the two men were facing each other. Tom regarded him with open curiosity, and there was a silence while Nick framed his questions in his mind. Finally, he decided just to come out with it and ask directly. He said, 'What happened with John last night?'

'Not much.' Tom shrugged. 'He refused Jane's attentions. He is still, unequivocally, a virgin.'

Nick smiled. He had thought as much. 'Did you expect anything else?'

'He's almost a man. I thought … It doesn't really matter what I thought. He is different from me.'

'Yes, he is.' As different as the sea from the sun, Nick thought. Then he hesitated, wondering whether to ask more. Regarding Tom carefully, he tried to read the younger man's face, suspecting there was a darkness that lurked beneath the handsome features, an ugliness that found its outlet too easily in whores and drink. Scratch beneath the affable surface, he guessed, and he would find corruption: Tom had lost his innocence a long time since.

'John was almost incoherent when he got home,' he said. 'He was rambling about witchcraft and wickedness, asking for God's forgiveness.'

'A budding Puritan?' Tom smiled. 'Perhaps he will leave the playhouse for the Church.'

'Aye, perhaps,' Nick answered. 'He has always been sensitive – it is his greatest gift as a player. But last night was something different. I've never seen him so distraught. He threw himself at my feet. He held my legs and sobbed. I could barely prise him off me. I had to carry him to his bed and stay with him till he slept.' He kept his voice even as he spoke, acting to conceal the truth of his feelings, the sense of fear that John's distress had evoked in him. The boy had been terrified for the safety of his soul, shaking and crying as though he had committed some terrible sin beyond redemption. Nick had never seen such terror in another person, and it had unnerved him, awakening his own latent fears. He had slept badly afterward, haunted by dreams of the Devil, and he could not imagine what had provoked John's anguish. It surely must have been something more than the unwanted advances of a whore.

'How is he this morning?' Tom asked, returning to his stitching.

'Quiet,' Nick answered. 'Pale. He said nothing. How was he when he left you last night?'

Tom hesitated for half a heartbeat, but Nick observed it and knew the other man was hiding something. 'He was upset,' Tom admitted. 'Perhaps we tried too hard with Jane against his objections. I thought he'd come round. I thought it was just timidity.'

'But witchcraft?' Nick said. 'Why would he say he was bewitched?' He wasn't bothered about the sex or the pressure Tom and Jane had brought to bear on his virginity. Such things were a normal part of boyhood and becoming a man, especially on Bankside. But he persisted because he knew there was something more and that Tom wasn't telling all of it.

'My stepfather suspects witchcraft behind any sinful act,' Tom offered. 'Perhaps John's the same. Perhaps he thinks whores are daughters of the Devil.'

'It wasn't Jane he was accusing,' Nick said carefully.

Tom's breathing stopped for a moment and he left off his sewing, laying aside the satin breeches on the bench. Then he looked up at Nick across from him with his full attention for the first time.

'What did he say?' Tom asked.

'He said you truly are a witch. Not just a player in a play. He said that you bewitched him. You and your sister.'

Tom swallowed and dropped his head, eyes tracing the lines of the fabric in his hands, fingers smoothing out the creases. 'I am not a witch,' he said. 'And neither is Sarah. Surely you don't believe so?' He looked up then, searching Nick's face for an answer. 'Surely?'

'I don't know what to believe,' Nick replied. 'I only know that he was terrified and that you haven't told me all.'

Tom nodded, acknowledging the accusation, and Nick could see the struggle of his thoughts, the desire for concealment against his fear of the charge of witchcraft.

'Nick, please,' he said, after a time. 'Don't press me. Just believe that I am no witch. Please.'

Nick sat back, considering, regarding the younger man whose face was now taut with concern, his fear of discovery of whatever secrets he was keeping. It seemed unlikely after all that he had bewitched the boy. Perhaps Tom was right. Perhaps John's accusations were the product of an overwrought mind, his fears of the sins of the flesh. The boy was not going to last long in the world of the players if he kept up with such imaginings. It was a rough, tough life, and the Puritans were not wholly wrong in their assessment of its depravity. It was surely no place for the pious. He nodded, allowing

Tom the benefit of his doubt. 'But you must make it up with John before tonight. Or you sleep elsewhere.'

'Thank you,' Tom murmured. 'Thank you.'

Nick tilted his head in acknowledgement and got up from the stool. Then, at the head of the stairs, he turned back. Tom was still watching him, the breeches still on the bench. 'Where is your sister?' Nick asked. He knew very little of her parents but he guessed a night-time trip to the taverns of Bankside would be ill-received by all but the kindest of fathers. He hoped she hadn't been ill-treated.

'I don't know,' Tom answered, and Nick heard the concern in his voice, the same worry as his own. But he said nothing, only ducked his head and lowered himself down the steep steps that led down through the tiring house towards the stage and rehearsal below.

Chapter Ten

A PEERLESS KINSMAN

In a break from rehearsal, Tom lowered himself down the steps from the wardrobe and sauntered out onto the stage. The players were gathered in small groups, chatting, eating, going over their lines. John was with Nick and Will and John Heminges, seated behind the yard in the lowest tier of the gallery, but he sat a little apart from them and his attention seemed elsewhere.

Tom hesitated, unsure if he should approach him now when he was with others or if it would be better to catch him alone. With others he guessed would be safer, so he dropped down into the yard and made his way across the open space to sit beside him on the bench. John watched him approach and Tom could see the tension in his jaw and posture, eyes following his every move, wide and child-like. He took his seat on the bench with enough distance between them that there was no chance of them touching, and the memory of the taste of him filled his senses, making it hard to focus on the words he needed.

'How goes it, John?' he asked.

The boy half nodded, half shrugged, then threw a glance along the bench, seeking reassurance from the presence of the other men. Nick looked up and caught Tom's eye for a moment of shared understanding.

'Forgive me,' Tom murmured, 'for last night. I didn't mean to frighten or to hurt you. I thought you wanted it as I did.'

John was silent, biting his lip, but his eyes never left Tom's face, watchful and full of distrust.

'Say something,' Tom said. 'We must work together. We must be friends.'

'I cannot share a bed with you,' John whispered. 'You must find somewhere else to sleep.'

Tom nodded, angry with himself for his failure. He had moved too soon, too suddenly, and wrecked his chances of success. And too, he had lost the roof above his head. He would have to find lodgings somewhere else, an expense he could poorly afford.

'I understand,' he said. 'I expected no less. But please, no more of this witchery business.'

He had thought of it all through the morning, the implications sinking in, the understanding he could lose his life at the end of a rope if John chose to press the claim. And if the accusation of witchcraft failed to stick, he could hang for being a sodomite. He cursed himself for his impatience.

'I do not trust you,' John breathed. 'So keep away from me.'

Tom nodded again, eager to pacify the boy and keep him sweet. He lifted his hands palms outwards in a gesture of conciliation.

'I am not like you,' John went on, 'so do not seek to make me so. As God is my witness, I detest all that you are and all that you want from me.' Furtively, he touched his fingers to his chest and traced a tiny outline of a cross. It was a small movement, almost imperceptible, but Tom was regarding him closely and he saw it.

A secret Papist then, he realised. Not a Puritan after all. He wasn't sure which was worse – both creeds would condemn a witch or a sorcerer without a second thought, and neither would have mercy for a sodomite. His heartbeat quickened. The risks had not seemed real before when he was safely alone in the wardrobe. They had seemed distant, a vague and unlikely possibility that he could easily avert with the charm and wits he had always used in the past. But faced now with John, the terror and hatred plain across his features, he began to fully understand his danger. His mouth turned dry as sweat broke out along his spine and under his arms, and he could feel his shirt as it clung wetly to his back. He forced himself to breathe slowly.

'I swear to God,' he said, 'I won't touch you again.'

'Don't even look at me,' John snarled softly. 'Because I can see the lust in your eyes, the presence of the Devil inside you. You are not your own master and I cannot trust your promises.'

Tom shifted back away from the hatred, afraid of what he had unleashed. He dropped his gaze away from John for the first time. 'Forgive me,' he whispered.

'It's not in my power to forgive you. Only God can do that. But I will pray for you because I do not think you will pray to save yourself.' Then he got up from the bench and, sliding out past Tom's knees, careful not to touch him, he walked away across the yard, lifted himself up onto the stage and disappeared into the tiring house behind.

Tom watched him go, observing the narrow back and slim hips, the tight movement of his arse, and in spite of everything, he still wanted him, desire only fanned by the challenge and the risk, John's anger only making him more beautiful. He shook his head at himself, at the tenacity of his lust. Perhaps he really was infested by the Devil, he thought, and blackened beyond redemption.

The conversation along the bench had stopped and he became aware of the attention of the others. He turned towards them and pasted a smile on his face.

'How are the costumes coming along?' Will asked. 'Are there any that are ready yet? May we try them?'

He forced his mind back to the wardrobe, trying to recall his work that morning. He had sewn in a haze, his mind only turning on John and the memory of the taste of him, and he struggled to remember.

'Almost,' he said.

'Good.' Will nodded with a smile of satisfaction. 'I find it helps to rehearse in costume, do you not?' He turned to Nick, who nodded. But it was obvious to Tom that Nick was barely listening, his attention wandering towards the tiring house where John had disappeared, and wondering what had passed between them.

∽

Later in the day Tom found new lodgings – a narrow third-floor chamber in a crumbling house of similar rooms west of the theatre. But it was dry and relatively clean, with fresh rushes to cover the boards and a soft straw pallet on the bed. Linen and blankets and candles supplied for sixpence a week. A place to lay his head at night and nothing more. She was a widow, he guessed, Mistress Overbury, renting out the rooms of her home to make ends meet. Downstairs had once been a potter's shop, the sign still swinging above the door with the symbols rusted and faded out of sight, and it was her living quarters now, the rest of the house rented out to journeymen and hired workers such as himself.

With the first week's rent paid, he took the few coins he had left and met the other players in the Green Dragon for his supper. He took care to sit away from John and ate his stewed beef without attention or appetite, saying nothing. His silence was noticed.

'Are you quite well, Tom?' Henry asked. 'I've never known you with nothing to say for yourself before.'

Tom forced a smile. 'Quite well, thank you, Master Condell. Tired merely.'

'Too much sewing?'

He cocked his head. 'Perhaps.'

'Too much ale and too many women, more like,' John Heminges teased.

'That too,' Tom replied. He glanced up with a smile. Nick was watching him with the same intent scrutiny as earlier, as though he would see beneath the surface, beyond the words and smiles. He dropped his eyes once more to his food, uncomfortable to be so observed, and wondered if Nick had guessed more than he was saying, or if John had told him more of the truth. Tom risked a look towards the boy, and he too was sitting silently, examining his hands on the table in front of him, his food and ale untouched. Then Tom cursed himself once more for being a fool.

Tom left the tavern early, the others still drinking and talking over the day's rehearsal, and went out into the clearing cool of the night.

The street was quiet, with few people about. Torches flickered at the doorways, and across the way the windows of the church glowed and glimmered from the light of the candles within. He shivered and looked up. The sky was clear and black, stars shimmering brightly, a waning moon. He stood for a moment, head tilted back, taking in the vastness and the beauty and the mystery of it. Then a beggar child scurried past him in the narrow street, too close, and he snapped back to his surroundings, one hand reaching for the knife at his belt, the other checking to see if the child had taken his purse while he was dreaming. It was still there but he glanced around him anyway, wariness a habit in this part of town, and when he was satisfied he was safe, he set off at a good pace away from the river toward his stepfather's house.

In Narrow Lane he slowed his steps, and took a moment to observe the house from a distance. It was a good house, timber and brick that had belonged to his own father first – three spacious storeys above the tailor's shop, his own room and Sarah's behind the little windows high in the gables. It was his birthright from his own father, and though he had never thought of it much before, the realisation it would never now come to him fanned his hatred harder. He spat into the mud at his feet in disgust but the bitter taste in his mouth remained.

The shop was closed, shutters drawn, and he guessed the household would be gathered after supper in the first-floor chamber above it. He ran his mind across the image: his stepfather in the big hard-backed chair to one side of the hearth, reading aloud from the Bible on his knee, asking questions and quick to temper if the answers fell short. Or he might be at the table with Tom's mother at his side as he checked the day's accounts, every last farthing counted and accounted for. Simon would be there too, hanging on his master's every word, spineless and servile. Tom had detested him always. And Sarah?

He searched the image in his mind, trying to place her before the fire with sewing or a book in her hands, or simply staring into the flames. But he could not see her there and a sudden fear billowed through him, goading him into action. Doubling back on himself he found his way easily in the darkness to the overgrown alley that ran behind the row of houses, and vaulted the wall into the back garden with practised ease. He still had his copy of the back door key, and the fact that his stepfather had never known of its existence gave him a grim satisfaction.

Letting himself in silently, he wondered if the terrier had heard him from its place at the hearth. Sarah had told him once she always knew when he came and went, the dog's ears pricking up, listening with a slight half-bark of recognition, before settling down once more to sleep. Sliding through the dark, he passed the kitchen and the door to Simon's room behind the shop, then found the staircase that ran up alongside it. At the foot of the steps, he crouched to take off his boots, and his stockinged feet made no sound on the wooden boards, the creaky ones well known and avoided. He was up and past the first-floor chamber and in his attic room in moments.

In the utter blackness he crept across to the window and drew back the curtain, letting in a faint glow from outside to give enough shape to the shadows so that he could see to grab a handful of linen and his spare set of breeches from the chest at the foot of the bed, folding them deftly into a bundle. Then, hurriedly, silently, he closed the chest and, leaving the curtains open to the night, he padded back across the small room and opened the door. On the landing outside, the weak light spilled through and caught on the key in the lock on Sarah's door, glinting softly. It took a moment to understand the significance but then he turned it silently, sliding into the room. Inside was dark, no candles, no fire, but he knew straight away that she was there, his senses attuned to the night.

'It's me,' he whispered into the gloom. 'Tom.'

She was standing at the window, a black shape silhouetted against the softer dark of the night behind her. At his voice she turned with a soft gasp of breath, and in a moment she had reached him, holding him tightly against her. He held her, smoothing her loose tangled hair with his fingers, his face close.

'What happened?' he murmured.

She lifted her head from his chest. In the half-light he could just make out her eyes, searching his face, pleading.

'Later,' she breathed. 'Take me with you now.'

For an instant he hesitated. It was one thing for him to be cut free from his father, his family: he was a grown man who could make his own way in the world. But Sarah was little more than a girl, innocent and dependent, no rights to her own life under the law.

She sensed his doubt. 'He's going to marry me to Simon,' she whispered, 'and forbid me to see you, forbid me the playhouse. You must help me.'

He swallowed, thoughts spinning rapidly with all the possibilities, all the risks and dangers. But he had promised her once he would always take care of her, and he could not leave her to such misery now. With a quick sigh he nodded, aware he would probably regret it, as she reached under her bed and grabbed a bundle she had already packed. In spite of the danger, he smiled, impressed. 'Your boots? Your cloak?'

'By the front door.'

'Come,' he said. He took her hand and led her out, careful to close and lock the door behind them. She followed him down, her hand still in his, soft-footed as he was, skills learned early in life.

At the first-floor landing they paused to listen: this was the most dangerous part of the journey. The door could open at any time – anyone might step out to head downstairs to the privy – and there was nowhere to hide. They listened. Their father's voice was rumbling its nightly sermon, odd words carrying out to the passage, and they half walked, half ran along the landing, gaining speed on the last flight of steps. Sarah paused to find her cloak and her boots and then they were outside in the back garden, running together across the damp grass. Tom took the wall first and leaned down to help her as she struggled, her small hands gripping his hard as her feet kicked against the wall to lift herself up. When they landed in the safety of the back lane, she cried out and he turned to her, holding her arm in one hand, bending to see into her face.

'What's the matter?'

'Nothing.' She shook her head. 'Let's go.'

Then they walked away quickly and he wondered what he had done.

They moved in silence for a time, slower now. She was less sure in the darkness than he was, less accustomed to finding her way, and she held tightly to his arm. She seemed to be limping, and he shortened his stride to keep pace with her. Finally she stopped. 'I must rest a moment.'

He looked down at her, surprised, and in the flickering light of a nearby torch he saw her face was wet with tears.

'Sarah?' He lifted his hand and wiped at her cheeks with his fingers. She tilted her head towards his touch and sniffed.

'Forgive me.'

'What's the matter?' he asked her again. Doubts began to bubble through him. He was responsible for her now, her only protector, and the prospect of it terrified him.

'He beat me,' she told him. 'It hurts to walk.'

'Oh God,' he murmured. He knew too well the pain she was suffering, and he could only begin to guess at her humiliation. It had been bad enough for him as a boy to have his arse and legs exposed before a man he detested, but for her it must have been a torture, every bit as painful as the physical hurt. A fresh hatred for his stepfather burned inside him, and he vowed the old man would pay. Taking Sarah's bundle from her hand, he put his arm around her waist and drew her in close to his own body.

'We'll take it slowly,' he said. 'And I'll support you.'

He felt her lean in to him and they set off again, moving with small, careful steps through the night.

He took her to the theatre. His new landlady had been most insistent that he should not bring women to the house, and he dared not disobey so soon after moving in. He could not afford to lose the room, his money almost gone. In the morning he would think again, but tonight they needed somewhere safe and warm where she could rest and recover.

It took an age to climb the wooden steps that led to the wardrobe.

'Why here?' she said, when they were at last inside. 'Why not Nick's?'

'I've moved into lodgings,' he replied. 'A room in a house. No women allowed.'

She nodded, too weary with pain and emotion to question him

further.

'Tomorrow, we'll find you somewhere else,' he said, clearing the couch for her to lie down. He knew from experience it would be a while before she could sit without pain: the old man used to make him sit on the hard wooden stool in the shop for hours of Bible study after a beating, keeping watch as he worked. 'And I'll find some salve for the welts.'

'Mother has some,' she said.

'Mother is out of our reach,' he replied, wondering if she understood she was renouncing all of it: fleeing her father meant fleeing her mother also.

'For now,' she said, so that he realised she didn't yet fully understand.

He helped her to the couch and eased her down gently. 'Sleep now,' he said, sitting himself down on the floor by her head, smoothing back the hair from her face.

She smiled. 'Thank you.'

He watched her in the light of the single candle, eyes flickering quickly into sleep while he stroked her head as he used to do when they were children. She was peaceful in her sleep, he thought, pale and soft and pretty, but he was sleepless himself, wide awake with the turmoil of his thoughts. She could not stay at the playhouse for long. Really, no one should ever stay, and if the others in the Company knew how often he spent his nights there, he would possibly find himself out on his ear.

But where could she go? Become a servant somewhere in a household? For one of the sharers, perhaps? Master Shakespeare? Master Burbage? Or Nick? He ran his thoughts across the possibility. It was easy to see her there with Nick as her master, an honest servant and helpmeet; she would find her way from there to his bed for sure. If he could persuade Nick to take her on, it would be the perfect answer, and for the first time since he had led her from her chamber prison, the load seemed to lighten on his shoulders a little. Relieved, and sleepy at last, he reached for the nearest thing he could find to cover himself – a single blanket – then, resting his head on his arm, he curled up on the rug by the couch and drifted quickly into sleep.

Chapter Eleven

BLACK AND DEEP DESIRES

❦

S arah woke abruptly, startled by an image in her dream, and it took a moment to remember where she was. Dim morning light filtered in through the window and she blinked to clear her vision, memory of the night slowly returning. She lay still, allowing the recollection to come, then ran her gaze around the room, looking for Tom. He was sleeping on the hard floor beside the couch, covered by a single blanket, curled into a ball. He must have been freezing, she thought, and wondered why he hadn't found more blankets to use.

Carefully, she raised herself to sit up on the couch, and winced as her skirts brushed the welts on her thighs. Hesitating, she planted her feet firmly on the floor and, using her hands to steady herself, pushed up to standing. Once upright, she paused, allowing the slight dizziness to subside before she took an experimental step towards her brother. She could feel the tightness of the weals in her skin as she moved, but the soreness was tolerable and she bent carefully to wake him, placing a gentle hand against his shoulder. He woke groggily, slowly, evidently surprised to see her before he blinked himself fully awake and sat up.

'You're half-frozen,' she said. 'Why didn't you use more blankets?'

'I slept fine,' he answered, but he was shivering, so she fetched another blanket from the couch to wrap around his shoulders. He accepted it with a smile and drew it round him before he got to his feet.

'How are your legs?' he asked.

'Sore,' she replied with a shrug. 'But bearable.'

'It'll ease in a couple of days. I'll get some ointment today.'

'Thank you,' she said, and she meant for more than just the ointment.

He nodded, understanding. Then he said, 'You can't stay here. We have to find you somewhere to go.'

'I know.' She had thought of little else since her beating, her options spinning round in her mind. And last night she had cast her fate to the gods, asking for a new path to open.

'I thought as a servant somewhere?' Tom suggested. He sounded hesitant and unsure, as though he expected her to refuse him outright. 'Perhaps for Nick? There is only Joyce, who comes in during the day to look after the house. There would be enough work for you if he would have you. And you could still earn money with your needle.'

She nodded. 'Do you think he will have me?' She saw the image of Nick in her dream, taking her hand, kissing her fingers, leading him towards her. It was the answer she had prayed for.

'I think he will.' He paused again, eyes wandering the boards, and she waited, watching him. He looked weary, his skin pale and sickly, cheeks gaunt. Then he raised his face to meet the look. 'But it will ruin any chance for a good marriage for you. Your good name will suffer.'

She shrugged. 'I have run away from home and rejected my father, so I have no dowry. I work at the playhouse. Three nights ago I wandered the Bankside taverns with a whore and drank ale with a company of players.' She gave him a wry half-smile. 'I think the damage is already done.' If a good marriage meant Simon, she could wear the loss without sorrow. And though she knew the easy comfort of her former life had gone for ever, she had few regrets – the comfort came at too high a price.

'Besides,' she said, 'where else can I go?'

'One of the others in the Company? A bigger household with a family, women.'

'I would rather go to Nick's,' she said softly, and he laughed.

'Of course you would.' He pushed himself to his feet. 'I will ask him for you, gentle sister.' He stepped forward and touched a finger to her cheek and she rubbed her face against his touch, like a cat. A memory of his touch in her dream forged unbidden into her thoughts, her breasts against his ribs, his member against his belly, and she swallowed, guilt blushing over her, denying the sense of desire. All her other transgressions slid away under the sin of this.

'What's the matter?' he asked.

She backed away and shook her head, eyes lowered, appalled at herself. He followed her and all she was aware of was his closeness, the shape of his body under his clothes.

'Sarah?'

'Nothing,' she said. 'I'm fine.'

'Second thoughts? It's still not too late to go back.'

'No, it isn't that,' she mumbled, in her confusion. 'I don't want to go back.'

'Then tell me,' he urged. His hand held her arm and she could feel the warmth of his breath against her hair.

'I can't,' she whispered.

'Tell me,' he insisted again.

She shook her head once more and he took her chin between his fingers and tilted her face up towards him. She struggled to look away but his grip was firm and his mouth was close to hers. 'Why can't you tell me? You've always told me everything.'

She swallowed again. Tears began to rise and there was nothing she could do to stop them. 'Please don't, Tom.'

He let her face go and folded her into his chest, his arms holding her tightly. She stood quietly, forcing down the tears, forbidding herself to cry. But she did not relax into him as she had always done before, and his closeness was not a comfort but a torture, all her senses alive to the maleness of him, forbidden need suffusing her. She wanted only for him to let her go. He sensed her reluctance and loosened his hold, stepped back one pace and looked into her face again.

'What have I done?' he asked.

'I had a dream, is all,' she answered, because she couldn't bear to see the pain in his eyes, the belief he had done something to hurt her. 'It's nothing.'

'A dream is never nothing,' he said. 'You know that more than most. Tell me.'

She hesitated. He was right: her dreams had foretold the future many times. It was a gift she knew Tom envied, and he had helped her in the past to find the meanings they contained.

'We can puzzle it out together,' he said. 'What did you dream?'

She sighed, unable to resist any longer. She had never been able to say no to her brother: he had a capacity for persuasion she was sure he used often and well. And perhaps, after all, it meant something other than it seemed. Perhaps he could help her to see it.

'Come, Sarah, tell me.' He held her fingers gently in one hand, his face still lowered and close to hers. A warm desire fanned from her belly and she kept her face averted.

'We were naked, you and I,' she whispered. 'You touched my breast, and your ...' She stopped, searching for the right word. Even with her brother, she had never talked of such things.

'My ...?' he prompted.

'Your ... manhood ... pressed against me. Against my belly.' She watched him closely, trying to judge his reaction, but his expression remain unchanged: there was no trace of the revulsion she had feared, and hope gave a little spring inside her. For a moment he said nothing and she waited, aware of her breath in the silent room, her brother's eyes searching the floor for answers. A sliver of the same desire from her dream crept through her blood, and as she wound her fingers more tightly in his, he lifted his head to look at her.

'Did it ... please you?' he asked, returning the pressure of her fingers.

She nodded, biting her lower lip in shame, gaze tethered to the boards at their feet. 'I wanted you,' she whispered.

He let out a long breath, so that she knew even he was taken aback by it. Then he said, 'Tell me the rest of it.'

She told him as quickly as she could say the words, without emotion. The forest, the four men, the prediction each of them had made. When she had finished, his fingers were still entwined with hers and he rubbed at them gently.

'They were choices,' he said, after a time. 'Choices for you to make. You rejected the first two. You can reject the third also.'

'Perhaps,' she agreed. 'But the dream led me to give up Father and Simon: I could reject them in my waking hours because it was the path I took in the dream. And in the dream you led me to Nick. Though in the daylight I know it must be wrong because my head tells me so, my spirit disagrees and still rises with desire.'

He was silent, considering her words, and after a moment he let go of her hand. With the contact broken, she breathed out as though released from a bond.

'What are you afraid of?' he asked.

She took a deep breath, and the fear coalesced into meaning at last. 'I'm afraid,' she said, 'that I must follow the path the dream has set. That I must reject and choose as it guided me. That if I go another way I will lose all power of choice.'

'You're afraid of losing Nick?'

'Yes. And of losing the freedom to reject Father and Simon.'

He nodded in agreement. Downstairs they heard a door slam, a man's voice in the yard. Both of them looked towards the stairs; the Company was arriving for rehearsal. 'We'll talk more later,' Tom said. 'But first we must find you somewhere to go. And before even that,' he went on, 'I must find some breakfast.'

She smiled. 'Fetch me something too.'

He touched a finger to her face and in a moment he was gone, his lean frame dropping through the hatch onto the ladder, his footsteps light and quick on the rungs. She turned away, fingers straightening her hair, brushing down her skirts. As she bent to retrieve the chamber pot, she heard Tom calling out to bid good morning to someone he passed on his way out, and wondered if it was Nick. Then she wondered if she should have told him, if they were being tempted into something evil. But her dreams had never failed her before, never been wrong, and the meaning had seemed very clear. Fear and guilt and desire mixed into excitement, and the soreness of the wounds from her beating was forgotten. She turned once more towards the steps and carefully lowered herself down through the opening to face the day.

Downstairs, the players were getting ready to begin. John was centre stage, pacing softly, hands gathered before him, lips moving in a silent murmur as he practised his lines. The tension of his nerves was palpable. Nick stood at the door to the tiring house, the daggers held loosely in one hand, awaiting his entrance, watching.

Moving with care, Sarah found a spot at the edge of the yard and leaned against a pillar. Other members of the Company lounged around the theatre, and Will stood to one side of the stage, leaning, arms folded, impossible to ignore.

'Tis strange, Sarah thought, how some men have such a power in their presence that you know when they enter a room by a change in the air, a different atmosphere that follows them: they can lighten a room or darken it. Will was such a man, and the others let him lead them readily; she suspected this play would have faltered already without him. He was the kind of man that others would follow willingly to battle, she realised, and for some reason the thought made her glad.

Tom approached, holding a packet of still-warm bread that filled the theatre with its scent. She took the piece he gave her with a smile of thanks and nibbled at it absently, still watching the stage, waiting for the scene to begin.

Will clapped twice to call the Company's attention, and nodded to John, who was watching for his cue to begin.

> 'That which hath made them drunk hath made me bold;
>> What hath quenched them hath given me fire.
>> Hark! Peace!
>> It was the owl that shriek'd,
>> the fatal bellman ...'

The boy changed before her eyes. The rangy, awkward limbs of his youth straightened into elegance, his chin lifted into the tilt of a woman's head as the nerves of before slipped away. Sarah smiled in appreciation of his talent and flicked a glance to her brother, standing beside her. Tom was rapt, chest lifting with deep breaths, eyes bright and dark with something that was more than admiration. She swallowed, seeing in him the same excitement she felt watching Nick, the same desire. She hadn't known her brother's lusts ranged so far, and the realisation stuck in her chest, catching at her breathing. He would have to be careful – such desires were forbidden. Gently, she touched her brother's hand and he turned immediately, an impatient question in his look.

'You're staring,' she whispered. 'You'll give yourself away.'

He said nothing, but slid his gaze hurriedly back toward the stage. She regarded him a moment longer, noticing the flush that coloured his sallow cheek.

She switched her own gaze to Will, who was talking to the actors now, discussing some nuance of their lines, and wondered whence the inspiration came to have witches to set Macbeth upon his path of self-destruction. For why did they choose to topple Macbeth? What gain for them? And such witches – seers, sorcerers, conjurors – they could summon up the gods and the spirits, raise the dead. It was witchcraft beyond her knowledge, a magic steeped in evil. Dark witches she had heard of, wicked souls who spat their curses onto others and summoned unnatural forces to hinder and to harm. But these weird sisters that Will had brought to life hailed from a darker realm: they were barely human, spirits from a netherworld. Daemons. Words of sorcery, words of conjuration – the witches' incantations reached far beyond her own simple spellcraft, and their powers tapped a different, darker source. They frightened her: words spoken contain a power, no matter if they're said by actors on a stage or by witches round a fire. No wonder Will had nightmares when his mind was filled with spirits such as these, their speech upon his tongue. Though she had seen in the shewstone that his dark imaginings had opened doors to shadow realms, she had barely understood it at the time. But now she'd heard the witches' words of sorcery as they worked their malice to warp a man into a tyrant and to send his Lady mad, and the visions of the shewstone had come to seem as destiny, a fate that was hewn in rock.

Shaking her head against the thought of it, she turned her mind once more to the actors on the stage. The scene came to an end and the players moved away. Tom turned to her again. 'Say nothing,' he said.

'Of course.'

'I'll talk to Nick.'

Tom crossed the yard to speak with the man she hoped would soon be her master, and Sarah saw him cast a furtive glance towards John, who had found himself a quiet spot in the gallery to practise his lines. Wondering if John was the first boy Tom had wanted or if there had been others before, she looked away with a sigh, then, conscious that she barely knew her brother after all, she turned her gaze to him once more and watched him as he spoke to Nick.

The two men talked for what seemed like an age, and she saw Nick's gaze flick towards her once or twice, saw him nod and smile and, finally, when she was sure he must have said no, he beckoned her towards them. Taking a deep breath to steady herself, heart hammering, she stepped across the yard, made a small curtsey and stood before them.

'Your brother tells me you're in need of a position as a servant somewhere?' Nick said. His smile was kind, lines forming at the corners of his eyes, and she dropped her head away from it, afraid she was wearing her feelings too plainly in her face.

'Yes.' She nodded. 'I've left my father's protection ...'

'I know,' Nick replied. 'Tom has explained all.'

She waited, raising her eyes to Tom for a quick glance of understanding. His head dipped briefly and relief surged through her in a wave. She forced herself to breathe deeply, to calm herself, suddenly aware how afraid she'd been that he wouldn't take her after all.

'You can have the attic,' he said. 'It'll need a clean, but you're welcome to it if you think you can bear to serve a couple of players.'

She lifted her eyes to meet his then. He was regarding her closely, waiting for her answer. 'Thank you. I can think of no one I would rather serve – a couple of players will suit me fine,' she whispered, dropping her head once more in a small bow of gratitude. 'I'll serve you well.'

Nick smiled. 'And I'll try to be a good master.' He looked across to Tom. 'Or I'll have your brother to answer to.'

She returned the smile. 'I'm very grateful.'

He reached out to touch her arm with a movement of gentle reassurance. 'It's my pleasure,' he murmured. 'We'll talk more on it later.'

She nodded, curtseying again before she walked away, and the ground felt like air beneath her.

When the Company broke for lunch, Nick found Sarah in the wardrobe upstairs, sewing one of the dresses that John would wear as the Lady. She was alone at the bench, standing, the dark silk spread out before her. The door was open to the bright winter cold to let in the light, and she had wrapped a blanket about her shoulders. Her breath condensed in little clouds before her.

She turned at his footstep on the stair and laid down her needle carefully, threading it through the fabric to keep it safe, waiting. He could see the slight hesitation now that the relation between them had changed. They were no longer simply fellows in the Company and neither was quite sure how to act. Dipping into a brief, respectful curtsey, she kept her head lowered as he stepped across the boards towards her.

'How goes it?' he asked.

'It's John's gown for the banquet scene – it's very fine.' She fingered the fabric lovingly, her eyes still turned away from him.

He smiled. 'It is. But I wasn't asking about the dress.'

'Oh.' She lifted her face then and there was a smile at the edges of her mouth. He observed her for a moment, the smooth, pale cheeks, flushed now with cold and her nerves, the full lips, the bright and curious eyes. Her hair was pulled back sharply from her face, and he wanted to loosen it and let it fall about her shoulders. She would be pretty with her hair about her face.

'I am well,' she said.

'But not well enough to sit.' He gestured to the stool that was set away from the bench.

She licked her lower lip and her gaze still wandered everywhere but to him. 'No. Tom tells me it will be a couple of days.' She looked up. 'He has more experience of such things than I.'

There was a silence. He remembered his own beatings as a child before he too ran away to the playhouse to escape them, and the thought of such violence against the girl before him raised a bitter taste to his mouth. But though he understood her desire to flee her family, he wondered if she knew how stark and hard would be the road; she was risking a very great deal for her freedom. It was no easy thing to be a woman at the mercy of men. 'I am glad I can help,' he said.

'I'm very grateful,' she murmured and curtseyed again, awkward.

He smiled. 'I should get back,' he said.

She nodded, and when she looked up again, he had gone.

'Methought I heard a voice cry, "Sleep no more.
Macbeth does murder sleep ..."'

She tore her eyes from the stage and searched the playhouse for a sign of her brother, but he was nowhere to be seen. The other players were scattered about, lounging on benches, studying their lines. To one side of the yard, two hired men she barely knew were practising their swordplay, the same feint drilled over and over as they took turns. She leaned her shoulder against the pillar and returned her gaze to the stage.

Then the slam of an outside door broke the spell, and the stocky figure of her father barged in and strode across the yard towards the stage. Instinctively she shrank back, holding her breath, and the welts on her thighs began to throb.

'Why, worthy thane,
You do unbend your noble strength, to think
So brainsickly of things. Go, get some water,
And wash this filthy witness from your hand...'

John paused in his line, his attention distracted by the interruption.

Nick looked up at the hesitation, following John's gaze to light on the newcomer. Sarah saw the brief look of question they exchanged, but Will, standing in his usual place at the edge of the stage, recognised the intruder straight away; there had only ever been hostility between the two men, the first husband's friend resented by the second husband, who had tried and failed to cut him from the family's life. Will crossed to centre stage, murmured something to the others, and they followed him down the steps to greet her father, standing at a distance to cover Will's back, or so it seemed to her. All eyes were watching the scene as it unfolded, the whole Company tense with attention, and she cast another searching look across the playhouse for Tom, flinching in surprise when he appeared as if by magic at her side. He placed his arm around her shoulders and drew her in tight against him. She gave him a small smile of gratitude and they moved out from the gallery together and into the yard to hear better what was said.

'Where is my daughter?' Stone demanded.

Will said nothing, still taking the other man's measure. She could see the distrust and contempt in his eyes. They should have told Will straight away, she realised. He had a right to know.

'Where is she?'

'She is here,' Will answered then, lifting one arm to gesture towards her at her father's back. Stone swung round to see and Tom led her forward, but he did not let go of her hand. She gripped it hard, drawing courage from his touch, sure of his protection.

'She is mine and I want her back.' Her father's shout rang through the playhouse.

Sarah swallowed, breath coming hard and quick, heartbeat hammering. Be brave, she told herself. Be strong. 'I'm not coming back.'

Her father took a step towards her but as one man, every player braced and readied, and Nick stepped forward to Will's shoulder, speaking soft words in his ear, explaining. Will nodded as he understood, then addressed her father again.

'Come, Master Stone.' He gestured to the table and stools that were set close to the stage, pages of the play strewn across it and a basket of apples that someone had brought holding the sheets in place against any breeze. 'Let us sit.'

Stone breathed heavily from his exertion loudly through his mouth, and his eyes travelled over the assembled men, weighing his disadvantage. He was out of his depth here, the playhouse an unknown milieu. Perhaps he had thought he could triumph with bluster; if so he was sadly mistaken. This was Bankside, its inhabitants not easily cowed, and if he believed he could bully them as he bullied his family then he had misjudged his enemies. But still Sarah watched him with nervous eyes, and her heartbeat thrilled fast in her chest. Reluctantly, Stone crossed the yard toward the table and seated himself on one of the stools. Will beckoned to Sarah and Tom to come closer with a gesture of his head, and when Will had taken his seat, Nick settled himself on the remaining stool. The other players moved off a ways but their attention remained. Sarah was one of theirs and they would fight to keep her.

She stood near to Nick's shoulder, and he turned his head and lifted his eyes to her with a small smile of reassurance. Her father saw the exchange and half rose in his seat before he remembered he could not beat her into submission here amongst these men and lowered himself back down. Tom squeezed her hand.

'Master Stone,' Will began, 'Master Tooley has agreed to take your daughter into service.'

Stone blew out a hiss of air.

'A twelve-month contract,' Nick said. 'I am in need of a servant.'

'My daughter,' her father breathed, 'will never be a servant for the likes of you.'

'She is young yet,' Will countered, his voice calm and even, as though he held meetings such as this every day. 'And it is usual, is it not, for girls her age to enter service for a while before their marriage years? My own daughter did so.'

'She answers to me,' Stone said. 'And I say again she will not be contracted to service with a Bankside player. I have already lost my son to this den of sin, and I refuse to lose my daughter the same way.'

Will sat back slightly and looked across to Nick, then briefly to Tom and Sarah, composing his response.

Then he said, 'You understand, of course, that we are the King's Men? That Master Tooley is a servant to the King himself? A sharer in the Company?'

'I know all of that.' Her father waved his hand in dismissal. 'And if the King chooses to sanction your evildoings, then he must look to his own soul. But the girl is mine by right and I will take her home and use her as I see fit.'

Tom's fingers tightened again on hers. It was easier to be brave with him beside her and with Nick's protection too. She was moved by Will's defence of her. 'I will not come,' she heard herself saying.

'It is not your decision to make!' Stone stood up again, shouting with impotent rage, outnumbered and friendless. The flesh on his jaw wobbled as he spoke, and spittle flew from his lips. She looked away, repulsed. 'The law will be upheld. I will have my rights!'

'Let her stay, Master Stone,' Will advised. 'What gain otherwise?'

'She is my daughter. She owes me obedience.'

'A year in service,' Will said. 'And then you may have her back.' He flicked a quick glance to Sarah to stave off her objection. Reluctantly she held her peace, understanding the strategy and the need to win one battle at a time. 'She is young yet,' Will was saying.

Her father was silent, seething, his fat hands writhing together on his lap. She could see the fury in the flush across his face and the grinding of his jaw – in his haste to reclaim her, he had miscalculated. Had he imagined he would just stride in and drag her home? He stared at her, at a loss to know what to do next – he would win nothing here today and he knew it.

'I will have a contract drawn up,' Will said in the silence, 'and sent to your house.'

Stone said nothing. Nick lifted a brief glance to Sarah, who smiled, relief rushing through her in waves. Her father got to his feet and gave a curt nod towards Will, pointedly ignoring the others, before he turned on his heel and strode with all the dignity he could muster across the yard and out of the door. Sarah turned to hug Tom and then wheeled back to face Will, who had risen to his feet with a weary smile.

'Thank you, Master Shakespeare,' she breathed. 'I can't thank you enough.'

'I did it for your mother,' he said. 'I've hated the old bastard since the first day she married him.' The smile widened. 'So you are very welcome, Miss Stone.' He dipped his head in a bow and walked away, back toward the stage, his mind already returning to the business of the play.

She watched him ago, touched by his loyalty, then realised that Nick was at her side. She looked up and he was smiling.

'Welcome to my household,' he said. 'It's now official.'

She returned the smile. 'Thank you,' she replied. 'Thank you.'

He dipped her a nod, then moved away from her, lightly taking the stairs back onto the stage to resume the rehearsal. Within minutes it was as if the scene with her father had never taken place and the only world that existed was the world of *Macbeth*. But all the emotion had wearied her, and carefully, her legs too weak to stand any more, she lowered herself onto one of the stools to watch and distract her mind from the soreness by the magic of the play.

In the afternoon they played one of Will's early comedies – *The Taming of the Shrew*. It was a play that Sarah hated, all her sympathy with Kate as she chafed against her social bonds. Though with Nick as Petruchio instead of Burbage, she found she hated it less: she could better imagine herself being tamed by Nick. But the play was unequivocal in its lesson – our roles in the world are defined by our birth, and happiness only comes with acceptance. Was that the truth of things, she wondered, or could happiness be found beyond such narrow strictures? Her dream had offered her a different path – she had defied her father and refused her fate. What future awaited her now?

Then she remembered the vision in the shewstone and thought that after all, none of it mattered. Death would claim her soon, and the path in the dream was no more than a fleeting illusion of freedom. Depressed by the thought of it, she turned away from the stage, climbed wearily to the wardrobe upstairs, and set her mind to focus on her sewing.

In the evening, she walked back to the house next to Nick, John trailing silently a few paces behind. They walked slowly, still mindful of the soreness of her legs, and he gave her his arm to hold. It was a cloudless night, clear and crisp. The moon was yet to rise but the stars' glow brushed the blackness of the sky with light. Torches burned brightly in their sconces at the doors of the buildings they passed, the ground was packed hard and cold underfoot, and she felt like a lady walking out with her beau. They were talking of *Macbeth*.

'Why does he allow her to persuade him?' Sarah asked. 'Why does he not refuse?'

'He's hungry for power. He wants to be king.'

'But still ... murder?'

'She questions him as a man, pricks his pride. He loves her, so he needs to prove himself to her. And he believes it's fated. The sisters have foretold it, so he must act to make it happen – it's not his choice to make.'

She said nothing, remembering her dream, the shewstone. The same conundrum – blind faith in the rightness of the spirits.

'But would he still do it without her urging?'

'Ah, who can say? She plays on his ambitions, his desires.'

'The same as the witches do.'

'Aye.' He nodded in agreement. 'And when the spirits foretell what you wish to be true, it's tempting to believe them, even if you know the path can lead only to evil.'

'And the Lady?'

He shrugged. 'She wants to be queen.'

'John?' She turned to address the boy behind them and they slowed, walking backwards for a few steps to face him. 'What do you think?'

He looked up, startled to be addressed. But then he said, 'I think they are both bewitched, maddened by the weird sisters' spells. They have lost their true natures, and their souls are blackened and corrupted.' His voice was harsh and bitter, as though he spoke of real people he had once loved and lost.

In the dim light she slid a glance to Nick. He met her look and she saw a mirror of her own concern.

'It is a good play,' Nick said. Then they turned forwards again and walked on and talked of other things.

~

She slept before the fire, refusing outright the offer of Nick's bed. 'I am your servant now. It wouldn't be right.' And despite his pleading and the temptation a soft mattress offered her aching legs, she remained firm.

'Then tomorrow we must clean out the attic,' he insisted.

She agreed and they retired early – for her sake, she guessed. But in spite of her tiredness, she could not sleep, lying restless and uncomfortable before the hearth, her mind turning on all that had passed and the knowledge of Nick in his bed in the room above, the scent of him in the quilt that was wrapped about her.

She wondered where Tom was now. Drinking probably, or at sport with a whore. The image from her dream flicked across her thoughts and she brushed it away: to go down that road would be madness. The spirits could guide us, she thought, but our souls are our own to nurture or deny. To choose to couple with Tom would be akin to Macbeth's decision to murder – a desire indulged that should have been denied. Whatever the spirits had promised, it was for her to decide her fate, and she could not take what they offered on such terms. Besides, she reflected, she had come so far already: her father and Simon rejected, and she a servant in Nick's household. Surely her desire was almost in reach.

But the memory of her brother's touch still fed a craving inside her, tempting, dangerous, and forbidden. In these last few days she had begun to know her brother more. She had seen his lust for John, forbidden fruit just as she was, and she knew Tom wouldn't scruple to follow his desire for the boy. There was a darkness in him she had never before suspected, and his pursuit of pleasure seemed more than a youthful exuberance: there was a need that drove him, a corrupting lust for knowledge of all things. What else would he do to fill that need? Corrupt his sister? Perhaps. He hadn't refused the possibility, after all.

The image passed through her mind once more and she let it linger this time, allowing the warmth to spread through her belly. Then she followed the dream away from her brother to the man who lay now upstairs, and the warmth flickered more brightly, heat between her legs. Briefly, she recalled that he still loved another, the woman at Court, but she pushed the thought away and held the image of him from the dream in her mind: his body strong and hard, his member erect. In her thoughts she stood before him as she had in the dream, naked, but without the dream to guide her she was hesitant, uncertain how to go on. She remembered he had touched her breast and she touched her own now, gently, as he had, caressing, imagining it was him.

Then, carefully, hesitantly, a sense of her own sin suffusing her, she reached beneath the linen shift with her fingers and searched out the source of the heat that lay between her legs, fumbling gently to explore this unknown part of her body. The pleasure from her dream began to engulf her, the memory of the hard warmth of Tom's member against her stomach, the touch of Nick's hand on her breast. She quickened the movement of her fingers, more sure of her touch now, and the heat rippled through her in waves, building until it exploded into a light that consumed her.

Afterwards, she lay still, silent, understanding for the first time the drive of desire and the pursuit of the release, the brief moment of satiety. So this was what Tom sought in the brothel and with John, even perhaps with her. Now she understood. Gazing up at the ceiling, hidden in the darkness, she thought of Nick's body above it, so close, and another wave of lust passed through her. Smiling in the darkness with her fingers resting lightly on the part of her body she had no name for, she drifted finally into sleep.

Chapter Twelve

COME, YOU SPIRITS

On Sunday there was no rehearsal and the household went to church. Sarah had not been to worship at St Saviour's before; her only knowledge of the inside of it came from the night with the six-fingered child, though she had passed its dark stone walls often enough. The parish consisted of players and whores, drinkers and gamblers – the souls her Puritan father would cast out of his church as unbelieving sinners who defile the sanctity of worship. He had no time for a universal church; God's love and salvation was reserved only for His elect. Immediately she loved it, delighted by the buzz of conversation and laughter all around them as they found a place to stand. It seemed more like a marketplace where people gathered to while away the time than a church, and it was a world away from the dismal seriousness of the worship she was used to. People seemed glad to be there, and there was a cheerfulness shared amongst them that was infectious.

She spotted Jane and smiled and the girl sauntered across to join them, dropping a coy curtsey to Nick, who dipped his head in the briefest of bows of acknowledgement. Sarah watched, intrigued, and saw the frank appreciation pass across her master's face.

'Is your brother here?' Jane asked her in a low voice, stepping to her side.

'I haven't seen him,' she replied. 'Does he usually come?'

'Sometimes. Enough to avoid paying the fines.' She smiled. 'As do we all.'

'But I love it here,' Sarah laughed. 'I'm used to a Puritan church …' She trailed off. There was no need to explain any further.

Jane cast a glance around the gathered congregation. 'No Puritans here,' she agreed with a smile.

The minister arrived and took his place at the lectern, and the service began. She stepped back to rejoin her household, taking her place once again at Nick's side and waiting for the hush to fall, but though the volume of the banter dipped a little, the talk continued. She was astonished, barely able to hear the service above the chatter.

Tom arrived. He looked haggard, as though he had not slept, and he took his place to stand quietly beside her. John slid him a distrustful glance and moved away, stepping back and moving to stand on the other side of his master. She exchanged a brief look with her brother, questioning, but he made no answer, apparently straining to listen to the minister's words.

The sermon was brief and mostly unheard, and after a hymn that was more reminiscent of a drunken ballad at the alehouse than a song of worship, the congregation knelt on the hard stone floor to pray. For the first time, the church fell silent, and Sarah cast a look along the line beside her. Nick's head was bowed, lips moving in prayer, and John knelt beside him, hands clutched together before his heart as though he were afraid his soul would escape. On her other side Tom leaned in close to her.

'I've thought more about your dream,' he said. 'Come to the Grove at midnight and we'll talk.'

She nodded to show she understood. Then she lowered her own head and closed her eyes, though she could not bring herself to pray to a God who denied all she knew to be true, and who would demand her death as a witch in His name. But the endless childhood hours of Scripture had left their impression nonetheless, and she could not shake off a guilty taint of sin for the desires of her dream nor for the pleasure she had learned to give herself last night. Automatic words of confession stumbled through her mind, supplications for forgiveness she thought she had forgotten, but even as they ran across her thoughts, she was conscious of the two men either side of her, their masculinity, their scent and warmth stirring up desire. Confused, she shook her head against the uninvited phrases of confession in her thoughts and grasped her brother's hand, waiting for the prayers to end as her knees grew sore on the flagstones. He squeezed her fingers gently, but the contact did nothing to reassure her.

'All rise.'

The silence ended, chatter resuming with the movement as the congregation stumbled to its feet. Letting go of his hand, she risked a smile at her brother, who returned it with a tilt of his head. Then she turned the other way and saw that John had remained on his knees, lips still forming words of prayer, face lifted now in fervent appeal to God. She swallowed, made uneasy by his devotion: there was something desperate about it. She had seen such confessions before at her father's church, the wicked and sinful pouring their souls out to God for forgiveness and filled with self-loathing. Nick touched John's shoulder lightly and the boy swung towards them as though Nick had dealt him a blow. He stared at Tom.

'What are you doing in here?' he hissed. 'Witch!'

'Get off your knees,' Nick said. 'The service is ending.'

'Get him away from me.' John's whisper carried and the worshippers nearby left off their conversations, turning to look. 'How can you be here?! How can God tolerate your presence in His house?' He staggered to his feet, and his eyes, wide with fear and hatred, never left Tom's face.

Nick grasped John's shoulder more firmly and stepped forward, placing himself in front of the boy. John struggled, trying to see Tom around the older man's body. Nick flicked a glance over his shoulder.

'Just go,' he said to Tom. 'Go.'

Tom turned and left without a word, and Sarah watched as Jane ran out after him. She was torn, wanting to follow but needing to stay. When she turned back, Nick was shaking John by the shoulders.

'What is wrong with you?' he breathed. 'Get a hold of yourself.'

John stared up at Nick's face in a moment of bewilderment before all the emotion seemed to leave him in a wave and he slumped, falling limp in Nick's hands. Sarah stepped forward to take one arm. His body was slight, the arm narrow in her grip, and between them they held him easily.

'Let's get him home,' Nick said.

They almost dragged him from the church – his feet shuffling on the ground and barely supporting him – stepping out into the brightness of the morning beyond the church doors, where the willows were still bare with winter. The yard was already full with people milling – deals being struck, arrangements made, arguments flaring. She searched briefly for a sight of Tom or Jane, but they were long gone and she wondered if they were together now, if Jane was at work. An image of the two of them together flickered in her thoughts, and she forced her mind away from it before she turned her attention once more to John, hanging almost limp against her, and the effort to get him home.

≈

At the house, Nick lifted and carried John to his room while Sarah set to laying the fire. By the time Nick returned, it was burning well, the room warming, and she was setting out bread and cheese and ale on the table. She looked up at his approach.

'How is he?'

'Almost insensible,' he replied. 'He's praying again now. On his knees. I could get no sense from him, so I've left him to it.'

'What do you think is the matter with him?'

'He thinks your brother is evil. He thinks Tom's bewitched him.' He lifted his hands in a shrug of bafflement.

She said nothing, turning her attention back to setting the dinner. But she knew of Tom's lust after John and could only guess that John had learned of it too. She remembered the fate she had seen for them in the shewstone and wondered if this was the start of it – the first steps on the road to their deaths.

'Sarah?' Nick's voice was low and he came to stand close at her shoulder. 'Do you know something of it?'

She swallowed. She must have let her thoughts show in her face. She had never been good at hiding her feelings – her mother had always known when she lied. She had no idea what she should say, and Nick's presence so close flustered her thoughts. She shook her head, her voice failing her, no words she could think of to say. Nick laid a hand on the muscle of her arm and his touch pulsed through her, her breath coming short. She lifted her head, and his face was but inches away. She could feel the warmth of his breath and she dropped her eyes away from the question in his.

'Sarah?' he said again, gently. She wanted to move away and put distance between them to gather her thoughts, but the pressure of his hand on her arm was insistent. 'Tell me the truth.'

She was silent, eyes still lowered.

'You're protecting Tom?'

She let her gaze meet his for a moment then, and nodded, grateful for his understanding. 'It's not my secret to tell.'

He lowered his hand and moved back a pace, but his eyes were still searching her face for clues, still hoping, she guessed, she might confess after all. She was tempted, wanting his approval, his regard. But her fears for Tom were greater and she could not yet be sure of Nick's response. The moment hung between them until he turned away, disappointed, and she breathed again. He moved to the fire and stood before it, stretching out his hands to the heat, more for something to do, she suspected, than for the warmth. It was a good fire, drawing well, and the room was already warm. She poured him a cup of ale and took it to him, and he accepted it with a small smile.

'I'm sorry,' she said.

'I won't judge him,' Nick said. 'But I cannot help John unless I know.'

She nodded, still torn.

'And if John keeps crying witch, then Tom is in danger. You saw how people stared in church. How long do you think it'll remain a secret?'

'I know,' she murmured. Nick's stark assessment frightened her: she had seen the end of it in the shewstone. Whatever the truth of things, Tom was in danger. She clasped her hands before her and turned this way and that in front of the hearth, tortured with indecision. Nick watched her, sensing her weakening, and once more lifted a hand to touch her, taking her fingers in his, and drawing her closer to him until she was filled with his nearness. She kept her head lowered, staring down at his boots, only inches from the hem of her skirts.

'Tell me,' he urged, rubbing her fingers. 'I can't protect him if I don't know.'

She took a deep breath, the decision whirling, coming finally to rest in a choice. But she needed also to find the courage to do it, the words to say. Lifting her head finally, she said, 'I will tell you what I know.'

He nodded and stepped back, guiding her to the chair at the fire-side, placing a cushion on the seat. She eased herself down carefully. Then he drew up a stool and sat close by her. She leaned forward, elbows on her thighs. She couldn't look at him.

She said, 'I have little enough to tell you ...' She lifted her eyes in a small movement of apology. 'But I know that Tom lusts after John. Perhaps something has passed between them ...'

She took a deep breath, the words out at last, and lifted her face to meet Nick's. He nodded. 'Thank you.'

She allowed herself a half-smile of surprise at his reaction. 'You aren't shocked?'

He almost laughed, and patted her wrist. 'I'm a Bankside player and I've haunted the stews and taverns of Southwark since I was a boy. There is little can shock me now.'

She lowered her head, feeling foolish, tears prickling at the backs of her eyes as the emotions and fears ebbed and flowed. Nick tucked a finger under her chin and lifted her face.

'Don't cry,' he said. 'I understand you wanted to protect him.'

With his kindness the tears she had kept in check began to spill and flow, and she found herself held in his embrace, her face against his chest, his lips against her hair. The image of her dream welled inside her, his nakedness beneath the clothes, the memory of his hand on her breast, and she struggled to force it down, but the craving swelled, burning her. She shifted and as he loosened his hold, she lifted her face to him.

He looked down at her for a moment and she thought once more that he would kiss her, but then he let her go and stood in one quick movement, stepping across to the table, taking his place there to eat. She sniffed and wiped at her eyes, breathing deeply to order her thoughts and quell her emotions, breath still catching in tight small sobs. It seemed he did not want her after all, in spite of her dream, that she still meant no more to him than as a servant and friend.

'Come,' he invited, gesturing to the table. 'Have some food.'

She nodded and stood up carefully, smoothing her skirts and her hair back from her face, where it had become tangled from his embrace. Then she joined him at the table.

Dark drew in early, bright cold surrendering to the night and a heavy sky that promised warmer weather and rain. There was no moon, no stars, and she slipped from the house unnoticed to walk swiftly away from the life of the city towards the ancient peace of the forest, lighting her way with a torch. As the last of the houses dwindled away to the south, the lane petered into a narrow path that was shadowed by trees. She kept walking, following the path as it wove deeper into the forest amongst the great beeches and oaks, and out of sight between them she could hear the movements of fallow deer and foxes, halting in their stride to mark her presence. She was not afraid: the way had been well known to her since childhood by daylight and by night, and her skin prickled with the familiar sense of excitement as she turned off the path at last to thread her way between the trees toward the sacred Grove.

Tom was there before her: she could see the fire he had lit in glimpses through the trees, drawing her in, and she quickened her pace as she drew closer, eager for its warmth and his company. Then the trees opened out into a narrow clearing that was guarded by the gnarled and ancient yew tree, looming black against the brightness of the fire beyond it, branches dipping close to the ground. She trailed her fingers across the bark as she passed beneath its boughs, breathing in the magic of its age. Tom looked up when he heard her footsteps and came forward to greet her, taking her hands in his with a smile of welcome. She returned the smile, then gazed around her. The protective circle was already prepared, marked out on the soft grass with branches but not yet closed, and a single candle stood at each of the cardinal points. Two blankets lay folded close to the fire, and three more candles marked the points of a triangle a little distance away. Though they had cast a circle together many times before, a sense of trepidation heaved in her gut; it had always been the three of them together – mother, brother, sister – enacting the sacred rites. That this was something different she knew by instinct. She lifted her face to her brother again.

'What do you think?' he asked.

'I think,' she began carefully, 'you're planning something wicked here.'

'Not wicked,' he was quick to say. 'Magical.'

'What is this?' she asked, turning her eyes back to his face. 'You asked me here to talk.' He was watching her, eyes glinting dark in the firelight, but she understood the glow she saw in them, and the memory of her dream tugged inside her. She dragged her eyes from his and passed her gaze once more across the circle, letting understanding settle in her thoughts.

'It's just magic, nothing more or less than we've done before.' He shrugged, dismissing it, but she knew that he was lying. This was far beyond the spellcraft and the natural magic of the earth she had been born to. This was something altogether darker and more dangerous. She could sense it.

'What magic? Where did you learn of it?'

He gave no answer to her question. 'Come,' he said instead. 'Sit with me.' She followed him into the circle and he let go of her hands to crouch and spread the blankets out in front of the fire. It was a good fire, burning high and well, and the flames licked keenly into the darkness. She sat beside him, and the heat brushed against their faces. Then he swivelled to face her, taking her hands once again in his, long cold fingers wrapped around hers.

'What is this?' she asked again.

'I thought more about your dream,' he said, and she snapped her gaze away from the fire to meet his eyes. His face was near to hers and his expression was serious, earnest, eager.

'What did you think?' she asked. She was almost afraid to know, skin still alive with apprehension.

'We can make magic, you and I, together, to gain what we desire.'

'How?' she breathed.

'It's very simple,' he said, eyes sliding to the flames for a moment before returning to her face to meet the question. He hesitated, apparently searching for the right words to use. Then he said, 'When two people … lie together … there is a moment of ecstasy, and that moment has great power in the realm of the spirits. Done rightly, we can call on the spirits to give us what we want. Done rightly, they can only obey.'

She was silent, attracted by the possibility. She thought of Nick's mouth close to hers earlier that day, the want for him that had almost undone her, the disappointment when he turned away. And though she was certain he was tempted, she had not won him yet, his desire seemingly still bound up with the woman at Court. Then she remembered the dream and Tom's body pressed against hers, leading her on the path toward Nick.

'It's what the dream told you to do,' Tom said as though reading her thoughts. 'To go through me to have Nick. And this is how we must do it.'

She swallowed. Her heart was racing now, and desire was pulsing through her for both of them. 'You told me I could win him without magic,' she said.

'I was mistaken,' he answered. 'But this will bring him to you for sure. The dream has told you so.'

'Can we?' she whispered. It didn't seem possible that her love for her brother could be turned in such a way, that they could join in the flesh to lead her to a higher love again. A part of her rebelled at such a joining, aware of the sin of it – forbidden love, wicked.

'Of course.' He smiled. 'Why not? Who but our father's Church forbids it? For aeons past, the ancients knew the power of coupling, the magic possibilities of love. You don't yet know the bliss of it, the lighting of the spirit.'

'I have a little knowledge of it,' she whispered. 'I have tried alone …'

Tom laughed, surprised. 'Then you know.'

'But we are brother and sister. Did the ancients not forbid such unions also?'

'Nothing was forbidden.'

She nodded. She wanted to, and the awareness of the danger of it, the wickedness, merely fuelled the want. Only a small resistance remained, somewhere lodged inside – the voices of her childhood morality, the hard lessons of right and wrong drilled into her at the joyless church of her father. She dared not ask her brother again where he had learned of such magic.

'Will we go to Hell for this?' she asked him.

'There are many realms,' he answered, with a slight shrug. 'Who knows where we'll go?'

'You're not afraid?'

'A little,' he conceded. 'But I gave up on the teachings of the Church long ago, and if there is a Hell I am bound there regardless.'

She said nothing, letting the thoughts and emotions roll through her mind and body, giving herself to them, waiting for the answer to come. It took only moments and it came as a clarity, a lightness, a brightening of desire. She turned to her brother.

'What must we do?'

He smiled and lifted her fingers to his lips to kiss them.

'First we must bathe,' he said.

They got up together and he took her hand again and led her to the stream that ran beyond the clearing, through the trees. They stood on the bank a moment before he let her hand go and began to undress, the whiteness of his skin ghostly in the half-light. She watched him, hesitant to undress herself, still searching for her courage, and then he was before her as he had been in the dream, naked and aroused. Instinctively, she blushed and looked away, made shy by the reality of him. It had been different in the dream – there had been no sense of doubt.

'I'll help you,' he said, reaching for the ties that fastened her bodice, loosening the laces, cold fingers brushing her skin as he worked. She stood still, aware of the whoosh of the blood in her head, her breathing quick and shallow, and the doubts still lingered. Then she was naked too, shivering not only from the cold, and he stepped in close, skin against skin, his lips just brushing her temple.

'I'm afraid,' she murmured.

He said nothing but took her hand again and guided her down the bank, keeping her steady as her bare feet gripped against the shifting pebbles on the riverbed. The water was icy and she gasped and laughed instinctively as he drew her deeper in toward the middle of the stream until the water lapped about her hips and waist, making her shiver. With a deep breath in for courage, she bent her knees and dropped until the surface of the water touched her chin. Then she rubbed at her body with her hands, washing, cleansing, purifying, until she was sure she was clean, and together they left the stream and climbed up the bank. It was hard to look away from his naked figure next to hers, tall and white and lithe, but she forced herself to look forward, doing as he told her and focusing her thoughts on the image of Nick as her lover, the goal of their magic. Goosebumps rose, her nipples growing hard in the cold, and she shivered.

They stood before the fire on its western side, hands outstretched to its warmth, skin reddening, until finally he turned towards her again. She waited, uncertain and a little afraid of him, brother become lover, a different aspect.

'Then, as always, we must step into the circle and close it behind us.'

He took her hand and led her inside the circle and drew the branch across the opening to seal it. Straightening out the blankets close to the fire, he told her to face the east and to kneel and wait while he prepared the circle. She half listened to the rise and fall of his voice as he spoke the incantations, letting the unfamiliar words wash over her, lulled by the rhythm of the sacred syllables as he turned to each of the four points of the compass, addressing a summons to each and invoking the Elements with a rough-hewn wand she hadn't seen before. Watching him, her eyes grazed across his pale body as he moved, the long limbs and taut muscles, the smooth, round buttocks. Then as he turned to the west she saw him proud and erect, and the desire of her dream surged through her. She closed her eyes, remembering she was to think of Nick, and listened once more to the words as he spoke now to the west.

'Gabriel, archangel and guardian of the West, may I partake in the mysteries of water. May your blessings descend in the name of EL.'

He circled to the north.

'Auriel, archangel and guardian of the North, may I partake in the mysteries of earth. May your blessings descend in the name of ADONAI.'

Then he returned to stand before her in the east.

'I beseech Thee, O Lord God, that Thou will deign to bless this Circle, and all those who are therein to preserve us from evil and from trouble: grant, O Lord, that we may rest in this place in safety through Thee, O Lord, who livest and reignest unto the Ages of the Ages. Amen.'

When at last he fell silent, she opened her eyes. He was kneeling before her, and holding a piece of charcoal in his hand. He said, 'Don't be afraid – I will always keep you safe.'

She frowned, not understanding, until he smiled and from his memory began to trace out the figure of a sigil between her breasts, imbuing her with its power. For a moment she was terrified, holding her breath. This seemed dark magic indeed, and all the fears of the evil that the play had stirred rippled through her before she forced herself to recall that Tom was her brother and he had promised to keep her safe. So she lowered her eyes to watch him make the lines, marking her with the sign that would call to the spirit who owned it, and as he worked she could feel the weight of its latent darkness: it was no idle drawing. Finishing the symbol, he drew back a little to admire his work. What daemon would it summon? she wondered. What spirit would come? Her breath quickened with her nerves, and for a moment her instincts cried out against it. This was sorcery beyond her knowledge, a dangerous path.

'Trust me,' Tom said. He dropped the charcoal and smiled at her again, reassuring, but his gaze travelled over her body with open desire and she lowered her eyes, made shy by his attention and the sudden full awareness of her nakedness, of all that they were doing, her body his now to take. Then he reached out his hand to touch her breast, and shifted nearer. As his mouth closed in to kiss her, her shyness was forgotten, all sensation converging on the pleasure of his touch.

His lips moved on hers, tongue searching inside her mouth, and it took her a moment to understand the rhythm as he used his weight and arms to lower her onto her back, his body weighing down on hers, their mouths still pressed together. Then his hand was trailing down across her belly, between her legs, seeking out the secret places, rubbing and probing, and the unfamiliar sensations took her breath away and sent heat through her blood. It was hard to remember to think of Nick when her desire was bound up with Tom, but she brought her mind back to him again and again, imagining it was his hand, his member, and sending out her desire to the spirits.

Then Tom began to speak again but not to her, half-heard words vibrating close to her ear:

'I conjure you ... by the virtue and power of his divine majesty .... and by the innumerable powers that you and your superiors possess ...'

She let his voice encase her, wrapping herself in the power of the words as his fingers still rubbed and probed the openings that led inside her body. Pain mingled with the pleasure as he forced his fingers deeper, fire burning so that she could no longer have said what part of her he was touching, only that she knew he had reached inside her, the gates to her body breached.

His voice was still murmuring the words close to her ear, but she knew they were not addressed to her.

'That wherever you are you should rise up from your place without delay and seduce the heart and mind of Nicholas Tooley to the love of my sister ...'

She was aware of his cock against her, testing with its tip, touching first one entrance then the other, his hand still rubbing, heat still burning. Then a searing pain engulfed her as he pushed himself inside her and she cried out and tried to struggle, her first instinct to escape, but his weight held her fast, pinning her, so she surrendered to the pain, shifting her legs to let him move deeper, and the pain ceded swiftly into pleasure. He slowed his movements, aware of the change, but he was still murmuring to some unseen being and she was suddenly conscious that they were not alone: another presence was with them and witness to their union. She looked up wildly but saw nothing except the shifting shadows of the firelight's flicker.

'Ask for him now,' Tom's voice commanded in her ear, bringing her back. 'Send out your desire for him.'

He began to thrust harder, deeper, faster, and she did not want to think of Nick, her whole body wracked with the pleasure of her brother, but she forced her mind over and over toward the image of the dream, ecstasy building, consuming her, and she held the image of Nick in her mind as she climaxed, overwhelmed by the sin and the pleasure of it until slowly the waves began to ebb and faded to ripples of a warmth that suffused her. She lay quietly, still trembling in the aftermath, aware now of everything as though her senses had opened up new doors of understanding. She could feel every inch of Tom's body against the skin of her ribs and her belly, the slick of sweat between them, the distribution of his weight, the rough woollen weave of the blanket under her back, and his hands cupping her head, holding her gently. He had stopped talking and the sense of company had gone – whatever it was he had summoned had left them. He lay quite still inside her, sensations pulsing through her, but she felt no more desire to escape. It was a part of her and she let it be, accepting all that was.

They lay for what seemed a long time until at last he pushed himself up on his arms, lifting his weight off her body and withdrawing. She lay still, waiting, and was surprised when he moved down her body, his hands parting her thighs again, his tongue probing her secret place, warm and soft against the tender flesh. Then he lifted himself back over her and lowered his head for a kiss, sharing the seed he had spilled in her and the blood of her maidenhead. She tasted it, salt and sour but sweet nonetheless, and smiled. Tom smiled in reply, then lay down beside her and pulled a blanket across to cover them, holding her close against his chest, his lips against her hair.

'Sleep for a while now,' he said softly. 'Then I'll take you home.'

Still floating, still drifting in the aftermath, she gave herself up to the drowsiness and slept.

When she woke, the fire was almost out, embers pulsing, a small blue flame here and there amongst the remains of the logs and the ash, and the night was cold. Tom was no longer lying beside her. She turned onto her belly to look for him and saw him sitting, fully dressed, close to the fire, watching her.

'It's late,' he said. 'We should go.'

She nodded and he handed her her clothes, still watching her as she stood up to dress, but she was not ashamed of her nakedness in front of him now. When she was ready he stamped out the fire and took her hand, and together they left the Grove and wove through the trees towards the living world. The streets were still busy despite the hour, noise and light spilling from the stews and the taverns, whores and drunkards in the street. She saw them with different eyes that understood the pleasures that they sought. She was one of them now, a sinner too, and her whole being vibrated with connection to it all.

They walked slowly and she was conscious of a new soreness between her legs as she moved. But the ache spoke of pleasure and she did not mind it. She moved closer in beside her brother, tightening her grip on his arm, and he smiled down at her in the dark. A new love for him filled her, forbidden and delicious, and Nick was forgotten: at this moment she wanted only Tom. Neither of them spoke as they walked, connected by the closeness of their bodies and the ritual they had shared; there was nothing more to say and when they reached Nick's house, too soon, Tom took his leave of her with a peck to one cheek and a simple bow. She looked for him for a long time after he disappeared into the darkness, feelings she couldn't name or understand vying for attention in her body, her thoughts drifting and uncertain. Then she slipped silently into the house and crept without a sound to her bed in the newly cleaned-out attic.

Chapter Thirteen

SUMMER SEEMING LUST

At the playhouse, she took her sewing to the topmost gallery so she might watch the rehearsal unnoticed as she stitched. The sky stretched pale grey and damp above the roof, and a weak sun glimmered through in patches, teasing with an offer of warmer, brighter days to come. She lifted her face to the light, the cool air soft against her skin. It was her favourite part of the theatre, this close to the gods, so high above the drama of below and beyond its reach to touch her.

Looking down, she saw the players were in serious discussion: Will, chin in hand, considering; John waiting with intense attention for direction. He seemed recovered today, subdued and calm, but she had seen a new mistrust of her in his sidelong looks which frightened her, as if he had divined her new closeness to Tom and the magic they had wrought together, seeing the witch in them both. Perhaps the boy was right and her brother had bewitched him after all: Tom's lusts and knowledge were beyond her skill to understand.

She watched the players for a while with half her thoughts, her gaze flicking back and forth from the stage to the fabric in her hands, the needle deftly marking out the stitches, until a footstep behind her made her turn in surprise – the top gallery had always been her preserve: no one else had ever disturbed her here. It was Nick, and she smiled in delighted surprise, an automatic hand smoothing back her hair, her back straightening. He returned the smile.

'May I?' He gestured to the bench beside her.

'Of course.'

He stepped over the bench and sat himself down. ''Tis strange but I've never sat up here before,' he said, looking around. 'I can see why you like it.'

She nodded. 'It's peaceful, and I like to be so close to the sky.'

'I'm disturbing your peace?' he asked. 'I can go if you'd rather be alone. I just saw you here, and ...' He made a move as if to stand and she answered hastily.

'I can think of no one better to share the peace with me.'

He smiled then and settled back into his seat. 'I wondered if you would read with me – there are lines I need to practise and John is busy.'

'I'd be honoured,' she said, placing her sewing on the bench beside her and reaching for the pages he held out for her. His finger marked the place on the page and their fingertips brushed as she took it from him. She was aware of the flush rising over the skin of her neck, nerves colouring her breathing, and she kept her gaze lowered to the words he had shown her, but for a heartbeat neither of them moved, the contact unbroken till she slid the pages away from him and held them tightly. Her eyes were fixed on the written words before her, though they held no meaning, all her thoughts wrapped in the presence of the man at her side.

'From there,' he said softly.

She nodded, struggling to bring the small writing into focus.

'Whenever you're ready.'

She took a deep breath and began, the words tumbling out too fast, stumbling.

'How now, my lord! Why do you keep alone...'

'Slow down,' he said. 'There's no need to be nervous.'

She risked a glance towards him. He was regarding her with a smile that she could not read, and the flush deepened across her neck and cheeks; she was making a fool of herself.

'Try again,' he said gently. 'Take your time ... It's harder than it seems, is it not?'

She nodded, grateful for his kindness, but her face still burned and her mouth was dry and hot.

'*How now, my lord! Why do you keep alone ...*' she read, raising her eyes to him for a moment of question.

'That's good, go on.' He nodded, smiling his encouragement.

Heartened, she found the place on the page again and read on.

'*Of sorriest fancies your companions making,*
Using those thoughts which should indeed have died
With them they think on? Things without all remedy
Should be without regard: what's done is done.'

At the end of the speech she looked at him once more for his approval – she had heard John's delivery in her head as she spoke, and her own voice had sounded weak to her in comparison. Nick was regarding her closely and his gaze was lit with surprise and admiration. She waited for him to speak, aware of the greenness of his eyes, the flecks of red in his beard, the straightness of his teeth, but he was silent, watching her.

'It is your line, sir,' she whispered.

His lips curled into a smile and he nodded, as though to call his thoughts back to him. 'Yes, it is. I ... Forgive me. Give me the last line again.'

'*What's done is done,*' she said.

'*We have scorched the snake, not killed it ...*' he said, and with the words he became another man for her, transforming himself, his expression changing, the timbre of his voice, the way he held himself. She was in awe of this skill of a player to inhabit another, and bring a new soul into life. She listened, rapt, forgetting herself as the Lady, overwhelmed to be so close to a king.

'*Treason has done his worst: nor steel, nor poison,*
Malice domestic, foreign levy, nothing,
Can touch him further.'

He stopped and turned to her, still Macbeth for a moment, until his eyes met hers and he became Nick again and laughed.

'Your line,' he said.

She cursed herself for a fool, dropping her gaze to the page again, searching desperately for the line. 'I'm so sorry ... I just ... I couldn't help but just watch you ...' she mumbled, but she could not find the place on the page however hard she searched, the written words seeming to bear no relation to the speech she had just heard.

Nick placed a hand on her wrist and she swung her head to look at him, startled by his touch. 'Sarah?' he asked. 'What's the matter? Do I frighten you so much?'

She swallowed and shook her head, dropping her eyes away and down, hating herself for her foolishness. How could he want her now, after this? Why would any man want her? There was a silence and the weight of his hand on her wrist seemed an unbearable load, but she could not bring herself to move it away from his touch. Then he brought his other hand to tuck his fingers under her chin and tilt her face towards him.

'Look at me,' he said softly.

Reluctantly but unable to disobey, she turned her eyes to meet his. He searched her face and she wondered what he saw there, if he understood her need and her distress. Tears began to rise and she slid her eyes away from his though she knew he would see them anyway.

Gently, he wiped away the tears, tracing the line of them across her cheek with his thumb, bringing it to rest finally against the centre of her lower lip. She drew in a sharp breath of shock and very slowly lifted her gaze to meet his once again. The light in his eyes had changed: they were darker, the laughter gone, and she could see more of Macbeth in him now, a hunger and a lust. She remembered her dream and her breasts prickled in the hope of his touch. Dragging his thumb across her lip, he lowered his mouth to hers and kissed her, sliding one hand behind her head to cradle it, the other hand against her back. She moved with him and into him, and all she wanted was more of him, to merge with him as one. Then, too soon, he drew back, sliding his hands down her arms to grasp her fingers. They regarded each other in surprise. She could see the doubt now in his eyes, the fear of taking a new and unknown path.

'Forgive me,' he whispered.

'For what?'

'I did not mean to take advantage ...'

'I did not want you to stop.' All her nervousness was forgotten now. He had kissed her, wanted her as a woman, and he had no memory of her foolishness. A power suffused her, a knowledge of its rightness, its perfection – the spirits she had called with Tom had willed this union, this love, and soon it would be fulfilled.

A shout of laughter from the stage broke the connection between them, Nick's attention turning at the noise, drawing him back to the playhouse. But her fingers remained in his and she waited patiently for his thoughts to return. After a moment, his eyes passed back to her and he smiled. 'I should go down,' he said.

'We didn't finish reading your lines.'

'No matter. Later. We can read them later. At home.'

She nodded, returning his smile, and then he lifted her hands and brushed his lips against her fingers, as he had in the dream. Briefly, she closed her eyes, and when she opened them again, his gaze was still intent on her face. But the flicker of his doubt remained beneath the smile and she understood that she had not completely won him yet.

'Till later then,' she said, and slid her hands free of his fingers.

He stood up with reluctance, still watching her. Then he turned and walked away and her gaze followed his retreating back until she could see him no more.

Later, after the afternoon performance, the men went to the King's Head on the High Street, where the food was good. Tom was the last to arrive, having tarried to take leave of his sister, and the only spare stool at the table was the one next to John. He hesitated, waiting for John to look up and realise, but the boy was intent on the talk that was passing across the table. Tom watched for a while, standing on the outside looking in.

The conversation was about the new play and it seemed each man had something they wanted to say. He watched the comments batting back and forth, lively, animated with laughter and argument. In the centre of it all John was silent and still, and Tom realised his attention never wavered from the face of his master. Sliding onto the stool beside him, he kept on watching, starting to understand where the boy's affections truly lay. There was a break in the talk as the subject brought forth a round of laughter and John turned abruptly, suddenly aware of the man at his side. Tom saw the conscious effort not to flinch, finding a strength instead in a stillness of his body that was quite beautiful. It was the same elegance he brought to his portrayal of the Lady, Tom thought, an innate quality of composure he could call on at will.

'How goes it, John?' Tom asked.

'Well, thank you,' the boy replied stiffly. 'And your good self?'

'I am also well.'

In the pause that followed, Tom leaned across for the jug and poured himself wine, then held the jug above the cup that John held in his hand, in a questioning gesture. After a moment's hesitation, John nodded and Tom poured. Then he said, 'And how is my sister faring as your servant?'

'She is no servant of mine,' John answered.

'But she is of your household now. I am just curious to know how she does.'

John slid a furtive glance towards Nick before he answered. 'I believe Master Tooley has nothing to complain of.'

Tom nodded. 'He is kind to her?'

'He is always kind,' John replied in barely more than a whisper so that Tom had to lean in to hear him. 'Always.'

'I am glad to hear of it.'

They sat in silence then, and he could think of nothing else to say, no way to tease John away from the company of the others, no chance to try his luck once more. Giving up the hope that he might make John his that night, he turned to the players, helped himself to the slices of salted radish on the table, and added his voice to the conversation.

The wine was strong and when they finally left the tavern not one man among them could hold a straight line. Tom walked with them, his own lodgings along the way, and he kept close to John so that sometimes their arms brushed together as they walked. They were at ease with each other now – Bacchus had done his work – and Tom's mind was whirling, plotting the night's seduction. He turned to Nick on the other side of him.

'How does my sister as your servant?' he asked.

'She does very well,' Nick answered with a smile that Tom suspected held other thoughts. 'Very well. You didn't talk to her today at the playhouse?'

'I did,' Tom said, 'but I wanted to hear it from your lips. She is not one to complain ...'

Nick's answer was swift and sure. 'I hope she has no cause to complain. I am sure I have given her no reason ...' He turned towards Tom, questioning, concern in his voice. 'Has she given you cause to doubt that?'

'Not at all,' Tom replied.

They walked on in silence for a few paces. Then Nick turned to him again.

'Why don't you come home with us now?' he said. 'See her there for yourself?'

'Yes.' Tom nodded. 'I would like that.' Smiling to himself in the darkness, his arm brushing against the boy's, he felt the heat pass through him and knew he would gain his desire tonight.

Sarah was waiting when they reached the house, a good fire burning, spiced wine warming at the hearth, fresh rushes on the floor. It was a house that was good to come home to now, and Nick was glad that she was there. She opened the door and dipped him a small curtsey, which he met with an answering bow. Her cheeks were flushed from the warmth of the fire and her pleasure to see him. She showed no surprise to see Tom but he guessed she was used to her brother's unpredictable ways.

'He came to check on you,' Nick explained. 'To be sure I'm not mistreating you.'

'I am fine, dear brother.' She smiled. 'As you can see.'

They went into the hall and settled themselves before the fire, warming their bodies after the chilly dampness of the night outside.

'Wine, wench!' he ordered, with a smile. 'And remove my boots.'

She gave him a low playful curtsey and brought wine for them all, then knelt before him, her hands resting on one of his boots, ready to drag it off. He leaned forward to stop her with a touch to her shoulder. She looked up, their faces close, and he thought again how lovely she was with her grey-blue eyes and the small perfect breasts that pressed now against the top of her gown. 'A jest, merely, Sarah.' He smiled. 'I can take off my own boots.'

'I am here now, sir,' she replied, dropping her eyes, coy, hands still placed against the soft leather. 'And it is no trouble.'

He swallowed and sat back, stretching out his leg for her. 'Then I thank you.'

With one hand against the heel and the other across the arch, she paused, lifting her face to meet his smile for a moment before she deftly pulled the boot from his foot, allowing her hand to graze along the stockinged foot along the way. Her touch pulsed through him and he drew in a breath to steady himself as she readied to draw off the other. When it was done and his feet stretched out towards the heat of the fire, she did not get up but remained seated on the floor by his chair, only turning a little to face more to the fire. Some strands of her hair had come loose from their binding and rested on the pale skin of her shoulders. It was hard to take his attention from the nape of her neck and the thought of how it would taste against his lips, his tongue. But he was aware of her brother on the other side of the hearth and John, sitting on his heels on the rug, fidgeting with his cup. He took a mouthful of the wine. It had a different spice, a bittersweet taste he did not recognise that lingered on the tongue beguilingly and invited you to more.

She turned once more towards him. 'The wine is to your liking?'

'Yes,' he replied. 'Very much. What is it that you use?'

'A family secret.' She smiled. 'Passed from mother to daughter.'

Tom flicked his sister a glance that Nick could not read, sensing a history behind her words, a deeper meaning. But the wine was warm and intriguing and he took another mouthful.

Tom drained his cup and stood up, stretching like a cat before the fire, a theatrical yawn. Then he said, 'And now that I have seen that you are happy and well here, dear sister, I fear my bed is calling me.'

Nick smiled, aware Tom was excusing himself so that he and Sarah might be alone. He was sure that Tom had never in his life been the first in a party to take to his bed and he wondered if Sarah had told her brother what had passed between them in the gallery, or if Tom had simply guessed. It was hard to judge the closeness between them and know what secrets they shared. His own sisters he barely knew, and it was a kinship he could only imagine.

'John's bed is big enough for you to share,' he said in an automatic offer of hospitality, before he recalled what Sarah had told him of her brother's desire. Lulled by the wine and the fire and his lust for Sarah, he had quite forgotten John's fear of Tom. He watched the boy and waited, interested to see what he would do. Perhaps it would do him good to lose a little of his innocence, he thought, and Tom was surely the man to take it. John stared for a moment, gaze flicking between Tom and his master. Nick thought he saw a glimmer of interest, and he saw no signs of fear. After a moment John dropped his head and swirled the wine in his cup before he drained it off.

A new tension fell. Another look passed between brother and sister, an exchange of confidence that he could not share, and the beginnings of a jealousy bit at his innards. He drank more of his wine and Sarah rose to fetch the jug to refill his cup. He smiled his thanks as she poured, but he could see she had registered the change of his temper in the tension of her jaw and the tightness of her grip on the jug.

John had got to his feet and was standing now awkwardly before the fire, fingering the empty wine cup.

'Come,' Tom said, with a smile. 'Let's to bed.' He held out his hand to take John's cup, then walked across the room to place it on the sideboard before he went toward the door.

Nick felt the gust of cold air as the door opened and gave an involuntary shiver. Sarah caught the movement and smiled at him, taking her place once more on the rug near his feet, close to the warmth of the fire.

Then the two boys were gone and he was alone with her at last. They sat in silence, listening to the uneven sound of the footsteps climbing the stairs, the low rumble of their voices in the room overhead. They waited to hear the door close, and when it had latched to, Sarah turned herself to face him. He observed her for a moment, aware that she would have him in a heartbeat if he wanted, the desire plain in the brightness of her eyes, the slight parting of her lips. Above him, he heard the thud of boots hitting the floorboards, the back and forth of a conversation whose words were lost to him.

He knew that her brother was happy for him to have her, tacit approval in the way he had gone early to bed. But Tom did not know the whole of it, and he wondered if he'd be so keen if he only knew the truth.

Sarah was smiling, waiting, and he was unsure what to do. She was different from the women he usually bedded, whores and harlots who were ten a penny, or bored ladies at Court who liked the danger of a player when the Company played there for the King. An image of Catherine fell across the thought; it was hard to believe now that he had ever loved her, and the realisation took him by surprise – he could not remember the moment of his change of heart. But Sarah would be no idle fuck; she was no plaything to use and cast aside as soon as he was done. She was under his protection now and he owed her more. Did she have hopes of marriage? he wondered. Or just a first taste of love?

She shifted forward to kneel between his feet, still looking up, breasts tilted at an inviting angle, the dark crease between them a promise offered. He could not look away. 'Do I not please you, Master Tooley?' she asked.

'You please me,' he heard himself answer. 'Very much.'

'Then why do you hesitate?'

'You are my servant,' he whispered, leaning forward, placing his hand against her cheek, cupping her jaw to tilt her head closer. 'And a maid. I don't want to use you badly.'

'I would give my maidenhead to you,' she offered. 'If you will take it.'

He was silent.

'Will you take it?'

Her hand was on his leg, her face inches from his own, and he struggled to think of anything beyond the warmth of her palm on the muscle of his thigh and the rise of her breasts against her dress.

He swallowed, forcing his thoughts to coherence. She was waiting, ready to give herself to him, and the temptation to deceive her filled his blood, running through his veins and hard to put away. But he liked her too much to lie to her. Slowly, he lowered himself from the chair to sit beside her on the rug. He kept his eyes trained away from her, watching the flames dance and flit in the fireplace, but he could still see her anyway in his mind, the soft curve of her breasts, the full lips, and his thigh still burned from her touch.

He forced the words to his mouth and turned towards her to say them. 'I cannot marry you.' He watched her, trying to judge her reaction and know if it was indeed marriage that she hoped for, but there was no change in her expression, no flicker of surprise, and relief began to burn inside him, desire rising. She said nothing but lifted her hand to his face, fingers tracing the line of his cheek towards his mouth. Then she placed her thumb on his lower lip as he had done to her in the gallery that afternoon, before she leaned in to kiss him. With her kiss all will to resist her fled him and he gave himself up to the desire.

Afterwards, they lay together half-naked before the dying fire. Languidly, Nick reached out to poke it, stirring the last life from the embers to throw a little more warmth into the room. They shuffled closer, smiling, both reluctant to move and bring the moment to an end.

When he had finished with the fire, he replaced his arm around her and she lay with her head against his shoulder, fingers moving lightly across his chest. So different from her brother, she thought, solid and firm and strong against Tom's boyish slightness. She nestled in closer.

'We should go to bed,' he said. 'It would be warmer.'

'Soon,' she replied. 'Just a little longer here.' She was comfortable with her back to the fire and her body alongside his, and reluctant to disturb the closeness.

He smiled and gave an exaggerated shiver, so she peeled herself away, sitting up to watch him, her gaze tracing the lines of his muscles and the strength of him. Instinctively, she reached out to touch, trailing her fingers along his shoulder, over his chest, still amazed that she could. Then he got to his feet and held his hand to help her up, and they stood together for a moment at the hearth before he squatted to scoop up their clothes and led her out of the room, up the stairs and into his bed.

Chapter Fourteen

INNOCENT OF THE KNOWLEDGE

'Why can't you marry me?' she asked.

At rehearsal he had come to find her again, taking his place beside her on the bench in the gallery while she sewed. On the stage the Lady was losing her mind and it was hard to look away and give her attention even to the man at her side.

They were awkward with each other now: the intimacy of the night had left them and they had yet to find a way to be with each other in the day. They sat close, almost touching, and though words were hard to find, she knew that he wanted her again. But she was intrigued by his admission that she could not be his wife and her thoughts had been turning it over all morning. She shifted to face him now. He was leaning forward, forearms resting on his knees, hands lightly clasped, eyes lowered to the boards beneath his boots. At her question he bit at his lip, took a breath as if to speak, and said nothing.

'Nick?' she said softly, and laid a hand on his arm.

With her touch he looked up and she could see the indecision in his eyes, gaze flicking to and fro, not meeting her own. 'Why did you say it? I had no expectation that you would …'

'I was afraid to mislead you,' he said, stilling his gaze at last, eyes coming to rest on her face. He placed his own hand over hers, absently rubbing at her fingers. The closeness of the night was returning and she smiled, pleased that he had thought enough of her to care, and her judgement that he was a good man had proved correct.

'So now you must tell me why not. My curiosity is aroused.' She smiled, encouraging. 'Please?'

He nodded, looked away, and she could see the struggle. Then he turned his eyes back to her and said, 'I already have a wife. And a child.'

Even though she had known, for there could have been no other reason, his admission came as a shock of disappointment and surprise; she hadn't realised just how much she had hoped for him herself.

'But …?' she heard herself say. She could find no words, thoughts refusing to cohere into order.

'Where is she?' Nick formed the question for her.

She nodded.

'We never lived as man and wife – she remained at her father's house.' His voice was low and reluctant and she could hear the pain within it. 'And I have never seen my son.'

Sarah found her voice at last. 'What happened?' she asked, entwining her fingers through his.

'Her name is Rebecca. Becky,' he said, dropping his eyes once again.

She clasped his hand tighter, hoping he would look at her again. She felt she could bear to hear anything if only he would look at her.

'She was the daughter of my lawyer, of Burbage's lawyer at that time. He drew up the contract of my apprenticeship when I was fourteen. By fifteen she and I were lovers. By sixteen she was with child. I had no choice but to marry her.' He lifted his eyes to her and shrugged. 'What else could I do? But I could not keep her, so she stayed at her father's until the time came that I could provide for her.'

She nodded to show she understood. 'And now?'

'And now she refuses to come to me. Despite my house and my income, she will not come.'

'How so?'

'She has taken to her father's Puritan ways. The playhouse is evil, a den of sinners, she says, and while I am a part of it she will not live as my wife.'

'But you are her husband and she belongs to you. She gave herself to you – she is subject to your will.' Then she thought of her father and her own disobedience. Perhaps it was not so different. She wondered if the same thought occurred to Nick.

'Aye. In law I have the right of it. But do I seem to you the kind of husband who would beat my wife to obedience?'

She smiled and shook her head. 'Do you see her still?'

'No. Nor my son. And believe me, I have tried.' He stroked her fingers, watching the movement of his hand. 'It pains me that my son will never know his father.'

'You would be a good father,' she said. 'Firm but kind.' She thought of her own father and the strap across her legs, across Tom's, and could not imagine that Nick would ever give such hurt to a child.

He gave her a wry, sad smile. 'I doubt I'll ever know.'

'And Becky? Do you still …' She stopped, wondering if after all she wanted to know.

Nick waited for her to finish, and she forced herself to say it. 'Do you still love her?'

He shrugged. 'I love the thought of her, of what could have been. But we've not met in more than eight years and I can barely even remember her face …' He trailed off and his gaze slid away from her, his fingers falling slack in hers.

She swallowed, emotions confused and conflicting. Jealousy and hurt raged with anger at his wife for causing him pain, and she wished she could think of some words to say to give him comfort. But nothing came to her and so they sat in silence a while, letting their attention be gradually drawn once more to the drama below.

The players were gathered on the stage, all of them, though no scene was being acted. Voices were hushed and tense and they could not make out the words. Nick slid a look towards her.

'I should go down,' he said. She nodded her agreement and followed after him.

By the time she reached the yard he was already on the stage, and she approached it slowly, aware that something was wrong. Her senses prickled in warning and instinctively she sought to find Tom among the players, seeking his reassurance. She found him quickly and as soon as he saw her he jumped down and took her elbow in his hand, ushering her away from the gathering.

'Go,' he breathed. 'Get out of here now.'

'What?'

'I'll explain later. Just go …' Then, 'Go to the church. St Saviour's. I'll meet you there.'

She handed him the sewing that was still in her hands and turned and fled as he had told her. The morning was bitter outside, a chill wind that blew straight off the river, but her cloak was still in the tiring house and the cold cut through the wool of her dress, biting at her skin beneath. It was hard to recall the warmth of the fire and Nick's arms as she ran through the streets for the shelter of St Saviour's, and the church tower loomed up solid and dark against the pallor of the sky behind it.

Inside was warmer, out of the reach of the wind, but she still shivered, arms wrapped around herself as she wandered the church, searching for some warmth, waiting for her brother to come. A sense of foreboding weighed on her spirit, and the sombre church oppressed her: she could not pray to the spirits, couldn't seek the guidance she needed. Tom had been so urgent and afraid when he sent her here, and she fought to piece together what she had seen, desperate to understand what had happened. But she could remember only her conversation with Nick and the sudden realisation that all the players were gathered, that something was wrong.

Forcing her mind to see the stage again, she worked to place each man in the group. They had been gathered about the figure of John, she realised, in his nightgown as the Lady. The gown she had sewn, embroidered flowers at the neck and on the sleeves, a nightgown fit for a queen. But she could not find the words they spoke in her memory and she paced the church impatiently, waiting for Tom to come.

At the playhouse Tom watched her go, making sure she was safe and away before he turned back to the scene on the stage. John was kneeling, hands clasped before in prayer, face wet with tears.

'I am bewitched,' he was wailing. 'Forced to wickedness ... poisoned ... cursed ...'

Tom vaulted back onto the stage to join the others. Though instinct warned him to flee with his sister, he remained in spite of it, aware his escape might be construed as evidence of guilt. He hoped Sarah had left unseen, but in a quick glance around the assembled men, Nick caught his eye with a questioning look. Tom gave a slight tilt of his head, evasive, and turned his attention back to the kneeling boy in their midst.

John was still mumbling prayers, *sotto voce* now, attention turned inwards. Nick was squatting next to him, a reassuring hand on his shoulder, trying to coax him up off his knees and away. John resisted, apparently oblivious to his master's presence. Then, with a shout that startled them all, he screamed at Tom, pointing, spittle flying from his lips with the words.

'Witch! Witch! It is no act – he is an agent of the Devil. Brother and sister together! She gave me potions that unravelled my mind. They wove their spells to bind me in their wickedness. They made me do it. I am undone, bewitched, condemned ...' And then he fell once more to mumbled prayer, face contorted with the agony of his spirit.

All eyes turned to Tom, who shrugged, lifting his hands in a gesture of bafflement. But his heartbeat raced, his mouth was dry and for the first time in his life, he was truly afraid. For himself, but more for his sister.

'His mind is undone,' he managed to say. 'The play has addled his wits – the witches, the madness of the Lady ...'

Several of the players nodded but no one said a word in his defence, and Nick's gaze did not leave his face.

～

'Where are you going?' Nick's hand was firm on Tom's shoulder as he caught up with him in the street outside. Tom hadn't heard the other man come up behind, and his sudden appearance set his own heart racing again, fear prickling over his skin.

'I'm going to find Sarah,' he said. 'She's at the church.'

Nick gave him a look of puzzlement.

'I sent her there, out of John's way.'

'And last night? What happened last night?'

They walked to the river. It was high tide, the water murky and swirling, and the watermen in their wherries strained to keep their course in the current. Two whores beckoned from a brothel door but Nick waved them away with a gesture of his hand. The women shouted abuse for a moment, then turned toward a group of other men, merchants by the look of them, arriving at the dock with money to spend, climbing the steps from the river. Tom turned to face the other man and hesitated, unsure how much to tell, if the truth of his own forbidden lust might save them from the charge of witchcraft. It was a risk of course – sodomy could also lead a man to the gallows, but it carried less danger. And Nick was no Puritan: he had lived a long time on Bankside, where sodomy was only one of many perversions. Tom swallowed and the fear of before rose through him again. In the cold afternoon he was sweating, streams running down the crease of his spine, his mouth dry.

'Last night ...' he began. God, he thought, how could he phrase it best? 'Last night John and I ...we fucked ...' He raised his hands in a gesture of helplessness and searched the face of his companion, desperate for his reaction, his fate, Sarah's fate, dependent on it.

'You and John?'

There was no disgust at least, Tom thought. Nor even surprise. So he had suspected it and let them go to their bed together regardless, his own desire for Sarah stronger than his care for John.

'Did you force him?' Nick asked.

'No,' Tom answered quickly. 'Of course not. That's not my way ... He liked it. He wanted it. And ... that's why he thinks he was witched.'

'You tried before and he refused you.'

Tom saw the other man piece it together and nodded.

Nick turned away, jaw working with anger, shaking his head. 'Dear God, Tom!' he said then, swinging back. 'What were you thinking?'

'I ... wanted him.' Tom shrugged. 'Same as you wanted Sarah. And he wanted it too. I swear I did nothing to coerce him, nothing but give him pleasure.'

There was a silence and Nick sighed, jaw still tight with fury, eyes following the boats on the river. Some young gentlemen in a pleasure craft were shouting and waving at the whores on the bank, and one of the women lifted her skirts to entice him. In spite of himself Tom turned to Nick with an eyebrow raised and the two men exchanged a wry smile.

'But we must scorch these accusations of witchcraft,' Tom said. 'Not only for me but for Sarah. You must tell John – I fear he doesn't know what he's saying, where it will lead.'

Nick nodded. 'I'll do what I can, though it may already be too late – such things spread like wildfire. But for now keep away from him, and for God's sake keep your cock in your breeches.'

'And Sarah?'

The actor hesitated, jaw still working, hands clenching and unclenching absently. Then he drew in a breath and turned his eyes to look hard at Tom.

'She has nowhere else to go?'

'Nowhere.'

Nick nodded, still considering for a moment. Then he turned to head back to the playhouse, where John would be waiting for him, undoubtedly still kneeling in prayer, still pouring out his sinful soul to God. Tom watched him go, the strong figure striding along the bank, ignoring the calls of the whores, before he hurried towards the church to find his sister.

At the playhouse, John was still distraught, tearful and jumping at shadows. Nick put an arm about his shoulders and led him to the upstairs gallery, away from the others, where it was quiet and the sky was broad overhead.

'Tell me what happened,' Nick said.

'I cannot,' the boy wept. 'I need to see a priest. I need to confess.'

Nick tipped back his head in frustration and lifted his eyes to the heavens above him. Dear God, the boy was a Papist. That was all they needed. He said, 'You cannot see a priest. There are no priests. If you need to confess anything, you will have to confess it to me.'

John stared. 'Why you?' he asked.

'Because I'm as close as you have to a father and no one else is going to help you.'

'And you will see them hanged for witches? You will keep me safe?'

'I will keep you safe,' Nick promised, laying his hand on the boy's arm. 'But you must tell me all first.'

'Do you not believe me?'

'You have told me nothing. Only that they are witches. You have not told me why you think so or how they have bewitched you.'

'She has bewitched you too. She took you to her bed, didn't she? She cast her spells on you as well. The wine ... there was something in the wine.'

Nick gave a wry smile. 'She needed no spells to get me to her bed, John.' The wine had been unusual for sure and a half-doubt played on the edges of his thoughts, but he dismissed it at once: he had wanted her long before that. Tom was right – John's wits had been undone by his own forbidden lusts, and the play had put witchcraft in the front of his mind.

'But you would not know,' John was saying. 'The Devil's kind are clever, Master Tooley—'

'But you say you know a spell was cast on you.'

'Because they enticed me to unnatural acts. Acts against God, against nature.'

'They?'

'*She* made the potion that made me fall, that stripped me of my senses. It was her doing – poisoning me as a gift for her brother. I would swear it.'

The words sent a chill through Nick's blood. He could understand the boy might believe that Tom had bewitched him, but why Sarah?

'You coupled with Tom?' He gave the words a casual tone.

John dropped his head, made a furtive cross with his fingers above his breastbone. 'Yes,' he whispered. 'And I must confess or I will burn for it.'

'There are many who enjoy such things,' Nick said gently. 'God made us capable of pleasure – it does not mean you were bewitched.'

John slid his eyes finally to meet those of his master. 'But you don't understand. God made me as I am to test me, to test my faith, and I failed. With Tom. Of all people. To fall with such a man, a servant of the Devil ...'

'You fell,' Nick agreed. 'But you failed God's test by your own weakness. Not witchcraft. Not spells.'

'You think God sent Tom to test me? You think he is a servant of God?'

Nick fought to suppress a smile. It was hard to think of the dissolute Tom as a servant of God. 'Perhaps,' he said. 'It is possible, after all. We can only be tested in adversity.'

John was silent for a moment, mulling over the thought, and Nick waited, hoping he had said enough that John would leave off his claims of witchery. Then the boy brought his gaze to rest on Nick's face and the light in his eyes glimmered with despair. Nick's heart turned in pity.

'I thought it was you,' John whispered. 'I thought it was you God had sent to test me. Not Tom ...'

Nick stared, thoughts groping stupidly to comprehend the boy's meaning, reluctant to believe what he had heard and searching for another possibility. But there was none. He said, 'You lusted after me?'

'Not lust.' John shook his head. 'Never lust. Love ...' He trailed off, sliding his eyes away to stare down at the floor between his feet.

Nick took a deep breath and rubbed at his temple with the fingers of one hand. He had never suspected, never thought. He trawled his memory, searching through the images, trying to recall something he should have noticed, a hint that he had missed. He had known the boy admired him and was eager to please, but he himself had once felt the same about Burbage: it was the natural regard of a boy for a more experienced man, for his master. But there had been nothing untoward he could remember, no indication that John felt anything more. There was only his reluctance at the brothel, and he had put that down to shyness.

When John spoke again, it was a whisper that Nick had to lean in close to hear. 'And she has taken you from me – you have eyes only for her now. She has willed it so.'

Nick sat back and lifted his eyes to the open sky above them. The clouds hung low and heavy and dark, and the air was filled with a dampness that warned of rain to come. Dear God, he appealed again, how do I make this right? He turned once more to the boy.

'Sarah and I …' he began, stumbling and unable to find the words he needed. Then he said, 'There is nothing between us but the natural regard of a man for a woman. She is pretty and I like her, and …'

John's gaze slunk towards him, lips tight, eyes dark, and in their light Nick stopped talking. 'She has you in her thrall,' John snarled, 'and you cannot see her for what she is. She is a witch and between them they will destroy us both.'

Frustrated now and beginning to lose his patience, Nick turned on the bench to face the boy, placing a firm hand on his arm. It was thin and frail beneath his palm and it was hard to imagine how Tom could lust after him. Sarah or no, John's desires would never have borne any fruit. 'You must not say such things.'

John kept his head lowered.

'Look at me,' Nick commanded.

Reluctantly the boy lifted his head, and the eyes that held Nick's were brimful of distrust and doubt.

'They are not witches. And if you say otherwise, they will die at the end of a noose.'

'It is no more than they deserve,' John spat, and Nick saw an ugliness in the boy he had never suspected. It lit an anger in him and he grasped at John's arm hard, enjoying the wince of pain it brought.

'And you?' he demanded 'Do you deserve such an end, for what you did with Tom? For your sinful desires – for him? For me? You have no right to judge them. What is it that Christ says – let him who is without sin throw the first stone?'

With his words all the tension drained from the boy in a wave that left him slumped and miserable on the bench so that Nick felt like a bully. But he was afraid and confused, and desperation had made him willing to be cruel. He let go of John's arm.

'We all of us deserve to burn,' John murmured. He lifted his eyes and cast them once around the playhouse. 'This is a wicked place, a wicked life, and we are all of us sinners. Even you that I love. Even you. May God have pity on all our souls.' Then he dropped to his knees in the cramped space between the benches, clasped his hands at his breast and began once more to mumble his confessions.

Nick sat and watched him and did not know what to do. Word would have spread by now; the rumour of witchcraft lured all kinds to be witness. Gossip would be passing through the taverns and alehouses, the murmurs growing and changing all over Bankside, taking on a life of their own until they reached the ears of someone in authority who would come to arrest Tom and Sarah, their guilt already decided, their trial already heard in the whispers of the streets.

He thought of Sarah, bound in prison, and he had to repress the urge to strike John across the ears, fingers twitching with his help-lessness. But it would do no good – the words were said, the reports already exerting their power to harm. Words said could not be unsaid, and over time truth transforms: belief makes things untrue become true. And there was nothing he could do to stop it if he couldn't make John retract his charge.

'John,' he tried again, placing a hand (gently this time) on the boy's shoulder. 'Sit up. Talk to me.'

John prayed on, apparently oblivious.

'John.' His voice was firmer, sharper, and the mumbles ceased. 'Sit up with me. Let us talk some more.'

Unwillingly, John pushed himself back onto the bench and sat beside his master, but his head remained bowed, eyes turned defi-antly away.

'You say you love me,' Nick began. 'Do you? Truly?'

John nodded, but his face was still averted and Nick could not judge the reaction to his words.

'Then as you love me, you will do this for me.'

Slowly, John turned. 'Do what?'

'Take back these accusations.'

The boy stared, an expression in his eyes that Nick couldn't read. He pressed on. 'If Sarah were to die because of me, because I love her, I would also die.'

'You said you liked her,' John replied.

'Like her, love her …'

'You wish to marry her?'

'Aye,' Nick said. 'I do.' He took a deep breath, finding an unexpected truth in the words. 'I would make her my wife if I could.'

John shook his head. 'It is not a true love, Master Tooley. It is a love born of magic and spells she has woven to entrap you. Once she dies you will be free of it.'

'You are just a boy, John,' Nick said gently. 'And you know very little of the ways of love. I have loved before and now I love again, and it is a love born in the heavens, a pure and godly love …'

'If you marry her,' John said, 'if you say your vows before God and he does not strike her down, I will believe you. Then and only then.'

'And if we handfast in church until the banns are called?' Nick asked, desperate to buy some time. 'If we exchange our promises before God? Then you will leave off your accusations?'

Reluctantly John nodded.

Nick swallowed. It was the best that he could do for now and he nodded his acceptance, though his heart still beat quick with fear for the lie the promise was based on.

'Come,' he said. 'Let's get you home.'

Then they walked home in silence in the darkening afternoon, and the cold closed around them with the coming of the night.

Tom found his sister huddled in the chapel, arms wrapped around herself against the cold, shivering. He sat beside her, put his own cloak around her and drew her close in to his body.

'What happened?' she asked. 'Why did you take so long to come?'

It had seemed liked hours she had waited in the cold, light growing dim in the oncoming night, pacing for warmth until she grew tired of it and found a sheltered spot to sit and wait. Fear had abated with the cold and boredom, but now, in the half-light of the candles, she could see the pallor of her brother's cheeks, the gauntness beneath the bones, and the glimmer in his eyes reawakened her disquiet. He gave her a smile of reassurance that did not meet his eyes, and fear lurched in her belly. She spun herself to face him.

'What?' she demanded. 'Tell me.'

'John has charged us with bewitching him …'

'Us?'

He tilted his head in affirmation.

'Did you?'

'No,' he whispered, taking the fingers of one of her hands in his, stroking them gently. 'I had no need – his own desire was enough. That, and the wine you prepared … mandragora?'

She nodded. 'And herb of grace.'

'Come,' he said then. 'Stay with me tonight. 'Tis safer that way.'

'And give fuel to more charges against us?' She shook her head. 'Take me home.'

'To face John?'

'To see Nick.' She wanted to be away her brother; their desires for each other were too dangerous and frightening. Her love for Nick was simple, the natural want of a woman for a man. She felt safe in his bed and she knew that he would fight to protect her.

'As you wish,' he replied, and though she felt the coldness in his tone, he did not argue.

He helped her to her feet and held her hand as they made their way through the gloom and hush of the church to the colder air outside, close to the river. She shivered, and he drew her under his own cloak, his arm around her to share their warmth. Close again, she lifted her face to look at him. What had he summoned that night at the Grove? What dark force did they awake with their magic?

'How did you learn your sorcery?' she asked. 'Who taught you?'

He smiled. 'I learned it from a book.'

'What book?'

He shook his head and squeezed her shoulder tighter by way of answer, and she asked no more as they hurried on through the dark towards the house in Water Lane. Perhaps it was better not to know after all.

~

Tom saw his sister safely to the house, then turned back to make his own way home. He walked slowly, oblivious to the press of life in the tenement buildings around him, weaving through the narrow lanes in automatic abstraction. Sarah's question turned in his thoughts as he walked, and the cold night went unnoticed. He hadn't thought of his teacher for years; he could no longer even picture the man's face. But he could recall his initiation well enough – the young boy seeking knowledge, his innocence offered to the spirits as he had offered Sarah's. For the whole of his sixteenth summer he had milked the man for his learning, allowing him to use his body in exchange, and when the shadows from the man's past had caught up with him again and he had no choice but to flee, Tom had stolen from him the ancient grimoire with its densely packed pages of ritual, dark powers contained between the worn leather covers. It lay hidden and buried now beneath the stage at the playhouse, his most treasured and secret possession, though much of it he could barely understand. And though he knew there was danger in it, he still consulted it often, enjoying the weight of it in his hands and the latent power it gave him, unknown magic in the handwritten pages – inks mixed with blood, rituals enacted in their writing. All the sorcery he knew was in that book, but there was far more yet to learn: words of magic he could not decipher, spells in foreign tongues and symbols that were still unknown to him. So he continued to spend his nights quizzing the travellers that he met in the taverns and the stews, searching for more knowledge, for deeper understanding.

Briefly he wondered what had become of its previous keeper, but the thought didn't linger long as the cold finally pried its fingers inside his cloak and he quickened his pace towards the warmth of his bed.

When Sarah reached the house in Water Lane, Nick was waiting for her and John was nowhere to be seen. Nick leapt from his chair to greet her and held her tight against him. She nestled into him, absorbing the smell of him, the strength of his body, his warmth. His lips were against her hair, brushing it with gentle kisses, and she wondered what insanity had turned his wife away from such caresses; the God of the Puritans surely demanded too much. After a time, he loosened his hold on her and she drew back a little, but she remained in the safety of his embrace. 'Where is John?' she whispered.

'Safely asleep. We stopped at an apothecary on the way and got a sleeping draught. He is peaceful now, praise God.'

She nodded and they turned, still holding hands, and stepped to the fire. She settled herself before it and he sat close to her so that when she lifted her head she could only meet his eyes, staring intently into hers, his mouth but an inch from hers.

He said, 'John accused you of bewitching me.'

She frowned, searching to understand words that seemed to make no sense. 'But I thought it was because of Tom,' she said. 'Because he thinks Tom seduced him through witchcraft ...'

'It is that. But he also claims you have bewitched me to love you.'

'He has lost his mind,' she said. But the truth of the charges frightened her, for truth has a way of being heard and she knew of no magic against it. She had never thought to harm anyone, only to stir up Nick's passion more keenly and to act on his desires: she had never sought to bring him to her against his will. And why should it matter to John, anyway?

'There is more,' Nick said, lifting her chin with a finger and tilting her head up towards him. He was watching her as though he would read every thought through the window of her eyes. She tried to smile, but dread was weighting the very blood in her veins and she could barely summon the strength she needed to move her lips.

'He has said that if I marry you before God and He does not strike you down, he'll believe you are no witch.'

'But you cannot marry me.' The pity of it struck with new force and she hated his wife afresh.

'We can handfast in church, and it will buy us some time.'

'A handfast is binding,' she said carefully, though the thought of it was tempting. 'You're not free to make me promises you cannot keep. You'll end up in prison.'

'Better that than you at the end of a rope,' he answered.

'No,' she said. She couldn't let him endanger himself on her account. He was innocent of all of it, and she would have him stay that way. 'There must be another way.' She needed to talk to her mother – her mother would know what to do.

'There is none,' he said. 'And I would happily bind myself to you whatever the consequence.' He lowered his face to meet hers, mouth against mouth, one hand holding her head, the other searching out her breast. For a heartbeat she resisted, needing to think and to plan, but his fingers against the skin of her breast undid her and she gave herself up to the passion, awareness of her danger sinking with his touch.

When Nick woke, the bed was empty beside him and for a moment he thought he had dreamt of her there again. Such strange dreams he was having of late, dark images that faded into air as soon as he awoke, leaving him only with memories of darkness, shadows that trailed his waking thoughts. But last night had been no dream – she had shared his bed, her body soft and warm, and now she was gone. Reluctantly, for the room was cold, he threw back the covers and swung himself out of bed, reaching for his shift and shrugging into it. He shivered. Then, without bothering to light a candle, the way well known, he crossed to the door and opened it, pausing on the landing to listen. The new crescent moon shed a quiet light through the landing window and cast tall shadows across a silver film.

He paused at John's door. Hearing nothing, he assumed the boy was still sleeping. He hoped so, praying that sleep would calm John's madness and bring him back to peace. Creeping downstairs, no light glimmered around the hall door, but he opened it anyway, peering into the gloom. The curtains were drawn and a deeper blackness hung in the room. He went in and drew back a curtain to allow a faint light to seep in, but the room was empty, so he drew it closed again and stepped out once more into the passage, following it through to the back of the house, past the kitchen and down the step that led to the back door and the yard. The door was ajar and a jolt of apprehension tugged at his innards – had someone broken in through the night? But as he drew the door wider open he saw the figure of Sarah on the grass, her white shift shining in the moonlight, the shape of her body outlined against it, long hair trailing down her back. He smiled to himself, enjoying what he saw, and for the first moments he imagined she was dancing. Her arms were raised above her head, her body swaying. But then he realised that it was not a dance as he understood it and held his breath. At the same moment she sensed his presence and turned, and he saw the smile that lit her face on seeing him there. She came towards him and took his hand and they sat on the step by the door.

'What are you doing?' he whispered.

'It's a beautiful night,' she replied, which didn't answer his question.

'Sarah,' he urged. 'Tell me truthfully. What were you doing?' He held her hand tightly and peered into her face. Her eyes were shining, lit with laughter, and her lips were curled with a smile. He had never seen her look so beautiful. She lifted a hand to his face and smoothed the rough cheek with a gentle finger.

'Nothing,' she murmured. 'I was doing nothing.'

He twitched his head away from her touch. 'I'm not a fool,' he said. 'Tell me the truth.'

She let her hand drop and he saw the uncertainty cross her face before she spoke to him again. 'I was dancing,' she said, but her eyes gave the lie away.

'You'd leave me with suspicions and doubt?' he replied. He would rather know the truth of it than the horrible imaginings that were starting to crowd his mind. He thought of John, raving like a lunatic and terrified, and for the first time suspected there might be truth in his words.

She swallowed and turned her face away, watching the narrow moon once more as it slipped behind the clouds, allowing the darkness to reclaim the night. He examined her in profile, the high cheekbones and strong nose, the full lips, pursed now in thought. It seemed impossible she might be a witch, so young, so beautiful. And he, so in love with her. He squeezed her hand again and prayed to God in his heart that it was not true. With the pressure of his hand on hers, she turned to him again with a small sad smile on her lips.

Her chest rose with a deep breath as though she were about to say something, but she paused and took another one before she finally spoke.

'I do a little natural magic,' she said. 'Nothing evil, nothing dark – a few herbs, a few words chanted over them, a healing here and there. A cunning-woman is all, a gift from my mother. You know she is a midwife?'

He knew. But he had seen her praying to the moon; she was not telling him all.

'You pray to Hecate?'

'I pray to the moon and the earth – to the forces in the cosmos that move us and give us life. Only that. Nick, please believe me.' She touched her finger to his cheek again and turned his face to hers. 'Please believe me.'

He wanted to believe her. The touch of her aroused his desire for her, love for her brimming through him. But John's charges rang in his mind: she had bewitched him and made him hers – it was not a natural desire.

'Am I under your spell?' he whispered, their faces close, his own hand raised now to her cheek, her skin soft and smooth and cool against his fingers. 'Have you bewitched me?' He remembered the strange spice of the wine and the passion between them afterwards, but with the memory his desire overruled the logic in his head. He didn't care if she had bewitched him, for what was love anyway but a spell of nature to make us mad? He bent to kiss her, one hand reaching down to gather up the hem of the shift and find the soft flesh underneath. She sighed and moved into him as his fingers sought out her secret places, but even as he laid her down on her back on the cold grass and slid himself inside her, a shadow trailed across his thoughts, a fear that she was something other than she seemed who would lead him down to Hell.

Chapter Fifteen

PALE HECATE'S OFFERINGS

'**H**ow now, you secret, black and midnight hags? What is't you do?'
'A deed without a name.'
'I conjure you ...'

Sarah watched in silent fascination, echoes of the rite she did with Tom pulsing in her mind. *I conjure you, I conjure you ...* She could hear her brother's voice, whispers in her head – this was sorcery indeed, spirits summoned, mischief made. Her veins seemed as ice and she was frozen to the spot, unable to tear herself away, though all her instincts bade her run and just keep running.

'Speak.'
'Demand.'
'We'll answer ...'

Tom as spirit now, obedient to Macbeth's summons – witch, daemon, creature of the darkness – and she shuddered, afraid of what the words might invoke, conscious of their power. She slid her gaze to Will in his usual place at the edge of the stage and wondered at his knowledge. No wonder he had nightmares when his head was filled with scenes like these, his thoughts composed of words of occult ritual that could open doors to powers of darkness. Did he truly understand what he had done? For how did he know of such things? It was hard to credit he possessed such arcane learning. But all her certainties had slipped away since the vision in the shewstone: everything she thought she knew and felt and understood had shifted underneath her feet, and she could only watch and wait. The fate she foresaw never left her mind, trailing all her thoughts and dreams, a dark destiny waiting – it was simply a matter of where and when. But she had trained herself to shut it in a corner of her mind, for Death hangs over us all, awaiting his chance, and there is nothing any soul can do but live out the time allotted.

Her glance strayed across the playhouse. All eyes were rapt, spell-bound by the scene before them. And John, close to the stage and staring at Tom in terror – pale, sweating, trembling. She followed his gaze to watch her brother too, transformed into something other than he was, withered and wild and dangerous, and she began to understand John's fear.

Later, when the play had moved on to more worldly matters, her mother came to the playhouse, climbing the outside steps to the wardrobe and pausing at the door to regain her breath after the climb – it was a tall flight of stairs. Then she stepped down into the room where Sarah was stitching a witch's dress and drew up a stool at the workbench, fingering the black wool automatically, giving a slight instinctive nod of approval at its quality, a tailor's wife in her core.

'Mother.' Sarah gave a small nod of greeting.

'Daughter.'

There was a silence. Sarah put down her needle and waited, forbidding herself to speculate on what news her mother brought, schooling herself to patience.

Finally her mother spoke. 'You are in love with Nick,' she said. It was not a question. 'Tom came to me last night and told me all.'

Sarah wondered how he had done so without her father's knowl-edge, but she did not ask – her brother's capacity for secrecy had always amazed her.

'Everything?' Surely he had not told her all?

'Everything.' Her mother raised an eyebrow and nodded in affirmation, and Sarah dropped her gaze, ashamed for her mother to know such things about her.

'Nick will handfast with me,' she said, 'to keep John from proclaiming me witch.'

'He isn't free to do so,' Elizabeth replied. 'And it will not help.'

Sarah was silent – there was no answer to her mother's bald statement of the fact. She had turned it over again and again in her own mind that morning as she cleaned and swept Nick's house before leaving for the playhouse, imagining herself as mistress there with the house as her own, thinking she would have been a good wife to him and borne him many children. And though she knew it was but idle fantasy, it had been easy to picture their life together. It was a cruel game his true wife was playing, to hold him yet deny him his due. She had loved him once, and it seemed a strange path for a Puritan to take. Perhaps he should have beaten her after all, Sarah thought wryly, or at least demanded what was rightfully his.

'Sarah?' her mother called her attention back.

She slid her eyes from her sewing towards her mother, who was observing her intently, shrewd eyes narrowed and questioning, and Sarah felt like a child again, in trouble for some misdemeanour. She lowered her head once more and stared at the stitching that lay on the bench. Her mother said, 'We must ask for help and bring the world back into balance.'

She swallowed, forcing down the doubt and fear. 'Where?' she asked.

'The Grove. Midnight.' Her mother rose. Then she slid from the stool and was quickly gone. Sarah watched her till she moved out of sight beyond the door before turning her attention back to sewing the witch's gown for Tom.

In the afternoon, they went to Whitehall, summoned by King James to play a comedy. Sarah had never been to Court before, but her excitement was tempered by nerves, fearful that John might bring his charges again before the King, whose interest in witchcraft was famous and his sympathies not in doubt: he had written a book on daemonology and prosecuted witches in Scotland himself.

She sat close to her brother on the boat that bore them up the river, the Company's costumes in a trunk behind them, and said nothing, but she knew he understood her fears. A rising crescent moon rode low above the city, peering through a shifting veil of cloud, but she drew no comfort from its presence, and the journey seemed long as the boatman laboured against the tide, the water lapping and surging against the bow until she began to feel sick with the movement. A pair of swans bobbed beside them, indifferent. Instinctively she nestled closer in to Tom, who turned his head with a smile and squeezed her hand.

'Don't fret,' he murmured. 'He wouldn't dare.'

'How can you be so sure?'

'Trust me,' he replied.

But she was uncertain if he truly meant it, or if they were empty words that merely hoped to reassure her.

Finally, the great walls of the palace at Whitehall loomed at the bend in the river, and she was glad to step off the boat and onto the landing stairs. With solid boards beneath her feet at last, she stood and breathed deeply to quell the unease in her gut as Tom and the boatman heaved the trunk onto shore. But though the nausea began to abate, the sense of danger remained – her skin still prickled with trepidation and her mouth felt dry.

The other boats arrived, and she followed the men of the Company as they wound their way through the corridors towards the Great Hall. They strode with confidence, self-assured – they were the King's Men and this was their rightful home – so she had little time to look around her as she hurried to keep up, until abruptly she found herself in the doorway of the Hall and stopped instinctively, casting her eyes around it, amazed by its vastness. Great stone walls supported a steeply pitched roof, and multiple windows admitted the last of the afternoon light through dozens of clear panes of glass. Richly dressed servants with tapers moved like ghosts, and the walls began to glimmer as hundreds upon hundreds of candles flickered into life, drifting a sweet honey scent across the air. The biggest hearth she had ever seen roared with flame, and her fears were forgotten amidst the splendour. She stared, mouth agape, until she became aware of her brother beside her, laughing.

'It's impressive, is it not?' he said.

She returned the smile and nodded. It was hard to imagine that people could actually live in such a place.

'Come,' Tom said, and he led her toward the curtained-off area behind the stage that had been erected for the evening's entertainment. The men were already busy at work, donning make-up and costumes, stretching out the stiffness of their limbs, muttering their lines. She caught Nick's eye across the room and he winked. A flush of pleasure sighed inside her and she smiled, aware of the heat across her cheeks. He looked very fine in the robes of the Duke, and she had begun to make her away across the room to help him dress before she noticed John at his side, absorbed in a struggle with the laces of his dress. She stopped mid-step, reluctant to go near him, fearful of his reaction. Nick, observing her uncertainty, caught her eye again and shook his head, but it was too late. John had seen her and he froze in his movements, ignoring her hopeful smile of goodwill, his limbs held tense and in readiness, eyes wide and wary. She flicked another glance to Nick, who tilted his head in a small shrug of helplessness as John shifted backward and away.

'Don't come near me!' he hissed. 'Witch!'

The murmurs in the small room halted abruptly, and while the men did not pause in their dressing, she was aware of the heat of their attention. Briefly, she wondered where her brother was, but she didn't dare to take her eyes away from the boy. She lifted her hands, palms outward in a gesture of peace.

'I wish you no harm,' she said softly.

There was a silence. Beyond the curtain they could hear the hubbub of the audience drifting to their seats. A man gave a sudden shout of laughter that set off others in a ripple of hilarity.

Then Nick said, 'Come here, Sarah,' and reached out his hand toward her. 'Help me with these damn ties.'

John shot him a look of hurt confusion, then dropped his head and turned away. Sarah waited a moment longer until the boy had begun once more to attend to his costume, then she went to her master and fumbled with the laces at his wrists with trembling fingers.

Nick said nothing, but ran a quick and gentle hand across her hair. It did nothing to reassure her and she had to fight against the tears that prickled behind her eyes.

The heavy tension in the room was broken by a fanfare of trumpets that made her jump, and the chatter beyond the curtain quietened to a sudden hush. Will peered through the gap in the curtains, and Nick took a deep breath, straightening up with a nod to Sarah that he was ready. The musicians began their song and he strode toward the curtain. Then, at Will's signal, the two men stepped out onto the stage.

'If music be the food of love, play on ...'

With the beginning of the play, Sarah's unease began to ebb. John transformed into Viola, and all his fears seemed forgotten – onstage he was a different person. She watched as best she could through the small chink at the curtain's edge, and then Tom came to stand behind her, pointing out people in the audience whose names she might know.

It was her first glimpse of a king, and she found she was disappointed: there was nothing remarkable about him, no quality that marked him out as monarch. His clothes had seen better days and his hair hung lank and greasy – she had seen more regal-looking kings on the stage at the Globe. But still she was fascinated, watching how awkwardly he sat in the great high-backed chair with his head leaning close to the fair young man beside him.

'Robert Carr,' Tom whispered, in answer to her silent question. 'The King's favourite. 'Tis said they're lovers ...'

He shrugged, as if to imply such a thought was beyond his understanding, and she had to turn her head away to stifle a giggle. Then he showed her others.

Lancelot Andrewes, chaplain to the King: she had heard him preach at St Paul's on the devilry of the gunpowder treason – he had a way with words to rival Will, and a voice that could have out-acted Burbage.

Richard Bancroft, Archbishop of Canterbury, more like a Bankside wrestler than a cleric, with thick, stubby hands that gripped his knees, and an air of boredom he could not quite disguise, as though he would rather be elsewhere – interrogating Papists, perhaps.

Robert Cecil, Earl of Salisbury, the true power in the land; Thomas Egerton, Lord Chancellor; Queen Anne and the princes. She had never seen so much finery before, but her interest in silks and jewels soon waned and her thoughts drew her back, as always, to the world of the stage.

> *'There is no woman's sides*
> *Can bide the beating of so strong a passion*
> *As love doth give my heart ...'*

Her brother was forgotten, her attention rapt once more in the play.

> *'... She never told her love,*
> *But let concealment, like a worm i' the bud,*
> *Feed on her damask cheek: she pined in thought ...'*

John – boy as girl as boy, lamenting his secret affection. She flicked a glance to her brother, still standing close, and he met her look with small smile of understanding.

Later, at home, she pleaded a headache and retired to her own bed, so it was easy to slip from the house unseen in the darkness. The crescent moon rode high now above a chill mist that drifted off the river and searched inside the wool of her cloak. But she welcomed the freshness, standing for a moment in the lane, letting her eyes adjust to the gloom, breathing in the night air that was hard in her lungs. Then she checked her bundle, making sure of the piece of paper that detailed John's offences before she turned her back to the river and set her footsteps through the maze of lanes that led towards the woods. She was glad to be on her way at last – the waiting had nurtured her fears, making her jump at every footfall in the lane, expecting arrest at any moment, the dread of the noose around her neck.

She was first to arrive, the way to the Grove well known. Even in the darkest of nights, she had never lost her way to this sacred clearing, led rightly by Hecate's power. It was a place of great magic, infused with the goddess's presence, but it had taken on a new significance now, other magic conjured there, other spirits called through her union with her brother. She had not asked him what it was he summoned – she didn't want to know – but it was a different brand of magic, a new world opened, and in spite of everything, she had no wish to take it back.

She was not there long before Tom arrived, appearing silently beside her so that she laughed in delighted startlement. He took her hands in his as she greeted him with a kiss to both cheeks, and though he was just a shadow in the darkness, she knew his face was close to hers, could feel the warmth of his breath. She smiled, reassured by his presence and love, the power of their connection.

'All will be well, good sister,' he said. 'Hecate will see justice done.'

She nodded and took her hands out of his, and they parted to gather wood for a fire. As they worked together in silence, the cold wood felt good in her hands, solid and real, and when the pile of branches and twigs was big enough, Tom knelt to light it in the centre of the clearing. The dry wood caught quickly and the flames sent a merry light through the Grove, shadows dancing. They stood side by side in the glow in silent contemplation, preparing themselves for the ritual, awaiting their mother. There was no need for words, their bond sealed in the rite to come, the rites they had already shared. Then Elizabeth was standing beside them and neither had heard her arrive.

They set to work, Tom casting the circle around them, calling to the quarters for the Dragons to attend and defend them against the forces of harm. A brief image of the last time flickered through her thoughts – Tom's naked body, skin ghostly in the firelight – and she let the memory rise and fall away. When the circle was ready they stood together at the fire, and though only Elizabeth's voice called out to the night, she spoke with the heart of all of them.

'Oh, Great Goddess of Darkness, unruled Sorceress, teacher of Mysteries,

we call upon you to attend this rite and send back the evil that is sent against us.'

The fragrant scents of juniper and rosemary mingled with the earthier smell of woodsmoke as they threw herbs onto the flames, and the words vibrated through the stillness of the night, borne upwards in the smoke.

Sarah's fingers gripped the folded sheet of paper she held out before her. John's wrongs against them hung above the fire. A stillness descended, a greater darkness, and an owl hooted overhead. She could hear the flurry of its wings as it took flight, and she knew that Hecate was with them.

Elizabeth's voice sounded out again, louder now, stronger.

'Dark Mother, Queen of the night, there are those who stand against us.

Let their efforts fail. Let them be always lost in the darkness with no light to guide them.

Dark Mother, we are your children, protect us and keep us safe to follow thee ...'

Sarah stepped forward, and the heat of the flames licked at her legs through her skirts as she held the paper above it.

'Crush the evil that is sent against us,' she called out.

'Sweep its remains back against him who sent it.'

Briefly, she bent to touch the corner of the sheet to the flame and held it out in her fingertips for a moment, watching it curl and burn before she let it drop into the centre of the fire, where it shrivelled into ash and was gone.

'Hecate, Dark One, hear our plea.

Bring justice now, we ask of thee ...'

She stood back and watched the smoke rise from the fire, John's accusations contained in the ashes that burned within. There was nothing more she could do, their fate in the hands of Hecate now. When the last remnant of the paper was gone, she spoke once more.

'We thank thee, O Hecate, Dark Goddess, our Queen, and we bid thee farewell.'

Afterwards, they sat silent in the fire's dying light, allowing themselves time to come back to the earthly realm, each still infused with the magic of the rite, heart and senses open, the chill of the night unnoticed. The embers pulsated with the last of their warmth, and when, finally, the fire was cold, they got to their feet, packed away their things, and made their way silently back to the world of men.

At the door to the house, Sarah paused. She could hear the soft footsteps of her brother receding along the lane, and in her mind she watched him go, savouring the last few moments of connection before stepping back into her daylight world. Then a sound beyond the door snapped her back to the present with a shudder of apprehension: the morning was still far away and the household should be sleeping.

Aware of the knocking of her heart, she slid the key into the lock and turned it, inching the door open so as not to make a sound. The entrance hall was empty but a light flickered at the head of the stairs, and as she stepped forward and closed the door behind her, she could see the figure of John in his night shift, his face lit pale and ghastly in the light of the candle he held. Hot wax dripped onto his fingers unnoticed, his eyes were wide and staring and there seemed to be no life in them.

Placing her bag down at the foot of the stairs, she swung her cloak from her shoulders. Then, with a deep breath to calm herself, she crept up the stairs towards him.

'John?' she said softly.

He did not hear her.

'John?' She said it louder this time, and her voice sounded strange in the silent house.

'Sarah?' Nick's voice answered. 'Is that you?' He appeared on the landing close to John, legs bare under his night shirt and his hair still tousled with sleep. 'Where have you been?'

'With my mother,' she said quickly. 'But no matter. What's the matter here?'

'As you see,' Nick said.

John turned at his master's voice so close to his ear but seemed not to see him. Instead he took a step forward towards the stair and

Nick reached out a hand to stop him, palm coming to rest on the boy's outstretched arm. The touch jolted through John's body, and he swung his head towards Nick in abject terror as his body bent and backed away, candle held out before him now as a weapon to defend himself.

'Hush, John,' Nick soothed. 'It's only Nick. I wish you no harm. 'Tis a dream you are having ...'

The boy stared, eyes apparently still unseeing, and Nick took a step back, hand outstretched in concern. He flicked a glance to Sarah, still on the stairs.

'We must get him back to bed,' she said.

'Aye,' Nick answered. 'But how?'

They watched him for a moment, bewildered, and then John spoke, startling both of them. Sarah sidled up the stairs behind him to stand with Nick, reaching for his hand, which he took with a small, uncertain nod of reassurance.

'Why did God make me so?' he whispered. 'Why can I not wash this sin away with prayer? I must confess, I must confess ...'

He knelt, perilously close to the top of the stairs, and Nick took an instinctive step forward, but Sarah's hand on his arm stayed him before he could touch the boy again. She was aware of his breathing beside her, ragged and hard, and her own heartbeat knocked hard in her chest. They waited, watching.

'It is too long since my last confession ... Forgive me, Father, for I have sinned ...'

Sarah turned to Nick. 'Hear his confession,' she whispered. 'Be his confessor.'

He swallowed. 'Tell me your sins,' he said softly, with a shrug towards Sarah. Neither of them knew the rite and he could only guess at the words. But they seemed to have their effect.

'I have wicked desires. I have lusted after men,' John murmured. His head was bowed and his words were hard to hear. 'And I have lain with a man...'

'And do you repent of your sins?' Nick asked with a quick glance at Sarah, who nodded, encouraging. He seemed to be doing it right.

'Yes, Father,' John whispered. 'Can I ever be forgiven? Can I ever be forgiven? Can I ever be forgiven ...'

'If you truly repent,' Nick answered. 'Then God will forgive you.'

'What must I do?'

Nick looked to Sarah for help, but she could think of nothing. She shrugged.

'You must pray,' he said desperately. 'You must ask God's forgiveness and you must pray.' Then, inspired, 'But first you must rest and find your peace in sleep.'

John nodded and in one swift movement lay down on the floor where he had knelt at the top of the stairs, the candle tumbling from his hand. Sarah leaped forward to snatch it up, then went to fetch a blanket from John's bed to cover him, and a pillow for his head. When he was settled and apparently peaceful in sleep, she sat with Nick on the stairs, one step below him, resting her arm against his leg. He stroked her hair and she rubbed her head against his hand.

'He is losing his mind,' she said.

'Where were you, Sarah?' he replied.

She looked up sharply at the distrust in his tone. He was observing her, searching for a new truth, and though his hand still caressed her hair, she knew he was seeing her differently, as a stranger.

'With my mother,' she said again. 'A midwife's duty.'

'I did not hear her come for you.'

'She sent a boy. I was awake and I heard him in the lane before he knocked.'

'A local woman?'

'A whore on Bankside.' She hated lying to him but this truth he could not know. He was still watching her and she could see the tension in his face, the uncertainty. John's accusations had taken their hold and he doubted her now. Tom's fault, she thought. Tom and his forbidden desires. She nodded towards the sleeping form of John. 'Do you think he'll be all right?'

Nick shrugged and finally drew his gaze away from her. 'Who can say?' He stood up and reached down a hand for hers. She took it and got to her feet and stood beside him, fingers still entwined in his.

'Shall we sleep a little?' he asked.

'Sleep?' She smiled, and squeezed his hand, head tilted and coy.

He returned the smile. Then he said, 'Yes. Sleep. You've been awake all night.'

It was true, but she felt calm and vibrant, a gift of the goddess to her followers. 'I don't feel sleepy,' she said.

'Well, I do,' he returned. But he led her nonetheless to his bed, and when she stretched her body out beside him and touched her fingers and lips to his skin, he made no word of complaint.

Chapter Sixteen

GOOD THINGS OF DAY BEGIN TO DROOP AND
DROWSE

In the morning when they woke, John was no longer asleep on the landing but dressed and downstairs, pacing before the hearth. He refused to take breakfast.

'I'll have nothing from your hands, witch!' he snarled, and took himself off out of the house without another word.

So Nick and Sarah sat at the table and broke their fast without him. They were quiet with each other but at ease again; Nick's doubts seemed to have ebbed even in the backwash of John's vitriol, and he was reluctant to leave her for the playhouse, lingering for one more goodbye kiss at the door.

'Farewell, my witch,' he whispered finally, with a smile in his eyes and his palm against her cheek, and she could not say if he was jesting or in earnest.

'Farewell,' she replied. 'Anon.'

She watched him go with his confident stride towards the town, and at the bend in the lane he looked back, saw her and waved. She waved in return, watching him until he was out of sight. Then, with a sigh, she stepped back inside and began her work for the day.

She answered the knock at the door halfway through the morning without a second thought, wiping floured hands on her apron, the pastry still in its bowl in the kitchen. On the doorstep were three men she didn't recognise, middle-aged and poorly dressed, and at the sight of them a jolt of fear passed through her: she knew at once who they were.

'Sarah Stone?' the eldest of the men enquired. He was balding with greasy hair combed across his pate, and his face was lined with life's disappointments.

She nodded, fear taking her voice, and stepped back instinctively as the man's hand lifted to grab her arm. He wasted no time, pressing forward, fingers digging into the flesh of her upper arm. 'You're under arrest, witch,' he said, dragging her forward. Out of instinct, she resisted and one of the constable's men stepped in to take her other arm.

'Better come quietly,' he breathed into her face. She turned her head away from the sourness of his breath. 'Or it'll be so much the worse for you.'

'Joyce!' she called out, straining back over her shoulder. 'Joyce!'

She heard the older woman's hurried footsteps in the passage.

'God in Heaven! What is all this fuss?' Joyce shoved her way through and stood blocking the doorway, hands on hips, a wiping cloth still in her hands, flour on her forehead. She was not a small woman and her bulk loomed large.

'She's under arrest,' the constable said. But Sarah noticed the change in his tone, the subtle failing of confidence under Joyce's directness.

'On whose authority?'

'Master Wickham, madam. Magistrate. Justice of the Peace.'

'I see. And does our master know of this?'

'Your master?' The constable was clearly ill at ease now, his authority thrown into doubt. The two younger men looked to him for leadership.

'Our master. You can't just take off servants willy-nilly, without his say-so.'

'We can,' he said, squaring up to her, finding his courage. 'When his servant is a witch.'

Joyce sucked in a hiss of air, a tremor of fear and shock passing across her face. Sarah locked eyes with her for a heartbeat and was uncertain what she saw there. 'Where are you taking her?'

'Master Wickham's house.'

Sarah suppressed a shiver and was suddenly aware of the pressure of the men's hands about her arms, the violence of their grip.

'For questioning.'

'Then you may expect a visit from Master Tooley shortly. The King won't be happy, you know, when he learns the leading actor in his company has been treated so discourteously.'

Sarah swallowed, watching the constable's hesitation, a moment of hope. But then he shook his head. 'I got my orders,' he said. With a nod to his companions, they manhandled Sarah out of the door and into the lane.

'I'll go to the playhouse,' she heard Joyce calling. 'I'll let the master know …'

'Thank you, Joyce,' she tried to call back, but the jerk on her arm when she spoke was savage, so she said no more as they dragged her down the lane between them, away from the house.

The magistrate was waiting for her at his house just off the High Street when the constable shoved her roughly through the door. The men let go of her and she shook herself as though she could free her body from the memory of their touch. Her arms burned where the men had held them. She cast a quick glance around the room: dark wood furnishings, a Turkey rug beneath her feet and a single fine tapestry on the wall – the Witch of Endor summoning Samuel's ghost intricately woven in the finest of wool. A good fire blazed in the hearth and the room was warm.

The magistrate, Master Wickham, looked up from his desk and she observed him carefully. Her fate depended on this man, his kindness and credulity. He was well dressed and greying, and from his garb and the fineness of the house, she judged he was a merchant of some sort. He had a thin face and a worried look, but he did not seem to her to be unkind – there was a curiosity in his eyes that she hoped would be to her advantage. She waited, breathing deeply, searching to find reserves of peace within, but she could only feel the dryness of her mouth and the sweat between her shoulder blades. She wondered if Joyce had found Nick yet, if he knew. Then she thought of Tom – had John accused him also?

Wickham dismissed the constable and his men, who shambled out of the room with reluctance. 'Miss Stone?' he spoke softly and her hopes lifted a little.

'Yes, sir,' she replied, and dropped slightly into a curtsey of respect.

'Do you know why you are here?'

She hesitated. The next few minutes were crucial, her words her only source of protection now.

'He ...' she began, with a glance over her shoulder towards the door. 'They ... called me ... witch ...' The bewilderment in her voice was feigned but the fear was real enough.

He nodded and sat. There was a chair next to where she stood but he did not invite her to sit in it, and she thought she must be wary; he was harder than he seemed. Kindness could also be feigned. Wickham examined her with a cool disinterest, and she submitted to the scrutiny with her hands clasped before her and her head dropped modestly. Then he spoke again and with his voice she looked up.

'Who taught you your witchcraft?' he asked. 'When did it begin?'

She shook her head. 'I don't know any witchcraft,' she answered. Deny everything, she thought. John's word against hers.

'Did the Devil come to you as a young girl?' he said. 'Did he seduce you?'

She shook her head.

'Where are your familiars?'

'My familiars ...?' A witch's companions, agents of the Devil. Lines from the play echoed through her head – *'I come, Graymalkin!' 'Paddock calls'* – and it was easy to believe they existed, dreamed into life by Will and given substance by the players, dark life created to alter fate. Her fate. Tom's. 'I have no familiars, sir,' she said.

'No pets? No small creatures you suckle and feed?'

'No, sir.'

'So if I send for women to examine you we will find no witch marks? No teats for the Devil's creatures to suckle at?'

'You will not, sir,' she replied.

He was silent for a moment, fingers resting on the papers before him on his desk, eyes travelling across the written lines as though searching for some new truth. From where she stood she could not make out the letters, but she guessed it was the accusations against her – John's words. She waited, head still lowered, forcing herself to breathe slowly, but she was aware of the sheen of sweat that collected along her spine and the rapid thud of her heart. She had never thought she might die on a gallows.

After an age, he lifted his head to look at her again. 'You understand that you have been accused of witchcraft?'

She nodded.

'And what do you say to that?'

'I would say …' she breathed, searching for the right words, the right tone. 'I would say … who has accused me?'

'A boy that is known to you.'

'I don't understand, sir,' she said. 'What am I accused of doing?'

Wickham let out a sigh, as though the whole business was a matter he wished had not come to him. 'You are accused, Miss Stone,' he said, lifting his eyes from his desk to regard her. She set her face carefully to betray no expression. 'Of bewitching the boy to perform lewd acts with your brother.'

'Lewd acts?' Then, 'What boy?'

'I think you know the boy in question, Miss Stone. Your act of innocence is convincing, but I am already aware the accusations have been heard by many in the last few days and are therefore not unknown to you.'

She swallowed and ran her tongue across lips that felt dry. Panic started to well up from her belly and she forced herself to breathe, to remember the calm of last night and the power of Hecate. All would be resolved, she told herself. Trust in the goddess and all will be well.

'But …' she started. John's charge at the playhouse had not been so specific – he had accused her of bewitching him, of making him do evil things, but he had not given details. She must remember how much she should know, how much to keep hidden.

'I thought he was raving …' she said. 'I didn't know what he was talking about … lewd acts with Tom? What lewd acts?'

'You have recently left your father's house?' he said.

'Aye. I wanted to go into service.'

'And not marry your father's choice of husband for you?'

She nodded. There was no point in denial – he had obviously done his research and her position was not so uncommon. Most girls of her class went out to service before they married.

He sighed again and she could not read the meaning behind it. Boredom, perhaps? Impatience? Disbelief? She was starting to feel weak, the sleepless night beginning to tell at last. Her legs felt unsteady beneath her and she wished he would invite her to sit. The sweat was still gathered along her spine.

'You will not confess, then?'

'I have nothing to confess, sir,' she said.

'As they all say.' He stood up and stepped out from behind the desk. He was tall and thin, and when he stood before her he towered over her by more than a head. She dropped her gaze but she could smell the perfumes in the velvet of his tunic and the wine on his breath.

'Well,' he said then, cupping a hand under her chin and tilting her head up towards him. 'Let's see if you're telling the truth. Take off your bodice.'

'Sir?'

'Are you deaf?'

'No ... but I am a maid, sir ...'

'Or should I do it for you?'

She shook her head and fumbled at the laces of her bodice with fingers that trembled and could not prise the tie loose. Finally she managed to work it free somehow and let it gape open. He nodded at it, gesturing with his hand and, hurriedly now, wanting to get it over with, Sarah pulled it loose and dragged it free of her body. Then she stood before him in her linen shift and waited for what he would tell her to do next. Did he truly want to look for witch marks? she wondered. Or did he plan to rape her? She could sense his eagerness and his impatience to see her body, but his intentions she could not guess.

'Pull down your shift,' he ordered.

She shrugged it down so that her shoulders and breasts were

exposed, shivering as the air touched her skin, despite the warmth of the room. He came close and though she kept her eyes averted, she recognised his lust. 'Do you see any witch marks, sir?' she asked.

'Not yet,' he said. 'But the Devil is cunning – he places them secretly, in the hidden parts of the body.'

She swallowed, all senses alert and tingling, breathing short and shallow. He was not interested in witchcraft, didn't care a fig one way or the other, but she could hang just the same if she played this wrong. She forced herself to be calm and to slow her breathing. As she closed her eyes, her thoughts travelled unbidden to Tom, always her protector, but with a sudden burst of clarity she understood he had no power this time to keep her safe; there was nothing he could do to help her here, and she was on her own. Turning her attention inward, she searched her spirit for peace, finding memories of the Grove, a connection to the moon, bringing her thoughts to rest in its immortality. Her body he could defile, she thought, but her spirit he would never touch.

He stood close and trailed his fingers across her throat, across her breast. She could feel his breath against her hair, and it took all the force of her will not to shudder. Slowly he moved around her, the velvets of his tunic brushing her skin, his fingertips tracking across her shoulders and down the line of her spine. Tears pricked behind her eyes and she blinked to stop them falling.

'You don't like that?' he murmured.

'I am a maid, sir,' she whispered.

'Perhaps,' he replied. Then abruptly he turned and moved away from her, retreating behind his desk, his back turned.

'Get dressed,' he commanded.

She bit back the bile that rose in her throat, nausea threatening in her gut. She pulled up her shift, shrugging her shoulders into it rapidly, anything to cover her body and hide her flesh from his gaze. Her bodice took longer, the laces hard to tie with trembling fingers, and when she was finally dressed he turned to face her again. She stood silently in front of him, hands clasped, head still modestly lowered though her spirit was bright with her fury and humiliation. Words of evil gathered in her throat – curses she had never spoken, spells she had never cast – and she swallowed them down, aware they would not help her here. He nodded in approval and resumed his seat behind the desk, tidying up the papers, brushing it down, making it neat.

'Did you find any marks, sir?' she asked. She was surprised she could find the words, that she still had a voice.

'I did not,' he said. 'But I will have women sent to examine you further. Your examination will be on Friday. You will face your accusers and I will hear all the evidence. Until that time you will stay at the Marshalsea.'

She nodded, forcing down her fear of what the prison held, keeping her thoughts off her face. Then he went to the door, opened it and called the constable back in.

'Take her,' he said, and the constable grasped her arm to lead her down the passage and out of the house, before escorting her through the busy afternoon streets to the prison. She was conscious of the attention of passers-by, peering and curious, but she kept her eyes fixed on the ground a yard before her feet, jaw set firm against any desire to cry until finally she was shoved into a tiny, barely lit cell that contained nothing but a dirt floor strewn with filthy straw and the figures of three other women who sat with their backs against the wall. They lifted their eyes briefly at her entrance, and the despair she saw in them turned her heart with dread and pity. She stood still for a moment, struggling to breathe, while the gaoler retreated and locked the door, then she sank onto her knees in the straw and buried her face in her hands to weep.

Nick was surprised to see Joyce at the playhouse. She had never come there before, having no interest in plays, and he knew straight away from the crease above her eyebrows and the pucker of her lips that she bore bad news. She stood at the edge of the yard, uncertain, and he got up from his place on the side of the stage where he was watching the rehearsal and crossed the yard toward her. Taking her arm, he guided her into the lower gallery, where they could sit and talk undisturbed. A sense of foreboding crept through his limbs, and the memory of a forgotten dream wavered at the edges of his thoughts.

'Mistress Curtin,' he said. 'What brings you here?'

'Sarah's been arrested,' she answered. 'The constable's taken her to the magistrate's house.'

'On what charge?' he asked, though he already knew. He could feel the thud of his heart in his chest, fear that she might hang.

'For witchcraft.' She gave him a searching look, but he said nothing and his eyes scanned the theatre instinctively for John before he realised he hadn't seen him all day. So the boy had made good on his threat. Had he accused Tom also? He brought his gaze back to Joyce. She was still watching him, still trying to understand. 'It isn't true, is it?' she said. He met her gaze and saw his own doubts reflected in her eyes.

'Of course not,' he replied, automatically. 'Why do you even ask?'

'Because ...' She hesitated, reluctant to give words to the thoughts. 'Because her mother is a cunning-woman, a midwife ... and some say there is witchcraft in such things ...'

He shook his head. 'Nonsense. A knowledge of herblore and experience is all. Nothing evil.' He gave her a smile of reassurance that he hoped would convince her though his own doubts remained. He remembered again the taste of Sarah's wine and the passion that had passed between them. 'I'll go to her,' he said. ''Tis a misunderstanding, nothing more. Do not fret.'

She stood up then and with a hurried curtsey took her leave, eager to be gone and away. He turned and watched her go, skirts swinging, then went to seek out Will to tell him. Tom, he could not find.

They went together, he and Will, guessing she would be taken to the Marshalsea, and weaving through the late-morning streets that were crowded with stalls and carts and livestock. Cutting through the market, the stench of fish caught at his nostrils, and though Nick breathed through his mouth it made no difference. To distract himself he tossed a coin to some beggar children who had followed them from the playhouse. The boy who caught it ran off, chased by the others with wails and howls of protest. A slate-grey sky glowered overhead, low and pregnant with rain, and the dampness fingered his neck beneath the collar of his cloak, chilling him.

'Tell me the story,' Will said as they walked, and Nick explained it as best as he could, though he kept his doubts to himself. He was unsure how the playwright would take it: the two men were not close and Nick found him a hard man to judge. But Will only listened, thoughtful, and said nothing till they reached the gates of the prison in the High Street. Mediaeval brick loomed above them, blackened with age and damp, and the thick wooden doors had begun to rot. Nick did not want to guess at the misery behind them. He turned toward his companion, whose face was grave as his eyes seemed to search the road for the words he needed.

'Talk to Sarah if you can and find out what's happened,' Will directed. 'Give the keeper money for bedding and food. I'm going to tell her mother. I'll find you later.'

Nick nodded and watched the other man go, the slim upright back disappearing quickly in the crowd. An old woman approached him, ragged and half-blind, hands held out in supplication, but he turned away from her, thoughts intent on Sarah. Raising his fist, he hammered on the door. It took time for someone to come, and when the door finally opened a slovenly man stood drunkenly before him. He looked the visitor up and down, making his judgements about how to treat him, how much coin to charge. Evidently, Nick passed the test, because the man lowered himself into an unsteady bow and stepped back to let him enter.

'I wish to see Sarah Stone,' Nick said, pressing a sixpence into the man's filthy palm. 'She was arrested this morning.'

'Right you are, sir,' the man replied, examining the coin before he yelled out a woman's name. Then they stood just inside the door, waiting, as the porter nodded and swayed where he stood. Eventually, when Nick was beginning to think that no one would come after all, a middle-aged woman appeared. She stopped when she saw them, her arms folded across her chest, shrewd eyes narrowed under a tatty cap.

'Sarah Stone,' Nick repeated. He was beginning to lose his patience, eager to get this over with.

The woman tilted her head to one side, considering. Nick held up pennies in his fingers, watched the light change in her eyes. She stepped forward and snatched at the money with bony hands but he did not let go. 'Take me to her,' he said. 'And the coins are yours.'

The woman shook her head. 'No visitors.'

'The money is yours,' he coaxed. 'And there is more, if you take me.'

He could see the indecision, her eyes resting on the coins, her mouth working as she struggled with her greed. He held out his hand towards her as though he were tempting a reluctant horse with a carrot. Long seconds passed until finally she nodded and snatched the silver from his fingers.

Then she led him into a courtyard that was filled with debris and filth, mud slimy underfoot. A whipping post stood next to a water trough, and he turned his face away from it to focus on the back of the woman as she led him through a low doorway and into a dimly lit passage. He followed her along, aware of a press of unseen humanity around him, disembodied voices echoing amid a miasma of abject misery. He swallowed, a bitter taste in his mouth, and the thought of Sarah here amongst this filth and roughness, this brutality, lit an anger in his gut it was hard to suppress. He wanted to rage and hit out, abuse this drab woman in front of him, but he only clamped his jaw tight, balled his fists and kept walking. Finally, they stopped at a door and the woman slowly sorted through her keys to find the right one while he balled and unballed his fists with impatience. When at last she opened it, he pushed past her roughly to get inside.

The cell was less than three paces wide and almost dark, the only source of light a small opening high in one wall. The stench almost dropped him to his knees and he had to force down the reflex to retch. He stood by the door for a moment to compose himself, taking in the presence of the other women, who watched him with hopeless eyes. Sarah stood against the far wall, and even in the gloom he could see the heaving of her breath and the fear in her look.

'Nick!' she breathed when she realised it was him, and then she was in his arms, her face buried against his chest, her small body tight against him. Her hands were icy where they touched his neck, and he wrapped his arms around her, his lips against her hair, taking in the scent of her. With the touch of her he no longer cared about the truth of things. He loved her, whatever the cause, and the love was real and not to be denied.

'Sarah, my love,' he whispered, over and over. 'Sarah.'

After a time, she drew back from him a little, and when she raised her face to look at him her cheeks were wet.

'Did they hurt you?' he asked, fingers brushing at the tears.

'He examined me for witch marks …'

He nodded but could think of no words to say, and his mind was full of the image of her body and another man's hands against the flawless skin, her humiliation. He tried to think if she had moles or birthmarks, anything a court could see as a Devil's teat, but his recollection was of unmarked perfection, smooth and clear and soft.

'Did he find anything …?' A mark more than anything else could condemn her, and he held his breath for her answer.

She shook her head.

'Thank God,' he murmured. 'Thank God.'

'The examination is on Friday,' she said. 'Will you come?'

'Of course,' he replied, finding his voice at last. 'Of course.'

'And Tom?' she asked. 'Have they taken Tom too?'

'I haven't seen him. I don't know.' He had not thought of Tom since leaving the playhouse, but he remembered John's fear of him and the charges against him spitting from his lips. He wondered if John truly understood what he had started. 'I'll find him and I'll bring you news if I can.'

She gave him a small smile of thanks as the door scraped open behind him. The dishevelled woman stood in the doorway, keys rattling in her hand.

'I must go,' Nick whispered, his lips close to her ear, her cheek cold against his. 'Keep your courage,' he said.

She dropped her head away from him, too sad to watch him leave, and, outside in the passage, when the door was once more locked between them, he gave a half-crown to the woman. 'For food and blankets. Make sure she gets them.'

The woman nodded, then turned to go, and he followed her once more along the dismal passage towards the brighter light beyond the prison wall.

Tom was at the brothel when he heard the news of his sister's arrest, a messenger sent from the playhouse to find him. He withdrew his hand from under Jane's skirts and shoved her from her place on his lap, all levity forgotten, all thoughts of anything but Sarah sliding from his mind. Jane watched him and though he saw the jealousy and hurt across her features, he did not care. He had to find John and lure him out of his madness.

Tossing the girl a coin for her time, he grabbed his doublet and made for the door, then halted in the lane outside, reorientating himself to the day. It was still afternoon, a warm drizzle in the air with the first hint of spring. A street seller stood across from the brothel door selling apples from a basket, and he crossed to her, picked out the largest and handed over a penny in exchange. Then he rubbed the fruit against his jacket, buffing the skin to a pleasing shine before he bit into it. The sweetness was welcome after the bitterness of ale, and he stood for a moment in the lane, chewing, considering where to begin his search for the boy.

Deciding after a moment that the church would be his best bet, he lifted his eyes to the tower that loomed over Bankside in futile hope of spreading God's message across the streets of sin around it, and set his footsteps towards it.

John was there, as he'd expected, on his knees before the altar, hands clasped in desperate supplication. Tom paused a moment in the nave to quell his rage and his passion: his instinct was to beat the boy unconscious for all that he had done, and it took all his will to force his breathing to quieten and check the racing of his heart. It would do no good to give way to his anger – for Sarah's sake he needed to be cunning. Taking a deep breath, forcing out all the tension that was coiled inside him, he stepped forward and knelt beside the boy. John jumped in shock, swinging round with startled eyes.

'What have you done?' Tom whispered, careful to keep his voice soft and even, not to frighten John any further.

'She is a witch,' John replied, so low that Tom could barely hear him. 'She cursed me and made me want you, forced me into evil.'

'No one made you want me,' Tom said.

'I won't be free until she dies.'

Tom shook his head. How could he make him see his desires were his own?

'The magistrate believed me,' John said, his voice cracking as though he were hurt by Tom's unbelief. 'The physician too.'

'You saw a physician?'

'The magistrate had him examine me. There's no doubt I was bewitched, he said. No doubt at all ...'

Tom drew in a deep breath, mind racing. A lunatic boy on his own might be denied, but a physician? This was ill news indeed. He cast his eyes skyward towards the vault of the church in a silent plea to Hecate. John saw the movement.

'You pray?' he whispered.

Tom smiled. 'Yes, John. I pray.'

'And does God answer you?'

Tom nodded, instinct guiding his answer. He searched John's face, hoping for clues. The boy dropped his eyes away for a moment before lifting them once more towards the cross beyond the altar, appealing to the hanging Christ in his agony. His eyes were bright with tears.

'He does not answer me,' he murmured. 'And I don't know why.'

Tom laid a gentle hand against John's shoulder. 'Perhaps he answers but you cannot hear him,' he said.

Turning fully to face Tom at last, John subsided into sobs and Tom drew him close, arms around him, holding him, comforting. He remembered the slight frame in his embrace in the night, the pleasure he had given and taken, and his limbs and the muscles in his jaw tightened with regret for the price that pleasure was costing now. He should have left the boy alone, he thought, should have sensed the fragile soul within. But Bankside was a rough-and-tumble place and the weak did not last long: you either hardened or you sank.

When the sobs ran dry at last and Tom's knees ached from

kneeling on the cold stone, he coaxed the boy to his feet with reassuring words as though he were a child, and they stumbled from the church. With Tom's arm still around John's shoulders and his weight pressed close against him, they made their slow way home to Water Lane. When Joyce opened the door to them she let out a gasp of surprise, expecting to see her master, but she let them in and set out bread and a pie and ale on the table, and they sat and picked at it without appetite. Tom was impatient for Nick with news of his sister, and it was hard to resist the temptation to go out to find him. But there was a good chance of missing him between here and the prison, and he needed to stay with John and keep him sweet.

The afternoon hours dragged. They spoke little, shifting after lunch to sit before the newly lit fire. John passed the afternoon staring sadly into the flames as Tom drifted in and out of a doze in the chair at the hearth, idly wondering what thoughts occupied John's mind, if his fears and delusions still clawed at his sanity. But the boy seemed peaceful at least, and content enough in Tom's company as the grey afternoon slowly turned to dark beyond the windows. Joyce came and went, crouching to stoke the fire, closing the curtains against the oncoming evening.

It was almost dark before Nick's footsteps sounded at last in the lane outside. Joyce, hovering all afternoon, was quick to get the door, and Nick started in surprise at the sight of the two men at his hearth, though only Tom was aware of it. He waited while Nick spoke hurriedly to Joyce, giving her the news before he sent her home for the day. Then he got up from his chair and stood with Nick at the fire. John paid them no attention.

'How is she?' he asked.

'Afraid,' Nick answered simply. 'And alone. The magistrate found no witch marks.' He lifted his gaze to Tom's face and Tom couldn't say if the words were an accusation. Then he said, 'Will went to tell your mother.'

Tom nodded and turned away. There was nothing more to be done except to bring all his charm to bear on John. It was going to be a long night.

Chapter Seventeen

THE NIGHT HAS BEEN UNRULY

I n the morning Nick woke early, the night still dark and the house quiet with sleep. He lay for a moment in the warmth, letting his mind drift, hoping to find answers in the lazy space between sleep and waking. Images from his dreams caught at his thoughts, ephemeral and hazy, and he let them go so that only the shadow of their darkness remained.

Sitting up, he rubbed his face, yawned and stretched, trying to stir some energy into his limbs. Then, still weary, he swung his legs out of bed and got up. Downstairs he heard Joyce arrive and the noises of water being drawn, a fire being laid, and he wondered if finding Tom at the hearth had startled her, if inviting him to stay had been a mistake. They had talked late into the night, bound together by their fears for Sarah, but still Nick did not trust him, suspecting something dark beneath the surface and corruption in his soul. He dressed hurriedly in the cold, then padded downstairs in his stockings to begin the day.

In the main chamber the fire was already burning, warmth seeping through the room. Tom was nowhere to be seen, no trace of him at all. Joyce appeared at the door with a tray and bid him good morning.

'Did you see Tom this morning?' he asked.

'Tom?' She looked puzzled, then shook her head. 'No, I've seen no one but you this morning.' She set the tray down and he sighed, took his place at the table and allowed her to serve him ale, and bread and cheese, which he ate without interest. Vaguely, his mind still sluggish, he wondered what had happened to Tom.

By the hour to leave for the playhouse, John had still not appeared. Beginning to worry, Nick climbed the stairs to the boy's chamber, averting his eyes from the stairs that led to Sarah's attic room, refusing to think of where she slept now. Opening the door, he peered in. John was still sleeping, his pale face peaceful in slumber, limbs spread and relaxed. Relieved, he swallowed before his eyes lighted on the figure of Tom, who was dressed and seated on a stool at the window.

'What are you doing in here?' he hissed. 'Come out!'

John stirred with the voice and turned in the bed as Tom rose obediently to follow the older man out of the room and downstairs to the hall, which was empty now, the table cleared, a setting laid out neatly on the sideboard for when John should finally wake.

'What in God's name were you doing up there?' Nick demanded.

Tom let out a sigh of hesitation. Then he said, 'I talked to him last night after you were abed. I could hear him moving about overhead, so I knew he wasn't sleeping.'

'Talked to him? Or buggered him?'

Tom smiled. 'Both, actually.'

Nick lifted his face in silent appeal to the heavens. Tom's nonchalance took his breath away. How could any man be so reckless? He was silent, unable to find words, his thoughts too hard to pin down.

'I wanted him to recall his own desire,' Tom said.

'And did he?'

Tom tilted his head. 'Yes. And the pleasure of it.'

Nick took a deep breath and turned away, leaning his hands on the mantelpiece and staring into the fire. Tom was silent, standing across the room, fingers resting lightly on the back of the chair, waiting. The pause lasted a long time and he heard Joyce in the passage outside, the quick, irregular footsteps, the swish of the broom. Finally, when the heat from the fire had become too great against his legs and belly, burning, he turned back towards the room. 'And how will that help Sarah?'

'He will know 'tis his own sinful nature,' Tom said. 'No spiced wine to blame.'

'Don't …' Nick lifted a hand and shook his head, lips curling in disgust. Tom's lechery knew no limits and Sarah's fate was no more than a poor excuse to indulge it. 'Can you not control yourself for one night?'

Tom's face closed in anger at the insult and Nick saw the flush that lit the pale cheekbones, blue eyes turning grey and cold in the light of his emotion. Dear God, Nick thought, but he was beautiful. He swung his own eyes away, confused by the sudden, unexpected sweep of attraction.

Tom stepped forward, standing close. 'Nick,' he said, his voice soft and persuasive. 'Nick.' With a sigh Nick looked up, unable to resist. 'I took pleasure last night, yes,' Tom said softly. 'I won't deny it. But John is afraid of me again, filled with the desire I awaken in him and the sin of it, and that can only help us. 'Tis better he accuses me than her.'

'But he hasn't accused you. It is your sister that is under arrest.' Tom's reasoning made no sense to him, and he was still aware of Tom's beauty and the tension that hovered between the two of them.

'I know.' Tom touched fingertips to Nick's arm in a gesture of reassurance, and he flinched. The younger man lifted his hand away with care. 'You must trust me.'

Nick held Tom's gaze then. 'I do not trust you.' His sense of the other man's beauty began to diminish, but the memory of it lingered and only served to feed his mistrust. No wonder John had thought himself bewitched: against such power of seduction, he had never stood a chance.

The church bells struck the hour. 'We should be gone,' Nick said. 'I'll wake John. I'll see you at the playhouse.'

Tom nodded and gave a curt bow of farewell. Then he turned and walked away to the door and Nick watched him leave, aware of the trail of disturbance Tom left behind him; the man possessed a charm that could win his way into most anyone's bed, man or woman, and the sudden knowledge that even he, Nick, might not be immune sickened and disgusted him. Swallowing hard, he forced the feeling down and headed up the stairs to wake John.

～

At the playhouse, Tom tarried a while in the yard to watch the rehearsal of the final scenes – Macbeth's last battle, his death – and Nick was magnetic to watch. He was a better Macbeth than Burbage would have been, Tom thought, a younger and more physical energy that well fitted the warrior king. There was a passion and strength in him that was hard to look away from, and it was easy to understand his sister's eagerness: Tom would not have said no himself. He recalled with satisfaction Nick's brief confusion that morning, the half-conscious recognition of an unwelcome lust.

'Turn, hell-hound, turn!'

Macduff's cry rang out through the empty theatre. Strange how different the voices sounded without an audience, hollow somehow and lacking substance. It took an audience to bring the sound to fullness. He kept watching, filled with pity for Macbeth: he was too aware himself of the lure of ambition and the power of promise to judge the laird harshly for his folly. But Macbeth's downfall had been his trust – trust in the witches, trust in his wife. Surely a man should know to ponder deeper meanings – the spirits seldom promise an easy truth, giving glimpses instead of unseen possibilities, unlooked-for ways to meet our fates. Choices offered, possible futures. What we do with the knowledge is for us to decide, and Macbeth sealed his fate the moment he chose to take their words as gospel truth, immutable and destined.

The rehearsal broke for a moment, Nick and John Heminges stepping aside to practise their swordplay. Tom got up from the bench and made his way backstage to the tiring house, climbing the stairs to the wardrobe where his work awaited. He had not been working long when John's head appeared through the hatchway and halted, hesitant, apparently unsure of his welcome. Tom laid down his needlework and turned with a smile. 'Come up,' he coaxed. 'Come sit with me.'

John returned the smile and climbed up into the room. He looked around as if he had never been in it before, and Tom recalled that the last time had been for his first attempt at seduction. No wonder the boy was nervous.

'What brings you to my lair?' He smiled.

John rested on one of the high stools by the bench and Tom noted the distance he had carefully put between them. He had been less reluctant to get close in the night.

'I don't rightly know,' John said, with a small half-smile of uncertainty. 'I wanted to see you.'

Tom smiled. John seemed to have returned to himself, the unsure, eager boy he used to be before all this. 'Then I am glad.'

They sat in silence for a while and Tom returned to the doublet he was altering. It had last been worn by Burbage for *King Lear* and the waistline swam on Nick. Even without looking up, Tom could feel the heat of John's attention on him, desire in the bright green eyes. He finished the seam and tied it off. Then he lifted his head to look at the boy.

'What are you going to say on Friday?' he said.

'Friday?' John looked confused.

'Sarah's hearing,' Tom reminded him.

John drew in a sharp breath, remembering. 'I ... I ... don't know,' he stammered.

'Do you still think she bewitched you?'

John dropped his gaze away and bit his lip.

'John?'

John spoke without looking up, avoiding the other man's gaze. 'I don't know,' he whispered. 'Perhaps.' He edged his eyes back towards Tom. 'Why else would I ... would we ...?' he offered, trailing off with a shrug, unable to put words to his desire, his acts.

'Why would Sarah do that to you?' Tom asked.

'For you. Because she loves you,' John said.

'Of course she loves me, she's my sister.'

John hesitated, taking two quick breaths of indecision.

'Tell me,' Tom said.

The boy shook his head, too afraid or ashamed or uncertain to say more. Tom waited, and in the silence took up his sewing once more, focusing his attention on threading the needle, placing one neat stitch after another. After a while he said, 'So you will hold to your accusation on Friday?' He paused in his needlework and lifted his eyes from the doublet.

John was silent, lips compressed, eyes bright and evasive. Tom took a deep breath. He had hoped this might go more easily, that he could turn John's beliefs with more gentle persuasion, but his sister's fate rested on John's evidence: he needed John to doubt himself.

'It was not my sister's doing,' Tom said, 'that brought you to my bed.'

John's breathing quickened and his hands began to fidget with the reel of cotton before him on the bench.

''Twas your own desires. Your own sin.'

The boy shook his head rapidly in denial. 'I would never have acted so wickedly ...'

'The flesh is weak,' Tom said.

'No! It was the Devil's doing!'

'It was your own desires, your own lust and weakness. Did you not take pleasure in it?'

John stared, barely breathing. Tom laid down the sewing and slid off his stool, moving round to stand close to John, almost but not quite touching him. He could feel the boy quivering with fear and lust, and his own lust started to rise. Ignoring it, he leaned in to place his mouth close to John's ear. 'Were you not satisfied?'

John dropped his head away as Tom slid his arm along the boy's shoulder. 'She made me,' he whispered, lips barely moving. 'She made me do it.'

'And I?' Tom murmured, pressing closer, using all the power of his charm.

John straightened a little, trying to find his strength, but Tom could hear the tears in his voice when he spoke again. 'You are a wicked man, Tom Wynter,' he said, 'a sinner. And your black soul will surely burn in Hell for all eternity. But your sister is a witch. She sports with the Devil and she has bound me to you with dark and ill-gotten spells. She has sent her imps into my dreams and fed me with a madness, and until she is dead I won't ever be free.'

Tom stepped back and let his arm slip from John's shoulders. 'And last night?' he asked, his voice soft and casual. 'Who compelled you last night, when we lay together and you took your fill of me? When you loved me? Was it madness then?'

John's face began to crumple, tears beginning to brim and fall, small sobs breaking his breathing. Tom stepped closer again and drew John to him, the boy's head against his chest, his arm around him, holding him.

'It was love, John,' Tom murmured. 'We loved each other and that was not the Devil's doing. God gave us the gift of love.'

He felt John tense in his arms and shift back, lifting his head to look up. 'Love?' John asked. 'Was that love?'

'Did you not feel it?' Tom said.

John was silent, considering this new possibility. Tom took the boy's hands in his own with a gentle grip and drew him up from the stool so that they were standing together, close, hands still inter-linked. With a quick glance to the head of the stairs to reassure himself they were still alone, he lifted one hand to touch John's face, and very gently kissed him on the mouth. The boy's face was still wet with his tears and his lips tasted sweetly of salt.

'Does that not feel like love to you?' Tom said with a smile, using his fingers to softly wipe the tears from John's cheeks.

Still uncertain, John nodded, swallowing. Tom could feel the confusion and the doubt, and he understood it was the best he could hope for now. But the danger still remained. He had lain awake through the night next to John's slight and naked form as it sprawled beside him, and as the hours had passed, he found himself imagining the constriction of the rope around his neck. How would it feel, he had wondered, to struggle hopelessly for breath? Putting his own hands around his throat, he had squeezed with his thumbs to simu-late the moment, but he couldn't hold it for long. He had heard once that there were whores who would choke a man in the throes of passion to enhance the climax, but it was said to be a rare skill, and he had never yet found a whore to try it with. Regret flickered through him: so many experiences he might never know. Perhaps he should conjure the daemon again, he thought. Perhaps he should consult the secret book. But for what? The rites in the forest would bring Hecate to their aid, though the goddess had her own brand of justice and he was still afraid.

'John,' he said quietly, now that he had restored the intimacy of the night. They were still standing close, the fingers of one hand still entwined. 'What did you tell the magistrate?'

John shook his head, and a shadow of panic flickered across his face.

'John?'

'I don't know,' the boy murmured. 'I have no memory of it. None at all.'

Tom closed his eyes. He could see no way out. John's descent into sin, his fits of madness, his forgetting – all could be laid at Sarah's feet, and whether or not it was witchcraft it was Tom who had seduced him into sodomy. They were both of them in danger and if anything else happened now to John, it would surely be seen as the Devil's work. Sighing, delving deep to recall his trust in the goddess, he touched the backs of his fingers once more to John's pale cheek. 'You should go,' he said. 'I have work to do.'

John smiled and nodded, and backed away, letting his fingers slide free of Tom's. Then he turned and walked away, and Tom watched as his head descended out of sight down the stairs before he turned once more his stitching.

❧

The afternoon performance of *Julius Caesar* was a success. Though they still missed Richard Burbage, they were learning to manage without him, the parts rearranged and rapidly learned, the play familiar to them all, and afterwards the players went en masse to the tavern to celebrate. The sky had broken at last and a cold rain whipped through the lanes, soaking them in moments. The torches in their sconces could barely stay alight. At the Green Dragon they dragged tables together and ordered wine and food and the chatter was full of the new play.

Nick raised his cup in toast. 'To *Macbeth*,' he said, to a chorus of cheers and whistles of approval. Then, turning to Will at the head of the table, 'And to Will, who makes it all possible.'

The others lifted their glasses in Will's direction and there was a moment of silence as all of them drank. The wine was cheap and strong, and on an empty stomach its strength hit Tom hard. He was aware of his head growing light and the loosening of his tension. He loved this feeling – he had learned to seek it early as an escape from his cares. When he filled himself with the pleasures of the flesh in the stews and the taverns, his stepfather had lost the power to hurt him; he had treated the pain of a whipping more than once in the insensibility of wine and sex.

Now he drank to blur the fear he refused to acknowledge. He thought of Sarah still at the Marshalsea waiting on her fate, and looked across to Nick, who met his gaze with an uncertain look. There was little understanding between them – too many secrets, Tom guessed, for them ever to be close. Next to him he was conscious of John's attention, the boy quiet as always in company, listening to the talk of the others. Tom wondered how much of it he ever understood: even now, he retained the same air of innocence as in his very first days with the Company, something naive and incorruptible about him. Such purity would do much in his favour in Court – most men would instinctively see him as victim.

Under the table, John's tentative hand touched his thigh and Tom turned to him with surprise and a smile. Perhaps he was learning after all, less innocent at last. Then Jane appeared and rubbed herself against her favourite customer, her arm across his shoulders, her bosom level with his face. Automatically he lifted his face to smile at her and he felt John's hand withdraw from his leg.

'Not tonight, Jane,' Tom murmured.

She gave him a theatrical pout, coy and disbelieving. 'No?'

He shook his head lightly but still she stayed. Her feelings for him had clouded her whoreish instincts for business. 'No,' he said, more firmly. He could sense John growing tense beside him and he lifted her arm from his shoulder and shoved it towards her, ignoring the hurt look on her face.

'Not tonight,' he said again.

She stepped back and he swallowed with a slight sense of pity. But she was just a whore, after all, and he had only ever paid her for her time. Within a moment he had dropped her from his thoughts and turned his attention once more to the boy at his side, bestowing his most charming smile, the full light of his focus. But John was staring and rigid, and at Tom's smile he shifted back along the bench as far as he could before the body of Nick, whose back was turned, prevented him going any further.

'You like her,' he breathed. 'You want her.'

'She is just a whore.' Tom shrugged. 'Nothing more to me.'

'I don't believe you. Was it love with her too?' His voice was rising and Tom flicked a glance around the table to see who had heard. But the tavern was noisy, the Company was raucous and laughing, and no one else seemed to be listening.

'I remember what you wanted me to do with her,' John said. 'Did you laugh with her about it? Did you mock me together?'

'No! No, it was always you I wanted,' Tom answered. 'But I thought you might like to know a woman first.' It was true enough, he thought, although wanting John had never once lessened his lust for Jane. And now he longed for the ease of a simple fuck with her, pleasure taken without consequence. Without the boy beside him he would have gone to her tonight, hours in her bed well paid for and both of them happy. With the thought of it he raised his eyes to search for her again and found her at a nearby table with her arm around another man. Fat and twice Tom's age, his hand was already up Jane's skirt. She let him feel her, an instinct for money, but still she looked over his head to scan the room, always searching for a better prospect. Tom watched her, waiting for her gaze to light on him, and when they finally locked eyes, she gave him a rueful smile and a slight shrug. An unexpected ripple of jealousy turned in his gut and he had to look away. Beside him, John sat silently watching and Tom turned his attention to him once more. 'You like her,' John repeated. 'You still want her.'

'She's good at what she does,' Tom replied with a lightness he did not feel. 'You should try it.'

'Am I not enough for you?' John leaned in close, his voice lowered, so that Tom could only just hear him over the rowdiness in the room. 'Do I not satisfy you?'

'It's different.'

'Different how?' John demanded. 'Tell me.'

'I can't explain it,' he answered gently, lightly touching John's leg beneath the table, fingers resting on his inner thigh. John's own hand clamped over his, squeezing it tight.

'You want me to go to her?' John lifted his eyes to search Tom's face and there was fear in his look, and a desperation that was disturbing.

'Only if you want to,' he replied with a smile.

John said nothing, but his hand still gripped Tom's with a vice-like fury as his eyes searched for Jane among the crowd. Sensing the tension at his back, Nick turned to see and gave Tom a questioning look. Tom replied with a small shrug of bewilderment.

'Have you drunk enough yet, John?' Nick said, smiling, lifting the jug to refill their cups.

John jumped, startled, and his hand sprang open to release Tom's, shoving it away from him as if it were poison. 'No,' he answered, smiling weakly. 'Give me more.' He held out his cup and Nick poured.

Tom's cup Nick refilled without asking, and both men lifted their drinks together in a silent salute. Then Nick turned to John. 'What think you of the play now that we know all of it?'

John hesitated. Then, 'It's good,' he said with a feigned shrug of nonchalance.

'You don't like it?' Nick asked.

The boy's glance flicked from one to the other as though they were bullies who had cornered him. 'I like it ...' he began. 'It's just ...'

Nick nodded his encouragement and Tom sat back, his interest waning and his thoughts drifting towards Jane again. She was still flirting with the fat man but she had removed his hand from her skirts. Perhaps she had decided he might not pay her after all. He half listened to the conversation at his side.

'It's just ...' John was still stammering. 'It's very dark. The witches frighten me. It is they who lead Macbeth and his Lady to their fates, with their promises and lies. Without them ...' His eyes slid towards Tom. 'And Tom frightens me as one of them.'

'The illusion is convincing,' Nick agreed quickly, trying to draw the boy's attention back to himself. 'And your portrayal of the Lady ...'

John looked up, hopeful for praise.

'I can't think of anyone who could do it better.'

The boy smiled, flushing with pleasure, and Tom got up. John's head snapped round towards him.

'I need to piss,' Tom said. 'I'm coming back.'

Behind John, Nick shook his head gently and gave a wry lift of his eyebrows. Tom smiled in response then turned and walked away, heading out to the courtyard at the back. From the stables at the far end he could hear the restlessness of horses, their stamps and whinnies competing with the drum of rain, and he kept close to the wall, sheltered by the wooden gallery that serviced the first-floor row of rooms for rent above him. Holding his breath against the stench, he relieved himself in the corner by the stables, then moved hurriedly away to breathe in fresher air, beginning to sober with its touch.

The wind was swirling round in bursts, trapped in the square of the yard and blowing the rain into confusion. The eaves of the gallery offered scant protection from its reach. He shivered and wrapped his arms around himself but he tarried anyway: he was weary of John and his own desire, and it was easier to forget it in the tumult of the rainstorm.

He should have left John alone, he thought again, but how could he have known where it would lead? He, Tom, had been a much younger boy when he first gave himself to a man, and the man had been a stranger and far less gentle than Tom had been with John. But there had been pleasure in the pain, and the experience unlocked doors to a whole new world he hadn't known existed; he had never once regretted the rough initiation. But his own corruption of John had opened different doors, gates that led to realms of danger, and he could think of no way out.

A trio of riders arrived, hooves clattering loud on the cobbles, the horses' breath puffing in clouds around their faces. The riders clapped their gloved hands with cold as they dismounted and the ostler's boy came running to lead the horses away. Tom watched the men disappear inside, ducking through the low doorway, a rush of noise and warmth spilling into the yard. The horses clopped across the stones and into the stables; he could hear the boy talking to them as he led them, voice sing-song and reassuring. Then, when they were stabled out of sight and the boy's voice was lost in the storm, he took a deep breath and headed back into the hubbub of the tavern.

Inside, the heat and noise assailed his senses. He paused in the doorway a moment to readjust before he headed across the room to the table he had left. Only Nick and Will were still there and he slid into his place and lifted the jug to pour himself another cup.

'Where's John?' he asked when the men's conversation paused.

'He went out to piss,' Nick replied.

Tom shook his head. 'I didn't see him.' A sudden tension grabbed at his innards. 'So where is he?'

The three men scanned the room and Tom stood up to see better. His eyes grazed the sea of heads but there was no sign of him. And, he realised with a new jolt of unease, there was no sign of Jane either. The fat man was still at his table. Without a word to the others, he moved back across the floor toward the door that led upstairs. When he got near, one of the other girls stepped into his path, breasts offered up to him with a none-too-coy tilt of the head.

'Where's Jane?' he asked her. He had had her once, he recalled, but he could not remember her name. After Jane she had been a disappointment. But then, most of them were.

'With your friend,' she simpered. 'Didn't you know?'

'My friend?'

'The boy. The pretty boy.'

The unease lurched into fear and he pushed past her, almost running in his haste. He knew the way well, taking the narrow stairs two at a time, forcing a descending customer to flatten himself against the wall as he pushed past him. The man shouted after him with a half-heard curse as Tom ran along the landing to the end of the corridor and the rooms the whores used. Outside it he paused to take a breath. Perhaps he was wrong, he thought. Perhaps Jane was in there now giving John the time of his life, drawing him back to the normal pleasures of the flesh. But he knew that it was not so. Deep in his blood he could feel the darkness, the knowledge of foul forces at work.

He raised his fist and knocked. There was no answer. He didn't wait to knock again but threw open the door and burst in. Jane was sprawled across the bed as he had seen her many times, her skirts lifted, her head turned on the pillow towards the door. For a heart-beat he thought, hoped, she would speak to him, but even in the flickering light of the pair of candles that lit the room, he knew the stare in her eyes for what it was, unseeing and lifeless.

Briefly, he flicked his gaze across the chamber just to check, but the window was open and John was long gone. Squalls of rain swept in through the opening and the pale curtain billowed in the wind. He stood stupidly for several breaths, struggling to make sense of it, his insides hollowing out with an unexpected grief that was ferocious; he had never known such pain was possible. Then, gathering his strength and forcing himself to reason, he stepped forward and lowered her skirts to cover her legs. Had John fucked her before he strangled her? A final act of lust that had destroyed his fragile mind beyond repair? Why? Why had he done it? He recalled the desperate look in John's face – *Was it love with her too?*

His legs buckled under the weight of his grief and he sank to his knees beside the bed. Jane's blind eyes seemed to follow his move-ment but there was no anger in her look, no blame, and he was grateful for that. He took her hand but it was already cold as stone and so he let it drop, unnerved. Footsteps behind him, men's boots on the boards, and then Nick and Will were beside him.

'Oh my dear God,' Nick murmured. 'John did this?'

'The other whore said he went with her,' Tom answered. His voice sounded loud in the quiet room and absurdly, it bothered him he couldn't remember the girl's name. Nick touched his fingers to Tom's shoulder and Tom was thankful for the contact. Then a rustle of fabrics at the door was followed by a woman's shriek. Nick turned and strode toward the girl, the whore whose name Tom couldn't remember, and grasped her arms in strong hands of reassurance and command, bending so that his face was level with hers.

'Send a boy for the constable,' he told her.

The girl nodded but did not move, her eyes wandering over and over to the lifeless form of her friend on the bed. Her face was ashen.

'Go,' Nick said gently, stepping back from her. 'Go now.'

Taking a deep breath, the girl picked up her skirts and fled back down the passage. They could hear the patter of her shoes on the wooden steps, hurrying down them.

'Should we stay?' Tom lifted his head.

'We should,' Will replied. Then he shrugged, as though to say the decision whether or not they would was beyond him.

Tom tried to think, to plan, wondering if it would look better or worse for him to remain, but the wheels of his mind would not turn and his thoughts moved heavily, like a cartwheel through winter mud. He shook his head in frustration, trying vainly to clear his head. He was vaguely aware of Will and Nick as they talked in low voices, and he heard them close the door on the gathering onlookers in the passage. But even through the fog, he understood that this murder might buy Sarah's freedom. John was the criminal now, a murderer, and with no one to accuse her, Sarah would be free. Hecate had turned John's darkness back upon himself as they had asked of her and Jane had been the sacrifice, the price to pay.

'Get up now,' Will was saying. Tom lifted his head, forcing himself to think, to concentrate. 'Get off your knees. The constable will be here soon. You found her, is all. You came looking for John and this is what you found. She was nothing more to you than a whore.'

The same words he had used to John about her that very evening. He wished he had been nicer to her, that she could have died knowing that he cared. But in the end she was just a whore, he told himself, and very few of them ever grew old. He pushed himself to his feet and shook the stiffness from his knees. He felt as though he had aged ten years.

Then the three men stood in the silent room and waited for the constable to arrive.

There was no sign of John at the house. The constable followed them home in case John in his madness had gone straight there, but after a cursory check through the rooms he left to report the story to the magistrate.

Nick squatted to light the fire that Joyce had laid, and Tom went to the kitchen for wine. Will stood at the hearth, waiting for the warmth to begin. They were all of them drenched and dripping, and the night was still wild outside. They could hear the wind as it wailed in the chimneys, and the fire danced and flashed in the hearth. Then they drank and after a moment, they moved to settle themselves more comfortably. Tom reclined on the cushions with his back to the heat of the fire and nursed the cup between his fingers. It was good to be indoors.

'Well,' Will said at last. 'This changes things.'

Tom exchanged a glance with Nick: neither knew how much Will knew or suspected. More than he was saying, Tom was sure.

'Where do you think he would have gone?' Nick asked.

'Church,' Tom said without hesitation. 'He'll be praying for his soul and wishing he had a priest to confess to.'

'Perhaps he does, at that.'

Tom sat up. He had heard rumours years before that Will was a Papist too, another one among them with a secret faith. But this was an admission: it had become a more dangerous secret since the gunpowder treason a few months since, a Catholic plot coming close to blowing the king and his Parliament into dust. Every Papist was a suspect now. It was no longer just a question of faith but of loyalty.

'Does he?' Nick asked, and Tom knew the question was far less casual than it sounded.

Will nodded. 'There's an ex-Jesuit priest who recanted to save his life that haunts the brothels on Bankside. He lives as a hermit in a hut in the forest. He comes and goes, disappearing for months at a time, then reappearing to tend to the broken souls who need him.'

Tom looked once more to Nick but the actor's gaze was fixed on Will. 'You took John to him?' he asked.

'When I first saw the boy's soul was troubled. I thought it would help him.' He shrugged. 'I thought he was overwrought by the play – the illusion of the witches and the Lady's madness. I thought the Jesuit would bring him back to himself.' He shook his head. 'I should have known where it would lead. I should have seen.'

'How could you have seen?' Nick demanded. 'No one could have foreseen all this.'

Sarah had foreseen it, Tom thought. All of it. She had warned Will where the play would lead them, and he had refused to believe in the truth of it. And now she was paying the price.

Will tilted his head. 'I've been away from the faith for too long. I had forgotten what it means to be a Papist. The priest would have told him to make his accusations, that the safety of his soul depended on it. I put Sarah's life at risk.' He nodded towards Tom. 'I put both your lives at risk ...'

Tom looked down into the remnants of the wine in his cup, the dark blood-red liquid that held the light from the fire at his back. It seemed that Hecate had saved them, the power of the old goddess undimmed by the new religions.

'Take us now to this priest,' he said, half rising, ready.

Will gave a half-smile and shook his head. 'For why?'

'To find John.'

'And if you find him, what then? Will you give him to the authorities yourself? Hand him over to die after all he has been to you?'

Tom sank back onto his haunches. So Will knew all of it. 'To save my sister,' he said.

'Your sister will be saved,' Will said. 'There will be no one to accuse her at the hearing, only those of us to speak on her behalf.'

Tom looked up then. Will must suspect the truth of John's charges, yet he was willing to lie to save her. Tom felt a rush of affection – the other man's loyalty to his mother through the years had never abated. And now this. He smiled his thanks.

'And how and when John meets his fate is not for us to decide. Now I must go,' Will said, draining the last of his wine and standing up.

'Stay,' Nick offered. 'It's late and the night is rough.'

'Thank you. But I sleep better in my own bed these days.' He smiled. 'And there is the small matter of the play to consider ...'

'I'll walk with you,' Tom said. He had planned to stay himself but it would be safer for Will in the night with two of them, and he had nothing more to talk over with Nick.

They left the house together. The night was beginning to clear at last, the rain blown elsewhere by the force of the wind, which still rattled the branches of the trees in the lane and set the dogs to howling. Now and then as they walked, the sliver of moon broke through the shifting clouds and Tom was glad to see it.

'I'll send a message to your mother,' Will said.

'Will there still be a hearing? She must still face the Grand Jury?'

'She must. But it can only be a formality now. I will stand bond for Sarah tomorrow and she will be free to come home.'

Instinctively, Tom's eyes turned in the dark in the direction of the Marshalsea, unseen behind the houses. It hurt him to think of her there in the mire and misery, the cold. Nick had described to him the cell, and the thought of it made his skin crawl. Of all things for his sister, a cage would be the worst – she was a creature of the air and sky. He hoped Will was right about the court proceedings: he was a person of status, welcomed at Court by the King; his word must surely count for much. For himself Tom had little faith in the justice of the system. And John was still out there somewhere, still alive, still with his faith in his bewitchment. Until Sarah was acquitted by the court and truly free, there could be no certainty.

The two men parted ways close to Tom's lodgings and he watched the playwright walk away into the darkness. Then he doubled back and made his way to the playhouse to unearth the secret book from its hiding place and search for a different answer.

Chapter Eighteen

THESE TERRIBLE DREAMS

They moved Sarah into a different cell and bound her naked to a stool. Allowing her neither meat nor rest, they hoped, she supposed, to weaken her into confession. The hours uncoiled with agonising slowness, moment by moment in a series of battles with the weariness that sent her swaying, brought up short each time she began to fall by the rope that was curled around her neck. The manacles that held her chafed against her wrists, rubbing them raw, and her legs pained from the pressure of the stool against them and no ability to move. The cold and stench she barely noticed any more.

Her mind wandered – the natural inclination to escape the confines of her body's suffering – but the thoughts were scattered, broken, fragmented, like the shadows in the dreams of a fever. Lines from the play whispered out of order, seeming out of nowhere, and the playhouse seemed a haven of impossible safety now. Images of its warmth and laughter flickered in the corners of her mind, intangible and fleeting, and for a while she could think of nothing but the stitching on the Lady's nightgown, details of the intricate embroidery impressing on her brain.

She wanted to picture Nick. Coaxing her thoughts from the playhouse, she tried to see the bed they had shared, following the mental trail, his hand on her breast, between her legs, the thrill of when he entered her. But the images eluded her: she could neither recall his face nor his voice, all memory of him lost. Grief-stricken, she turned instead to thoughts of her brother and found his presence was close and real: the soft reassurance of his voice murmured in her ear, and she could recall every detail of the touch of his hands, his lips, his member. She could bear anything with him beside her as her protector, she realised, and she held the images tightly, binding herself in his presence as armour against her fear.

Now and then men whose names and offices she did not know came to witness her humiliation and ask once more the same questions, pacing around her, thrusting their faces into hers, jabbing at her body with bony fingers:

Where did you learn your witchcraft?

When did the Devil first come to you?

Where are your familiars now?

She kept her eyes averted from the contempt she saw in theirs, and her answer was always the same – *I am no witch.*

The morning lightened slowly as the sun dragged its heels, discouraged by the gathering clouds that swept in from the river and made everything grey. When they finally came to fetch her and dragged her from the stool, she could not stand, so they had to hold her upright while they dressed her, fat male fingers struggling with the women's clothes she had not the strength to fasten for herself. Clothed now and unbound, she unearthed the remnants of her strength from deep inside, and though her legs could barely support her as they hauled her from the cell, she was conscious that her spirit remained intact. They would force no confession from her yet.

The examination took place at the magistrate's house in the same fine room she had been taken to before. She was acutely aware of her own smell with its foetid stench of prison, and she had to swallow down the sense of shame it aroused. It was not her fault, she told herself. It was not of her own doing. Lifting her eyes, she saw the

woven Witch of Endor gazing down from her tapestry and took
courage from her presence.

She faced Wickham across his desk, and when he bid the guards
step back away from her, her legs buckled and she fell. From her
place on the floor she heard him sigh before she felt herself being
lifted into a chair by the rough hands of one of the guards. Briefly,
she wondered how long it would be before her strength returned
and she was able to stand. Wickham dismissed the guards and stood
for a moment observing her. Then he moved round to the front of
the desk and leaned against it just to one side of her, arms folded,
still observing. She swallowed, eyes lowered now, aware that this
man held the balance of her life in his palms.

'Are you ready to confess?' he began.

'I have nothing to confess,' she answered. But she did not look
at him.

'If you treat plainly with me and confess the truth, it will go better
for you.'

'I have done nothing to confess,' she repeated.

'But if you continue in your lies I will make sure that you hang.'
He leaned forward, closer, and instinctively she shrank away. 'I know
the truth about you, Sarah Stone,' he said. 'And you'll come to confess
it in the end.'

She was silent: he had the power to grant bail or withhold it, and
the thought of more days on the stool without sleep, without food,
spun panic through her guts. Her weakness threatened to over-
whelm her, and she blinked against the tears that prickled behind
her eyes.

'So I'll ask you again – where did you learn your witchcraft?'

'I am no witch,' she whispered. But even to her own ears there
was little conviction in the words. Time and ill treatment would
surely wear her down in the end. She sent her thoughts to Tom,
drawing his strength into her to bolster her own flagging will to
resist. Was he here now? she wondered. Had he been arrested also?
She did not dare to ask.

'Your victim says otherwise,' Wickham said, straightening,
looking down at her, aslant. She refused to lift her eyes.

'He says you gave him potions to inflame him with illicit lusts. He says you sent your imps into his dreams to turn him mad.' He gestured to the papers on his desk. 'It is all there …'

She swallowed, sensing worse to come, and in the pause she could not help but raise her head to look at him.

He gave her a grim smile. 'Just as well, since you maddened him to murder and he is gone.'

'Murder?' The word escaped her lips instinctively and ice closed round her heart. Not Tom, she pleaded silently. Please, not Tom. 'Who? Who is dead?'

Wickham tilted his head to appraise her response. Could he see her confusion, her fear? she wondered. Did he believe it?

'Who did your imp provoke him to kill?'

'No one,' she breathed, before she understood the trap.

Wickham smiled and, unfolding his arms, he rubbed his palms together. 'At last, a confession.'

'No,' she said and weakness suffused her, her mind struggling to make sense of things, thoughts clouded by starvation and by weariness. 'No.'

'You did not send your imp to the boy to stir him to murder?'

'I have no imp.'

'Just to drag him into madness.'

'I have no imp.'

'And to inflame him for your brother's lusts.'

She shook her head, overwhelmed. And the fear that Tom was dead stripped the last of her strength away. 'My brother …' she murmured.

Wickham bent close to her again. 'Your brother …?'

She lifted her head to look at him. His face was near to hers, thin lips pressed tight together, eyes narrowed. Everything else paled beside her need to know. 'Is my brother dead?'

The magistrate sat back and laughed. But he did not answer her question.

'Tell me, Miss Stone, how you bewitched the boy.'

She shook her head, words failing to come.

'You will not tell me? You would prefer to go back to your cell? We can wait. It is two weeks or more until the assizes. How long do you think you can last without meat or rest?'

She was silent.

'You'll tell me in the end,' he said. 'But if you tell me now, you may be granted bail till your trial. A soft bed, a warm hearth, meat in your belly ...'

She closed her eyes against the temptation he offered. She could feel her will ebbing low, and the threat of more days in that cell on the stool was like poison in her mind. She shook her head as if she might dislodge the thoughts.

'There are people in my hall,' he said. 'People who are waiting to speak on your behalf. People who will no doubt tell me of your honesty and purity, your godliness. But we know, don't we, Sarah, you and I, that you are neither honest nor godly, whatever your friends or your mother may believe. And until you tell the truth and beg for God's forgiveness for your evil and your lies, I will not hear them speak.'

Her mind groped for some solution, but the weariness and fear had made her drunk and her thoughts would not cohere into sense. And still she did not know if Tom were dead. She tried to sense him as she had before in the cell, reaching out to his spirit to come to her, but she could not bring her mind to focus and her thoughts were scattered and broken.

Wickham, growing impatient, stood up. 'We've proof beyond doubt that John was bewitched,' he announced in a change of tone, peremptory, commanding. 'We have the word of the physician who examined him. He is here too, waiting to give his evidence against you. I just need your word of confession. One word. One little *yes* from you and we can proceed. We are all waiting, Sarah.'

He stood behind her chair. She could feel him there, looming. Then he bent to speak in her ear. 'Do you want to keep your friends waiting? I'm sure they have other places to be, important matters to attend to. Men of substance, I believe. King's men. Do them a favour, Sarah, let them give their statements and leave.'

She realised she was shaking. Would he really keep her here all day? Surely not. Surely there would come a point when he would have to hear the others. But by then she would be back in her cell, bound and sleepless and starving. And Tom, she thought. What has happened to Tom?

'I am not a witch,' she whispered. 'And I have nothing to confess.'

There was a silence. He moved out from behind her, circling around to take his place once more behind his desk. She felt safer with him there, distance between them.

'The Devil chose well with you,' he said. 'A loyal servant indeed. I'm sure he'll have a warm place ready for you after you hang. As you wish then. We will proceed.'

~

The guards came and dragged her out, and she sat slumped against the wall where they left her in a small room that smelled of wood shavings and mice. Everything around her was blurred and shifting, and though she strained to hear the voices beyond the door, listening to the footsteps that came and went, when they came to fetch her again she was asleep on the hard wood floor. She came to with difficulty, blinking hard to force her eyes to open, to focus. The guard held her upright, allowing her a moment to come round.

'Can you stand, miss?' he asked, kinder now that his master was not watching.

'I think so,' she answered. 'Maybe just a little help?'

He took her arm and led her out through the door and into the passage where her friends were waiting to greet her. Tom was the first to get to her and she collapsed against him as the guard let go of her arm. He held her in his arms, supporting her weight, and she pressed herself against him, drinking in the reality of him, solid flesh and warm breath. 'I thought you were dead,' she breathed.

'Hush,' he murmured. 'Let's get you home.'

'I can go?' She tipped back her head to look at him in surprise.

'Will posted bail.'

She turned to find him, and though his face was no more than a blur, she smiled and nodded her thanks, a curtsey beyond her, and hoped he understood. Then, with her brother's arm around her and Nick close on her other side, they stepped out of the magistrate's house and into the street. Above them the sky was low and grey and full, and she tipped her face towards it, breathing in the fresh-sour air of the river, the cool damp welcome against her cheeks as the small party shuffled along the lane towards the High Street. When she thought she could trust her voice to speak, she turned her head to Tom. 'What happened with John?' she asked.

Tom's eyes locked briefly with Nick's above her head before he spoke, and fear pulled at her guts.

'He's disappeared,' Tom said. 'Last night at the brothel … he … it seems he strangled Jane.'

'Jane?' she managed to whisper. She had never thought he might have murdered Jane. 'But why?' It made no sense to her. To kill Tom or herself she would have understood. But Jane had no role to play in any of it. 'Why Jane?'

No one answered, too much to say here on the street.

'At home,' Nick said, tucking his hand under her arm, so that most of her weight was supported between the two men. 'We can talk more there.'

She nodded, and with a brief farewell to her mother and to Will, she watched them walk away side by side, deep in conversation. Then the two men she loved most in the world walked close beside her through the damp Southwark streets to her home.

At the house, they gave her into Joyce's care and Nick could hear the two women on the stairs, imagining the hot bath to come, the fresh linen, Joyce's motherly touch. Relief to have Sarah home suffused him, and he took his seat at the table in the warm main hall, the fire burning brightly, meat and bread spread out ready. Tom joined him as he poured ale for them both, and they ate for a while in a comfortable silence. He was learning to stifle his distrust, conscious that in spite of everything there was nothing Tom would not do for Sarah. United in their love for her, they were bound together, their fates entwined with hers. He ate the food that was before him without interest or attention and when they had eaten their fill, Tom turned to his host. 'What do you think will happen to John?'

Nick shrugged and said nothing: he did not want to think about it. His nights were laced now with bad dreams, John's guilt interwoven with Macbeth's, madness in them both and a lust to kill. He had woken that morning afraid of himself, recognising pleasure in the blood on his hands, the lure of the power to give or take life. For the first time in his life, he began to understand his father's viciousness, the satisfaction that came with acts of violence. In his dream he had killed them all as he lay with them – John, Sarah, Tom – and the early morning had found him on his knees, praying for God's forgiveness for the evil that dwelt within him. For what normal man had such dreams?

'Nick?' Tom's gentle question brought him back to himself.

'Forgive me. I am tired – I had strange dreams in the night.'

'Aye.' Tom nodded. 'It is hard to believe he could do such a thing. That any of us could,' he said, as though he had understood Nick's nightmares and the fears that lay behind them.

Nick looked away, remembering the dying face of his companion in the dream, the struggle as his hands gripped Tom's neck, squeezing, his own thrusting into climax as he took another man's life. The image sickened him and a thread of vomit rose in his throat. He swallowed it down and washed the taste away with more ale. 'What power can drive a man to kill?' he murmured, more to himself than to Tom. It was a question he had pondered often since he was given the part of Macbeth, but now it had a new urgency and resonance and his nightmares had gifted him some small understanding.

'How could we not have seen it coming?' He lifted his eyes then to Tom. 'One moment he was there, drinking at the table with us, and then ... How could we not have known what he was thinking?'

'Who can ever know the thoughts in another man's mind?' Tom replied. 'And who would want to? But thoughts are not deeds. Which among us has never harboured evil thoughts?'

'What evil do you dream of, Tom?' he asked. It was not hard to imagine Tom with wicked thoughts.

Tom smiled. 'It is best left unsaid. You of all people know the power of the spoken word, the potential of language for magic.'

Nick said nothing but he observed the other man with his languid, easy movements, the almost womanish elegance, the changing blue-grey eyes that met his own now, bright with amusement at the scrutiny. He had seen the same look in his sister. A brief shadow of the attraction he had felt for him flickered inside and swiftly died.

'What?' Tom laughed. 'What evils do you think me capable of?'

Nick lifted an eyebrow, answering Tom's humour with his own. 'I wouldn't like to hazard a guess, my friend.' But he was conscious of the darkness in Tom, a lust for something beyond the usual vices of the brothel and the games of chance, an appetite for sin. Whatever else, he had no doubts that Tom would find his eternal rest in Hell.

Tom laughed again, comfortable in his role as sinner and enjoying Nick's unease at confronting it, and a sense of pity for John rippled through him. The boy had never stood a chance against Tom's seduction: such confidence brooked no resistance. Then he remembered the rising of his own brief desire for Tom and wondered if he would have fallen too, if Tom had chosen him instead. Before the dreams of last night he would have been sure of his own strength to resist, but the nightmares had shown him a part of himself he did not recognise and he was no longer so certain of who he was.

Sarah's appearance at the door distracted him from his thoughts. She was clean and bright and pretty again, the matted hair washed and brushed, a fresh gown. She smiled at the sight of them.

'Will you eat?' Nick gestured to the food still spread on the table.

She slid onto the stool next to her brother, at an angle to Nick, and took a little bread and cheese. Nick poured her some ale, which she sipped at.

'You must be hungry,' Tom said.

'A little,' she replied. 'But my belly has shrunk.' She looked down briefly and touched a hand to her stomach as if to reassure herself it was true, and Nick wondered how badly she'd been used in the prison, if hunger had been the worst of it. Rage at her treatment simmered in his blood and he tensed his jaw against it, making himself remember that she was home now and with him, the danger and humiliation passed for a time. She caught his look as he watched her eat and smiled, and the affection in her smile reassured him. He touched his fingers to her arm. 'I'm glad you're home,' he said.

'No more than I,' she returned.

When she had eaten all she could they sat at the fireside, and she settled herself in the cushions at the hearth while the two men sat in the chairs either side of it. He wanted Tom to leave. He wanted Sarah to himself, but her brother showed no signs of going. Will was working around them at the playhouse today, rehearsing scenes without them, and a performance in the afternoon that needed neither man. But Tom showed no interest in attending to his duties as company tailor. Nick lowered himself to the cushions to be closer to her, and she smiled as he reached up to smooth her still-damp hair back behind her shoulder.

Tom watched and Nick was sure he understood, but still the younger man made no movement to leave. He sidled in closer so that his body was almost touching hers and she dropped her face away, shy of his touch before her brother. He stroked the line of her jaw with his fingers and she rubbed her head towards the caress. He lifted his head to look at her brother. Go, he mouthed, with a gesture of his head toward the door. Leave.

Tom hesitated for a moment, his eyes searching Sarah's, and in the exchange that passed between the two of them, Nick suddenly understood something new: Tom had known Sarah before him, and the look he saw now was ownership. Confused, uncertain he had read it right and hoping he was wrong, he dropped his hand from her face and backed away from her, gaze switching from one to the other, praying to see a different truth. Sensing the change, Sarah sat up straight and the fearful glance she flicked to her brother only served to confirm his suspicion.

'What is it, Nick?' She turned to him and touched her fingers to his arm. The skin burned with the contact and he drew his arm away.

'He seduced you too?' he managed to whisper. 'You too?'

She swung her head away from him but he slid near her again and grasped her chin in his fingers, drawing her face round toward him so that he could look at her. Blue-grey eyes that changed in the light, the same as her brother's. They flitted away from him now, trying to reach Tom but he held her head firm.

'Tell me the truth.'

She swallowed and he could feel the unevenness of her breath, her hesitation. But even as he felt cruel for pressing her after all she had been through, his need to know overrode his pity. Was it this need that drove a man to kill, he wondered, an instinct that overthrew all else?

'Tell me.' His fingers gripped her chin tighter and she flinched, but he did not loosen his hold. 'Tell me the truth.'

There was a silence, the only sound the roar and crackle of the fire at his back and his own heartbeat loud in his ears.

It was Tom's voice that broke the deadlock. 'Yes.'

Nick's head snapped round to face him.

'I seduced her in an act of magic to win your love for her. Now let her go. You're hurting her.'

Nick's hand dropped from Sarah's jaw and he backed away, lifting himself into the chair again, elbows resting on his knees, head lowered. His gaze grazed the rug at his feet, examining the fine weave, the delicate pattern. It had been one of the first things he had bought with the money he inherited and he was still proud of it: it was the finest thing he owned. From the corner of his vision he saw Sarah move towards him, kneeling beside him, a tentative hand reaching out then withdrawing. His breathing was hard and short, his thoughts in turmoil, and he could not raise his head to look at her. His body sank with the weight of this new knowledge, and his limbs felt unlike his own. An image of Sarah from his dream cut across his mind before transforming into Tom, face contorted in the moment of his death, and his own arousal as he thrust himself inside him. The recollection excited him now, and to his disgust he felt himself beginning to harden.

'Nick?' Sarah's voice whispered close to his head. 'Say something.'

Slowly, he turned to look at her. 'My mind is poisoned,' he breathed. 'Get away from me.'

She backed away, towards her brother, and when finally he could bring himself to lift his head, they were together: Tom on the chair and Sarah on the floor close by his legs, her brother's hand resting on her shoulder, her fingers holding his. Even in his misery Nick thought how beautiful they were, watching him with those blue-grey eyes that would haunt him always now.

'What else is true?' he heard himself ask. 'Did John have the right of it after all? Were we bewitched?'

'Love is a spell of the gods to torment us,' Tom said. 'You should know that.'

'This was no spell of the gods,' Nick spat. 'This was your doing.'

They were silent and he knew that he was right. 'And John?'

Tom let out a snort of derision. 'I needed no spells to win John. He was mine the moment I set my heart on it. His sins were all his own doing.'

He said nothing, his mind struggling to make sense of it all, but he could hardly bear to take his eyes away from Sarah. She was watching him, her hand still holding her brother's, and the thought of them together sent a shudder through him, hairs lifting on his arms.

'Love born of love,' she said, letting go of Tom's hand, approaching him once again. He let her come, too weary now to force her away. And in spite of all he knew, he still wanted her. The spell had done its work well – no matter what she had done to win him, his love for her remained.

'Will I ever be free?' he murmured.

She reached a hand to his face, her soft, cool palm cupping his jaw, her lips close to his. 'Is that what you want?' she replied, leaning in, her mouth pressing into his mouth, the warmth of her tongue against his teeth. Desire erupted through him, heat in every part of him, and he cradled her head in one hand, fingers twisting in her hair, their mouths still pressed hard together, joining them.

He was dimly aware of Tom as he laid her down on her back across the cushions, hand lifting her skirts, pushing her thighs apart, fingers searching, opening, preparing. Then he freed himself from his breeches and pushed himself inside her. She yielded easily, warm and slippery and welcoming, and though he remained aware of her brother watching, it did not decrease his desire nor the building of his pleasure as he moved in and out, Sarah moaning with her own pleasure underneath him. He would make her his again and erase her brother's touch with his own. Close to his climax, he chanced to look up and the two men locked eyes. Tom was pleasuring himself as he watched, and the contortion of his face as he came near his own orgasm was the same he had worn at the moment of his death in Nick's dream. Nick tore his eyes away, confused, but his arousal drove him on, thrusting harder, deeper, wanting now to hurt her for the prisoner she had made of him, the instincts of his dream goading him on. Her moans of pleasure ceased and he could feel her hands against his shoulders trying to push him off and out of her, beating at the muscles, her mouth forming words that he did not hear. But she was pinned beneath him and he did not stop, hands pressing against her legs to force them wider, allowing him deeper. He came, finally, in an explosion of light and heat through his body, and her struggle beneath him stopped as he let her legs go and laid himself down, his weight on hers, her hair against his face, tickling.

When he came back to himself, he rolled away and lay beside her, staring up at the ceiling. He barely understood what had just happened, his desires running out of his control. He had never tried to hurt a woman before, never been watched in the act of coitus, and a sense of falling gripped him, uncontrolled and dangerous. Is this what happened to John, he wondered? Was it this that had driven him mad?

He forced himself to sit up, rearranging himself in his breeches, watching Sarah lower her skirts and make herself decent again. Tom he pointedly ignored. She shifted to sit close to him, her fingers caressing his arm and he realised that after all, she had liked the roughness. She was not the innocent he had thought her to be, her purity corrupted by her brother's darkness. He found himself wondering how hard her seduction had been, how much she had resisted her brother's desires. Not much, he guessed sadly, remembering the look that had passed between them, Tom's hand in hers. Not much. He lifted a hand to stroke her cheek and she leaned up to kiss him again, gentle this time, her lips soft against his.

'You never needed to bewitch me,' he murmured. 'I would have come to you of my own free will.'

'I wanted to be sure.'

'And now that you have me, will you keep me?'

'Of course,' she said. 'Of course. I will never let you go.'

He rested his forehead to hers, and knew he was her prisoner.

∾

Later, when they were alone together in the dim warmth of his chamber, she stood at the window looking out into darkness beyond. The clouds were unleashing their load once again, rain driving into the earth and spattering off the roof into the lane below. Nick stood close to her and his eyes were on her face: he was oblivious to what lay outside the glass. He said, 'What spell did you use to capture me?'

She turned towards him. 'Does it matter?'

'You said, "love born of love." What did you mean?'

She took a deep breath, knowing him well enough to know he would not let it go until she answered.

'Sarah?'

'A love spell, is all,' she evaded, sliding her eyes once more to the blackness outside. The sickle moon was hidden by the rain – she would have liked to be able to see it.

'Sarah.' He took the ends of her fingers in his hands and turned her gently to face him. 'I'll accept all that you are and all that you have done, you and Tom; I ask only you don't lie to me.'

'Some things are better for you not to know,' she answered with as much gentleness in her voice as she could find. She lifted her hand and stroked the rough cheek.

But as she had known, he would not give up. 'You lay with Tom to win me?' he asked.

She sighed and rested her head on his chest. He was warm and strong and good, and she had bound him to her: he deserved to know at least some of the truth. 'Yes,' she said. 'We lay together.'

She heard the sharp intake of breath – even though he had asked, had guessed at the truth, her answer still shocked him.

'What did you do?'

'Nick, enough.' She tried to laugh.

'No. I want to know.'

'You never give up, do you?'

'No.'

'Fine,' she said. 'Then I'll tell you. We did a rite in the forest in the waning moon.'

'Dear God!' he breathed. 'Like a witch in the stories. Did you ride on broomsticks too? Sup with the Devil?'

'We walked there,' she told him. 'And we have no truck with the

Devil. He belongs to your church, not mine.'

'So ...?'

'That is all.'

She saw him sweep his gaze away and down, trying to imagine it, but she could not tell him the rest of it in all its sacred power and beauty. His forehead creased in pain and the line of his jaw tightened.

'And did you like it?' he asked, after a moment, returning his gaze to her face. 'Was he good?'

She let out a laugh of exasperation. And perhaps of embarrassment too. 'Yes,' she said. 'I liked it. But it was a rite. It was different from what we do. It was not just about the pleasure of it, the love. There was a purpose.'

'You would not lie with him otherwise?'

She shook her head to reassure him but her denial was a lie. She had remembered their coupling often, desire burning. She loved Nick as a man, as her master and her lover – she would be his wife in a heartbeat if the Fates allowed – but her brother kindled something else: theirs was a bond of a different kind, forged in knowledge and magic and darkness, ineffable and sacred.

'And you'll not lie with him again?'

She tilted her head in evasion.

'Sarah?' She heard the hurt in his voice.

'If I were your wife ...' she whispered.

'You would be my wife?'

'Ah, Nick. You know that I love you,' she said, moving in closer to him, her hands resting on his shoulders, her breasts just touching the leather of his doublet. He lowered his head so that his forehead rested on hers. 'All I did was only to be with you, like this.'

She felt his hesitation, the doubts that battled with his faith in her, his love. 'Love me again,' she breathed, lifting her head to expose her neck to his lips, waiting for his kiss. But it was his hand not his mouth that touched her throat, fingers spread and pressing hard against it, stopping her breath for a seemingly endless moment of fear until his hand slid away gently from her neck to touch her breast, and his teeth found the delicate skin instead, biting hard, allowing her to breathe again.

'You have made me your slave,' he said, pressing himself hard against her, her back up against the wall beside the window. 'But I cannot be without you.'

'Let us go to bed,' she murmured, sliding her hands along his arm, disengaging herself. She wanted to slow him down and dampen the conflict in his passion, afraid that something wicked had been woken by the knowledge she had given him and the passions she had stirred with Tom as witness. No man wished to be bound as she had bound him to her, and his hand against her throat had scared her – a reminder of a witch's fate, the end she had seen for Tom in the shew-stone. She must treat him gently and bring him back to the memory of the love they shared together. Taking his hand, she led him to the bed, and slowly, teasingly, as they had done before, she undressed and lay down, arms up to welcome him into them.

They made love again but slowly, tenderly this time, with gentle caresses – fingers, lips, teeth – exploring the hidden places of each other, giving pleasure with the lightest touch. It was beautiful and she wanted it never to end. For all the excitement of the passion of the afternoon, it was this she loved with Nick, this quiet and tender intimacy. She wished she could be his wife and share this with him all through their life to come.

Afterwards they lay together in the soft, warm bed, Nick on his back, Sarah on her side alongside him propped up on one elbow, fingers of the other hand resting on the firm muscle of his chest. So different from Tom's slender frame and pale, soft skin, she thought, Nick so much more of a man. She loved the hair that grew in the dip of his chest, trailing down across his belly towards his cock, and her fingers curled themselves around it, teasing it gently.

Nick looked at her and smiled.

'Am I forgiven?' she asked. 'Do you love me still?'

'I have no choice but to love you,' he answered. 'But I would love you regardless, witchcraft or no. And yes, you are forgiven.'

'I'm glad,' she said, laying her head on his chest, her hand still caressing his belly, the smooth hollow where his pelvis met his thigh. He stroked her hair and then, leaning over, he blew out the one remaining candle and in the utter darkness they fell into sleep.

Chapter Nineteen

SOUND AND FURY

The next rehearsal was fraught and angry. John's madness had rattled them all, his charge of witchcraft hanging in the theatre's air and leaving shadows that infected the corners of their thoughts. No one spoke of it, wary of lending unnamed powers a voice, but the same thought was shared by them all: ill luck was woven in the fabric of the play, its darkness reaching out beyond the confines of the stage, and every one of them wished they could play something else instead.

The boy, Francis Gage, who had taken John's place, struggled with his lines. He was still young and green, and though he had shown some skill as Lady Macduff, Lady Macbeth was beyond him, crippled as he was by the fear that his own fate might echo John's if he gave himself to the role. They watched him try to be John, mimicking the other boy's inflections, but he was afraid of the passions in the words and, not daring to touch the darkness the role required, the lines fell flat and lifeless. There was no weight in his performance – he was an innocent made to recite words that terrified him.

Halfway through the morning Nick's patience broke at last. Unable to get beyond their first scene together, the same lines repeating over and over, the same mistakes and no feeling between them, he threw up his hands in exasperation and, to spare the boy's feelings, walked silently away.

'I'm so sorry, Master Shakespeare.' The boy was close to tears. 'I'll try harder. I'm so sorry …'

Will patted his shoulder without a word and turned away to follow Nick into the tiring house. The rest of the players said nothing. It was clearly not going to work – less than a week till they played and they had no Lady. The raised voices of Will and Nick drifted out from the tiring house in snatches.

'What are we going to do?'

'What can we do?'

Then a silence and low murmurs that the listening company could not catch. Sarah laid down her sewing on the bench beside her and got up, conscious of the eyes of all the watchers as she took the steps up onto the stage, walked across it, and entered the tiring house. Both men swung towards her and she stopped short, made nervous by the anger she could see in them. She waited to be asked to speak, aware of her uninvited intrusion and the gravity of what they were discussing.

'What is it, Sarah?' Will spoke in a polite tone that she knew masked a slew of other emotions.

She took a deep breath, conscious that her words might be unwelcome, hesitant to say them. But it was an answer and it could save the play. 'Tom could play it,' she managed to say.

The two men looked at each other, unspoken questions hanging between them.

'There is no one else.' Will shrugged and turned away with a sigh, and Nick sought out Sarah's gaze with his own. They met for a heartbeat before she dropped her eyes away from him, disturbed by what she had seen. 'And someone must do it,' Will said.

'Does he have the skill?' Nick asked.

Will lifted his hands in a gesture of helplessness. 'There is no one else,' he repeated. 'Without Richard, without John, we are truly short of actors, and someone must play it.' Then, to Sarah, 'Is he here?'

She motioned upstairs with her head.

'Fetch him,' Will ordered and she hurried past them to the stairs and climbed.

Tom descended reluctantly.

'Will you do it?' Will asked. 'Will you play the Lady?'

She saw her brother's hesitation, the glance he threw towards Nick, who had turned his back, and the question in his eyes for her. She had known when she suggested it that neither man would like it: they had not spoken to each other since Tom had left them last night, still sprawled and breathless on the rug after making love. Tom was silent and she knew he was waiting for Nick to turn around and give him his permission to play. Long moments passed and all eyes rested on Nick's back, waiting. Finally, when she thought he would never face them, he wheeled slowly round. His mouth was fierce with tension and his hands were tightly balled, knuckles white.

'I'll play if Nick allows it,' Tom said.

'It's not for Nick to decide!' Will's fury was plain.

'Yes, it is,' Tom said, and his gaze remained on Nick's face.

Nick swallowed, the muscle in his jaw moving back and forth, fists stretching open and closed. She could see the hatred in his eyes and she slid her gaze away. She should have kept quiet, she thought. His anger would turn to her again for suggesting this, but in spite of everything, she could not let the play fail when a chance remained to save it.

Will looked from one to the other, bewildered by the sudden animosity. Last time he had seen them, walking Sarah home from the Marshalsea, the two men had been friends. He flicked a questioning glance towards Sarah, who gave him an evasive half-smile. There was nothing she could tell him to explain, and he could never know.

The silence lingered. Nick's eyes came to rest on Sarah, observing her as some unknown thing, a stranger he could not understand. She could see the implicit reproach within the anger: she had made him love her and then turned cruel towards him. At last he turned to Tom.

'What other choice do we have?' He shrugged. 'He can play.'

Will clapped his hands together in relief and strode out of the tiring house to tell the others. Tom followed him, eager to be away from Nick's hatred. Nick turned to her, brow creased, eyes dark with mistrust of her. She remembered how he used to be when first she fell in love with him, before all of this, when his mouth had been wide in smiles and the light in his eyes had been bright and full of laughter. She had done this to him, she thought. She and Tom between them had taken his happiness.

'Why?' he demanded. 'Why would you suggest Tom do it?'

She shrugged. 'I wanted to save the play.'

'But surely …' He trailed off, arms lifting in incredulous bafflement.

'There is no one else,' she said. 'Alexander, John Lowin – they could do it but they already have their parts. And Tom will be good.'

'John was good,' he snarled. 'John was perfect … until you and your brother …' He turned away, unwilling to put words to the thoughts.

She stepped towards him with a backward glance at the stage to check they were still alone. 'We did nothing to John,' she said, moving close to him. But he would not look at her. She stretched out a tentative hand to his arm, but he shrugged it off and took two steps away from her. She let her arm fall.

'Your brother has evil in him,' he breathed. 'It was his actions that sent John mad, by whatever means he used. He seduced him, corrupted him, pure and simple. And you …' He turned towards her then, chin tilted in aggression, words spat between his teeth. She stepped back, nervous of him now. They had crossed a line together yesterday and she no longer trusted him not to hurt her. 'Was it your idea, you and him? Or was it his?'

'I dreamed of it,' she whispered quickly. 'That it would lead me to you.'

Nick lifted his head and let out a laugh that startled her. 'A dream? Oh dear God. You had a dream.' He lowered his gaze to her, a wry smile across his face, and the crinkles at the corners of his eyes were beautiful. 'And when he suggested it for real, did you hesitate?' he asked. 'Even for a moment?'

Her eyes filled with tears and she could not stop them, so she turned her face away. 'Of course I did,' she replied. Her voice was trembling and she wiped at her eyes with the heels of her hands, but the tears kept coming. 'But I wanted you so much, and my dreams have always led me truly in the past …'

He shook his head. 'You foolish, foolish girl,' he whispered. 'I would have been yours, and willingly. I would have come to you freely. But now you have trapped me, and though I must love you, I'll hate you too for the chain you've placed around me.'

She was silent. There was no answer to his logic and she did not know how she could undo what she had done. She wiped at her face again. Nick watched her for a moment before he stepped across the boards towards her. She tensed, ready to meet his anger, but instead he placed a finger under her chin and lifted her face to his.

'Don't cry,' he said. 'I hate it when girls cry.'

She smiled, grateful for the humour, conscious of the wetness of her face, her breath coming unevenly in snatches. He returned the smile and gently wiped the tears away with his fingertips. This was the Nick she knew and loved. The Nick she had wanted. Tender and funny and beautiful. Then he folded his arms around her and drew her in to his chest and held her. They were still standing in their embrace when Tom reappeared through the door.

'The rehearsal is starting,' he said.

They moved apart and turned to look at him, his outline tall and narrow in the doorway against the light of the theatre. She remembered him watching them in the heat of their passion and a sliver of shame crept through her.

'They need you,' Tom said.

Nick nodded, and with a final squeeze of her hand and a small smile that lifted the corners of his mouth, he followed Tom out onto the stage to rehearse.

Tom's Lady was much different from John's. Stronger and less regal, with a darkness in her heart to match her husband's. And he brought a different passion to the role, a seductive quality that John had lacked.

> 'What beast was't, then,
>> That made you break this enterprise to me?
>> When you durst do it, then you were a man ...'

He followed the same movements as John had done, moving

close, embracing, a hand upon Nick's cheek. But the energy was something else entirely: though the words urged Macbeth to murder, it was pure seduction – Tom at his most dangerous, challenging Nick, questioning his manhood, pushing him. Nick struggled to meet the open eroticism Tom brought to the scene, and it was hard to shake the memory of Tom watching him with Sarah.

> *'And, to be more than what you were, you would*
> *Be so much more the man …'*

Nick felt the mockery implicit in the words, and his anger rose with the desire to prove himself. He wanted to turn Tom round, force him to his knees and assert his manhood. The conflict sounded in the words.

> *'If we should fail?'*
> *'We fail!'*

The Lady's answer was thick with derision, goading him, and though the lines belonged to the play, Nick was conscious there was something else at stake – a battle for power between them he could not fully understand.

> *'I am settled, and bend up*
> *Each corporal agent to this terrible feat,'*

he heard himself say, his will bent to the Lady's urging, though his conscience cried out against the deed. He had been seduced after all, and though he had done this scene a hundred times with John, he had never truly felt the weight of his capitulation, the true power of his Lady to bend him to her will. At the end of the scene both men looked across to Will for comment, but when no one spoke, they looked at each other for a brief exchange of concern.

'Was it not good?' Nick asked.

'It was good,' Will affirmed, pushing off from the wall where he had been leaning, crossing to centre stage. He nodded and stepped away, without another word. 'Let's press on … Banquo? Fleance?'

The other actors appeared from the tiring house doors as Nick and Tom left the stage, and the rehearsal moved on to the following scene.

∼

The rehearsal went late and most of the players went straight to the Green Dragon. Tom kept his distance from Nick and it was a sombre band that stepped through the doors out of the drizzle and into the close warmth inside. The last time they had come here was the last time they saw John, and out of habit Tom's eyes scanned the room for Jane, only recalling her absence when they lit on the girl whose name he still could not recall. She observed his search and swung her hips as she sashayed towards him, but he sent her away with a weary wave of his hand. He was in no mood for whores.

The players were subdued and though they ordered food and ale as they usually did, John's crime and the worries of the play hung over them all so there was little talk amongst them. Nick kept his head deliberately turned away; despite the good work they had done together during the day as actors, Tom knew the hatred simmered unabated. He shouldn't have stayed to watch them, he realised now. Blinded by his own salacity, he had misjudged the depth of Nick's feelings, and the violence with which he had taken Sarah made Tom cautious: there was only so far a man could be pushed before he snapped.

No one among them mentioned John, though his absence fell like a shadow on their company. He had always just been there at Nick's side, listening, speaking rarely, but always there. Tom wondered where he had fled to and what thoughts filled his head now. He would be hiding somewhere, perhaps with the priest. Was he filled with remorse, or did he still believe he was possessed? If he had any sense at all, he'd be on a boat and leaving England's shores, but Tom doubted it somehow. John lacked survival instincts; in time he would surely be caught and hanged. Tom sipped at his ale and let the scene play out in his head – John's slender form dangling from a rope above the crowd, head askew and thin legs kicking wildly as the piss ran down them. What would it be like, he wondered again, to feel the life force fail and no more breaths to take? He had considered his own death often; it was the awareness of his mortality that drove him to his recklessness. Life was short and hard and uncertain, and there was nothing in this world he did not want to know or taste or feel before he died.

He thought again of his sister – the slim, soft body, the tightness of her maidenhead and the blood that had trickled on her thigh. Recalling the taste of her, he felt the familiar lurch of desire. He had no regrets at all: his love for his sister was endless – she was the only person in the world who had ever truly touched him – and he would lie with her again without a second thought if chance allowed. Discreetly, he adjusted himself in his breeches and his eyes scanned the room to look for the nameless whore.

The girl saw him searching almost straight away and he smiled. She was learning fast. When she got to him she slid an arm across his shoulders and leaned herself against him. He breathed in the scent of her – cheap perfumes and soap and the stale smell of sex that clung to all the whores he had known – and one hand found her leg beneath the skirts, caressing the soft skin of her inner thigh. But he did not look up at her face and smile as he would have done with Jane. He didn't care who she was or how she looked. It was not the girl he wanted for herself but the simple release of the fuck. He would think about his sister.

He stood up. 'Excuse me, gentlemen,' he said to the others at the table. They all nodded with knowing smiles except for Nick, who looked away. Then he took the girl's hand and let her lead him to the rooms beyond the curtained doorway.

When he stepped through to the tavern again, only Nick remained at the table, still steadily drinking his ale. Tom stood in the doorway, undecided for a moment until he let the girl go with a fleeting word, took a deep breath and made his way towards him. Nick lifted his eyes from his cup and watched him come, and all Tom could see in him was hostility. He stopped with the table between them.

'You should go home,' he said. 'It's late.'

Nick drank more of his ale. His movements were deliberate and clumsy, and up close Tom could see the glassiness in his eyes.

'She'll be waiting for you however late you go, however much you drink,' he said.

The other man laid his cup down on the table with care. The muscle in his jaw was working and he was breathing hard. Tom stayed wary as Nick finally lifted his eyes to look at him.

'Don't presume to tell me what to do,' he breathed.

'Go home, Nick,' Tom said gently. He was reluctant to leave him there with such rage in his blood and an urge to violence – he would find a fight soon enough if he looked for it, and a knife to the guts in a tavern brawl with a stranger was a stupid way to die.

Nick shook his head. 'Bugger you.'

Tom smiled at the choice of insult. 'Come, I'm taking you home,' he said.

The other man shook his head and turned away as Tom moved round the table, but he did not resist when Tom lifted his arm across his shoulders and helped him to his feet to weave uncertainly towards the door. Outside, the night air was like a slap in the face and Nick straightened slightly, struggling to regain control. But when he spoke, the words were still slurred, and Tom retained a firm hold as they began to stumble home. They had not gone far when Nick stopped and jerked his arm free, turning to face him.

'Why?' he demanded. 'For the love of God! She's your sister! And I would have loved her anyway.' His eyes filled with tears, a drunkard's self-pity, and Tom swallowed down his irritation. He should have left him in the tavern.

'It's what I do,' he replied.

Nick regarded him closely and even through the fug of drunkenness, the contempt in his eyes was disturbing. Tom slid his gaze away and waited.

'Yes,' Nick agreed, nodding slowly. 'That's what you do. You corrupt people and drag them into your own pit of darkness. Why?' he asked. 'Is it lonely there that you need the company of others? Or is it that you can't bear seeing others happy in their innocence and purity?'

'You were happy enough to take my sister's innocence …'

'Except you had got there first.'

Tom shook his head. 'This is pointless.'

Nick was silent, staring off down the street, eyes following the erratic movements of a gentleman and his whore as they wove towards the river. Then he turned to lean on the wall behind him with one hand, supporting himself as he puked on the ground at his feet. Tom turned away, disgusted. When the sound of the splatter had ceased, he turned back. 'Better?'

Nick nodded and wiped his mouth against his sleeve. 'Better.'

'Can we go now?'

Nick nodded again as Tom took his elbow and guided him firmly towards the house in Water Lane. It seemed a long walk home.

Chapter Twenty

ALL OUR YESTERDAYS

Nick sat in the frontmost bench of the downstairs gallery
to watch the others rehearse the final scene, his own part
finished and Macbeth's head on a spike. He ached with
weariness and his head still throbbed from last night's drinking.
Sarah came to sit beside him with her sewing in her hands and he
did not welcome her company. When he saw her now, he saw the
shadow of her brother, and hatred bubbled in his gut. He gave her a
reluctant smile and, sensing the hostility, she left some space
between them on the bench.

They were silent, a new awkwardness between them. Twice she
opened her mouth as if to speak and closed it once again. He kept his
gaze trained forward – he wanted her to go and leave him to nurse
his wounds, and after a while she stood up again.

'You were wonderful,' she said. 'This morning … the scenes … I
couldn't look away.'

He lifted his eyes to her then. She was standing with her back to
the yard and her face was in shadow, but he could still see the sorrow
in her eyes, and regret for his coldness nudged at the hatred. He tried
to smile. 'Thank you,' he said.

Encouraged, she spoke again. 'It can't have been easy …'

He tilted his head and the smile this time was real and wry. 'No.'

She looked away, her eyes tracing the lines of the gallery above
them. He watched her, observing the fine narrow neck, the line of

her jaw, the soft, pale skin of her cheeks, young and perfect. She still carried an innocence about her and he remembered how much he loved her. Then Tom crossed the yard towards them in the corner of his vision and the shackle tightened on his heart. In spite of the love, he was her prisoner and she was no longer innocent. Her brother had seen to that. Tom reached them and Sarah turned at his voice.

'There's a messenger come for you, Nick,' Tom said. 'He's at the door.'

'Bring him to me,' he replied.

Tom turned with a nod and left. Sarah resumed her seat and picked up her sewing. It was the nightshirt for the Lady's sleep-walking scene, and it crossed his mind to tell her to leave in the pins.

The messenger arrived, a young man who was vaguely familiar though he could not have said from where. 'Master Tooley?'

'Aye.'

'My name is Marston. I am clerk to Master Roberts.'

Nick started. Roberts was his father-in-law, the man who had his wife's keeping. What on God's good earth did *he* want? 'He sent you?'

'He is dead,' Marston replied.

Nick swallowed, uncertain what to say, what to think. Sarah broke the silence. 'Your wife?' she asked softly.

He nodded. Then he turned to the messenger with a questioning look.

'The keeping of his daughter and grandson returns to you now. He has left no provision for her otherwise.'

He slid a glance to Sarah, still off balance from the news, so unexpected yet so long hoped for. But why now, he thought, when someone else had finally taken her place in his heart, in his bed? How could they be reconciled now?

'In law she is yours,' Marston continued. 'And he has bequeathed you a handsome sum to keep her.'

'But why?' Nick finally found his voice. 'He hates ... hated ... me.'

'I was not privy to his thoughts and feelings,' Marston shrugged. 'I am merely his clerk charged to bring you the news. But if I could venture a guess, she has to go somewhere. Someone has to provide for her and you are, after all, her husband.'

Nick was silent, aware of the trace of condescension in the man's tone, the judgement, but he cared nothing for the man's good opinion. His heartbeat was racing and instinctively he reached for Sarah's hand. It was small and cold, but her fingers squeezed his tightly and her presence was reassuring.

'You are to call at the house at your earliest convenience,' the messenger said. 'You can recall where it is? We will expect you.' Then he bowed and they watched him stride away, full of his own self-importance.

Nick swallowed, saying nothing, fingers still linked with Sarah's. He stared ahead, trying to compose his thoughts and his feelings, but they slipped and slid away, escaping his grasp, and he could make no sense of them. All the while he was aware of Sarah's attention on his face and the grip of her hand, but he could think of nothing to say to her.

The crash onstage of the trapdoor slamming shut broke the moment, and slowly he turned to the girl at his side.

'Are you all right?' she asked.

He shrugged.

'You should go to her,' she said. 'Bring her home. And your son. You've waited a long time.'

'And you? I cannot be without you. You know that.'

'I'll still be there, your loyal maidservant.' She smiled. 'You can love us both.'

He said nothing. He could not even begin to imagine how it would be with Becky now, so many years under the bridge, strangers to each other. She had loved him once as he had loved her, but she had accepted her father's law without question, put up not even a single spark of fight against him to be a true wife to her husband. The memory still rankled, the bitterness of it rising at unexpected times and catching him unawares. He had fought for her, and hard, but she had given him away without a single murmur of dissent. It had been a hard betrayal and ever since, he had held his heart in check, afraid to be so hurt again.

Until now, he thought. Until Sarah. He turned towards her, touched the back of his fingers to her cheek, enjoying the smile the movement brought to her lips, the flush of pleasure that brushed across her pallor. He could not give her up.

''Tis a pity we are not savages,' she said. 'Then you could have us both to wife.'

'You would be willing to share me?' His smile was teasing now – he could not recall ever playing so with Becky. Their love had been the earnest ardour of the very young.

Sarah's smile faded. 'Better that than lose you,' she said, taking his hand and bringing her lips against it, warm and moist. 'You know that there is nothing I wouldn't do to keep you.'

He nodded, swallowing, conscious they were not idle words. 'You're not going to lose me,' he promised. 'I will keep you both and love only you.'

She smiled with pleasure and kissed his fingers once again, and reluctantly he forced down the desire that the touch of her lips aroused. He would go to his wife's after the afternoon performance.

Tom slipped from the theatre and hurried through the morning. A light rain found its way beneath his collar as he half walked, half ran along Deadman's Place, busy now with stalls and shops – housewives and servants looking for bargains. A flock of sheep scattered as he wove his way between them, and a band of beggar children tried to sell him a handful of ragged flowers they had picked from somewhere, but he paid them no heed. Turning south into Red Cross Street, he slowed his steps a little, breathing hard, but it was not far to the Cross Bones graveyard and he cast his eyes across the unmarked mounds that held the bodies of the poor and unsaved of the parish – those souls deemed unworthy of the Christian rites, laid to rest in a winding sheet with a covering of quicklime and a shallow grave among the rank grass and barely tamed weeds. The place stank of death and instinctively he shuddered. But it was pity for the poor lives that had led them to here; it made no odds to him where a body ended up once it was dead.

By the far wall a pair of gravediggers laboured, and as he made his way toward them he saw the nameless whore, the gaudy colours of her dress bright against the dark, damp earth. She was standing beside the grave and when she saw him she flashed him a quick smile of gratitude for coming. The gravediggers stood back to rest a moment as he arrived, their shovels upright in the earth, and he moved past them to where Jane's body lay in its shroud. Kneeling, he beckoned to the girl to help him lift her: for some reason it mattered that she was laid in her final resting place with care. Reluctantly, the girl bent to take Jane's feet, and between them they managed to lower her into the grave.

When Tom had stood up again, the gravediggers went back to their work, and he watched as the cold earth fell onto the shrouded body. With a lurch of grief, he saw in his mind her face white and still, the decay of death already begun. She had not deserved such an end, so young and full of hope, and he hoped John was suffering now, remorse and guilt eating his soul and destroying his peace. It was no more than he deserved.

'You know she loved you,' the girl said, as he stood up once more. 'She hoped one day you might marry her and make her yours. Or at least take her as your mistress.'

He gave a wry smile and shook his head. 'Poor girl,' he said.

'Because she loved you?' the whore asked. 'Or because she died?'

'Both,' he answered. He did not need to explain himself, least of all to this girl whose name he did not know. He regretted he hadn't been kinder to Jane. It had crossed his mind more than once that he would like to keep her for himself: she had been good at what she did and he had liked her. But it took money to keep a mistress and he barely ever had enough even for his own meat and drink.

'I'll miss her,' he said.

'Come see me instead,' the girl offered. 'Jane taught me most of what she knew.'

He gave her a small smile and nodded. He had sampled her twice now and he knew she would never equal Jane for pleasure. 'Perhaps I will,' he said, because he knew she had cared for Jane too and he didn't want to be unkind.

'This afternoon?' The girl was persistent.

'Another time,' he said. 'I have work to do.'

He saw the disappointment but he was not moved, and, with a nod of his head, he took his leave of her and strolled back to the playhouse.

Sarah went with Nick to the Bankend stairs at the river and stood beside him while he hailed a wherry to take him across. The rain had stopped but a brisk chill wind had risen during the day, whipping the river into points and biting through the wool of her cloak. There were no pleasure craft on the water today. Sarah drew her cloak closer around her.

'Will you bring her back with you tonight?' she asked.

'I cannot say,' he answered.

She reached for his hand and squeezed it. Then a boat came alongside and he stepped onto it, leaving her on the landing stairs to watch after him as the boatman rowed them away from the shore. He kept his eyes trained on her form as he faded into the gloom, reluctant, it seemed to her, to face his future on the opposite bank. When the boat had been swallowed by the darkness and she could no longer make out its shape on the water, she turned sadly away.

How would it be between them now, she wondered, with his wife alongside them? It was hard to imagine Rebecca, God-fearing and passionless; Sarah already knew she would hate her. But they were bound together regardless in their connection to Nick – he was a prisoner of them both. She tried to shut her mind to the thought of it, regretting the cruelty of his shackles. She had only thought to love him better, and she had not truly understood the nature of the bond.

She found Tom in the Green Dragon. She was no longer afraid to go there, at home now amongst familiar faces, her own face recognised and known. There was safety in her connection to Nick and to Tom, and she was more confident now to rebuff the invitations of strangers.

Tom was drinking with a pretty young man she didn't recognise, the two of them sitting close together with their hands lightly touching on the table, but as soon as he saw her he pushed the boy away and turned his full attention to her. The boy gave her a filthy look and slouched sullenly away, but she paid him no mind and sat close beside her brother on the bench. The tavern was hot, but despite her new-found confidence she was reluctant to unwrap herself from her cloak. With her shoulders and her neck exposed she would still feel vulnerable, even in Tom's company.

Briefly she told him what had happened, her eyes on his face as she spoke, observing his reaction. He listened in silence, the thin, handsome face still with concentration, blue-grey eyes intent and bright. When she finished he said nothing for a moment, taking a sip of his wine, then offering her the cup. She took a mouthful to wet her throat, which was dry from nerves and the telling of the tale. Then he said, 'Are you truly willing to share him?'

'If I can have him no other way.'

'He is bound to you – he cannot give you up.'

'He is bound to her also, in law and in conscience. He will not set her aside.'

Tom nodded. 'Shall we scry?' he murmured.

'No,' she replied. 'I already know what the future holds, for both of us.' The images of the last time still haunted her thoughts, Tom's death and hers still beckoning. She had no wish to witness it a second time.

He shrugged. 'We should go.'

She nodded and got up, and they went together to the door. Just outside in the street before they parted ways, she turned to him. 'Who was the boy?' she asked.

He smiled. 'Just a boy. He'll keep.'

She shook her head with a rueful smile, still disconcerted by his appetites. 'You have forgotten John already?' she teased.

'Not forgotten,' he replied. 'Just replaced.'

'Just make sure this one doesn't lose his mind because of it,' she warned, and he laughed.

'I'll do my best.' He leaned in to kiss her cheek in farewell, and briefly she closed her eyes to savour the moment of his closeness and his warmth, his lips against her face. He must have sensed the lift her heart gave at his touch because he stopped and stayed near, his mouth still brushing her cheek. 'Are you jealous, good sister?' he murmured.

She was silent – she had not named the emotion even to herself, hadn't yet recognised its provenance. Was she jealous? she wondered. Did she truly care where Tom stuck his cock? Perhaps, she realised, and the new knowledge frightened her, but in the pause of her hesitation he slipped a hand inside her cloak to cup her breast and her insides heaved with desire. Gently he took her arm and drew her to the side of the door and into the shadow of the wall. Then his lips were on hers, his body pressing close. For a moment she resisted, head battling against the desire, but the pleasure overruled the doubts and so she gave herself to the kiss, and when he took her arm again to guide her into the lane alongside the tavern and placed her back against the wall in the darkness, his hands beneath her skirts, she did not protest.

Afterwards he held her, kissing and stroking her hair, and she could feel the warmth of his juices trickling on the inside of her thigh. 'Let's not tell Nick about this one,' he whispered.

She lifted her head but she could not see his face in the darkness. She cupped his jaw in her hand. 'We cannot do this again,' she replied. 'We mustn't.'

'Why not?' he asked. 'Because of Nick? Where is he now? Who is he with? Do you think he'll never lie with her again? She's his wife.'

'And you are my brother.'

'Ah. Yes,' he agreed. 'There is that, I suppose. But still,' he murmured. 'Who are we hurting really?'

She said nothing, his logic impossible to argue with. He lifted her chin with his fingers and kissed her again full on the mouth, and she knew she would never have the strength to refuse him. Perhaps Nick was right, she thought. Perhaps he truly was a force for evil, bent on a course of corruption. The pleasure of him was irrefutable, and she knew beyond doubt that she would give herself to him again without a moment's hesitation. It seemed impossible that they had come so far together without it.

'I'll walk you back,' he said then, stepping away, buttoning his breeches and allowing her to rearrange her skirts and smooth her hair once more into place. Then he took her arm and they walked together away from the tavern, moving slowly in spite of the wind, arm in arm, content simply to be close.

'What did you see?' Tom asked. 'When you scried before? What exactly did you see?'

She was silent. The images had remained clear in her mind,

visited in her dreams in the weeks since then, inescapable. But she had not talked of it again, reluctant to give the vision voice and grant it the power of words. Tom had not asked before, wary as she was. But now he would have her tell him and his hand pressed against hers on his arm as he turned his head to look at her, blue-grey eyes searching for an answer. She kept her gaze down and forward, watching the dark earth disappear underfoot with each step – she dared not meet those eyes. Slowing his steps, he turned her gently to face him, drawing her towards him to the edge of the lane. Behind him the windows of an alehouse blinked blankly, and through a small chink in the curtain, a sliver of light glowed bright just beyond his arm. She let her gaze follow its warmth; heat and life to counter the cold of the images inside her head.

'Tell me,' he said softly, taking the tips of her fingers, rubbing them lightly.

Unwillingly she lifted her eyes to meet his, glowing dark in the shadow from the torch on the wall behind him. How could she say no? She could refuse him nothing. A sigh left her lips, a deep breath of sorrow, and the words she needed were hard to find. 'To speak it …' she began, 'is to make it so, and I am afraid …'

He nodded but she knew he wouldn't give up. Would she, she wondered, if Tom had seen her death? She too would want to know.

'It's only one possible path,' he said. 'Nothing is immutable. Nothing is fixed. If I know, then perhaps I can act to change it.'

She swallowed.

'Tell me,' he insisted, drawing her closer to him, into the shadow of the wall, so that she could smell his breath and feel its warmth on her face. Behind her in the lane she heard the voices of men that were rough with drink insulting each other in jest as they passed by. She waited until the road was quiet again before she spoke.

'I saw our deaths,' she whispered.

'I know. But how? How do we die, Sarah?'

'You die at the end of a rope.' The words tumbled out quickly, no emotion. It was his death not hers she saw over and over, certain of its reality: the defiant leap into the noose, legs kicking wildly into the air, her own screams of grief as the life left his body and she dragged at his feet to hasten his end. His beautiful body hanging limp and unmoving, robbed of the spirit that she loved. She blinked back tears and moved in closer until he held her in his arms and she could drink in his warmth and life and beauty.

He was silent, holding her gently for a moment until he slid his hands to her shoulders and lowered his gaze to look into her face again. 'And you?' he asked. 'What happens to you?'

She swung her face away, staring down the street towards the river where a pair of young gentlemen were bargaining with a whore. She could hear the woman's cackle and the persuasive and expectant tones of the men. Tom waited, his hands still resting on her shoulders, until she turned her head back to face him, meeting his gaze at last. 'Grief,' she said simply. 'I die of grief.'

'Oh, Sarah,' he murmured, and drew her into him once again, holding her tighter this time, his lips against her temple, his embrace strong and firm around her back, wrapping her in a sense of safety she had known with him since childhood – a bond born of blood and magic and the darkness. He was part of her and she did not want to live without him; she doubted that she could. She wished they could hide like this in the dark for always and protect each other from harm.

Finally, they walked on, quiet with each other, the knowledge of their fates a heavy burden between them. All that had passed before seemed forgotten in the light of what was to come. She had rarely seen Tom so sombre – Tom who would joke in the darkest moments, Tom who would laugh in the face of his death. But not, it seemed, in the face of hers. Above them a full curtain of cloud obscured the stars and the moon, and the night was damp and dark. She held her brother's arm tightly as though the strength of their connection might yet keep them safe. At the door to the house they halted and the first drops of rain began to fall. They turned to face each other and Tom took her fingers in his.

'Will you come in?' she asked. 'Out of the rain?'

He shook his head. 'Nick would not welcome me.' Then he said, 'The future is never certain and there may be meanings we've not yet understood. The Fates rarely tell us all.'

She tried to smile but only nodded, lips pressed tight closed against the urge to cry.

'Have you told Nick?' he asked.

'And give him more reason to hate his bonds?' She shook her head. 'He has troubles enough of his own.'

'Good night then, gentle sister,' Tom said, and the kiss he placed on her cheek was pure and loving and brotherly. It felt good.

Nick stepped off the wherry at Temple Stairs with reluctance – it was many years since he had made this journey but the way was still clear in his mind. On the landing stage he paused for a moment as half-forgotten images circled in his mind – himself as a young man, John's age, ardent and full of hope, his purpose secret. He had been a different person then. Shaking his head to chase away the memories and to gird himself, he turned his back on the river and began to stride north towards Fleet Street and Carey Street beyond. The walk seemed to take no time at all, and close to the house he slowed his steps, approaching with a thudding heart, pausing a little distance away to look it over. A fine house with mullioned windows, it had grown in the intervening years, with a new wing on one end and established gardens, the trees grown up and mature. He remembered how it had seemed to him as a young boy fresh to London, a symbol of all the city had to offer. The lawyer's life had obviously served Roberts well.

He halted at the door, breathing deeply to calm himself, but he was aware of the sweat in the pit of his back and under his arms, and his mouth was dry. He had no idea what to expect nor even what he should hope for, but his heart was filled with a sense of foreboding. Swallowing, bracing himself for whatever he was about to meet, he lifted his hand to hammer on the door. With his knock, a dog started barking inside and he heard footsteps approach and hesitate before coming closer again. Then Marston opened the door and stood in the doorway, looking him up and down, condescension written plainly on his face. The man might have claimed to be just a clerk but clearly he held some position in the household, and in his master's absence he was enjoying a new-found power.

'I'm here for my wife,' Nick said.

The clerk stepped back and admitted him to a broad entrance hallway that was well lit by dozens of candles. He had no memory of seeing it before, though he knew he must have done so. Then he followed the clerk into some kind of reception room that was brightly furnished with Turkey rugs and tapestries, a warm fire in the hearth and wine set out on the sideboard.

'Make yourself at home,' the clerk said. 'I will tell Mistress Tooley you are come.' He backed out with a reluctant half-bow and closed the door.

Nick poured himself wine. It was some kind of Rhenish, and strong, and the buzz in his head that it gave him was welcome. He drank it off and refilled the cup, then took it to stand by the fire, warming the backs of his legs, but he didn't have long to wait. He could hear the double set of footsteps approaching on the flagstones beyond the door and he drew himself upright, taking a deep breath, preparing himself.

The door swung open on well-oiled hinges and then his wife was there, hands clasped modestly before her and her head bowed so that Nick couldn't see her face. The clerk hovered close behind her until Nick gave him a curt order to leave, and as the door latched shut with his exit, his wife ventured a few steps closer. He could feel her hesitation and the reluctance to meet his eyes.

There was a silence and he observed her carefully. She seemed very different from the girl he remembered: if he had seen her on the street he might have walked straight past. But perhaps it was the drabness of her dress, he thought, and the starched white cap that drew back her hair so severely from her face. The girl he recalled had worn thick auburn hair loose about her shoulders, silken in his fingers when he loved her, and there had been freckles and a ready smile. But the woman before him now had a furrow in her forehead and her lips were pursed and tight. It was hard to believe he had kissed those lips and loved them.

'Husband.' She curtseyed with her eyes still lowered to the ground and he realised she was afraid of him, afraid he might punish her for all that had gone before.

'Becky,' he replied.

At his use of her name she looked up, startled for a moment before her eyes flicked away again, avoiding his.

'I'm sorry about your father,' he said. He could think of nothing else and it seemed the proper thing to say.

'Thank you.'

There was another silence. He took a mouthful of wine. Her dead father's wine. Then he said, 'So he has handed you back to me at last.'

'Yes.' She nodded without looking up. 'Am I to go with you tonight?'

'Do you want to go with me tonight?' He stepped closer, trying to bridge the vast gulf that lay between them. There seemed to be no trace at all of what they had once meant to each other: they were utter strangers meeting for the first time.

'It is your decision to make sir,' she replied. 'I will do as you bid me.'

He hesitated, uncertain in the face of her subjection. Was this the obedience her father had demanded? Dear God, he thought, how could any man want a woman to be so afraid of him? Slowly, so as not to startle her again, he took another few steps towards her and touched gentle fingertips to her arm. He wanted her to look at him, trying to recall something of the spark that once existed between them. But she did not acknowledge the touch and her head remained resolutely lowered. Regret sidled through him. There was nothing left of the girl he remembered, the woman he had grieved for over so many years. And now they must make a new life together. He did not dare to ask if he could see his son.

He said, 'I thought after the funeral. So you have some time to adjust and to mourn with your family.'

'Thank you,' she said in a monotone, so he could not tell if she was glad or not.

He lowered his fingers from her arm, disappointed. He had not known what he hoped for, but this miserable subservience stirred an abhorrence in him, no hope for the days to come and the years of their marriage that stretched ahead.

'Then I'll bid you good night,' he said, dropping his head in a bow that she did not see as she lowered herself into an answering curtsey, eyes still fixed on the floor between their feet. Dismissed at last, she fled like a scolded child and Marston reappeared with a sheaf of papers, ready to discuss the details of the inheritance. Numbly, Nick half listened as the man explained at length and in detail, but most of his thoughts were with the timid creature who was his wife, and her terror of her husband.

The house was still empty when Sarah went in, Nick not yet returned from his wife, and she was glad. Time to compose herself and wash the scent of Tom from her legs. But first she lit the fire, needing the cheer it gave: without it the place seemed forlorn and sad. The wood took time to kindle and catch, and she had not long finished her toilet and settled with some wine at the hearth when she heard the door scrape open and Nick was home.

She got up from the hearth, stepping towards the door to greet him, but when she saw the sorrow in the lines of his face, his mouth grim with anguish, she hung back, uncertain how to be with him. The new presence of his wife had changed it all and so she waited to see how he would be.

'Get me wine,' he said, when he had taken off his cloak. It was heavy with the rain and when he shook his head and ran his fingers through his hair, drops of water splashed onto the rushes. She took the cloak and hung it on the hook beside the door, then went through to pour the spiced wine that she was keeping warm by the fire. He took the cup without a word and flung himself into his usual chair at the fireside. She waited again to see if he wanted anything else, but when he said nothing she settled herself back on the cushions and sipped at her own wine. He seemed oblivious of her presence.

He drained his cup and she leaned over with the jug and poured him more. He gave a curt nod of thanks and stared once more into the flames, which had settled now, the fire drawing well, the room warm and comfortable. She threw on another log and the hiss and crackle seemed to draw Nick's attention back to his surroundings. He sighed and sat forward, resting his forearms on his thighs, lessening the distance there had been between them.

'She's terrified of me,' he said, lifting his eyes to her at last with a wry smile. 'I've never seen such a beaten-looking woman. God only knows what her father told her about me to make her so afraid.'

Sarah could think of no words of comfort to offer and her own bleak future loomed over it all: the conversation with Tom had placed it frontstage and centre in her thoughts, impossible to ignore. She said, 'Did you see your son?'

He shook his head.

She tried again. 'So she will come here as your wife?'

Reluctantly he nodded. 'After her father's funeral.' Then he lifted his hands to beckon her towards him and she knelt between his legs and held him. Within the muscular strength of his body, she could feel his fragile soul, full of sorrow and afraid, and her heart turned in pity – he was a prisoner of them both and she didn't know how to set him free.

She held him for what seemed a long time until finally he drew back from her and took her face between his palms, lifting it to look into her eyes. His own eyes were dark and troubled and there was a light in them she had not seen before. 'Will you stay, even so?' he asked. 'Can I truly ask you to share me?'

'Where else would I go?' She smiled with a shrug.

'And will you be kind to her?'

She tilted her head, catching her bottom lip with her teeth, searching for the words for the lie.

'For my sake?' he prompted.

'She broke your heart,' Sarah said. 'And now that it's mended she would hurt you all over again ...' She trailed off. She wished the woman were dead; kindness would not come easily.

'This is not of her doing – I can promise you she does not want to come here.'

She said nothing but moved in closer towards him, resting her head against his chest, her arms wrapped around the muscles of his back, breathing in his warmth and strength and loveliness. Soon he would belong to his wife, his Christian soul chafing against the magic she had wrought to win him, aching to be free of it. Soon she would lose him, love given unwillingly shadowed with hate, and the sadness of all of it washed up in a wave that overwhelmed her. All the tears she had forced down before with Tom finally rose and broke and she was unable to stop them. She buried her face against him harder, trying to hide, but her shoulders were heaving with her sobs and her breath came in long ragged bursts. Nick held her tightly, broad hands strong against her narrow back, a different strength from her brother. But her love for them both was forbidden and this promise of safety was no more than a brief and tempting illusion. The cold, dark exposure of her future was waiting and soon none of it would matter any more, all of it meaningless in death. Then he could be as kind as he liked to his wife and she would neither know nor care.

He rocked her gently, soft sounds of reassurance on his lips, but the tears still flowed and she could only give herself up to them until slowly the tide of her weeping started to ebb and he loosened his hold on her, gazing into her face, wiping at her cheeks with a gentle thumb. Then she lifted herself upwards to meet him, her lips against his, her face cradled in his hands until he laid her down onto the cushions and loved her gently, tenderly, all their sorrow contained in their wordless union. And afterwards he held her tightly again, wrapping his limbs around her, her back reddening with the heat of the fire behind her.

They fell asleep at the hearth on the hard floor, the rug drawn across them for warmth, and they only awoke in the morning when Joyce arrived to make up the fire. She stopped in the doorway, just enough light still glowing from the dying fire for her to see them, and her instinctive disapproval struggled with her love for them both. After a moment she turned and walked away, closing the door behind her, and the two lovers smiled at each other.

'Never mind,' Nick said, twisting his fingers in her hair, wrapping the soft strands around his hand. She tipped back her head in answer and he kissed her upturned mouth, once, gently. Then he said, 'We should probably get up.'

Reluctantly, she disentangled herself from him, separating, becoming their two disparate selves once again. They watched each other dress, savouring the beauty of their bodies, his lean, strong hardness, muscles curved and taut, and her slight boyish frame, the small upturned breasts. She was sad when they were covered, too many layers of cloth between them. She wanted to undress them both again, to lie once more skin to skin and feel the thud of his heartbeat close to her ear.

When they were ready, he went to the door and called out to Joyce, 'We are decent now – it is safe to return,' and Sarah laughed, meeting him in the doorway on her way toward the kitchen.

He stopped her, holding her arms in his hands, bending his face close to hers. 'This will never change,' he whispered. 'It will always be so between us. I will make it so. Trust me.'

She smiled and nodded, wishing he had the power to make it true. Then she slipped out past him and hurried along the passage so that he would not see the truth in her face.

Chapter Twenty-One

THE WORD OF PROMISE

'They have taken John.'

The words took flight through the playhouse so that no one really knew who had said them first. They came to Sarah from the lips of Nick, who climbed the steep steps to the wardrobe to find her there sewing costumes with Tom. Brother and sister turned at once at his appearance and laid down their stitching. Nick was a stranger to this room; it was Tom's domain and she knew he felt at a disadvantage here. That he had brought bad news she knew without a doubt.

'They have taken John,' Nick said.

Her heart seemed to lift in her chest and pause in its beating. Her eyes slid of their own accord toward her brother, a shared look of despair.

'Do we know any more?' Tom turned to the other man, who had set his hatred aside to bring them the news.

'Not yet.' Nick shook his head. 'The word is that the magistrate examined him this morning.' His gaze moved from one to the other, and she saw her own fear reflected in his eyes. John's capture could hang them both, and the Grand Jury hearing would be the weighing of the balance of her life. Nick stepped closer and wrapped his fingers around her hand. 'It is only his word, against all of ours ...' he murmured.

'You will still speak for her?' Tom asked. 'Knowing what you know?'

Nick's fingers tightened on hers, muscles tensing. He turned slowly towards her brother. 'I will speak for her,' he replied. His voice was low and even, masking fury underneath, but still she was glad Tom had asked. It helped to hear Nick's promise. 'It was not John she bewitched.'

She was silent, thinking of the rite in the Grove, asking Hecate to return the harm against her to its source, and John's madness translating into murder. She kept her eyes lowered but she knew without looking the thoughts in Tom's head were the same.

'Thank you,' Tom answered.

'I need no thanks from you,' Nick snarled, leaning forward, an automatic hand resting on the handle of the knife at his belt so that Tom instinctively shifted back. Physically, they were unevenly matched. She tightened her grasp on his hand, calling him back, but he seemed unaware of her, all of his attention focused on Tom. 'Be sure that I would not say a single word that could save *your* skin. All of this is down to you. All of it.'

She saw Tom compress his lips and turn away, all the words gathering unuttered on his tongue and dangerous. Moving closer to Nick, her body up against his arm, she placed a gentle hand on his shoulder. 'Nick, please,' she breathed. 'It does no good.'

He wrenched his attention away from her brother and forced a small smile towards her. Then he said, 'I'm needed downstairs,' and with a few short strides he was gone, his head disappearing rapidly down the steps, boots thudding.

Silently, she moved back to the stool and picked up the gown she had been sewing – Lady Macduff's, green velvet with gold brocade. Just a while ago she had been admiring the fineness of the fabric as she made the stitches, the soft, deep colours that changed with the light. Now she was oblivious to its beauty, its richness against her skin unnoticed.

'It's over,' she whispered. 'The Fates were mistaken. I'm not going to live long enough to die of grief, Tom. I'm the one who'll die at the end of a rope.'

Tom took a deep breath and she waited, but he said nothing, merely shaking his head, no words he could offer her.

'He will say I cursed him to the murder and I will hang instead of him.' She laid the sewing aside, still careful with the fabric even in her distress, the habits of a lifetime, and her thoughts flickered back to the night before, Tom's mouth on hers, the rough wall at her back, the warmth of him inside her. All her senses pulsed with the memory, alive to the physical sensations, the lift and fall of her breath, the steady knock of the heartbeat in her chest. She let her gaze travel over the room around her: the colours seemed to brighten as she looked, and she became aware again of the softness of the gown under her palm. She was conscious of everything, her whole being opened to the universe, sensation pouring into her, filling her. Even the touch of the cold air on the skin of her hands, the slight warmth from the candle that flickered on the bench. But still it was not enough – she wanted to feel and touch and know everything, a desperate hunger to connect to the physical world she would soon be forced to leave.

She lifted her gaze to Tom. He was watching her with grave and curious eyes. Was this why he chased his pleasure with such reckless-ness? To experience the mortal world in all its mad entirety, aware of the nullity of impending death?

'And now you understand me, sweet sister,' he said softly, gesturing with a hand at the room around them. Her eyes followed the movement briefly. 'This is all there is and it is over in a moment.'

'I'm afraid,' she said simply. 'I'm afraid of the nothingness of it.'

'I'm afraid too,' he replied. Then he stepped around the bench and wrapped his arms around her, holding her close. For a moment she tensed, uncertain of his intentions, but the embrace was gentle and warm and she relaxed into him, trusting him again, her brother.

Chapter Twenty-Two

THE PRIMROSE WAY

'Come with me to the funeral.' Nick propped himself up on one elbow beside her in the bed the next morning, the other hand gently tracing the lines of her breast. They had made love on waking and now the daylight beckoned beyond the curtains. Neither wished to leave the haven of their bed.

She turned her head on the pillow to face him. 'I thought you wanted me to be kind.'

'I don't want to go,' he said.

'I know,' she said, lifting a hand to touch his cheek, his beard rough against her palm. 'But my being there would only make it worse. For everyone.'

He nodded reluctant acceptance, then turned from her, and as he rolled out of bed she propped herself up to see him better as he dressed, sad as his body disappeared beneath his clothes. She could have looked at him all day, drinking in the details of each line of muscle, the mole on his shoulder blade, the scar on his rib from a youthful brawl. Buttoning his doublet, he turned to her. 'You too.' He smiled, and lazily she swung herself up to sit, aware of his eyes on her breasts and her buttocks as she lifted herself out of the bed. She stood to face him, head tilted and coy, knowing he could not help but come to her again. He kissed her hard and she could feel the seams of his doublet press against her breasts as he held her close. Then, abruptly, he stepped back, hands held up before him in mock surrender.

'I must go,' he said. 'I must.'

She smiled and watched until the door latched to behind him, then listened to his footsteps on the stairs, the slam of the front door as he left. For a moment she stood naked by the bed, gathering her courage, before she turned to dress herself. Without the warm reassurance of his presence to shield her, the prospect of the trial loomed dark with its promise of death. The fear of it shadowed all her thoughts now, and she counted the days, terror always simmering just below the surface, only forced a little deeper out of sight in the pleasure of Nick's company. Tom, she could hardly bear to be with any more – it was like looking in a mirror – and though she knew her avoidance cut him deeply, she hoped he understood.

Taking a deep breath, her dress complete, she squared her shoulders, took her courage in her hands and went downstairs to face the day.

The funeral was at St Dunstan-in-the-West where he and Becky had married, and there were many mourners – Roberts's touch had spread wide, and Nick recognised familiar faces in the crowd that gathered in the church. Richard Burbage was among them, still hobbling and bent with a cane, and Nick moved through the mill to stand with him.

'How goes it, Nick?' Burbage seemed pleased to see him. 'I hear there've been a few problems.'

Nick tilted his head and smiled. 'Aren't there always?'

'Yes, but the female lead … murder and madness … that isn't usual. What did you do to the poor lad?'

'It was none of my doing,' Nick replied. 'I just played my part.'

'And what a good part it is.' Burbage lowered his voice, remembering where they were, realising his resonant voice was attracting attention. 'I am still sorry to have lost it to you, though I'll be interested to see what you make of it. And how is the new Lady? Losing

John must have been a bitter blow. Such a shame. Such talent gone to waste.'

'Yes. He was my apprentice,' Nick reminded him. If anyone should feel John's loss it would be him.

'And you will speak for him at his trial, of course?'

'Of course,' Nick lied automatically. Burbage was obviously less well-informed than he thought. but he was in no mood for explanations. 'But now,' he said, 'I must find my wife.'

He enjoyed the surprise on the other man's face but Burbage recovered quickly and smiled. 'Yes, of course,' he said. 'I'm sure you'll want to reclaim her now.'

Nick bowed and took his leave to make his way to the front of the mourners to find her.

She saw him approach and dipped low into a curtsey, eyes lowered to the stone floor at their feet. Her hand rested on the shoulder of a boy that he guessed was his son, but he too kept his eyes fixed to the floor. He was aware of the attention of the mourners around him and now was not the time to demand introductions. So he bowed to her instead, this stranger in mourning who now belonged to him, and took his place beside her as the service began.

He barely listened, repeating the words mechanically, without thought, aware only of the woman at his side who held herself so still and never turned her head towards him once, though he slid curious glances towards her often. She would be in his bed tonight, he thought, and tried to remember her body as he had known it before in their brief encounters, always clothed, always secret. Childbirth would have changed her, rounding out the youthful hips and breasts, putting flesh on her belly. In spite of everything, he was eager to know, to explore beneath the wall she had erected round her and force her to a response. She was his wife after all, and they must make a life together somehow.

The funeral dragged on and when at last the service ended he walked behind her as they accompanied the coffin to the grave, familiarising himself with the shape of her and the outline of the son he'd never met. Afterwards, as the mourners came to speak to her and pay their respects, he stood back to watch and observed an awful self-sufficiency about her, a detachment and aloofness: her expression never changed, and their son stood beside her with the same shuttered look upon his face. Perhaps it was the grief, he hoped, a mask to meet the trials of the day. But in his gut he knew it was not so and a cold dread of the future settled on his shoulders like a cloak. Finally, finally, only they remained, but she did not move or turn to him and he was forced to walk around her to stand and face her.

'Becky.'

'Husband.' Her voice was little more than a whisper.

He squatted before the boy, finding a smile from somewhere deep inside to wear. 'How fares my boy?'

The boy risked a quick look and immediately flicked his eyes to the ground again. 'Father.'

'His name is Michael,' Becky said. 'My father wouldn't allow me to call him Nicholas.'

He stood up, surprised by the offer of information. 'You wanted to call him Nicholas?'

At last she looked at him, a quiver of emotion running between them. She nodded briefly, then swung her eyes away.

'Come,' he said then, a tiny sliver of hope lighting inside, 'I'll take you home.'

He saw straight away that Sarah and Joyce had worked hard to prepare the house and make it welcoming. Bright fires burned in the hearths, fresh and fragrant rushes covered the flagstones of the hallway, and the air was redolent of baking: the scents of sweet pastry and cooked fruit drifted from the kitchen. Coming into the house out of the chill, Nick ushered his wife and son into the hall and bade them sit by the fire. The journey home had been almost silent, his early attempts at conversation dwindling in the face of reluctant and unwilling answers from them both.

Sarah poured wine and slid him a questioning glance he could not reply to. She turned away, apparently understanding all she needed from his look. Then she took the cup of wine to the hearth and offered it, and a watered ale to the boy.

'This is Sarah,' he said. 'One of my servants.'

'Your whore, you mean.' The words were said without emotion and Becky's eyes did not lift to meet his. He flicked a look to Sarah and saw his own horror in her eyes.

'My servant,' he said carefully.

'Don't lie,' Becky said. 'I saw the way you looked at each other. I know what she is to you. Have you brought me here to humiliate me? Are you flaunting her before me now to punish me?'

He hesitated. He had hoped that kindness might rekindle old feelings. He had hoped they might yet make a marriage together, friends and partners, a marriage bed, even if his heart belonged elsewhere. But this blank hostility and judgement stirred anything but kindness.

'You come into my house and dare to judge me?' he said. 'When you have refused me all these years, denying my rights to you as your husband and your master?' The surface scratched, the years of resentment began to surge through the crack. He was vaguely aware of Joyce moving round him, taking the boy to his new chamber upstairs, John's old room. 'You have no right to judge me,' he said, 'or set yourself above me.'

'I am your wife,' she replied. 'And she is your whore. As God is my witness, I have no need to judge you.'

He had thought her afraid of him, beaten, and this streak of casual cruelty took him by surprise. Instinctively, he responded in kind.

'There was a time when you didn't hesitate to be my whore,' he answered. 'When you were only too eager to have my cock between your legs. How do you think your son was begotten?' The crudeness was deliberate, an urge to provoke some answering emotion.

But the words seemed to have no effect. She merely lifted her face to regard him with a light of contempt in her eyes. 'Many years have passed since then, Husband. And now I am here as your wife, bound to serve you, as my lord and master. You may put your cock between my legs whenever you please.' Her gaze switched to Sarah, who was hovering close, the wine jug still in her hand. 'But not,' she spat, 'between hers.'

'Now?' he replied. 'Now you are here as my wife? And where have you been, Wife, these last eight years, when you should have been serving me as your husband and your master, warming my bed? Where was your Christian duty then?'

'Scripture tells us not to walk with sinners. And you, Husband, are a sinner.' Her gaze passed over Sarah and her lips curled with distaste.

He balled his fists against the urge to slap her. 'It also tells wives to obey their husbands.'

'Well, I am here now. So you have your wish.'

He looked across at Sarah. There was no answer to his wife's contrariness. She had rewritten the world to fit her story, convinced of her righteousness, and he knew it was pointless to argue: he had met such zealots before. They came sometimes to preach outside the playhouse or the brothels, and one afternoon he had spent several hours in argument with a Puritan at the bear-baiting ring. How had she become such a person? She had once laughed freely and given him her body with her love and her passion.

'What did your father do to you,' he asked, 'to make you so cold and hard, and to take all your joy away?'

The question seemed to catch her off-guard and she started, meeting his eyes for a moment, the first hint of a weakness.

'You used to be happy,' he said. 'We used to laugh together. You wanted to name our son after me. What happened to you, Becky?'

He saw his wife's eyes flick towards Sarah and with a gesture of his head, he told her to leave. She nodded her understanding but she left with reluctance, and briefly he wondered if she would remain outside the door to listen; he couldn't have blamed her if she did. But he gave it no more thought, his mind bent on salvaging the wreck of his marriage by finding some small spark between them that might yet be rescued. He drew up a stool to sit near his wife so their faces were level but she kept her eyes lowered now, as though ashamed once more. When she spoke her voice was low and hard to hear above the dancing roar of the fire.

'My father showed me the error of my ways,' she murmured. 'He turned my mind from the pleasures of the flesh to the glories of the Word. He made me see the body is as nothing against the sanctity of the soul. He taught me to pray and to ask God's forgiveness for my sins. He taught me to listen for God's voice in my heart, so that I would know I had been saved.'

'And are you saved?'

'I don't know,' she whispered. 'But Scripture says that by their fruits shall ye know them. Sinful actions and sinful thoughts are not the fruits of God's elect.'

He sat back a little to give her some space.

'I don't want to burn in Hell for the love we shared, Nick. I want to be one of the saved. I had to repent. I had to renounce you. We married only so that Michael would not be born a bastard. Not to save me. Do you understand?' She lifted her head to look at him, and for the first time he saw some of the softness of the girl he once loved, a light in her eyes he could recognise. Without thinking, he leaned forward and gently drew the cap from her hair, but what he saw as he lifted it away stopped his breath. The once-auburn mass was streaked with great bands of silver grey. She lowered her head again but not in time to prevent him seeing her tears.

They sat in silence awhile, the only sound the low roar of the fire. Once, he got up to throw on another log before he returned to the stool and watched it catch and burn and crackle. Eventually, though, he had to say something.

'Whatever has happened between us, Becky, we are man and wife under God. We can be friends or we can be enemies but either way we are one flesh.' He touched a tentative hand to her arm. 'Can we be friends?'

She sat up, shifting her arm away from his touch. He sat back slowly, conscious of the rebuff. Her face was dry now, no sign of her tears. 'We can,' she said. 'If you wish it. I will be an obedient wife. But the whore has to go.'

He closed his eyes for a moment, searching to compose himself, to find the right words and keep his temper in check. 'She is contracted to me as a servant for twelve months,' he said.

'It matters not.'

'Your father was a lawyer, Becky. Surely you understand.'

'She goes.'

'I will think on it,' he murmured, rising to his feet, spirit sinking.

'And I will leave you with Joyce to take care of your needs. I must go to the playhouse.'

His wife stood up also and sank immediately into a curtsey. He dropped his head to acknowledge it, then turned and strode from the room. In the hallway he met Sarah, backing rapidly away from the door.

'You heard?'

'Some,' she replied. 'Not all. But enough.'

He called out to Joyce to attend his wife and, taking down their cloaks from the hook, he draped Sarah's across her shoulders, straightening it carefully, hands lingering on the curve of her neck. She drew it close around her and they stepped out together into the morning. A grey sky glowered, dark pockets of cloud bulging with rain. There was a dampness in the air: the rain would break again before nightfall. Sarah linked her arm through his (to spite his wife?) and as they walked he filled in the words she had not heard.

'Will you send me away?' Her tone was casual but he heard the fear beneath it.

'Of course not.'

'And besides,' she said, 'come the assizes, it might no longer be an issue.' She turned her head to look at him, a small brave smile playing at the corners of her mouth. Her beautiful mouth. He leaned down as they walked, slowing slightly, to kiss her. In these streets on Bankside, no one even stopped to watch them and they continued on, walking more slowly now to prolong the journey even though the rehearsal was awaiting them.

At the playhouse they parted with a brief kiss and she made her way up to the wardrobe to make the last hurried alterations, the costumes all but finished. Tom was at the workbench, mending a seam that had split in some breeches, and he lifted his head and smiled at her. 'How was it?' he asked.

'Awful. She called me a whore and told him to get rid of me.'

Tom's eyebrows lifted in amused incredulity. Sarah dragged the cloak from her shoulders, hung it on the peg, and slid onto the stool across from her brother. Picking up a stray pin, she began to dig at a crevice in the wood of the bench. 'She wants to be sure she's one of the saved.'

'Are those her eyes?' He motioned to the movement of the pin.

'Regrettably, no.' She smiled and looked up, sorry she had tried to keep away from him. Now that she was with him there was nowhere else she wanted to be.

Tom laughed lightly, then pointed to a gown draped across the rack. 'The gentlewoman's. The embroidery is not yet finished.'

She got up again to get it and brought it back, laying it flat on the bench, smoothing it out with her fingers, struggling to remember the design she had planned. She was finding it hard to care. She looked up at her brother, aware he was watching her.

'I've missed you,' he said, reaching out a hand to hers.

'Forgive me.' She gave him a small sad smile.

'Of course,' he replied. Then, 'Don't give up, Sarah. Nothing is ever quite as it seems and the future is not writ in stone.'

She shrugged in a vain attempt at nonchalance, then forced her thoughts to turn to the sewing before her.

After the afternoon performance when the others wended their usual way to the tavern, Nick walked with Sarah to the house in Water Lane. She tucked her arm in tighter to Nick's and drew strength from his warmth and his nearness. At the door they both stopped, turning to face each other. He touched a gloved finger to her jaw and bent his head to kiss her lightly on the lips. 'I will not send you away,' he said. Then he turned and pushed open the door and together they went inside.

They found his wife at the hearth, reading her Bible in the light of the fire and a single candle on a side table set next to her chair. Michael was nowhere to be seen. Becky looked up at their entrance with the start of a small smile on her lips for her husband that froze when she noticed Sarah close behind him.

'Did you find her at the playhouse?' she said. 'Or at the brothel?'

'The playhouse,' he replied, and squatted to poke the fire. Then turning to Sarah he said, 'Some wine.'

Sarah bobbed in a small curtsey and hurried to the kitchen for wine. Joyce was there with Michael, who had evidently found his voice and smile again in the way that children do, now that he was away from his mother's harsh brand of discipline. He was eating bread and honey and in between mouthfuls they were playing a rhyming game.

'Good day to you, Michael.' Sarah smiled.

He lifted his eyes from his bread. 'Mother says I'm not to talk to you because you are my father's whore.'

Sarah bit her lip and forced the smile to remain. 'Well, your mother isn't here, so you can talk to me and it'll be our secret.' She winked and his eyes wandered slowly back to the bread and honey in his fingers, considering.

'What's a whore?' he asked, looking up again.

'A lady that men like more than their wives,' she answered with a sly look at Joyce, who shook her head and suppressed a smile. Then she went through to the buttery and filled the jug from one of the barrels.

'Does he want some spiced?' Joyce asked, gesturing to the pot.

'I don't think he cares.' The two women exchanged a look of understanding that promised further conversation.

In the main hall Sarah poured wine for the master and his wife, then withdrew once more to the kitchen to help Joyce prepare the supper.

They ate all together, the whole household at the table as was the custom, pausing for Becky to say grace. The prayer was long and Sarah risked a glance at Nick, who raised his eyebrows briefly. She lowered her eyes and smiled. Then, when grace was done and they began to eat, Becky spoke again.

'I will not eat with her at the table.'

'Then you will not eat,' Nick answered without missing a beat, his eyes still on the piece of chicken in his fingers. 'I am master in this house and I decide who sups at my table. You are my wife and my word to you is law. You've had your way for long enough. She is not leaving.'

Sarah lowered her eyes. In spite of everything it was hard to watch.

Becky did not flinch. 'Did you bring me here to insult me?'

'I brought you here because I had no choice.' He dropped the chicken bone onto the trencher and wiped his fingers. She had never seen him so cold – he seemed a different man from the Nick she knew. There was a long silence and nobody ate, all eyes lowered, waiting on their master.

When she thought she could bear the tension no longer, he got up and the stool scraped loudly on the floorboards as it shifted under his weight. 'I'm going to the tavern,' he said. 'I no longer like the company here.' And with that he was gone, the door vibrating in his wake. Sarah looked up and Becky was staring at her, a small smile of triumph on her lips. She pushed the remains of her own food away and got up also.

'And I'm going with him,' she said, which slapped the smile from Becky's face.

She ran the length of the lane before she caught up with him, breath coming hard. He slowed to let her recover but she could sense the rage pulsing through him, the urge to movement. Then he turned to her. 'Go home, Sarah. Where I'm going is not a fit place for you.'

'But I often—'

'Go home.'

'To her? She is my mistress now.'

'You have my permission to disobey her. And if she strikes you I'll strike her in return.' He made a sweeping movement with his hand. 'Just go.'

He turned and strode on towards the taverns and she stood in the lane and watched him go with no understanding of what had just passed, the cause of his anger at her. When she could see him no longer, she turned slowly to begin retracing her steps along the lane to the house before she changed her mind and turned again to follow his path towards Bankside. In the hubbub of the High Street she met Will, making his way home after supping at the George.

'Sarah?' He was surprised to see her. 'What are you doing here alone? Is anything amiss?'

She smiled and shook her head. 'I'm fine. I'm looking for Tom.'

He regarded her carefully so that she knew he was not fooled. But he let it pass, and she wondered how much her mother had ever told him, how close they really were. 'He left the George a while ago with a pretty young man named James,' he said. 'I believe they were heading to the Cocke.'

'Thank you,' she replied.

'But you cannot go alone, Sarah ...' he began. ''Tis not safe ...'

'I'll be fine,' she assured him, and with a brief curtsey and a smile of thanks, she cut away from him before he could protest. She felt his eyes on her back as she threaded through the crowd and turned off the main drag into a back lane out of his view. He was right, of course, the Stews on Bankside were not safe for a woman on her own, but how else could she find him?

She walked quickly, warily, all her senses alert. By the river she felt safer – the broad sweep of the water on her right, lively now with traffic, lights and the shouts of the boatmen, the plash of the oars, the excited chatter of the young men stepping off the wherry at Goat Steps as she passed. On her left the long white strip of bawdy houses stretched along the bank and she did not know which one was the Cocke.

A group of young men, apprentices by the look of them, lurched drunkenly towards her and she sidestepped them easily, but nonetheless she was afraid. Two whores standing at a doorway called out to her and she approached them carefully. Like the first time she had searched for Tom among the taverns, she thought, when Jane had helped her. It seemed such a long time ago.

'You looking for work?' one of the women asked. She was grubby and poorly dressed, but still young with pretty eyes.

'I'm looking for the Cocke,' she said. 'My brother is there.'

The whore looked her up and down as if deciding whether or not to help. Sarah waited, submitting to the scrutiny, and tried to keep the apprehension from her face.

'Third door down,' the woman said at last.

'Thank you,' Sarah answered and turned her steps towards it.

~

At the door she hesitated. The voices of men inside were loud and raucous, and a stale stench of ale drifted into the evening. Reluctantly, she pushed open the door and found herself in a low-ceilinged room that was thick with the smoke of cheap tallow candles and a low-burning fire, dirty straw strewn on the boards, and sundry tables and stools spread about. Three men at a table by the door lifted their heads to look at her, and she drew her cloak tighter about her as protection, though the room was close and hot.

Looking over their heads, ignoring them, she searched for her brother, eyes flicking rapidly across the gloom amongst the groups of drinkers until she saw him finally against the far wall. Swallowing hard, she wove through the tables towards him, aware of the looks that followed her. He was with the same pretty boy as before, who had his leg draped over Tom's, their bodies close and touching, and eyes only for each other. A knot of jealousy balled in her gut and she set her face hard to hide it as she drew up a stool to their table.

'Tom.'

He turned abruptly at her voice and shoved the boy's leg from his own, leaning forward across the table, taking her hand. 'Sarah! What brings you here? This is no place for you.'

She nodded, close to tears. The relief of finding him was almost overwhelming and she had no words to speak. He stroked her hand and smiled, and the boy beside him, ignored, stood up with a flourish and flounced off to find another customer. Tom watched him go and she could see the regret in his eyes.

'I'm sorry, Tom,' she said. 'I'm spoiling your pleasure.'

'He'll be here tomorrow.' Tom shrugged. 'Come. Let's go from here. Somewhere peaceful, away from all of this ...'

He moved to her side of the table and put his arm around her, holding her close and protected, shepherding her towards the door. Outside, she breathed more easily in the cool damp air: after the fug of the brothel the night felt fresh, even this close to the sourness of the river. They stood for a moment near the door, his arm still around her.

Then he said, 'The playhouse.'

She nodded and they walked in silence along the river, soothed by the running current on its way out to the sea, the life in its waters. She was aware of his closeness – the hardness of his body against hers, its physical reality – and the memory of the future she had seen pushed at the edges of her thoughts.

At the playhouse they entered their usual way up the outside stairs and into the wardrobe at the top, but she wanted the sky above her, so Tom picked up a rug and a blanket and they descended the stairs to sit together on the stage. They sat for a moment looking out into the silent darkness of the auditorium, and though it was empty she still felt exposed up there, watched and judged. She turned her face away from it and finally met his question.

'What happened?' he said.

Briefly she told him.

'He's tired of the drama of it, is all,' Tom answered. 'He's looking for peace in a barrel of ale or under the skirts of a whore he can use and forget. He feels bound by you both, and caught in between. He will come back to you – he has no choice.'

'And I understand,' she said. 'But I just couldn't be there with her.'

He nodded, and they sat together surrounded by the theatre's silence for a while. She was aware of him watching her but she did not mind – she was comfortable in his presence, content with all that was between them. It seemed natural now, inevitable. After a while she lifted her head to look at him, the narrow handsome face, the searching eyes. The image of his lifeless hanging body nudged in her mind again and she shoved it away.

'What do you think happens when we die?' she asked.

He gave her a half-smile. 'Our bodies turn to dust and our spirit returns to the universe.'

'But are we still us? I mean, will I still know that I exist? Or is it over? Nothing. No more.'

'I wish I knew. I have pondered it often. Perhaps there is an underworld ...'

'A hell?'

'No, not a hell. Hades, perhaps. Hecate would have no truck with the Christian Hell. No, I think Hades is just the realm of the dead, darker perhaps than the living realm. But not an everlasting torment. Only the Christians would wish that for anyone.'

'I wish it for Becky,' she said, and he laughed. But then she wondered if she really meant it. Here with Tom, her life with Nick seemed unreal to her, a life lived by somebody else. She said, 'If you were to die tomorrow what regrets would you have?'

He considered for a moment, tipping back his head, eyes searching the heavens. 'Very few,' he replied. 'I've tried most things I've wanted to. I'd have liked to see a little more of the world, perhaps. Rome? Athens? To see some of the wonders of the ancient world. But mostly, I am content.'

'You wouldn't regret never having fallen in love?'

'Who says I've never fallen in love?'

She looked up at him, surprised. He had never talked of anyone he might have loved, and her innards clutched in a twinge of hurt and jealousy. He touched her arm. 'What about you?' he asked gently. 'What regrets would you have?'

'I would have liked to have a child,' she said. 'To know the power of a mother's love.'

He nodded. 'It may still come to be,' he said softly. 'Don't give up.'

'Can we sleep here tonight?' she said then. 'I need to be near you.'

'Not Nick?'

'Not Nick,' she said. 'I love him and I'd have him as my husband in the blink of an eye if such a thing could be, but you know me better.' Her brother knew the hidden facets of her soul, nothing concealed, nothing secret, and she had no fear she would ever lose his love because of who she was. Tonight, it was Tom she needed.

He nodded and touched his fingers to her cheek, moving closer, lifting her chin to meet his kiss. Then he loved her gently, different from the other times, loving and tender, new pleasures given and received, and afterwards they lay together centre stage, wrapped in each other, the blanket barely enough for warmth. They snuggled closer for the heat of their bodies.

'How did we come so far together without this?' she whispered, tipping back her head to look at him. He was gazing up into the darkness, his face just a shadow in the gloom, but she knew every line of it, every sweet imperfection. She propped herself up on an elbow to see him better and trailed her fingers over his cheek. He turned his head towards her touch.

'You weren't ready before,' he said.

She was silent, no words to meet the unexpectedness of his reply, and in the pause he rolled himself to face her, kissed her once gently on the mouth. Then he said, 'I'm freezing. Can we go upstairs?'

She laughed and they got to their feet, moving slowly, still caught in the lazy aftermath of sex, and the cold air against their skin made them shiver. When they had straightened their clothes Tom rolled up the blankets, took her hand and led her back up the stairs to the comfort of the couch to sleep.

Chapter Twenty-Three

AN HOUR UPON THE STAGE

The morning brought the day of the first performance of *Macbeth* and most of the players came early to the playhouse. Nick dressed himself in the tiring room, fastening the armour with difficulty: the night had drained him. He had returned from the brothel in the early hours to an empty bed and Sarah nowhere to be found, and his only company at breakfast had been Joyce, hovering and ill at ease, which only served to feed his rage. The fury was still running in his blood as he donned his costume, and he had to breathe deeply to quell the urge to lash out and do damage to something, or someone.

The figure of Tom crossed the corner of his vision, half-dressed in his gown as the Lady. He was no longer playing a witch, the changes between scenes too quick, but the part of midnight hag had suited him better, Nick thought viciously: wreaking damage in others' lives, playing on their desires for his own amusement, the Devil in his soul – it was a role he could play with ease, the part he was born for. The two men caught eyes by accident and Nick turned away from the instinctive smile Tom gave him.

Will appeared dressed as King Duncan and called the players to the stage for some words before the performance. Nick half listened, his thoughts still turning over in anger, his jaw working, fists balled and eyes still searching for a sign of Sarah. Will finished and the Company withdrew to the tiring house behind the stage to complete their preparation. Nick locked eyes with Tom once again, the surge of hatred pulsing in his gut. He crossed the boards towards him. 'Where's Sarah?' he said.

'Upstairs,' Tom answered, his fingers teasing out the hairs of the wig he held in front of him, straightening, neatening. 'Last-minute stitches. As always.' He smiled again and there was something in his nonchalance that stoked the embers of Nick's rage.

Moving closer, he enjoyed the other man's sudden shift to wariness, the wig transferred to one hand and forgotten, muscles tensing. His own power pleased him. 'Was she with you last night?' he murmured.

Tom nodded. 'She was upset. She came to find me at the tavern.'

'And what did you do with her when she found you?' The words issued of their own accord and he regretted them immediately.

He did not want to know.

He already knew.

'We came here,' Tom answered with a shrug. 'We talked.'

'And after you talked?' He could not help himself.

'We slept.' Tom's tone had hardened, a warning within it, and Nick noted the change.

'And between talking and sleeping?'

'Why do you do this to yourself? To her?' Tom asked, voice low and harsh. There was an edge of danger in it and for the first time Nick saw a power in Tom, a quality of hardness and resilience he had not seen before. 'Why did you not just stay with her last night?' Tom breathed. 'You sent her to me with your petty anger and your jealousies. All she wants is to love you, and you drove her away. Where else does she have to go except to me?'

The other man's self-righteousness sparked the fuse of anger that had smouldered all day, and he lashed out savagely to smash his fist full-force against Tom's face, all his emotions and fury carried in the blow. Tom staggered and fell, caught off guard, and the wig slid across the boards where he dropped it. Nick moved in to strike again, lusting for violence, burning with the urge for blood, but within a moment the sinewy arms of John Heminges dragged him back and away as he kicked out with his legs, seeking to land a boot in Tom's guts. Other players launched forward to help, and rage spewed through his body in waves as he struggled to hurl himself across the room again and beat Tom's face into pulp; he had never felt such hatred in his life, never fully understood the urge to pure brutality until this moment.

He fought wildly to jerk his arms from the grasp of the men who hauled him away towards the wall, but they held him fast until at last the fury began to wane and he ceased to fight against them, once more master of himself. But he was breathing hard, the tension still running in his muscles, quivering. They let him go, standing close for a moment to be sure until he shoved them away and glanced between them to where Tom had raised himself up to sit, one palm pressed against his jaw. There was a satisfying trickle of blood from his lip and Nick allowed himself a brief grim smile of pleasure.

'What in God's name is wrong with you?' Heminges demanded, looking from one to the other. 'Both of you.'

Neither man spoke. Nick was aware of the baffled gazes of the other players but he felt no need to explain himself.

'Nick?' Heminges persisted.

Nick raised his head with a sigh and flicked a look towards Tom. 'Ask him,' he spat. 'Witch!'

All eyes turned to Tom, who was still nursing the split in his lip and keeping his distance, but no one said a word. Nick waited, and as the other men began to draw away, unwilling to push it further, he slid his body down the wall to sit against it and let the anger seep away. But no other emotion came to take its place and without his rage he was empty, a dark hole of nothingness inside him.

Beyond the door to the stage the playhouse began to fill. A slow trickle at the start, the first people eager to secure a good seat, swelling gradually to a stream of bodies from all walks of life, chatter rising, the playhouse coming to life. Sarah stood at the east door, collecting the pennies in the box – tuppence for the galleries and a penny extra for a cushion – smiles and curtseys. On a normal day, another performance, she loved these excited moments of anticipation, the expectant atmosphere intoxicating, heady. It signalled the start of something great, something magical – the beginning of the illusion. But today she had half heard the fight as she hurried through on her way to the door, and there had been no time to turn back to see as the first people started to arrive. Now all she wanted was to get them all in and close the door behind them so she could flee backstage and know what had happened. So she smiled and curtseyed till her cheeks grew weary and her knees began to ache, and the minutes stretched like days.

Finally, the last penny dropped into the box and she followed the gentleman in, closing the door behind him and squeezing her way around the back to deliver the takings to the tiring house. Then she took her place backstage to watch and help if she were needed. The house was full, the audience noisy and high-spirited, eager for the thrill of a brand new play. In spite of everything, she could not help but smile: the glow of expectation warmed her inside.

In the tiring house the witches were poised and set. Up above in the Heavens, she knew the cannonballs were ready in the thunder-run, and beneath the trap, the powder was primed for the smoke, merely awaiting a spark to ignite it. She cast her eyes across the room. The King's party, Will among them, stood to one side in a group, fidgeting in silent nervousness, their moment almost come. The fight had disturbed the usual balance – a darker tension pervaded the air and the pale hair on her forearms stirred and lifted. Against one wall Nick was slumped, head lowered, staring at the floor. He should be pacing, she thought, his usual ritual to prepare himself.

Foreboding filled her with a sense of heaviness, and though she took a step to go to him some instinct that he would not want her company held her back. Instead she trailed her gaze away from him along the wall and it lit on Tom, who was sitting on the bottom stair, watching her. He was dressed and ready in the fine gown she had sewn, holding the Lady's wig in his hands. She went across to help with the wig, and when she reached him she saw the livid welt across his jaw, his bottom lip split and bleeding. With a quick look behind her towards Nick, still gazing into nothing, she took the wig from her brother without a word and gently fitted it into place, taking her time to tuck the stray strands neatly and make it perfect. When she had finished he looked every inch the Lady. Except for the bruise that was already turning purple.

'What happened?' she whispered.

He lifted his chin towards Nick. 'He knows we were together last night.'

She sighed and moved around to sit herself on the step beside him. She was weary of it all – she only wanted it to stop and to be at peace again. A part of her wished that none of it had ever happened. But only a part of her. Tom placed his arm around her and she leaned into him, resting her head against his shoulder. 'Can we run away together, you and I?' she said. 'Somewhere where no one knows us? Somewhere safe?'

He smiled, painfully, and rubbed her arm. 'There is no such place and they would arrest us before we could set foot on the boat.'

She nodded, sadly. She had only half been joking. 'I know. It would be nice though, would it not? We could go to Rome. Or to Delphi, to see the Oracle.'

'Yes,' he agreed, squeezing her tighter. 'It would be very nice.'

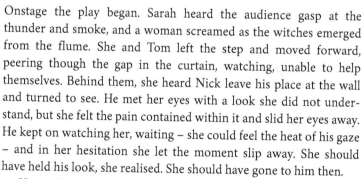

Onstage the play began. Sarah heard the audience gasp at the thunder and smoke, and a woman screamed as the witches emerged from the flume. She and Tom left the step and moved forward, peering though the gap in the curtain, watching, unable to help themselves. Behind them, she heard Nick leave his place at the wall and turned to see. He met her eyes with a look she did not understand, but she felt the pain contained within it and slid her eyes away. He kept on watching her, waiting – she could feel the heat of his gaze – and in her hesitation she let the moment slip away. She should have held his look, she realised. She should have gone to him then.

Henry Condell approached as Banquo, and Nick snapped back to the world of the play, meeting the other player's greeting with a smile of readiness. She turned away from him and trained her eyes back towards the stage, waiting with an uneasy heart for the scenes between Macbeth and his Lady.

They circled each other, wary and distant, untrusting. The audience was spellbound, tension rising. Sarah watched from backstage, mouth dry, pulses hammering as the Lady set their fate in motion, mocking her husband's doubts, entangling his reluctance with his prowess as a man.

Ah, but Tom was good, she thought: the seduction was absolute, and pitiless. Nick writhed beneath the insults, the Lady's courage to commit and dare all so much greater than his own. Always, this scene had borne the burden of their hostility, but there was something new in it today, a raw and painful battle of their wills.

Sarah held her breath.

'If we should fail?'

The two men stood close, Macbeth's hand raised to caress his Lady's cheek, the Lady's own hand covering it, head tilting in the pleasure of desire for her husband.

'We fail!
  'But screw your courage to the sticking-place,
  And we'll not fail ...'

Tom's chin was lifted, his words, his whole body, goading and provocative.

She saw the heave in Nick's chest, the moment of seduction when he bent himself to the Lady's will, the courage of his rightness failing in the face of her contempt for him as man and husband. She saw the smile of triumph on Tom's lips, and the sight of it eclipsed the bruise.

The audience hung silent and amazed, suspended in the drama, waiting, captive. Then sighed with relief as the next scene began. She turned to Will, who was watching at her side, and he lifted his eyebrows in wry recognition. 'That's almost what I wrote,' he whispered with a smile.

The play continued, descending into tyranny and madness,

murder heaped on murder, evil breeding evil, sinking towards its bitter end. She could hardly bear to watch.

'The Queen, my lord, is dead.'
  'She should have died hereafter ...'

Nick's voice cracked with grief, Tom's limp body cradled in his arms. The illusion was perfect, hatreds festering deep and hidden inside – she was surprised Tom trusted his head in Nick's hands. She watched, terrified, as Nick's fingers caressed Tom's pale throat, lips almost touching the bruised and swollen skin, uttering the words as though from great depths of grief inside him. But she could not look away, the familiar words taking on new resonance.

'Life's but a walking shadow, a poor player
  That struts and frets his hour upon the stage
  And then is heard no more ...'

For the first time since the opening line, she moved away from her spot at the curtain, unable to watch any more, the weight of the impending trial almost too heavy to bear. Briefly she paced in the tiring house, but the words beyond the curtain inevitably drew her back to watch, her own fate tied to the fate of the play.

'They have tied me to a stake; I cannot fly,
  But, bear-like, I must fight the course ...'

Macbeth, trapped in the curse of his own making and condemned to see it through.

The audience was tense and silent, the illusion complete, and even the hawkers had ceased to offer their cakes and ale. There were gasps as the final battle began, Macbeth and Macduff locking swords and fighting for their lives, and though Sarah had seen them rehearse it a hundred times, it had never looked so real before today. She flinched as every cut and blow seemed to find its mark, the actors grunting with the effort, steel ringing on steel. Then she froze as Nick staggered back and Heminges lowered his sword with horror on his face and blood upon the blade. A woman in the front row screamed. Another, further back, fainted, and not one person bent to care for her. Nick clutched at his arm and stumbled upstage; Heminges followed uncertainly, sword half-lifted.

Sarah held her breath and stepped away as Nick crashed through the curtain to the floor of the tiring house with John Heminges close behind him.

'What happened?'

Heminges lifted the bloodied blade and shook his head in wonder, then turned again to make his re-entrance on the stage as victor of the battle. Automatically, Sarah knelt to examine the wound on Nick's arm, her fingers lightly touching his hand to coax it free, but when the grip remained obstinately tight, she lifted her eyes to his in question and the look that met hers was charged with distrust.

'Don't touch me,' he hissed. Then lower, in a breath that only she could hear, 'Witch.'

'Forgive me,' she murmured. Then, overcome, she fled from the playhouse and down to the shingle on the riverbank to sit in the frigid afternoon and watch the water roll by, inexorable as time. Hugging her knees, she prayed to Hecate for courage. Her hour was almost done.

She sat for a long time until darkness claimed the day and she was frozen to her soul. The performance would be long finished by now and the theatre empty, the Company at play in the tavern or the brothel to celebrate. It had been a success after all, she reflected, in spite of the ill-wind that had followed it and the suffering in its wake. Brilliant and beautiful, a study in the madness of power. But at what cost? She wondered at Nick's injury and how the blades had come to be switched. Her first thought was Tom, seeking revenge, but she dismissed the idea at once – such brutality was not in his nature. An accident, then? Ill fate conjured by the words of the play? She didn't like to hazard a guess. But she knew it wasn't down to her, despite Nick's accusation.

She wanted warmth but she did not know where to go for it.

She could go home, she thought, to the house in Water Lane. In spite of everything, Nick must love and want her still. He had no choice: he was bound to her by the power of her magic, her prisoner.

She did not want him so.

She thought of his body in the night over hers, the strength of him, the beauty of his muscles. Loving her but not of his own free will, a slave to the passions she had wrought in him.

He was not hers by right.

Then she thought of Tom – their love exchanged in freedom, love desired and freely given. Love that was worth the taking. Love between two souls.

She had to set Nick free.

Uncertainly, but working out of instinct, she took out the poppet she still carried, the little protective figure she had fashioned out of yarn the night she scried for Will. It seemed so long ago now – she had been a different person then, a maid, barely more than a child. Carefully she unwove it, wrapping the wool around her fingers as she did so, watching the little figure diminish into nothing, and a slight fear touched the act for it had kept her safe till now.

When there was nothing left of the poppet but the yarn that was wrapped around her hand, she began to make something new. Working intuitively, she started to fashion two new figures of herself and Nick that were joined by single threads at the hands and heart and feet. A drop of blood from her thumb that she drew with her pocket-knife gave her essence to the one, and the key to Nick's house that she carried on a ribbon at her neck attached his essence to the other. She would tell him she had lost it. She let the two poppets be together for a while, holding them in her hands so that they touched gently, a last farewell. Then she cut the threads that joined them one by one.

'Once I cut to break the tie. Twice I cut for pain to fly. Thrice I cut the bond to cease.'

Holding the two figures separately now, one in each hand, she got to her feet and walked close to the water's edge to stand beside it, watching the tide bear the water seaward to the east for a moment before she raised her arm and cast the poppet that was Nick into the river.

'*I set you free,*' she murmured. '*Go with love and honour.*'

The poppet disappeared into the current, borne away on the tide to a different future. It was done. She sighed, twinges of regret pulling at her thoughts: she would never know his touch again. Putting the other poppet back in her skirts, she stepped away from the river, glancing upstream, trying to decide where to go.

She could no longer go to Nick's – that bond was severed now and the house at Water Lane was no longer her home – and though the tavern was tempting she was reluctant to intrude on the Company's gathering. They had worked hard for the play and they deserved to celebrate. She would be a burden and a worry and they would behave differently in front of her.

So she made for the playhouse.

The walk from the river warmed her a little and the feeling had returned to her feet by the time she climbed the stairs to the wardrobe door, the key still in her skirts. She fingered it as she made her way up the steps, warm from its closeness to her leg, the iron worn and smooth. But when she reached the top of the staircase and lifted her eyes to the door, she saw that it was already open and that candles were burning within. She stopped, startled, but curiosity drove her forward and she peered through the door and into the room that sprawled three steps below.

Tom was lying on the couch with a book in his hand, though he did not seem to be reading, eyes staring off into some distance only he could see. He swung himself off the couch when he heard her footstep on the stair and came immediately towards her. There was no trace left of the Lady and he was himself again, but the bruise was still livid and his lip had swollen more.

'I knew you'd come here,' he said, holding out his hands for her. 'Where else would you go?'

'Why aren't you at the tavern with the others?' she asked. She had never known him to pass up a drink or a night with a whore.

'I was waiting for you.' He took her hand and drew her into the room. A host of candles blazed on the bench and she stepped towards it, reaching out her hands to the warmth. 'Where did you go?'

'To the river.'

He nodded, understanding. It was good to be with him, no need to explain. She sat on her work stool and rested her arms on the bench, fingers extended toward the heat and light of the candles.

'It was the warmest I could make it,' he said with a shrug. 'It's not so warm ...'

'The riverbank was freezing,' she answered. 'My feet went to sleep.'

'Shall I rub them?'

She smiled and shook her head. Their mother had sometimes rubbed their feet as children – it had been a great treat. 'How's your jaw?'

'Sore,' he said. 'Your sweetheart makes a pretty fist.'

'He's not my sweetheart any more,' she said. 'I set him free at the river. I didn't think I knew how, but somehow I worked it out and let him go. We are free of each other now and his wife can have him after all.'

Here, close to Tom in this room that was their sanctuary, the words hurt less than she'd expected. The long hours at the river had worked their peace: it was not only Nick who had been freed. Then, reaching across the table and taking one of his hands, stroking the long cold fingers, she said, 'What happened?'

'He challenged me about last night so I told him he only had himself to blame – where else were you going to go but to me? He took offence.'

She gave him a half-smile. 'He doesn't understand,' she said. 'He thinks you're an agent of the Devil. He thinks that you corrupted me.'

Sliding off the stool she moved around the bench to stand beside him and examine his jaw more closely, tipping his head to one side, running her fingertips over the bruise. 'Mother will have a salve for it,' she said.

He nodded, then placed his hands either side of her waist, drawing her closer in, looking up into her face. 'And do you think I corrupted you?'

She smiled and ran her fingers through his hair. 'I think we corrupted each other.'

'So we're sinners?'

'If you believe in such things.'

He stood up and cradled her face in his palm, his mouth close to hers. 'Then sin with me again,' he whispered. 'My sweet, sweet sinner.'

She smiled and they kissed and it was the sweetest sin she had ever tasted.

~

In the morning she woke early in the silent playhouse and turned to watch her brother sleeping. His eyelids flickered in his dream, troubled, and she laid a hand lightly on his shoulder. The muscle was smooth and hard and cold, but he stirred with her touch and opened his eyes.

'You were dreaming,' she said.

He nodded.

'What did you dream?'

'Nothing,' he said, with a smile that hid the truth. 'It was nothing.'

She let it go. Perhaps he was right not to tell her – sometimes it was better not to know.

She rolled out of the makeshift bed, the piles of rugs and blankets they had made on the floor, and stood up to dress. He lay on his back with his head propped on his hands to watch her. Once she was clothed he got up too, and when both of them were ready, with the blankets stowed back in their proper place, he took her hands in his and looked down into her face. She could hardly bear to look at him, the day to come pressing on her spirit, draining the life from her blood.

'Are you ready?' he asked.

'As I'll ever be.' She nodded, raising her eyes to his face for a moment. 'I couldn't do it without you.'

'I know.' He smiled and lowered his head to kiss her once again and she could taste the salt of her own tears on their lips.

Then they crossed the room to the stair and, with a final look back at this haven she doubted she would ever see again, she ducked out through the door and into the dawning day.

They took a wherry for a penny to the courthouse in Kingston, the boat moving swiftly on the tide, too fast. She wanted the moments to slow, to savour every moment, every breeze against her face, every plash of the oar as it hit the river's surface. She held on to Tom's hand, aware of his body close to hers, and when the boat pulled in at the landing stairs, too soon, she was sad to step out of it and onto solid earth.

The day passed in a blur of faces and questions she did not know how to answer, her guilt assumed by the jury of men who examined her. John's reappearance had changed the stakes – he had charged her with bewitching him to murder, and the physician backed his claim. It was no longer a matter of a young boy lured to commit a sexual sin: Jane's blood was on her hands and she had no doubt they would send her to trial.

Everyone spoke for her, though they each spoke to the jury in private, taking turns, so she did not know what they said. Will and Nick and Tom. Her mother and others of the Company. She was grateful, but her blood churned in her veins, and the hard ball that was her stomach tightened and heaved through the hours. Finally, at the end of the endless day, she was committed for trial and led away by the constable to the Marshalsea to wait.

Chapter Twenty-Four

THE FATAL BELLMAN

The night before her trial she did not sleep, standing instead beside the small barred opening to the outside world to catch glimpses of a starless sky, brief moments of the young crescent moon as it peeped from behind a shifting shroud of cloud. She wondered if she would ever see the moon after this night or if this would be her final sight of the heavens.

She was aware of everything, senses alert to the smallest sensations, her heartbeats numbered, each breath treasured and precious. She spoke to Tom in her mind and hoped that he would hear her, recalling how he had been at the Grove, his body white and ghostly in the moonlight, and the beauty of his smile. She would miss his smile the most, she realised, more than anything else in this world. Unconsciously she raised her fingers to her neck, caressing the soft skin and fighting against her thoughts as they bent to imagine the roughness of the rope around it, tightening. The long hours passed too quickly, and when the guard came at last to fetch her with the dawn, his appearance took her by surprise.

The court was busy. Officers whose roles she did not know moved to and fro with sheaves of paper in their hands, and the twelve men who would decide her fate sat talking quietly amongst themselves.

She saw Wickham, who nodded his recognition, and her belly recoiled at the memory of his fingers on her skin.

She stood in her allotted place and wished they had allowed her a seat. The sleeplessness of the night had begun to tell in the weariness of her limbs, and she wondered how she could possibly stay standing for the duration of the trial. The room buzzed with business and chatter and she realised that for everyone but her it was just another day.

The judge entered and the room fell silent, every man rising to his feet until the great man had sat down behind his desk, arranging himself carefully, neatening the papers in front of him until he was satisfied and ready. Then he lifted his eyes from the hands that were clasped before him to look at the girl on trial for her life. He observed her carefully, forming his impression, and she struggled to calm the quickness of her breathing, the racing of her heartbeat. He was old, she thought, grey hair thinning, a neat silver beard, and the lines that scored his cheek and brow told of a life hard-lived. But his eyes held an openness that gave her hope.

The clerk read out the indictment – words of Latin she did not understand. When the clerk had finished, the judge pinned her with his gaze. 'How do you plead?' he said.

'Not guilty, sir,' she said and her voice sounded unlike her own as it cut through the expectant hush. She saw the clerk scrawling in the ledger, the words to come that would condemn her being transcribed in black and white.

'Who is the victim?'

John entered, the constable's hand on his arm, staring about him, still jumpy, still fearful. He seemed every bit as though he were under a curse, and any last glint of hope she'd held flickered and died. He stood behind the table as he was bid with the constable at his shoulder and, once he had taken his oath, he began to give his evidence.

He had seen her, he said, always watching him, muttered curses thrown his way.

She had stitched her evil into the seams of the shirt that he wore, charms woven in his clothes to inflame him with wicked lusts.

She had filled his wine with her potions, he said, to lead him to unnatural acts, to corrupt him into sin.

She had bewitched his master to lure him to her bed and trick him to adulterous love.

She consorted with the Devil. He had seen her in the playhouse, hiding in the topmost gallery, talking to the daemons of the night, conversing with unseen forces.

She had visited his dreams and forced herself upon him.

She had sent her imps to drive him into madness so that he confused right and wrong, good and evil, and everywhere he looked were shadows, Satan's creatures, tempting, cursing, corrupting.

She had provoked him to murder with her familiars and her ill wishes, and he had not stood a chance.

He had seen all this, he said.

And he could see her now, still sending him ill wishes, trying to stop his mouth with fear and madness.

He was her prisoner, and only her death would set him free.

He finished, and the courtroom was silent as he stood shaking and trembling, his face averted from Sarah, afraid to meet her eyes. She turned to regard the jury, trying to read their reactions, but their faces were closed to her and she slid her eyes away. She could feel herself swaying, hunger and sleeplessness taking their toll, and the officer beside her placed his hand under her arm.

'Are you all right, miss?' he asked, and she could have wept at his kindness.

She nodded and let him hold her steady while John began to answer the questions that were asked of him. She tried to concentrate on the words he was saying, but her head felt light and it was hard to make sense of it all. Tom's name was mentioned and her thoughts snapped back to attention.

'You had carnal relations with the defendant's brother?'

'Yes.'

'On how many occasions?'

John had to think. 'Three times.'

'And on each occasion buggery occurred?'

He shook his head. 'Not the first time.'

'What happened the first time?'

John's gaze darted from face to face in the courtroom, all watching him, waiting. He looked terrified but she felt no sympathy as she watched him along with all the others, curious for the details too.

'There was a whore,' he began. 'We went to the playhouse. I didn't know, I didn't realise … and she tried to kiss me … and touch me down there … but I threw her off.'

'You felt no desire for the whore?'

'No, sir.'

'Had you ever felt desire for a whore before?'

'No.'

'Had you ever had relations with a woman before?'

'No.'

'Tell the court what happened.'

'Tom sent the whore away. Then he took her place … He kissed me … he kissed me down there …'

'He … kissed your private parts?'

The hush in the room was uncomfortable, a new tension entering.

'Yes.' John's voice was a whisper.

'And did you like it?'

The boy nodded. 'I tell you, I was bewitched … corrupted. Sinful, sinful … I never would have … never would have done something so wicked …' He broke off into incoherent sobs and mumbles and the lawyer waited.

After a moment, he spoke again. 'And the next occasion?'

'At my master's house, sir …'

Sarah stopped listening, her mind drifting. The room was hot with so many people and she wished again that she could sit. She let her eyes graze the jury once again, looking for kindness, but she could not seem to read any of their faces and she forced her thoughts back once more to John's evidence. It was coming to a finish, John rambling now about the night at the brothel and Jane's last breath, but he was barely coherent and his madness was plain to see. Sarah's life hung by a thread.

When it was clear that he would make no more sense, the judge dismissed him and the physician took his place, confirming all that

John had said, declaring the boy had surely been bewitched. When he was done, Sarah's friends were allowed to speak for her at last.

~

They went in one by one. Nick, Will, Sarah's mother, Joyce. All of them spoke of her good character – a dutiful servant, a hard-working seamstress, a loving daughter, an honest friend.

Tom went in last, though she had not asked for him to speak for her, and he saw from her face as he took his place at the table that his presence was a surprise. He held her eyes for a moment, recalling them bright and full of fire for him in the night, his own pleasure reflected in their depths. Then he gave her a smile and turned to face the court.

'Please state your name for the court.'

'Thomas Edward Wynter.'

'And your relationship to the defendant?'

'Half-brother. We share the same mother.'

There was a sudden tightening of attention in the room, all eyes drawn towards him. He breathed slowly, deeply, and held himself straight, upright, allowing them to look and make their judgements. It mattered not. They could judge him as they wished: he had chosen his course.

'What would you like to tell us about your sister?'

It was now or never, and for a moment all his resolution threatened to leave him, his love for his sister giving way to the natural urge to life in all its barbarous, chaotic glory. Sliding a glance towards her, he took another deep breath and remembered the daemon he had conjured in the night, and the bargain struck. Sarah was watching him, her gaze fixed and tense as though with the first glimmer of understanding of what was about to come. He held her look, tears beginning to burn behind his eyes as he took his final breaths of freedom and set his foot upon a path he could not change. Still he hesitated, sniffing back the tears, wiping at his eyes with impatient fingers – he had not come here to cry. He felt the tension of the court begin to harden round him: everyone was waiting, expectant. Dragging his gaze away from Sarah, he looked out across the court towards the judge, though the man was nothing but a blur through the tears that filmed his eyes. Then he took the first step onto the path.

'My sister is innocent of all these charges.'

'You know her so well?'

'I know she is innocent,' he said. 'Because although John was indeed bewitched, he is mistaken in the author of the curses against him. It was not Sarah who bewitched him.' He kept his eyes trained away from her. He could not look at her again. 'It was me. I am the one who bewitched him.'

Sarah's scream cut through the sudden hubbub and he watched the court's reaction with a strange and weary detachment. It was done: his life in payment for hers. The shewstone had spoken truly after all, and the daemon would see that it was done.

Sarah was still screaming, her cries of *no* repeating and reverberating through the room. The officer beside her held her back as she fought to reach her brother, kicking and beating with her arms, hysterical. Tom turned to her and formed his lips to shush, but it made no difference: her grief was inconsolable. He wanted to hold her and stroke her hair and love her one more time, but it was over, and this would be his final act of love.

Gradually, the court came to order. Someone fetched a stool for Sarah and she sat obediently, but her eyes never left her brother's face. He could feel her gaze like a caress and he turned his head to look at her. She was beautiful in her wildness and her grief, her tear-stained face, her hair awry, and every fibre in him screamed with the pain of leaving her, of leaving the world, but he could not let her hang. He had dreamed of it, the coarse fibres of the rope tightening round her throat and squeezing out her life, the fear and pain in her eyes as she fought for her final breaths. Better that he should take her place – it was his doing after all that had brought them here, as Nick had said, witchcraft or no.

The judge was still conferring with his officers, but the rest of the court had settled again to subdued murmurs. Tom could feel the eyes of everyone upon him, but his eyes remained locked with his sister's. At last, the officers moved away from the judge's bench and the judge spoke, dismissing the case against Sarah, adjourning the court. Then with a flick of his hand toward Tom, he said, 'Commit him to the Marshalsea until we set a date for the hearing.'

The constable's grip on Tom's arm tightened grimly as he manhandled him towards the door. Sarah slid from her place and rushed forward, blocking the way for a moment, standing close. Tom leaned near to her and her proximity was intoxicating.

'You were the only girl I ever loved,' he said, softly, so that only she would hear. Then the rough hand that held him dragged him on through the door and into the cart that would take him to the prison.

Sarah sat through his trial mute and grieving. John had obliged the court by shifting his charges from sister to brother, as Tom had desired and planned he would. Witchcraft and sodomy – perversions of the Devil and punishable by death.

He had been misled, John claimed.

He had known at first that it was Tom that had bewitched him, he said, and there were others who could vouch he had named Tom witch on more than one occasion. Witnesses were called – men of the Company, worshippers at St Saviour's – willing to confirm the accusation, though Nick and Will were not among them.

Then Tom had beguiled him, using cunning spells that deceived and seduced him.

He had corrupted him and tempted him to sin.

He had forced him into sodomy and lured him into murder.

The Devil was in his hands to strangle Jane, his thoughts possessed by daemons raised and sent by Tom.

His mind had been poisoned: it had not been his own will to commit such a heinous sin. But he had been blind to the truth, for who but Tom would bewitch him to do such things?

Who indeed?

Sarah's mother sat with her through all of it, straight-backed, tight-lipped.

When Tom came to answer at last, he spoke not a syllable of truth: no mention of the Grove nor the magic of their sex; no word about divining with the shewstone or the rites they performed for

Hecate. Instead he wove tales of trysts with the Devil who came as a tawny owl named Solomon to suckle blood from a mole on his hip. He dropped his breeches to show it to the court, and briefly, Sarah turned her head away – it was too painful to witness his nakedness now: she preferred to remember the lines of his body in the night, when his hips had entwined with hers.

He had bewitched the boy, he told them, in revenge for John's rejection – he knew he couldn't win him otherwise – and he recounted the seduction in all its lurid detail. It was everything they wanted from a witch, meeting their belief, and the whole court hung on every word, lusting for more, their prejudice and prurience aroused. So he kept on talking, feeding their hunger in his final performance. No one from the Company came to speak for him and she hated them all for their cowardice.

Sarah's eyes never left his face, willing him, begging him in her mind to turn and look at her one more time. But he kept his eyes resolutely turned away and her mother's hand remained tightly held in hers. Only after sentence was pronounced and there could be no more doubt that he would die did he slowly turn his gaze towards her with a small and sorry smile on his lips, and a slight half-shrug of his shoulders. The sad beauty of the smile and the pain behind his eyes unravelled all her self-control, and then the tears flowed unchecked, sobs heaving, as her mother's arms wrapped around her and drew her into their embrace. She did not see her brother leave the court.

Chapter Twenty-Five

BORROWER OF THE NIGHT

With nowhere else to go, she returned to her father's house after her trial, her parents arguing long into the night to decide her future. She could hear the rise and fall of the trade of their desperate voices in the room below her attic chamber, but she did not attempt to make out the words. Instead, she stood huddled by the window staring blindly into the darkness beyond with her forehead pressed hard against the smooth, cool glass, and her only thoughts were of her brother in a prison cell awaiting his death. It was the fate she had seen for him, the fate he had chosen, and she would willingly have tumbled through the glass to plummet to the earth below: without Tom she could not bear to live and her future did not interest her.

So when finally, close to the dawn, she heard her father's footsteps on the stairs beyond her door, she did not even turn her head. He had no power to frighten her now – she was utterly bereft of feeling. He could beat her senseless for all she cared. He opened the door without knocking and she heard him close it behind him. Then he waited and it took her a moment to realise he was waiting for her to turn around and pay him respect, but she was almost paralysed with grief and sorrow, unable to bring herself to move, and so the silence continued for long awkward moments until he took a step closer.

'Look at me when I speak to you,' he said.

Reluctantly she turned herself to face him. He seemed a stranger to her now and she observed him with detachment, this man who possessed such power over her. Then she remembered his bluster at the playhouse and her fear of him, and felt nothing at all. He must have sensed her indifference because he drew himself up and took another step closer.

'For your mother's sake I have agreed to take you back.'

She waited.

'But I will expect obedience from you,' he continued. 'The playhouse, Bankside, Master Tooley – all of them are forbidden to you. Do I make myself clear?'

She nodded. It made no difference. She had lost all interest in the playhouse now: in her despair at Tom's fate, it was hard to understand how such make-believe worlds had ever possessed so much power to enchant her. Like a spell that had held them all in its thrall, and Will Shakespeare the master magician. Perhaps it was Will that should be on trial – it was the magic of his words that had set events in motion, his witches that sent John mad.

'Answer me when I speak to you.' Her father's command cut into her thoughts.

'I understand, Father,' she said mechanically. She would have agreed to anything he asked, and her thoughts trailed out once again beyond the glass across the Southwark rooftops towards the prison and her brother's cell. The memory of her own time there was etched in acid through her core – the stench, the cold, the hunger and despair – and she could see Tom standing by the tiny barred opening just as she had, gazing out to the sky beyond it and drinking in every inch of the world he could see, the world he had renounced to save her. The image lit a physical pain, guts clenching, breath coming short. He would barely sleep these last few days of his life, she knew, grasping every last and precious moment even in that foetid, brutal place. Sending her thoughts out through the night towards him with all her love and sadness, she wished that he had loved her less so she could die instead of him.

'Then we will say no more about it,' her father said then, in a gentler tone. 'And I am glad you are returned to us, a dutiful daughter at last. Perhaps you will be saved after all.'

She was silent. There seemed to be nothing more to say. Her

father hesitated, uncertain in the face of her silence. Perhaps he had expected more gratitude. Then he backed out of the room, the door rattling on its hinges in his wake, boots thudding loud on the stairs, and she laid herself down on the bed and finally allowed herself to sleep. For the first time in weeks, she did not dream.

The journey to the gallows seemed to be never-ending. She walked beside the cart as it was dragged through the streets, oblivious of the onlookers' jeers and the cold rain that swept into her face, the mud that churned underfoot, aware only of the still, pale face of her brother as he held her gaze with sad and steady eyes. Once or twice he tried to smile but she could see his tears behind the mask, and her own tears ran unchecked with the rain across her cheeks. A minister walked before the cart, but his words were lost amidst the splatter of the rain against the road and the roofs of the houses and the catcalls of the people they passed.

Twice the cart stopped to allow the prisoners to dull their fear with drink, and she passed him the cup of wine with trembling hands. He took it without a word and drank it off, and when he gave her back the cup his fingers lingered, brushing hers for a brief and final moment. His touch seemed to suck all the breath from her body and she staggered briefly. But still it seemed impossible that he would die: his light had always shone for her and the world would be a dark place without him.

The procession reached Tyburn at noon, and though she had heard tell of it before, nothing had prepared her for the sight of the great hanging tree with its three monstrous beams and the noise and clamour of the crowd of thousands who had come to watch, despite the storms. Her spirit threatened to fail, and she saw the fear that flickered in Tom's eyes as he stepped off the hurdle into the mud and took his final steps aboard the cart that would bear him to the noose. He moved awkwardly with his hands bound tightly before him, and she followed the cart in close, eyes locked with his as the hangman arranged the rope around his neck and swung the end up to the boy who was balanced on the beam to fasten it.

When all the prisoners were ready, the crowd quietened to hear any final speeches and the last words of the minister for the souls of the condemned. Two of the prisoners offered a short prayer for forgiveness, but Tom held his silence, a multitude of words contained in the look he shared with Sarah. Then the cart lurched forward as the horse was whipped away, and when the rope snapped taut she dropped her eyes for a moment, unable to bear to watch his final gasps for breath, the frantic kicking of his legs. When she lifted her face to him again, gathering her courage to pull on his legs to hasten his end, she saw he was already peaceful – his body swinging lightly, still turning gently from the force of his death. He must have thrown himself against the noose to quicken his own death, she realised. His eyes were closed and his neck was askew, and she knew there was nothing left of the man she loved inside the broken shell that hung before her. It was the fate she had foreseen. Lifting her eyes to the cloud-darkened sky, the cold, hard rain whipped into her face as she whispered her final farewell.

~

'Let's talk of graves, of worms, and epitaphs ...'

In rehearsal at the playhouse, Nick gave a sudden shiver, an icy cold crawling over his skin, and he lost the train of his thought. He paused in the line he was reading.

'What's the matter?' Will asked.

'Nothing,' Nick answered with a shake of his head. 'I just thought I heard something ...' His eyes trailed over the theatre as though looking for clues. But all seemed as normal. The hired actors were practising their swordplay for the afternoon performance, and small groups of players rehearsed their lines together as he was doing with Will and John Heminges.

'I heard it too,' Will murmured. 'The cry of a woman?'

'Aye.'

''Tis done, then.'

'It was a good thing he did,' John Heminges said. 'To save her.'

Nick nodded. In spite of his hatred, he could only applaud the depth of such love, for he knew he wouldn't have given his own life for hers. But still he would not mourn him, and unconsciously he rubbed at the wound on his arm. Tom's doing, he was sure – how else could the blades have been switched?

'I'll miss him,' Will said. 'I'll miss them both.'

John Heminges smiled his agreement, and Nick said nothing. He did not know what to say.

The night of Tom's death Sarah's dreams returned so vividly she was sure that they were real. Sleep had come as a blessed relief at the end of another day of grief, the moment of his death playing over and over in her mind: the fear and pain in his eyes and the frantic kicking of his legs no longer a fate foretold but a destiny lived, unchangeable. Now it only remained for her own death to come, the slow withering from grief she had foreseen in the shewstone.

In the sweet oblivion of sleep that night, her brother came to her again, his ghost reaching out across the void that lay between them now, and his silent presence ushered in a chill that hinted at the cold-ness of the grave. But she felt no fear as he lay beside her in the bed, only reaching out her hand in surprise and delight to caress his cold, pale cheek and touch the brutal bruise and welts that scarred his neck.

'Is it truly you, gentle brother?' she whispered. 'Or are you just a figment of my disordered brain?'

He said nothing but only smiled his lovely smile in answer and lifted a hand to smooth her hair behind her temple. His touch sent a shadow passing through her that chilled her to her soul, leaving her in no doubt he truly was a spirit from the dead. Questions clustered in her thoughts, but he placed a finger on her lips with a small shake of his head to silence her before she could begin to ask him anything. So she searched in his eyes for some understanding, and all she saw were dark and unknowable depths. With a sudden awareness she had glimpsed into realms of the dead, a shiver of fear rippled through her.

He smiled again as if to reassure her, then lowered his mouth to hers, and all fear, all thought, all reason, all grief were swept away in the transcendence of his kiss: if this was death, she wanted nothing more, the cold of the tomb that suffused her embraced and welcome.

A choice between life and death. A loveless life, or a loving death.

As he moved his body over hers, lifting her shift to enter her, she made her choice, surrendering all that she was to him, her mortal life as nothing compared to the bliss of this union with spirit.

Afterwards he stayed to hold her until the dream faded away into peaceful sleep, and in the morning when she woke, at first she couldn't say if she had merely dreamed him into life, an apparition born of a grief-stricken brain. But when she moved to get up and felt the stickiness between her legs, she understood he had truly come to her. Smiling to herself that she had not entirely lost him after all and sure that he would come to her again, she swung herself out of the bed she had shared with him in the night and got ready to meet the waking day with a lighter heart.

Within days she knew she was carrying his child. She could feel the life quickening inside her, a small gift of hope to light the darkness of her grief, and she knew without question it was his, sure of the night it was conceived – their last night together in the waking world.

As soon as she was certain, she sought out her mother in the garden behind the house, where she was tending the herbs she used to ease the trials of childbirth. A clear, light sunshine broke through the bright scudding strips of cloud, a water-blue sky behind them. Sarah's eyes wandered across the rows of budding greenery – motherwort and witch hazel, partridge berry and chamomile – and she fingered the leaves with a new and expectant curiosity. She would need them for herself very soon, but the thought didn't frighten her as once it might have. The child was Tom's parting gift to her, a piece of himself to love, and she had no cause to be afraid.

At Sarah's approach Elizabeth rose stiffly from her knees and wiped her forehead with the back of one hand, fingers dark with the dirt of her labour, cheeks flushed with the warmth of the changing season. The two women stood side by side in the warm afternoon and surveyed the garden. It was verdant and bright with new spring growth, and a pair of swallowtail butterflies flitted back and forth between the leaves in a complex dance of courtship. Sarah watched them for a moment, her gaze caught by the luminescent colours. Then she turned to her mother, who was observing her carefully with stern, shrewd eyes.

'You are with child.' Her mother spoke in barely more than a whisper even though they were sure they were alone. 'Tom's child.'

'Yes,' she replied. It never crossed her mind to wonder how her mother knew.

Elizabeth sighed and rubbed at her forehead again, smearing crumbs of earth across it. Sarah smiled and reached an instinctive hand to wipe the dirt away with the tips of her fingers.

'Then you must marry Simon after all,' her mother said. 'The child will need a father.'

She shrugged. With Tom gone she no longer cared. She must marry a man, any man, to keep her and her child, as her mother had married her father. It was her fate as a woman.

'We must work quickly,' her mother said. 'So the world believes Simon is the father.'

She nodded, recalling the words of the dream that had begun it all: *Wife thou shalt be, loving mother of children, though none of mine.* All of it would come to pass in the end.

Leaning forward, Elizabeth laid her hand on Sarah's arm. 'I will speak to your father tonight and tell him you're willing. It has long been his dearest wish for you to marry Simon – I see no impediment on our path.'

Sarah was silent. She would accept all that was arranged and become a dutiful wife. Except for Tom and his child, she cared about nothing. Sliding her eyes away from her mother's scrutiny, she wished, not for the first time, that she possessed some of Tom's skill to dissemble.

Her mother said, 'Does he come to you, in your dreams?'

She sighed. There was no point in lying. 'He comes to me most nights,' she whispered, 'as restless in death as in life.' And as real as day, she thought, to lie with her again and still her grief with his silent caress. Lying with his spirit in the night was all that mattered to her now. His touch, his body, his breath, his smile – these were the forces that sustained her, and the nights were all she lived for: she had no interest in the day.

'You must let him go, Sarah,' Elizabeth said. 'He comes because you call him, because he wants to ease your sorrow. Let him go. Let him go to his rest and give your love to the child. His child.'

She turned her head away, biting her lip, blinking back the tears.

'He loved you well,' Elizabeth said, and at the unexpected gentleness in her mother's tone, she slid her eyes back to meet her mother's look. 'And he left you a gift of himself. But the wheel has turned and we must turn with it. Let him go. Let him be at peace.'

She nodded, admitting her mother's wisdom. But her spirit was less easy to convince than her head, clinging fiercely to her desire to go to him and be with him again.

'Let him go, Sarah. Promise me. For your sake as well as his.'

She was silent, her heart in shreds and impatient for the night, to have him love her again.

'Sarah?'

She shook her head lightly, sniffing back her tears. 'I can't,' she whispered. 'I cannot give him up.'

Her mother said nothing, but her thoughts were clear on her face. Sarah waited, hoping for some word of understanding, some small offer of hope, but her mother simply turned away and knelt once more before the herbs, digging at the dark earth with the trowel. She watched her for a moment, still hoping, but when she understood her mother had no more to say to her she backed away toward the house. There was sewing for her to do, a shift for a local merchant's wife, and she took up her seat at the window in the first-floor chamber where the light was best. Then she picked up the linen and with a mind filled with nothing, started to make the stitches.

The morning of the wedding dawned with a blackened sky and a wind that chased the rain sideways so that it seemed as though the world had tilted.

'What have you done?' her mother asked as she helped her daughter dress for her marriage.

'Nothing,' Sarah answered.

'You did not let him go.' It was not a question, and her mother's hands stopped working at the ties of Sarah's sleeves. 'He still comes to you.'

Sarah nodded.

Her mother moved to face her, taking Sarah's chin in her fingers, examining her daughter's face. 'You must give him up,' she whispered. 'The life is already leaving you. Do you think I haven't seen? That I haven't been watching as you pale and fade?'

Sarah swallowed but was silent. She understood the bargain she had made.

'He wants you to join him,' her mother said.

'It was my choice. And the shewstone foretold it.'

'He should not have offered it to you. He gave his life to save you. Honour that sacrifice. Use the life he paid for.'

'In a life with Simon? What kind of life is that?'

'A life like mine,' her mother answered. 'What of your child, Sarah? I took the life with your father for your brother's sake – I made a sacrifice, a bargain if you like, of my happiness for the well-being of my child. And what of yours?' she asked again. 'Will you not do the same for him? For the gift that Tom gave you?'

'Why did he give it to me?' She still could not understand, and he did not answer in the nights when she asked him. 'What does he want from me?'

'I cannot say. I was never able to read Tom's heart as I can read yours. But perhaps,' she said, 'it was to give you a reason not to follow him, a way to turn your promised fate aside.'

Her father's footsteps in the passage outside her door stopped their conversation, and her mother finished tying the sleeves in silence and set to dressing Sarah's hair. But she had no interest in any of it, her mind turning instead on the fate of her child and her life to come. When she was finally dressed and ready, she stood up and turned to her mother.

'We should scry,' she said softly.

'Sometimes,' her mother replied, 'it's better not to know.' Then, 'Ready?'

'Ready.'

Together, they left the house and walked to the Puritan church of her father for the wedding.

~

Marriage to Simon wasn't hard. As her mother had promised, he was a kind husband, and in return she was a dutiful wife. Lying beneath him each night in their marriage bed in the room behind the shop, she let him fumble inexpertly to climax, patient with his efforts, unmoved. It was a world away from the passion she had known with Nick and with Tom, but she did not mind. He was gentle, afraid of hurting her, and she saved her rapture for the nights when Tom's ghost came to her while her husband slept. Only now and then she regretted her deception: he was an honest man and she had used him badly, though she was sure he would never suspect.

One morning close to midsummer, she answered a knock at the door to see Nick on the doorstep. She stared, startled. She rarely thought of him now, her world revolving instead around her child and husband, and the nights she spent with Tom. The playhouse seemed a different realm, an illusion she had dreamed of once upon a time.

'Goodwife Chyrche.' He bowed and she dropped him an answering curtsey.

He looked no different, she thought, the same reluctant smile and sad eyes, the same full lips. His beard was a little longer, and there was a weariness about him she had not seen before, but otherwise he had not changed. Only she could no longer see in him what she used to see, all desire for him faded out of memory.

'Please. Come in.' She stepped back to allow him to enter, and wondered what had brought him to her door. He followed her upstairs into the stuffy warmth of the main chamber and she poured him a cup of ale. He took it with a small smile of thanks, and with the smile his eyes glittered and crinkled and she remembered why she had loved him. She folded her hands before her skirts and waited.

'I'm sorry about your brother,' he said finally, when the silence had begun to grow heavy. 'I know you must have grieved for him sorely.'

'Thank you.'

'And congratulations on your wedding. And …?' He tilted his head, a small gesture towards her belly.

'Yes,' she answered the unspoken question. 'I am with child.'

He looked away into the bottom of his ale and she knew he was wondering if the child were his. 'It is my husband's child,' she told him. 'Of that I am sure.'

He lifted his eyes with a smile. 'Of course,' he answered quickly. 'I understand.' Then, 'And you are happy?'

At that she slid her eyes away. There were some things she could not mask entirely, and he would have noticed already her pallor and the gauntness of her cheek, her light dimming even as she tried to keep it bright.

She shrugged. 'Are you?'

He answered with a wry smile and a half-shrug of his own.

'Both of us unhappily married then,' she murmured. 'Both of us bound.'

There was another pause. Then she said, 'Why have you come here, Master Tooley? What is it you would tell me?'

She saw him swallow and glance down into the empty cup in his hand. She stepped forward and took the jug from the sideboard to refill it. His eyes followed her movements, and when she had finished he lifted the cup to his lips and drank. He took a deep breath.

'John died in prison this morning.'

'Poor mad John,' she breathed. She had barely thought of him of late but the news saddened her nonetheless. He had been undone by his own desire, the fear of his own sin. His was a delicate spirit, too fragile for the demands of his faith.

'He never regained his wits after the trial,' Nick said. 'So they kept him in prison, afraid he was still possessed by whatever evil spirit your brother had conjured.'

'You know it wasn't so,' Sarah said. 'No one ever bewitched him. 'Twas his own fear that undid him.'

And the words of the play, she thought, the curse she had foreseen in the shewstone. But she didn't ask how John died – she did not want to imagine it. She had spent dark days in prison, her own thoughts coloured with fear and desperate imaginings; she knew it would be easy to die in such a place.

Nick shrugged. 'It no longer matters one way or the other,' he said. 'But I thought you would want to know.'

'Thank you. I'm grateful.' Then, 'How goes the playacting business?'

'We are playing a comedy this afternoon. An old one. *A Midsummer Night's Dream*. Master Burbage is back.'

'No witches,' she said.

'Just faeries.'

They shared a smile, a little of the old understanding passing between them. They would have made each other happy, she thought, if the Fates had been kinder.

'I should go,' he said. 'A performance to attend.' He placed the cup on the tray on the sideboard and stepped to the door. Then he turned back. 'If I can ever be of service, Sarah, please, do not hesitate to call on me. You know where you can find me.'

'Thank you.' She knew the offer was genuine and that she would never take it up.

She stood at the door and watched him stride away, back towards his life at the playhouse, his gait well known and familiar. Then she turned back inside to return to her sweeping and closed the door behind her.

Chapter Twenty-Six

A BLESSED TIME

As summer ripened and her belly grew round, Simon began to leave her alone in bed, in awe of her and afraid to touch. She welcomed his reluctance, and they lived together as quiet and courteous friends. It was a life that seemed unreal to her, hours of pretend to endure in the daytime until the dark hours fell and she could be with her brother again in the only life that mattered.

But gradually, Tom came to her less often, missing a night here and there at first, then longer spaces in between, until at last the weeks went by and he did not come. Impatient for him to take her with him, she did not understand. Why had he left her? She had made her choice the first night that he came to her, her spirit fading and drawn towards the darkness, Tom's love awaiting her in death. The decision had seemed so simple: to die and be with Tom or to live without him. There had been no hesitation, not even for a moment. Tom was everything to her – without him she was incomplete, her life a half-life barely lived, and it seemed to be no sacrifice to leave it.

But without his presence to sustain her, her spirit began to falter, caught between two worlds. And as the life within began to kick sometimes and press against her organs, a reluctant joy began to bud in her forming child, love growing unlooked for and a reviving urge to life. Torn between her mother-love and her desire for Tom, she felt that she would drown beneath so much uncertainty.

When she was six months gone with child and had all but given up hope that Tom would ever come to her again, he spoke to her at last one night in the space between sleep and waking.

'Meet me at the Grove,' he whispered, and his breath was cool against her ear. 'At the next full moon.'

She snapped open her eyes to see him and to hold him again, but he had already disappeared, and she lay sleepless for the rest of the night. The days till the next full moon seemed to stretch endlessly before her.

It was easy to slip out of the house. Simon had no cause to suspect her, and her father no longer took an interest. He had given her to Simon and washed his hands of her – her sins were no longer his concern but a burden for her husband. Besides, Simon slept like the dead after long days in the shop, the familiar snuffle and snore, the narrow mouth hanging open. So different from the beauty of her brother when he slept in his pale and peaceful stillness.

With the whole household asleep, she took the front door, and in the street she breathed deeply. The London night had become an unfamiliar place to her now she was a respectable housewife and heavy with child, and she was wary of it: the confidence with which she had once slid through the night-time streets seemed to belong to a different person, a different time. Now she moved heavily and with caution, but as her steps led her closer to the Grove, closer to Tom, her pace quickened and she found her way through the trees without mistake. But always the question circled in her mind: had he come this time to collect her, to take her from her waking world into his realm of the dead? She could think of no other purpose, and the blood shivered in her veins at the thought of it, excitement stirred with dread.

When she reached the Grove it was bathed in moonlight: leaves that in the daytime were tinged red and gold with the oncoming autumn flickered silver and ash with the breeze. An owl called some-where in the trees, unseen. Hecate, she thought, come as psychopomp to accompany her into the dark. Wrapping her cloak around her against the chill of the September night, she lowered herself carefully to sit on the cool, damp grass, and settled down to wait. She did not doubt that he would come as promised, and her heartbeat quivered with nerves and pleasure.

He came just as the church bells tolling midnight faded into silence away beyond the trees, and Sarah struggled to her feet as he approached, off balance with her belly, heart racing with excitement and the effort and the fear of what was about to come.

He looked no different, only pale as he had been in her dreams, but a stale, deep cold emanated from him, a chill that rippled through the air between them as he came near to her, and when he reached out a hand to take her fingers, the blood seemed to freeze in her veins: instinctively she took a step back. He was silent, watching her, but he did not let go of her hand and she could not find the will to break the connection herself.

'Gentle sister,' he greeted her, and his voice breathed inside her mind.

'Tom,' she whispered. She held his gaze, blue-grey eyes black now in the night, and a light in them she hadn't seen before: another realm, the world of the dead. A shard of fear threaded through her, until the corners of his mouth lifted in a smile.

'Your fate is yours to choose,' he said, 'and the promise you saw in the shewstone can still be denied.' He moved closer, wrapping her in his coldness so that she shivered. But his nearness was intoxicating, his breath cool on her cheek and his mouth close enough that if she lifted her head she could kiss him. She wanted him with a fierceness that stole through her blood, but still she rested a protective hand on her belly and a part of her thoughts remained with the child, frightened for him to be so close to a spirit of the dead.

Tom said, 'Don't be afraid. He's safe. He was my gift to you and I would do nothing to hurt him.'

She nodded, aware of the burn of the tears behind her eyes as he tucked his finger under her chin and lifted her face to meet his kiss. The chill of him lit through her, stopping her breath, a death proffered. It seemed to her a good way to die and she kissed him harder, drawing the fate he was offering deeper inside her, opening herself up to its touch, the child forgotten in this final surrender to death.

The moment hovered, the chill spreading through her, until the child inside her kicked suddenly in protest. Both of them felt it, Tom's belly pressed close against hers, and they stepped apart instinctively. Tom placed his hand on her belly, testing for the life within, and when the child kicked again, he lifted his face to her.

'Stay,' he murmured. 'Stay for him. He needs you more than I.'

'Wait,' she whispered, understanding that this was a final goodbye and desperate to prolong the moment.

'It's time,' he said, and his eyes crinkled in the smile she loved so well.

She nodded, words too hard to find, eyes too filled with tears to see, and a new choice made.

He bent to touch his lips to hers one more time, and then he was gone, vanishing into the air, and her hands were left holding nothing but the soft autumn night.

She stood for a long time, gently caressing the tautened skin across her belly, and gradually the child settled and was at peace. Then, with a silent prayer of farewell that she lifted towards the moon, she stepped out of the Grove and into the forest to make her way home.

Also by Samantha Grosser

THE SORCERER'S WHORE - PAGES OF DARKNESS
BOOK TWO

England 1632.

25 years have passed since the first fateful production of Macbeth, and the forces of evil are about to be reawoken.

A cursed child ...

Six-fingered Mary Sparrow believes she was cursed at birth, and the bawdy house at The Cardinal's Cap is the only home she's ever known. Like most of the girls, she dreams of escape. But when an old man mysteriously drives her friend to madness, Mary begins to fear for her life.

A dangerous path ...

Toby Chyrche also has hopes for a better future, away from the confines of the tailor's shop where it seems his fate is set in stone. So when a chance meeting offers him a different path, he is only too eager to accept. Then the discovery of an old book of magic throws a new and shocking light onto the past - his mother had a brother, and that brother was a witch.

A price to pay ...

As the old man's shadow over Bankside lengthens, Mary is drawn into the growing web of darkness. Unable to escape its reach, she turns to Toby for help. But Toby has daemons of his own to face. Will possession of the book be enough to protect them? And what is the price they will have to pay?

In this compelling and seductive sequel to *Shakespeare's Witch,* nothing is as it seems ...

On Sale Soon! Read the first chapter at:

https://dl.bookfunnel.com/ucpxfaqybo

If you enjoyed *Shakespeare's Witch,* please take 5 minutes to leave a review at the store where you bought it. Thank you!

Acknowledgments

I'd like to thank the usual suspects who helped in the writing of this book. My husband Steve for unfailing enthusiasm, Dr Louise Pryke for encouragement, insight and inspiration, Jessica Gardner for edits, Deborah Frith for feedback, Bunny Star for eagle eyes, and last but not least, a huge thank you to all the players who have ever brought the Scottish Play to life.

Printed in Poland
by Amazon Fulfillment
Poland Sp. z o.o., Wrocław